GW00809074

TELL ME WHY: WHAT WILL THEY RISK FOR ANSWERS?

GEORGIE HARVEY AND JOHN FRANKLIN
BOOK 1

SANDI WALLACE

PRAISE FOR SANDI WALLACE'S BOOKS

'Aussie Noir at its best. Once again Wallace has tapped into the rural crime genre with an iconic sense of place beneath a black cloud of menace and intrigue. Her Georgie Harvey and John Franklin series just gets better and better.'

B. MICHAEL RADBURN, AUTHOR OF
TAYLOR BRIDGES **SERIES**

'Sandi Wallace's best yet! Engaging, fast-paced, and full of suspense.'

KAREN M. DAVIS, FORMER NSW
POLICE DETECTIVE AND AUTHOR OF
THE *LEXIE ROGERS* **SERIES**

'Unputdownable!'

L.J.M. OWEN, AUTHOR OF THE *DR*
PIMMS, INTERMILLENNIAL SLEUTH
SERIES

'A gripping twist on the bushfire threat all Australians live with.'

JAYE FORD, AWARD-WINNING AUTHOR
OF *DARKEST PLACE*

'Suspenseful, exciting, atmospheric rural crime; a riveting debut.'

'Worthy debut.'

'The police aspect of this novel has depth and believability...this debut is a cracker.'

'Sharply crafted and authentic... These are stories that linger, long after they are read.'

'Sandi Wallace packs as much punch into her short crime stories as she does into her novels.'

ALSO BY SANDI WALLACE

Georgie Harvey and John Franklin series

Tell Me Why

Dead Again

Into the Fog

Black Cloud

Short story collections

On the Job

Award-winning short stories

'Sweet Baby Dies' (*Scarlet Stiletto: The Eleventh Cut* – 2019)

'Fire on the Hill' (*Scarlet Stiletto: The Tenth Cut* – 2018)

'Busted' (*Scarlet Stiletto: The Eighth Cut* – 2016)

'Ball and Chain' (*Scarlet Stiletto: The Sixth Cut* – 2014)

'Silk Versus Sierra' (*Scarlet Stiletto: The Fifth Cut* – 2013)

Non-fiction

Writing the Dream (contributing author)

To Glenn, with love.

PART I

FRIDAY 12 MARCH

CHAPTER ONE

IN HER DREAM, SHE WAS STILL PLAIN AND PLUMPISH, HER hair streaked with grey. Beyond that, though, everything seemed off-kilter. The first thing she noticed was that she floated above herself as she stood in a paddock. She was without her obligatory glasses and wore a floral housedress, not overalls. The images in her dream distorted and reshaped and became even more unreal. Huge sunflowers covered what would really be their well-trampled top paddock. These flowers grew so abnormally bright that they glowed like miniature suns, and she had to shield her eyes with her hand. The brightness became hot, so hot that she moved a forearm over her face.

Then the cat growled, a long, guttural note that sounded a warning. He nipped her finger and roused her from the dream. More asleep than awake, she soothed him. What had upset the amiable puss?

Her husband shook her. She sat up in bed, puzzled. As she donned her glasses, she saw that he'd pulled on work boots and a woollen jumper over his long pyjamas.

'Quick!' he yelled, shutting their bedroom window.

They reached the front verandah but couldn't see anything for the hedge around the house except an orange flush in the night sky. They could feel the intense heat and hear the sinister sound of uncontrolled flames.

From the picket fence they saw billows of smoke. Several sheds were alight. Her husband sprinted for the hose; she for the telephone, to call the local fire captain.

Panic clutched at her chest while she filled buckets of water. Her knees nearly buckled as she dashed towards the outbuildings.

Which first?

The hay shed was fully involved; a lost cause.

The barn or machinery shed?

No animals in the barn tonight.

The latter, then, as it held the combustibles and expensive equipment.

She dumped the water. It did nothing but sizzle. She ran back to the house, detoured to the water trough and returned with soaked woollen blankets. She crashed into a wall of heat; so fierce it scorched her eyes.

As the hay shed erupted, it sent embers in every direction. She protected her face from those missiles of fire with her arm, mimicking her dream persona.

Wind fanned the roaring tongues, adding to the crescendo.

She coughed as smoke filled her lungs. Fire merged the sweet odours of hay and timber with acrid fumes of fuel, pesticides and rubber. Her eyes watered.

'Where are you?' she cried out to her husband. 'Are you safe?'

She fought the flames harder. She would never give up – on him or the farm.

Above the bellow of the fire and rupturing structures and terrified shrieks of sheep and cattle, she couldn't hear a thing. Throat blistered with heat, smoke and yelling for her husband, she couldn't tell if she managed to make a sound or if the screams were only in her head.

Then, a hand clasped her shoulder and something struck her temple. She crumpled to the ground.

CHAPTER TWO

Senior Constable John Franklin had been cooped up with Paul Wells for hours. Too long without a smoke or coffee because Constable-fast-track-Wells was driving and he didn't pay much attention to those who wore fewer than three stripes on their epaulette.

But that wasn't why Franklin wanted to throttle him. It was because Wells measured time, distance, temperature, power poles and countless other things. Plus he was a rigid perfectionist with as much personality as a dead carp. Franklin's workmates rated the bloke's neurotic traits with fingernails scratching down a blackboard. His two consecutive rest days relegated to distant memories by the OCD freak, he ruled it much worse.

'Four and a half minutes,' Wells said. He tapped his watch.

Franklin groaned. So today's general patrol took five minutes longer than the previous trip – *big deal*.

'Should not have stopped for Charlie Banks...'

And that's the difference between a copper from the country and a cockhead from the big smoke.

Franklin tuned out.

A lonely bugger, poor Charlie often wanted to chew their ears. On this occasion it was about his dog's arthritis, but it was just an excuse for company. Yet Wells evidently thought the schedule more important than a quick chat with the old codger.

Franklin scrutinised the intense constable as he unclipped his seatbelt. The bloke was third-generation cop with dad, uncles and grandfather all among the brass. Odds-on he'd be promoted and back to the city before most coppers learned to scratch themselves. They wouldn't improve him, so somehow they'd have to bide time until he moved on.

Granted, the real problem today wasn't Wells. It came from him. Because he was the single parent of a hormonal teenager with attitude and because after sixteen years in the same country town, he still wore a uniform. He chatted to lonely folk, changed light globes, chopped wood and mowed lawns for elderly widows, pointed the radar for hours on end and sorted out the same drunks, the same domestics. Those were the good days. One of his blackest days had seen him as pallbearer at the funeral of a road victim who was also a mate from the footy club. All a far cry from where he'd planned to be by his mid-thirties.

———

Some days start badly and end up your worst nightmare. She should have seen the ladder in her new pantihose when she pulled them on this morning—hell, the need to wear a bloody skirt and heels itself—as a damn omen. A sign that she'd end up here, two beers down, stomach clenched while she cursed Narkin.

'Bastard.'

The bartender shot her a glare, not the first for that afternoon.

She hadn't meant to say it aloud and grimaced. She resumed pushing the penne pasta around her plate.

Flight of the Bumblebee pealed. She fished through her bag and frowned at the mobile screen. Number withheld. She thumbed the call switch to answer.

'Georgie Harvey.'

'It's Ruby here.'

Georgie cringed. She had avoided the older woman since yesterday but was caught now.

'Michael and I are hoping you'll look up Susan...'

What was her name? Susan Petticoat, Prenticast? Her neighbour Ruby's supposedly missing friend. Whatever; Georgie wasn't inclined to drive to Hicksville on a wild-goose chase.

She was saved by Ruby's cry of *'You silly duffer! What've you done?'*

The phone clunked. Georgie necked some beer and considered hanging up. She couldn't.

'I'll have to ring back, love.'

The call topped off a crap day. Now she felt guilty about dodging her neighbours to boot.

Disgruntled, Georgie scanned the room. It ought to have been a wood-panelled bar with punters using the pool table, old-timers arguing companionably over the footy, the call of a horse race on the radio; cheerful, noisy and as comfortable as worn slippers. Not this stark, trendy joint, with its white paint, stainless-steel counter, blond-wood seats, piped music and ultra-slick patrons. Even the barman's hair had encountered an oil spill. But this was the closest pub to the courts, and a beer was what she'd needed after her run-in with Narkin.

She speared a mouthful of pasta. It was cold and tasted like spicy cardboard. She pushed the bowl aside.

'Can't smoke in here,' the bartender said.

Georgie glanced at the unlit ciggie between her fingers. She hadn't realised she'd reached for it. She wouldn't have lit up; it was just that beer and smokes fit together perfectly. Pity smoking in pubs had been outlawed. What'd be next, inside people's homes or Melbourne's entire central business district? And was it really a health agenda or simply political?

She flicked her black lighter.

'I wouldn't.' The voice came from behind.

She grinned as Matt Gunnerson slipped onto a stool and held up two fingers with a nod and smile.

'How's crime this week, Matt?' The barman had shot daggers at Georgie since her arrival yet beamed as he greeted Matty.

'It's keeping me out of the dole queue.'

Both men laughed. The barman served two Coronas, and Matty slapped his shoulder in that matey way of his. Georgie marvelled at his easy charm, a handy attribute for an up-and-coming crime reporter. She could do with a dose if she ever cracked a real writing gig, as opposed to scripting and editing boring business resources.

They clinked bottles and swallowed in unison.

Matty commented, 'Didn't go well then, Gee?'

'Have I got *loser* plastered here?' She slashed a line across her forehead.

'Which magistrate did you get?'

'Narkin.'

'Ah.' Matty's sigh summed up fronting Pedantic Percy,

as he was dubbed within the legal circle. By reputation he found against self-represented defendants – Murphy's Law, she drew him.

'Ah,' she mimicked. She tapped the file before her and said, 'Laird –'

'Laird's your ex-cop?'

'Yeah. He argued that Pascoe Vale Road's notorious for metallic reflection distorting radar readings. But their expert rebutted.'

'And Pedantic Percy agreed with theirs?' When she grimaced, he added, 'So you lost. No surprise. You *are* a lead foot.'

'I'm not that bad.'

'Sure...'

'Well, maybe I am,' she conceded. 'Anyway, I copped a fine, plus legals, though I *just* saved my licence.'

'Have you spoken to AJ yet?'

Georgie froze. Adam James Gunnerson, her live-in lover, also happened to be his brother. And he currently ranked high on her taboo list.

She was never happier to hear the *Bumblebee* tune.

While Georgie foraged for her phone, she noticed the sky had clouded over. In the tradition of Melbourne's contrary weather, the beautiful autumn day gyrated to bleak. Pedestrians on William Street scurried for shelter from the downpour or sprinted towards the train station. Except for one woman; she walked on in measured strides, stare fixed on the horizon of skyscrapers, bitumen and traffic lights. It was something Georgie would do.

'It's me again. Ruby.'

Damn. I should've known.

'Michael and I were wondering... Well, will you go to Daylesford for us?'

'I'm sorry, Ruby. Can't talk.'

'What was that about?' Matty asked after she disconnected.

'Nothing.'

Georgie squirmed. She couldn't avoid her neighbours forever. But it was easier to avoid the conversation than turn them down flat.

Just as it was easier to run from AJ's kicked-dog eyes.

Georgie evaded Matty's inquisition by heading for the cigarette vending machine in the tiny passageway to the toilets. It was one of those days when she'd need more than her ten (or so) Benson & Hedges allowance. She fed the machine a fistful of gold coins and pushed the button.

In the ladies' room, she pulled a brush through her hair, changed her mind and messed it up. She smoothed on lip gloss and examined her reflection in the mirror. She tried a smile, then tweaked her silky black top.

Georgie leaned forward and held up thumb and index finger to make an L on her forehead. Then realised it was backwards. She couldn't even get that right.

Definite loser.

————

'Um, John. Got a tick?' Tim Lunny said, crooking his finger.

Franklin's stomach flipped. Was he in trouble again? Or worse: about to be permanently rostered on with Wells?

Fuck no, anything but being stuck with that wanker.

He followed Lunny into his office and dropped onto the single visitor's chair clear of paperwork, discarded uniform or fishing tackle.

The sergeant aligned and re-aligned a stack of files. Finally, he said, 'Well, you see. Oh, hell, mate. Kat's –'

'What's wrong with Kat?' Franklin straightened, alarmed.

'It's nothing like that. She's in a bit of strife –'

'Shit. What is it this time?'

'She and her two cronies took a five-finger discount at Coles.'

Franklin groaned, raking his sandy-coloured hair. The trio had received a day's suspension for smoking in the school toilets three weeks ago and he'd grounded his daughter for a month. He'd given her time off for good behaviour, and here she was, caught shoplifting days later.

'She's in Vinnie's office,' Lunny added, patting him awkwardly.

Franklin clamped his jaw, squashed on his cap and plucked keys for the marked four-wheel drive from the board.

The ninety-second drive felt protracted. And so did the walk of fucking humiliation from the truck through the car park to the innards of the supermarket. Never before had he been as conscious of the downside of living and working in such an intimate community. He knew scores of Daylesford's permanent residents after so long in town.

Tight-chested, Franklin pushed through the two-way door to the labyrinth of offices and storerooms.

He and Vinnie shook hands, then the store owner cut to the chase. 'Frankie, we don't need to take this further for a handful of Mars Bars.'

Franklin lifted his palms and let them drop.

'C'mon, the girls are pretty upset,' Vinnie coaxed, then frowned. '*Except* Narelle King. If it was her alone,' he mimed spitting, 'I'd tell you to throw the book.'

'I don't know –'

'Frankie, Frankie! Put the fear of God in them and then let it be. Go!'

Still undecided, Franklin thrust open Vinnie's door. He saw Kat flanked by her partners in crime on the sofa. While she glared, Lisa turned grey-white and Narelle reclined, blasé.

'You two.' Franklin jerked his head at Lisa and Narelle. 'Out.'

When they'd gone, he used his daughter's formal name. 'Katrina. What happened?'

She scowled harder.

He waited.

Kat clasped a hunk of her long hair. She twirled crimped blonde strands in front of her face, looking through him with clones of his own eyes. While biased and blind to their many similarities, Franklin considered her a stunner. But she was ugly with insolence now.

He faced away and leaned on Vinnie's desk. He counted to ten, then twenty. When he turned, his daughter hadn't budged.

'What am I doing wrong?'

Parents had to shoulder some blame. It ate him up to realise he'd failed her somehow.

She eye-rolled.

'Smoking, now this. What next?'

Franklin hated to see Kat make mistakes. Her next rebellious act could end in heartbreak.

She sniffed.

'I've got nothing to say to you.' The utter disappointment in his voice made her flinch.

Finally, a reaction.

Franklin pulled open the door. Narelle stumbled, caught eavesdropping.

'We're going to the station.'

The instant Kat brought Narelle King home, Franklin had identified her as a brazen troublemaker. It wasn't her bottle-blonde hair, bazooka boobs or that she carried a street-savvy sophistication from living in Melbourne until she was thirteen. Pure and simple, she'd failed Franklin's attitude test then and perpetually since. Even so, he recognised the futility of forbidding Kat's friendship with King. You don't give your teenage daughter yet another reason for defiance.

He seized the scruff of King's neck and pushed her forward. Lisa Cantrell snuffled as she trudged in the rear. Franklin sympathised with her. Studious and timid, she was an odd fit with the other two.

Franklin shepherded the girls to the truck, feeling as miserable as Lisa. His aim was to let them imagine the worst possible outcome, while he tried not to think about local gossipmongers. He hid behind dark sunglasses and the peak of his police cap and zipped through the roundabout and two blocks to the station.

————

Slumped on the stool next to Matty, Georgie chomped peanuts and surveyed her companion in the mirror. His face was animated. Everyone else in this bar appeared happy too. It only made her crappy mood spiral further.

Outside was the same story. The brief shower had ceased. The road steamed warm air. After five on a Friday afternoon, the working week surrendered to the weekend. Men ripped off ties and undid top buttons. Women greeted friends as if they hadn't seen them for a month. There was saccharine sweetness all around but for her.

She slugged beer. Then the brew curdled.

Fight or flight?

Why not both?

Take time out from my messed-up life while I do a favour for Ruby. That works for me.

'I'm outta here.' Georgie slammed down her Corona, spilling it onto the stainless top.

'Need a lift, Gee?'

'Nuh, ta, I've got the Spider. Besides, you're not going anywhere near where I'm headed.'

'Where's that?'

'Daylesford.'

Before he could ask why, she hoisted handbag and court file, pecked his cheek and threaded her way to the exit.

'Gee!'

Surprised, she spun around. Half the pub froze.

'Should you be driving?' Matty pointed to the abandoned beer.

'I'll take my chances,' Georgie said, then mustered what dignity she could and merged into the commuter exodus on William Street.

CHAPTER THREE

THOUGH TEMPTED TO THROW THE GIRLS INTO A CELL, Franklin left them in the interview room. He found Lunny flicking the tip of his fishing rod towards the window, on a break from the endless paper shuffle.

'Vinnie doesn't want to make it formal.'

'Good call.'

'Won't it smack of favouritism? Plenty of people saw the girls in the truck.'

Lunny lifted both brows. 'You brought them here?'

Franklin shrugged, then asked, 'What do you suggest?'

'What would you do for other kids? Two of them are first-time shoplifters who've never come to our attention before, although they've no doubt caused their parents the usual headaches. And we haven't been able to make anything stick for the other one, so she's officially got a clean slate.' Lunny sipped from his World's Greatest Grandpa mug.

Instantly, Franklin said, 'Scare them silly with a warning.' The churn rate in his guts slowed a little.

'Sounds right.' The sergeant jumped up. 'I'll do the honours.'

Franklin followed Lunny to the cramped interview room and took sentry position in the corner, diagonal to his daughter.

The older cop folded his lanky frame behind the plain table and faced the girls. Minutes dragged. The threesome fidgeted.

Lunny tipped back and crossed his arms. 'I've known you two for years.' He pointed at Lisa and Kat. 'Kat, you've slept in our spare bed more than the grandkids. Lisa, remember you nearly chopped off your finger and I wrapped a tea towel around it and called your mum? And I've seen plenty of you, too, Narelle King.'

Even the incomer, King, was transfixed, and Lunny eyed her for a moment. 'I'm not talking about these girls, but I advise you to ditch the bad crowd you hang out with.' He leaned forward. 'And grow up.'

His voice climbed several decibels. 'Do you think the juvenile offender program's not for kids like you? That Daddy-dear,' he glowered at Narelle, 'or your copper-dad,' this was to Kat, 'can keep you out of court, detention centres and away from hardened delinquents if you keep stuffing up?'

He laid it on thick and reduced the girls to blubbering messes. However, Kat continued to shun her father's gaze.

The caution complete and trio dispatched outside, Lunny asked, 'What now?'

Franklin smiled wryly. Once the other families had been informed, police interest in Kat's affair was over, but he had to put on his parenting hat for the fallout. 'Oh, we'll deal with it, Kat and me. We always do.'

In the main office, he spoke with his offsider, Scott Hart.

Then he propped against the front counter and stared as the constable ushered the girls through the station. When Kat came abreast, he said in a flat voice, 'Hart will take you home.'

After the truck engine fired and faded, Lunny called, 'Righto, troop, reinforcements have arrived.' The night shift had straggled in over the past quarter of an hour. 'Pub?'

'Not for me,' Franklin replied.

The sarge materialised at the doorway. 'C'mon,' he urged. 'Harty'll join us down there. Slam's on his way.' He referred to Senior Constable Mick Sprague (aka Slam) who'd had a day off. 'C'mon. A quiet one or two –'

'Nah, boss.' Franklin shook his head, unable to face the inevitable debrief, the pity and then the ribbing. He didn't want to talk about it. Not even, or perhaps especially, with his two best mates, Harty and Slam.

———

Georgie stuffed up somewhere in her navigations, did a senseless loop through the city and onto Bolte Bridge. Car tyres swished hypnotically on the bitumen. The bridge's blue and white lights were sparklers on a birthday cake. She didn't think it was the alcohol talking; she was sober enough. Either way, set against the cityscape of skyscrapers with their white, blue and red neon advertising signs silhouetted against the moody sky, the vista was dramatic.

Georgie found space in the traffic. She flattened her foot against the convertible's accelerator. The 1984 Alfa Romeo Spider had cost less than a brand-new buzz box but looked a million dollars and had capital-A Attitude and lots of go. As it charged forward, she laughed, happy for the first time today.

She had the soft-top down. Faint odours tickled her nose: the peculiar Yarra River smell of fish and brine combined with rain and local industry smog. The wind in her hair diminished her stress where the beer had failed. Or it could have been because Richmond and Melbourne receded by the second.

She loved autumn. Her mum, Livia, reckoned it was because she associated it with her May birthday. But for Georgie it embodied vivid colours of dying foliage, memories of when she'd kicked up piles of crunchy leaves that Livia had raked for the compost bin and faced into bracing winds.

The West Gate exit loomed, breaking into her reverie. She swerved across two lanes and cut in front of a black BMW. Its driver blasted her. She shrugged him off. Not long after, she took the Ring Road, then merged onto Western Freeway. Now she was on track.

Georgie settled into the leather seat. It had been ages since she'd escaped the city. It would be fun to blow the webs off the Spider, even if the trip proved a wash-out. She expected to find Ruby Padley's pal tucked up in bed in a sensible white cotton nightie. Maybe she'd be knitting blanket squares or occupied with some such older-lady pastime. In all probability, nothing sinister had prevented her from ringing her buddy on Sunday as promised; simply forgetfulness or a crazy social life at the senior citizens' centre.

She thought back to yesterday.

Ruby's screen door had banged and rebounded. She'd beelined across the paving, calling out, 'Oh, love!'

Georgie had squinted in the morning glare and sneaked a glance at her wrist. She was late.

'Taking your car out?' Ruby asked.

The Spider lived in the pensioners' rear yard. Georgie and AJ had moved into their single-fronted Victorian cottage three years ago. Richmond had all the conveniences and diversity they wanted but couldn't afford to buy on her spasmodic income and his newbie solicitor wage, so they'd signed the lease on the unrenovated cottage, then fought over which car to house in their tiny courtyard. Two Taureans under one roof makes for Mexican standoffs, and this occasion was no exception. Georgie eventually capitulated but only because her neighbours insisted she park the Italian convertible behind their home rather than on the narrow Miller Street roadway. The Padleys neither drove nor owned a vehicle. More to the point, they loved to see their young neighbours, no matter the reason or brevity of the visit.

Georgie had nodded, then frowned. A grin typically split Ruby's plump face, yet it was blotched and tear-streaked now.

When she'd asked, 'What's wrong?' and patted Ruby's arm, the woman had blubbered about her friend, a strange phone call and Daylesford. Way too hard on top of a caffeine deficit; Georgie's brain had pounded.

It didn't matter that the Padleys seldom asked favours or that they'd do anything for Georgie and AJ. All she could think was *I'm late for coffee with Bron.*

Face it; she was a bitch before her morning mug of strong, black coffee.

Now, Georgie's cheeks flushed.

Well, gutless wonder, guess you'd better start mending bridges.

As she sped along the freeway, she activated her portable Bluetooth on the sun visor and clicked the mobile into its hands-free cradle. These necessary evils were the only blights to the car's original interior. She didn't even have a dash-mount satnav.

She dialled. Eight hollow rings. Nine. Michael Padley answered. Georgie explained that she was en route to Daylesford. She heard his walking stick tap as he shuffled across the wooden floorboards. He called out to his wife, and his shuffle-tap combination took him out of range.

Georgie played one-handed air guitar, then flicked the radio's volume down as Ruby picked up the receiver with a clunk.

'Oh, Georgie, love. Michael said you're in Daylesford!'

'Not quite.'

'You're a good girl. I knew you'd do the right thing.'

Thinking *I'm glad* you *did*, Georgie's stomach tightened. With that endorsement from Ruby, she'd have to go through the motions until Susan turned up.

She launched with, 'What made you worried about your friend? This Susan Prenticast?'

'Pentecoste!'

Georgie heard her neighbour plop onto the chair in the Padleys' hallway.

Sombre, Ruby said, *'It was my turn to call. We take it in turns.'*

She hesitated, so Georgie urged her on.

'I rang Saturday afternoon at our usual time and Susan seemed, I don't know, distant? She was so...flat. Normally she chats away. But...well, she didn't even ask about Michael's health!'

'Uh-huh. You told me yesterday that the call was cut short? What happened?'

'Oh, well, that's the thing.' The older woman's voice cracked. She cleared her throat and continued. *'There was a*

noise in the background, and Susan suddenly said she had to go.'

'What sort of noise?'

'I'm not sure. A sort of scratch or thump and then she called off.'

'So, Susan could have made the noise? She could've just stood up quickly and knocked something over. It's probably nothing to worry about.'

'Well, I suppose.' Ruby sounded doubtful. 'But either way she promised to call the next day. It was her turn then.'

'And she didn't call back, Sunday or since?'

'That's right, love. I've tried all week and haven't been able to...' Ruby honked her nose. Was she crying? Georgie wished she could hug her.

Ruby cleared her throat again. 'I haven't reached her all week.'

'And that's unusual?'

'Yes! Well, she goes away for a few days now and then. But to promise to do something and not do it, well, Susan just doesn't do that. We go back to when we were young tykes, and never, ever, have I known her to do that. Not even after the fire.'

Georgie started to ask what she meant, but Ruby's next words floored her. 'So I know something awful's happened to her!'

Concern crackled through the invisible telephone connection and hung in the air.

Georgie shifted her butt on the seat.

Ominous words or sensationalism of an older lady? She was contemplating which when Michael called out to Ruby and her neighbour left her hanging.

———

Several minutes later, Ruby said, *'I'm back. Sorry about that, love.'* She sighed. *'Poor Michael, it's no fun getting old.'*

Georgie wrinkled her nose and flipped the subject. 'How did you and Susan become friends?' She drove one-handed and noted details on a pad.

'We were both born and bred on farms in Wychitella, near Wedderburn. Do you know it?'

'It's between Bendigo and Mildura?'

'Close enough.' Ruby laughed. *'Well anyway, Susan has four years on me, and when I was just a tiny thing,'* Georgie grinned, unconvinced the large woman had ever been petite, *'she read books to me. You'd have liked her books, being a writer and all. Back then she loved old-fashioned romances and poetry.'*

Georgie read contemporary crime novels, mostly.

'I didn't understand the half of it, but it was dreamy.' Ruby drifted. *'Perhaps that's why I turned to theatre.'*

'On the subject of Susan,' Georgie prompted, not unkindly.

'Yes, yes, of course. Well, we shared a love of reading. And I can't remember which of us taught the other to dance, but we often partnered up in a paddock, sprucing our moves and singing.' Ruby sniggered. *'Actually, she was tone-deaf but made a good chorus line.'* She shrieked, *'Eik. We didn't see eye to eye on farming though. She was happiest mucking in with the men to get the job done, whereas I couldn't wait to escape. Would you believe that at nineteen my friend met her Roland at a church dance, fell in love and within a few months they were talking marriage?'*

Talking marriage at nineteen? Georgie winced.

Ruby shrieked again. *'Shock horror. I had my sights set on fun finding Mr Absolutely Fabulous, or many variations of Tall, Dark and Handsome, and she settled for marriage with a grazier.'*

She squelched with her mouth. *'Mind you, Roly was rather a dashing fellow – for a farmer.'*

Georgie waggled her head.

Perhaps sensing impatient vibes, Ruby picked up the pace. *'Well, within two years, they were hitched, and I'd hit the highway; seventeen, been kissed and moved to Melbourne. After that, I went back to Wychitella a couple of times to see my parents and never stepped foot in the place again after they died.'*

'But what happened to Susan? And her Roly?'

'Well.' Ruby thought for a moment. *'They started out in a cramped bedroom in his parents' homestead and then moved to their first property in Nhill.'*

Why a young couple would choose Nhill blew Georgie's mind, having passed through it on the way to Adelaide as a kid. She could only recall a budget motel and a roadhouse that served watery scrambled eggs. She cringed at the thought of living in the place.

The older woman's pitch deepened. *'About then, Susan had to have an emergency hysterectomy.'* She paused. *'Devastating their grand plans for a horde of children.'*

Over their years as neighbours, Ruby had made no secret of two things. She regretted not trying her luck on Broadway and couldn't be happier that she'd never had kids, not even stepkids via her twilight marriage to Michael.

When she repeated *'A horde of children'*, the words shuddered.

Georgie wondered how she'd feel if kids didn't eventuate – relief or regret? Whatever; it was irrelevant to Susan's welfare or whereabouts, and she shook her head, annoyed with her own digression.

'It was years later,' Ruby continued, *'that they moved to Abergeldie in Hepburn, and she's lived there alone since she lost Roly.'* She exhaled loudly. *'You know, it really was such a – oh, Michael, what're doing to yourself? Hang on, Georgie.'*

Although her friend couldn't see her, Georgie nodded. While Ruby scolded her husband in the background, her thoughts drifted to Hepburn, one of the tiny townships bordering Daylesford in Victoria's popular mineral springs region. Aside from the historic bathhouse and a multitude of spa and massage establishments, she'd found the area had good bookshops and was arty, foodie and pretty with rolling countryside and a couple of lakes. It made for a great weekend getaway, and while she couldn't imagine living there herself, she'd take it over Nhill or Wychitella.

Several minutes later, there was a thud of the receiver and Ruby said, *'Where were we?'*

'Hepburn, and the fact that you and Susan have known each other for, what, over forty years?'

'Darling,' Ruby replied in a Grande Dame voice, *'it's impolite to discuss a lady's age, indirectly or not.'* She returned to her normal tone. *'Actually, more like fifty or thereabouts.'*

'And how often would you have seen each other since you left home?'

'Our face-to-face contact? Rare as hen's teeth, particularly since she lost Roly.'

'Yet you've stayed friends?'

The actress echoed Georgie's wonder. *'Amazing, isn't it? I love Susan, but I detest the country, and she feels the same but the other way round. We've turned out to be chalk and cheese, but our phone calls are gold. Isn't it just the way? The one time I'd love to go see my old friend, Michael's*

27

health isn't up to it. It'd take us a train, bus and cab to reach Abergeldie. And even I'm conscious of my age all of a sudden.'

It all translated to: one – they didn't have mutual pals; two – Ruby was clueless about Susan's other close mates and failed to recall the names of her friend's siblings; and three – their regular telephone calls tended to dwell on their meagre common ground of distant childhood and ageing woes.

As Georgie hooked left onto the Daylesford turnoff, the call dropped out, cutting off whatever Ruby was about to add.

———

Franklin changed into his civvies—well-worn Levis, teamed with a simple black T-shirt—and strode off, leaving his Commodore in the station car park. He often did; the beauty of living a block and a half away.

He toyed with going home as he inhaled the night air, warm and balmy despite the brief shower a few hours earlier. Franklin loved autumn. For starters, he loved the crunch of dried leaves under his boots. Shot nerves alleviated by that simple pleasure, he lit a nicotine stick and blew a string of smoke rings. He was still pissed off, but hey, Kat was just a kid. Not a rotten kid and no angel, merely an ordinary teenager being a pain in the neck. Same as he'd been at her age.

Franklin approached their home on Raglan Street. Doof-doof music beat through the air and the house was lit up like the Melbourne Cricket Ground. He hadn't seen a footy match at the G in years, not since his Tigers lost by two points to Collingwood, of all teams.

His thoughts turned from feral Magpie supporters back to Kat. So much for his fantasy that she regretted her behaviour. He mashed the cigarette with his heel and frowned. There was no point confronting her.

———

Georgie grinned over produce for roadside sale by the old honesty system as she sped past humble farmhouses. *Great poo* and the misspelt *Cheep honey* were her favourite signs. The thought that the produce and cash would be pinched in a shot in Melbourne made her smile widen.

Soon the landscape changed and timber cottages hung on a hill, vying for views of the lake or over the village. The row of flashier B&Bs and guest houses adjacent to the water was a magnet for visitors every weekend.

As she climbed Vincent Street, the *For Sale* sign on a bungalow caught her eye, followed by the backdrop of Wombat Hill with its huge old trees and competing church spires. When houses gave way to shopfronts, she turned her gaze forward again.

A minute later she entered the main drag of town: one block edged by historic buildings on both sides between the two roundabouts. A horn honked, drawing her attention to the throng of slick machines, hoon mobiles and older-model modest sedans and utilities that reflected the mix of Melburnian escapees, local youths and their more sedate elders, everyone in a hurry to check into accommodation, pick up takeaway, select a pub.

Georgie was up for the latter as soon as she found a motel. She'd thrown a change of clothes into the boot that morning in anticipation of celebratory clubbing – *Huh!*

Definitely a jeans and boots girl, rather than stilettos and skirt, she couldn't wait to rip off the bloody pantihose.

The extended brightness of daylight saving aided her search for lodgings with a vacancy, without a two-night minimum tariff and well away from where she'd previously stayed with AJ.

The motel was inexpensive by Daylesford weekend standards, while exorbitant on a value-for-money scale. But she wasn't there for a holiday; it would do. It was a place to shower—though she wished she'd brought a pair of thongs, as things that belonged on a Petri dish bloomed on the floor —and kip for the night. Its flimsy curtains were shot with moth holes, but she didn't care as she stripped off the conservative court attire and donned jeans and a new camisole she'd bought at an end-of-summer sale.

With a few bars of service on her phone, she tried Susan Pentecoste's number. It rang out.

Perched on the end of the bed, with its much-stained, burnt-orange bedspread and springs that sagged to the floor, she considered the mobile phone. Then her thumbnails tapped the keys. She paused and hit send. Waited for the confirmation beep and sighed. She'd bought breathing space between her and AJ, but it would soon come to a showdown and a decision about their relationship, even if that decision wasn't what he wanted.

She tossed the phone into her handbag and left the dismal motel with a spin of gravel.

Georgie's previous visit to Daylesford had been for their joint birthdays, almost a year ago. They'd rented a Japanese-style cottage for the weekend and indulged in aromatic spa baths and heady sex before the open fire. When they'd emerged for a brief change of scenery, they'd tried a pub in the town centre and a trendy bar at the Convent Gallery.

This time she decided to sample a pub she'd spied near the market. Away from memories of a less complicated era with AJ, predating when he tried to make the L word head towards the Big M. Though she loved him, she was in no rush for marriage, kids or respectability.

———

Franklin hastened to the end of Raglan Street. Here the Trentham and Castlemaine roads intersected, and the town merged into countryside. But he wasn't there to sightsee; he needed a drink at the Wombat Arms.

The dining room catered for city slickers and local food buffs, sporting polished tables, antique armchairs and wacky art. He didn't mind the front part of the Wombat, though. In the bar and pool room, it was singlets and stubby shorts, vintage farm signs and stuffed animals, a fair dinkum Aussie pub. But Burke's was in spitting distance of the station and had all the pub essentials, so that was where the boys generally drank. The patrons there were regulars, in for a chat and ready to take the piss – which was exactly why he chose to drink at the Wombat tonight. Not that he could be anonymous anywhere in this town, but it would be less like broadcasting his woes via a megaphone.

Franklin settled on a stool in front of the beer tap, took a long draught and smacked his lips.

———

Ivy threatened to obscure the exterior of the Wombat Arms Hotel. But for now snippets of red brick walls, reliefs of cream trim and tall, arched leadlight windows showed.

Above the angled cut-off of the L-shaped pub, the walls rose to a peak at the 1857 establishment date.

Georgie pushed through the split door at the cut-off.

Now, this is a pub.

Rich wood panelling; rows and rows of beer bottles above the bar; hard-yakka types, mainly men, entrenched at the counter. The place was a sister to her old favourite in Richmond and received a big tick so far.

Aromas of garlic, herbs and spices reminded Georgie she'd barely eaten since breakfast. Her stomach growled as a cheerful woman wearing flowers in her blonde-and-black pigtails whisked by with plates of upmarket food. She scanned the three main rooms: crowded group tables, lots of couples, straight and gay, and plenty of happy noise. She smiled. Her Melbourne foodie friends and gay buddies, especially her closest mate, Bron, would all be at home here, and that ticked extra boxes.

A song that blended country and rock played in the background. Rock was her number-one choice, but her taste tended towards eclectic in music, drinks and friends, so she hummed along in her head.

Tension she didn't realise she held dropped from her shoulders.

A glimpse of a pool table at the rear sealed Georgie's approval. Yes, she could happily while away hours here.

Drink in hand, she leaned against the double doorway to the pool room and checked out the talent. She fixed on two candidates. One guy at the bar was not bad looking, although older than Georgie's usual type. He had to be mid-thirties, and she was only twenty-eight, with a penchant for younger men – like AJ, who was four years her junior. She saw several people wave and speak to him. He brushed them off and concentrated on his beer; not in a good mood.

She focused on the younger guy with a honed upper body and tight butt. He chatted with patrons and the female publican, and Georgie concluded he was also a local. He placed two dollars on the pool table and waited for a contender. He was spot on – a cute guy with a sense of humour, not too rough around the edges, probably generous with companionship and, most importantly, drinks. A mean pool player and an expert in harmless flirtation, Georgie anticipated a bit of hustle.

While she mentally rubbed her hands together, a ripple ran along her scalp and Ruby's earlier words echoed.

———

Franklin half-watched a pool game between a bird in black jeans and a bloke he knew from the footy club. Her creamy skin set off smoky brown eyes and a full mouth. She had a great arse and wore a g-string under the jeans. Though not big-breasted, she exposed nice cleavage as she potted a ball. She swished long, dark hair off her face every so often and flirted with her opponent. Franklin didn't recognise her and reckoned she had to be a tourist.

Over his second pot, he chewed on Kat's recent scrapes. This fell into one of those times he wished her mother had stayed on the scene. No, amend that. One of those times he wished he wasn't alone on this parenting roller coaster, on the proviso that the right person was alongside.

Franklin twirled his glass in his left hand and examined the layer of foam on its sides. A nod to Roz earned another. He scoffed a bag of chips and drained the third pot. Normally he was a master of slow drinking, so his brain took on a fuzzy edge.

Fuck it, he wasn't driving. Why not get quietly plastered and forget everything for a few hours?

———

Georgie managed to push her conversation with Ruby aside for half a game. But after she'd potted two long shots, she missed an easy one when her friend's voice echoed in her head: '...*to promise to do something...and not do it...I know something awful's happened to her...*'

She sensed that Susan Pentecoste needed her and she was letting the chance to help slip away.

Georgie blew out her cheeks.

Idiot.

She tossed her hair and turned her mind to the pool game and a fresh Corona.

———

Autumn again; it used to be her favourite time. She enjoyed the last flush of roses, bulbs sprouting the spidery heads of her treasured pink nerines and long, variable days hinting at rain for the parched dams and paddocks. Most of all, she loved the season because it marked when she had met her husband and best friend.

But now, instead of relishing the change of season, its withered brown leaves plagued her.

She'd tried all means of fighting it; depression hit weak people, not her, for goodness' sake. She had never been an overly emotional woman and was a great believer in a

stiff upper lip. Thus if she yielded, the tears were privately shed, wiped away and forgotten.

Why couldn't she stop blubbering now, then? Her body racked with tears because it was March and she missed him more and more every anniversary. That adage *time heals* was a lie. She ached and endured black dreams every day, but the wretchedness intensified each autumn. So much so that her faith scarcely sustained her and her desperation shocked her.

One way or another, it had to end.

She realised that knowing what is unproven leaves a gap for a spark of hope. That hope was not logical and definitely didn't ease the pain. That was why she needed action and answers, and as everyone else had given up, it fell to her.

Even so, as she stepped closer to the tragic truth, dread curled in her stomach like those dead autumn leaves.

SATURDAY 13 MARCH

CHAPTER FOUR

The chorus of Billy Joel's *Pressure* screamed inside Georgie's brain. The damn hangover squeezed her temples.

Eyes slit. Belly burning. Teeth furry.

The chorus repeated, either as a distraction device or sadistic form of torture.

A search through her sports bag unearthed zilch paracetamol and she'd used the last tablet in the Spider's glovebox yesterday. She likewise bummed out on a toothbrush. The closest implement was a de-clumping mascara brush.

Remind me again how the fuck I ended up in the sticks.

The vice tightened on her skull.

Desperate, she rubbed soap over her right index finger and buffed her teeth. It made a marginal improvement. However, there wasn't much she could do about the lack of clean underwear. If she rinsed her undies, the dampness might seep through her jeans.

At least she'd showered. If you could call the showerhead spitting irregular droplets of alternating hot and cold water showering. She'd had to run around the cubicle to get wet.

Now dry but naked, Georgie puffed on her third cigarette for the morning and hovered over the kettle. Finally it boiled. She poured two sachets of coffee into a cup and drank it, scalding hot and revolting. Still, the cheap powdered shit was a caffeine shot and kick-started the day. Another cup of the gross coffee later and Georgie set off to Susan Pentecoste's farm.

Abergeldie was on Grimwells Road in Hepburn. She'd swiped a tourist map from the motel and memorised the route, seeing as she didn't have satnav and could never be fucked trying to follow a map on her phone, especially with the mother of all hangovers.

She'd *thought* she'd memorised the route.

Five minutes later she stopped in front of the small post office in Hepburn Springs to recheck the map. And spent several minutes holding her aching head while trying to commit the directions to her foggy brain.

Too much to remember and much of it via roads she'd never been on before.

In the end, Georgie made the trip in legs.

Left turn before the Blowhole. Map check.

Turn left again onto Bald Hill Road. She lost her spot on the map, swore and refocused. Nearly there; she could do this.

Georgie hooked right at Howlong Road. If she reached Scheggias Track, she'd missed the Grimwells Road intersection.

Ta-da, Grimwells Road.

Georgie swung onto Grimwells Road and halted, appalled by the rugged track ahead. She normally drove the Spider at one speed—fast—but now eased the sports car into walking pace. Bumps vibrated through the suspension. Gravel struck the black duco as personal body blows. She cursed the Padleys and Susan Pentecoste and her voice jarred, aggravating her hangover.

She travelled a kilometre or so yet passed only one driveway before she saw the arched sign for Abergeldie. A mob of sheep stared from the front paddock as she manoeuvred through the entrance. The leader bolted as she slammed the gate, the rest following with anxious bleats. Cattle in a far field lifted their heads, then returned to their munching.

The gravel driveway had been recently graded, and Georgie's grip relaxed as she nosed the car through an avenue of large gums. Weeping willows overhung a creek that followed the road. Prior to recent record rainfall across the state, the creek bed had probably been dry and creviced for a decade or more. But water ran now. It rippled with the undulations of the land.

She passed several stone outbuildings that looked a century old. A comparatively new barn clashed with these, as did its attached hay shed chocked with golden bales and the machinery shed.

At last she reached a wall of lofty cypress bounded by a low white picket fence. Several terracotta chimney pots topped the windbreak.

Georgie drew a deep breath and pulled the Spider's handbrake. The crunch echoed.

What would she find beyond the hedge? Safe bet: Susan and that the tedious journey had been a waste.

Georgie finger-combed tousled hair and noticed sweat pooled at her armpits. It was already steamy under the cloudless blue sky. Enough to make anyone perspire, yet hangover and curiosity probably chipped in too.

'Ah, you're back,' said Tim Lunny, as Franklin and Wells entered the station. 'Wells, a bundle of documents needs picking up from the Rush. It's ready for you at reception, there's a lad.'

'Of course, Sarge.'

Smarmy prick.

The constable pivoted, his scowl observed by Franklin alone. Despite the arse-licking tone of Wells's reply, the sarge apparently read the set of his shoulders and the stiffness of his neck, because he smirked. They all enjoyed razzing Wells and it was too easy. Pleb jobs such as the pick-up from the hotel were shared among the crew but Wells always took personal affront. Although lowest in the station hierarchy, he believed his connections among the brass set him above such tasks.

Relieved to have the cocky constable out of his hair for even a short while, Franklin dropped his folder onto the counter and headed for the lunchroom, nodding to Harty on the telephone.

'No, that's Constable Scott Hart, ma'am...'

Pained, his mate pulled on a clump of hair. Franklin chuckled, mimed drinking and received a thumbs-up.

He scooped heaped spoonfuls of coffee into mugs. Set to add commensurable sugar, he heard the front door squeal open. A small sigh escaped. His cuppa would have to wait.

Franklin abandoned the kitchen to observe two women entering. Each pushed a pram. One gazed around, fascinated. The other wore an anxious expression. Scores of people had that manner with police. An innate guilty conscience or fear lurked in even the most do-goody sorts. It made the world kind of *us and them* and this used to irk Franklin. Back when he was young and idealistic.

He'd decided not to give a flying fuck if there was an *us and them* mentality around the time he'd realised childhood sweetheart, Donna, preferred one of the bad boys from school but settled for him because marriage was in vogue with her clique. Then she became increasingly negative about his job, took up with the other bloke and left him with the baby – and a cottage worth less than the mortgage in its semi-renovated state that nearly sent him broke when interest rates spiralled.

That was ancient history, but probably why nowadays he was unapologetically a cop.

So he approached the women with their prams with what he supposed was curiosity and helpfulness, tinged with arrogance. 'How can I help you, ladies?'

They exchanged glances. The younger turned on a saucer gaze. Up close she looked barely old enough to be a mother. Her cohort, aged mid-to-late twenties, bobbed her head. The latter's baby whimpered, and she pulled the child from its pram and cuddled it into her chest. Her youthful friend pushed a folded sheet across the counter.

The women watched Franklin unfurl it. They watched his eyes travel across the page, pause at the bottom, then reread it. They watched as he plucked the letter via fingertips to one corner and dropped it onto his clipboard.

He affixed a deadpan face. But a vein throbbed in his left temple.

'Shall we go through to the interview room?' he suggested. Dual motive, to guard the women's privacy and to keep the soon-to-return Wells out of a juicy case.

They manoeuvred their prams into the cramped room and Franklin procured the missing chair from the kitchen.

To his embarrassment, the teenager latched her baby onto her breast. Jesus, he'd seen boobs before, but they weren't supposed to be so out there during introductions.

The girl presented herself as Tayla Birkley. Her suckling son, Callum, was four weeks old, as was Lauren Morris's daughter, Millie. Tayla paused and positioned Callum on the other breast, triggering another uncomfortable *where do I look?* reaction.

He scratched his chin and concentrated on the second woman.

Lauren's hand trembled as she extracted a crumpled sheet from her handbag and broke the silence. 'We realised we'd both got one yesterday.'

Two? Holy fuck.

Franklin reached for the second poison-pen letter. He tried to rein in the buzz, but his brain raced ahead.

If there're two, there's every chance there will be more.

Outwardly calm, he compared letters. 'Identical.'

Tayla nodded. 'We got them roughly two weeks ago. I kept mine 'cos I thought it was pretty funny. Wouldn't've thought of it again if Lauren hadn't been so stressed.' She burped Callum.

Lauren blushed.

Her teenage friend laughed. She seemed to be enjoying the experience.

'Tayla noticed I was a bit off yesterday –'

'She looked *wrecked*,' Tayla clarified.

'Gee thanks.' Lauren mocked a glare, then confessed, 'New baby plus toddler. I've got permanent Santa bags under my eyes.'

Franklin smiled sympathetically. Sometimes his battle with his daughter's terrible twos didn't seem so long ago.

'But then I started to really worry about this –' She motioned to the letters. 'And yeah, I admit it. I'm wrecked.'

'I had no idea about *that*,' Tayla commented. 'I thought she might have post-natal depression. My mum worried I'd get it, being on my own. So, we'd had the *big chat* at home and it was on my mind. Not for me, though. We're fine, aren't we, Cal?' She rubbed noses with her infant and his neck lolled.

'So, Tayla made a fuss.'

'And she burst into tears. She mumbled something about Solomon, and I thought, *Hello*. We went back to Lauren's and she showed me her letter. We decided to tell someone, in case this Solomon's a psycho –'

Lauren interrupted, holding up her index finger. 'Only *one* person, so we can keep it quiet. Tell the wrong person in this town and you may as well've placed a classified in the *Advocate*.' Her face contorted.

'She wanted to speak to her priest.'

'But I haven't been to church since my two-year-old was born. It'd be hypocritical.'

'And I said, "What's an old guy with a dog collar going to do anyhow?"'

'So, we chose a policeman.'

Their story told, both women fixed on Franklin.

Lauren's expression seemed to say *Right, your problem now, fix it.*

He read Tayla's as *This is fun.*

'I'll try to keep it quiet,' Franklin said, massaging the crick in his neck.

Who'd have thought interviewing could be a spectator sport?

'No guarantees, though. Now, what can you tell me about this Solomon?'

'Nothing,' Tayla said. As he sighed inwardly, she added, 'That's why we've come to you.'

After twenty further minutes, Franklin had their background but little more and they departed. He placed the letters in evidence bags although he had two chances of the budget stretching to forensics or fingerprinting: Buckley's and none. What's more, he assessed the stock to be ordinary mid-range copy paper that could be picked up from any supermarket. Plus, the fingerprints of Tayla, Lauren and himself would probably obscure the perpetrator's dabs. Moreover, although the letters were handwritten, the calligraphic script could be contrived, concealing more than it revealed of the offender.

He jotted details in his battered daybook, his private log on matters that might never come to anything or that he wanted to explore in his own time and deal with in his own way. There would be no mention of Solomon on the day's running sheet and not even Harty or Slam would hear about it.

Franklin ran over Solomon's words and fought rising excitement. This was the case where he could step up, where he could score big points against Wells – the sweetest incentive of all.

The only dampener was whether the wacko stalker presented a harmless or serious threat.

CHAPTER FIVE

GEORGIE SLIPPED THROUGH THE GATE. HER SINUSES filled with the cypress pine scent trapped between hedge and weatherboard homestead. It was foreign enough to the city slicker for her to pause.

The well-worn tessellated tiles chinked underfoot as she stepped into the shade of the verandah towards the entrance. There was green wicker furniture in front of one of the two box-bay windows and green planters on either side of the door. Everything appeared cared for. Except that the foliage on the standardised rose bushes curled. Dehydrated; alive but suffering.

'What *the*?' she said, startled by her mobile. She glanced at the screen and shrugged. The caller would leave a message.

The heavy brass doorknocker gave a resounding bang. Her second bang was louder. The echo faded and again all was quiet but for the murmur of sheep and the drone of a distant tractor.

Her phone beeped. She listened to the message: David

Ruddoch, chasing a first-aid script. He could wait until later. Susan Pentecoste was her more immediate obligation.

Georgie followed the chequered paving around the old house, peered in and tested each window. Although the front door and windows were secure, the door at the rear opened at a twist of the knob.

Until that moment she'd wondered if it were fact or fallacy that country folk left their homes unlocked.

———

As Lunny entered the muster room, Franklin secreted his daybook under a pile of paperwork.

'How'd you go with Kat?'

'We had breakfast together. It was quiet.'

'Ah.'

'She's not talking to me because I grounded her – again. She thinks it's *so* unfair.'

Lunny chuckled. His children's adolescence deep in the past, he'd more than once admitted that he and Maeve enjoyed spoiling their grandkids when it suited and handing them back once they were sick of the monsters. 'She'll come round.'

'Yeah, I hope so. I miss hearing her chat away, even if every second thing is gay, stupid or too hard. We'd planned to take a ride after knock-off.' Kat had inherited her father's passion for tinkering with the Kawasaki Ninja and loved riding pillion on road trips. 'But that's not going to happen now.'

He didn't have long to dwell on personal problems. After a telephone call, he grabbed folder, daybook and keys to the police four-wheel drive. Wells arrived with the lunches and held up one finger, meaning *Wait. I'll be free in a minute.* Franklin waved and drove away.

Franklin 30, Wells love.

———

The callout was to a plain cream brick veneer on West Street. A woman stood on the forlorn nature strip. She balanced a baby on her hip and signalled Franklin to stop.

He immediately noted her puffy face and the blotched flush of recent tears. Her hand shook as she brushed away strands of black hair. The infant in his tiny sky-blue windcheater and jeans whimpered, affected by the atmosphere.

Franklin spotted the early model Corolla hatch before Christina van Hoeckel gestured towards it. Surprised that she hadn't exaggerated—all of the small car's windows *had* been smashed—he considered the determined effort and type of weapon needed to destroy automobile glass as he picked through chips on the driveway. The interior hadn't fared well either. Among the debris, the baby capsule in the rear was a mess of broken plastic, shredded fabric and shards of glass.

The child screamed and screwed his beetroot face into an alien mask.

'Bailey! You stop that.'

He bellowed again. Christina jiggled him. Her paunch and boobs shook in concert.

'Was he upset by the noise?' Franklin asked.

'What? Oh, no. We weren't here. I stayed at a...a friend's place last night. We found it when we got home. A little while ago. Then I rang you.'

Bailey took a fistful of his mother's hair and tugged.

'Ow! Stop it!'

'None of your neighbours let you know?'

'No.'

Franklin inspected the bonnet; in particular, the red smears over the white duco. He wiped a small area, rubbed the glaze between his fingers and sniffed. Synthetic, with a slight smell he couldn't quite recognise. Not blood, thankfully.

'Any idea what this is, Christina?'

'What?' she said. 'Uh, no. No idea. Look, I think Bailey needs a nappy change. I'll be inside.'

He narrowed his eyes as she scurried into the house.

What's your hurry?

Franklin examined the red smears again. Then he reinspected the whole vehicle. No sign of the weapon or other tangible evidence. Very little to note, yet he'd still have to complete a mountain of reports for some public servant in Melbourne to later plug into LEAP – the central database for the multitude of crap they accumulated every shift. From there, it would come down to witnesses, motives or a drunken braggart to get a body into court and a brand of justice for Christina. Otherwise the case would stagnate. Many did.

'Hello,' he called at the locked security door.

'What?'

She opened the screen but blocked his entrance. Over her shoulder, he could see a small living room; clean but scented with the baby smells of milk, spew and talc, and littered with toys in bright, primary colours. The beige walls, swirly tan and cream cut-and-loop carpet and a wall furnace announced a renter's house as much as the mismatch of hand-me-downs. A modern velour lounge suite and large flat-screen television were out of place.

'Can I come in?'

'Oh. I suppose.' She moved aside.

He correctly guessed that a cuppa wouldn't be offered. He watched, amused, as she sank onto the couch, then pulled herself upright on its edge. Seconds later, she jumped up and paced the floor, snatched Bailey from his colourful play mat and nestled him into her chest as she perched on the other armchair. She was definitely edgy, but it *had* been a violent attack.

Franklin extracted the basics and next inquired if anything had been stolen.

'Oh, no! No, it was nothing like...' Christina stopped. 'No, nothing was taken.'

She rubbed her free hand compulsively over her thigh. Bailey cooed and grabbed another handful of hair.

'What were your movements in the past twenty-four hours?'

'Okay. Well, we went shopping in the morning... *Don't do that Bailey, it hurts.* Yeah, after shopping, I went over to a friend's place...'

'The same person you were with later?'

'No. We had tea at home—*Bails, don't*—and I took Bailey over to my mum's—she lives in Hepburn Springs— and came back here for a bit. It would've been nineish, maybe, when my friend picked me up. I remember that the party across the road was cranking up. The Barker boys play their music really loud and finish late. Well, morning...you know. I think it must've happened while the party was on. Otherwise one of the neighbours would've noticed and called me.'

'And it couldn't have occurred before you were picked up?'

'No, I would've spotted it, for sure. I haven't had the car long and always check it before I go out.'

'Who was the friend you were with last night?'

She waved and avoided his stare. 'It's not important.'

'Do you live alone?'

'No! I live with my five-month-old,' she retorted.

'Only the two of you?' Franklin was undeterred. He needed a picture of the van Hoeckel family.

'If it's any of your business, I'm on my own. Okay? I don't live with Bailey's dad. Is that all right with you?'

He moved on. 'Have you had other recent trouble? Vandalism. Threats. Relationship issues. Something that this attack might relate to?'

'Hmm.' She rose and walked to the unlit wall heater, as if seeking comfort. 'Not that I can think of. It's just kids, isn't it?'

'Oh, have there been issues with youths in the neighbourhood lately?' Although nothing had reached the police station and it generally didn't take long for word to get around in this small town, the community could be dealing with strife internally.

'No. Not that I can think of.'

'Do you know who's responsible, Christina?' he probed.

She moved from the heater to the window overlooking the driveway and thus the damaged hatch. 'No. Of course not.' But the back of her neck flushed, and her voice sounded strained.

'You have no idea who or why?' Franklin pressed.

She shook her head.

'What about the red substance on the bonnet? Was it there beforehand?'

'Oh, it could have been. I'm not sure,' she replied.

She'd just contradicted her earlier statement that she

habitually checked her recently acquired Corolla.

'What do you think it is?'

'That's your job,' she spat.

'Is the car insured?' Insurance fraud was a possible motive. But if Christina was an innocent victim, he hoped she had the means to get the car back on the road.

'I could only afford third party, fire and theft. What's that got to do with it? Why don't you get on with your job? I have to put my baby down.'

Franklin clamped his lips, considering her mood swing from rattled to defensive. She was either pre-menstrual or concealing something.

Expelled from the van Hoeckel home, Franklin did a door-to-door of the neighbours. He made notes.

Christina hadn't told him everything she knew.

What's she hiding?

———

'Leaving the door unlocked is an invitation,' Georgie murmured. In fact, she'd been invited by Ruby, so she slipped into the kitchen with a tentative, 'Hello! Mrs Pentecoste?'

She hovered in the doorway, admiring the room's homeliness. It was large and well-equipped but simple with its laminate benches and painted two-by-one frame cupboards. The array of canisters and spice jars and the freestanding double oven suggested its owner loved to bake.

'Susan!' She raised her voice. 'Anyone?'

She scratched her arm. What harm in taking a peek? There was no one to see it, unless Susan lay in bed in her sensible white cotton nightie. Georgie couldn't go home and tell the Padleys she'd given up at the first hurdle. And in order to get this obligation off her back, she had to locate the farm woman sooner rather than later.

Georgie heard a clock tick. The ceiling creaked as timbers expanded in the heat. She sensed being watched. She did a quick 360-degree turn. Another 'Hello!' went unanswered, and she shook off the prickly feeling as her overactive imagination.

Apart from a small batch of clean dishes on the draining board, everything in the kitchen seemed in its place. There was no sign of life – or death. No indication a person had left in a hurry or under duress. Only a carton of soymilk past its use-by date stuck out.

In the walk-in pantry, Georgie spotted a packet of paracetamol. She hesitated, then swallowed three to assuage her thudding temples and tossing stomach. She reasoned it wasn't theft; Susan would've offered them.

Grandma Harvey would have said, *In for a penny, in for a pound.* Or perhaps, *A stitch in time saves nine.*

She nodded.

So stop bullshitting, Harvey.

Maybe Susan had left a handy note beside the phone. Or knocked herself out in the shower, left helpless on the floor. She'd come this far and so would search every nook of this house if that's what it took. Besides, she was getting more curious about Susan as she went along.

Adjacent to the kitchen were the laundry, toilet and sunroom. In the latter, a folded newspaper dated 6 March—seven days ago—sat atop a coffee table, along with a set of glasses. They were bulky, Clark Kent style.

Georgie tested them. The prescription lenses distorted her vision. She knew her dad couldn't have survived without his reading specs. If Susan Pentecoste was on a trip, why had she left hers at home?

CHAPTER SIX

GEORGIE MOVED TO THE BATHROOM NEXT. TIDY. BASIN and shower both dry.

Her phone beeped. She read the text. Rosie from the occupational health and safety committee had written: 'DAVIDS ON WAR PATH'. Her overuse of capitals and lack of punctuation irritated Georgie, who punched delete.

A bedroom opposite the bathroom was small and impersonal, unlike the next room. Here there were knickknacks on the dressing table, underwear (very sensible bone-coloured knickers and bras), and, in the wardrobe, a few equally conservative garments for an older woman with poor taste. The single bed was made up. Fluffy pillows cloaked in pure white embroidered slips matched the quilt. The linen still held fold marks. A regular female visitor, not a permanent occupant, used this room. She moved on.

'Ow!' She'd bashed her hip on the corner of a hall table. In a grab to steady the piece, she knocked the telephone handset. Georgie lifted it to her ear and heard a normal dial tone.

'Let's see...' She dialled.

The *Bumblebee* tune went off inside her handbag and with it the defective phone theory as explanation for Susan's silence.

She swore. There was no handy note by the phone either.

Then she heard scratching.

Georgie froze.

What the hell was that?

She strained. Considered abandoning the search and told herself not to be a wuss.

Eventually, she dismissed it as creepy rodents and entered the next bedroom. An initial scan here revealed no body—asleep, unconscious or otherwise—in bed or on the floor.

That established, she noted details. The mid-sized room was dominated by a suite of double bed, twin wardrobes and dressing table. The recently buffed veneer pieces were as new, but Georgie knew they dated from the 1940s and would've been second-hand when acquired by the Pentecostes because her Grandma Harvey had had a similar set when she was alive.

Georgie leaned over the dressing table. A muffled thump on the bed made the bedsprings rattle and robe doors vibrate. She jumped.

'Bloody hell! You gave me a fright.'

A fat tabby gazed at her with crinkled eyes, as if amused to have caused such a stir. Georgie approached, extending a downward-facing hand and let the cat sniff it, before she rubbed its glossy coat and tickled its chin.

She gently sat next to the cat and checked the small brass love heart on its collar. 'Hiya, Oscar. Where's your mum?'

The cat meowed. He rubbed his head against Georgie's side and climbed into her lap.

'Careful there, mate.' Georgie extracted one of his claws from her thigh. She petted his head. 'You don't seem hungry. Just lonely.'

Oscar shook his head, spittle flying. His pupils dilated simultaneously with a wail.

'Shush, Oscar. She'll be home soon.'

He purred. Georgie placed him on the floral eiderdown and resumed her inspection. The first wardrobe contained men's clothing, musty with disuse and mothballs. The second revealed well-ordered women's attire.

'Susan can't have taken much with her,' she told the cat. 'A few empty hangers. Couple of spaces for shoes...'

Georgie lifted the lid on the sole shoebox, finding a stash of letters. 'This'd be worth a closer look, don't you think?'

She put the box aside as Oscar jumped off the bed and headbutted her right calf.

'This your mum?'

The sepia photo she lifted from a group of three on a bedside table showed a young bride ducking through a confetti snowstorm as her new husband pulled her towards a Buick. She glowed with happiness and, by the way he tugged at his wife, Georgie imagined he itched for the wedding night. Among the cheery crowd was a minister with clasped hands and a euphoric expression.

The second, similarly framed portrait was of the groom: slightly older, still dashing and with a mischievous gleam in his eyes.

He was one of the subjects in the third photo, now middle-aged, wearing a charcoal shirt under a navy cardigan, hair and moustache silver-grey. A crease encircled his chin up to flushed cheeks in a second smile, and his pale grey irises were offset by the deep laughter trenches that surrounded them.

Georgie peered at the second subject in that photo. 'So you're Ruby's mate, Susan, all grown up.'

Susan had not aged as gracefully as her husband, Roly. She wore square, silver-framed glasses and a plain cross at the neck of her pinstriped, black skirt suit. Her mouse-brown hair was streaked with grey. Her upper lip had little puckers and her chin a frosting of bristles. But Susan's eyes shone as sincerely as Roly's, and girlish dimples imprinted her cheeks. The couple held hands at an open-air function.

Oscar swatted Georgie's ankles as she moved to one of the front rooms. It was a formal drawing room and brimmed with antique furniture, tapestries and prissy floor rugs. The cat stopped at the doorway. Georgie gathered no one went in there. He bobbed his chin as she abandoned it for the study.

Presented with a large desk, row of filing cabinets and wall-to-wall bookcases, the tabby yawned, exposing a set of sharp teeth and a black freckle at the centre of his pink tongue. He settled on the desk, in prime position to supervise Georgie.

'Okay, Oscar.' Georgie pointed to the top bills arranged by due date in a desk stand. 'Tell me why Susan hasn't paid these two when she's so orderly?'

Her headache flipped to full throttle as her phone rang yet again. David Ruddoch. She waited for the inevitable message and retrieved it.

He spoke through gritted teeth. The deadline expired yesterday. He'd give her until midday tomorrow to finalise the first-aid script or he would assign it and all further briefs to another writer.

Georgie's armpits dampened more. While she happily pushed out the deadlines on the boring OH&S projects, she needed the money and couldn't lose her most regular work.

She checked her watch and frowned. Less than twenty-four hours. She texted David a promise to deliver and sped through the rest of her search.

She scooted back to the hall. The phone had oversized digits and no memory buttons. *Damn.* She didn't find a personal address book on or in the phone stand and slammed the drawer shut. Georgie thumped her forehead in frustration. Redial would be useless; hers was the last number called.

'Stupid idiot.'

Oscar yowled.

'Who asked you, cat?' she spat back.

The offended feline shadowed her to Susan's bedroom. The shoebox and photos magnetised Georgie. She didn't have time to go through them now, as the script wouldn't write itself.

It was justifiable research, she reasoned.

Oscar oversaw her loading the borrowed items into the Spider, along with a photo album from the study. It contained more photographs of Susan's husband and newspaper clippings. She left its mate behind as it seemed to date further back. Apart from these meagre leads, her notepad had the registration number of Susan's Toyota Land Cruiser.

Georgie cranked her convertible's engine. With a headshake, she turned it off.

Back in the house, she fed and watered the cat. Instead of hoeing in, Oscar pawed at her leg and purred.

She deserted him reluctantly.

The blue feeling didn't improve as she left the property.

A cursory check of the outbuildings gave no clue as to the Land Cruiser's location or that of its owner.

———

'Where have you been?' Constable Wells demanded. He sounded more like a nagging wife than a colleague. Even had his hands on hips and lips pursed into a cat's-bum scowl.

Franklin ignored him. He wasn't compelled to explain himself to a junior officer, only did so if the other earned his respect, and Wells would never be confidant or mate.

'Here. Now,' Lunny demanded, beckoning to his office.

Franklin's guts tightened. He suspected what was going down.

The sergeant didn't offer a seat. He steepled his fingers and sighed.

'You made Wells pretty cranky. Apparently, he believes you've shafted him once too often. When you're rostered two-up, the *idea* is that you work in partnership. But I won't tell you how to suck eggs, Franklin. You know how to play the game.'

Franklin shifted his weight but remained silent.

'Wells even went so far as venting to D24.' Lunny referred to police central communications. 'Informing them that "Senior Constable Franklin is code 1, code 5, code 3."'

Out and about, at an address or meal break. I don't see the problem.

Franklin relaxed.

'"Or whereabouts unknown."'

Now I do. Fucking great.

'It's not advisable to exclude him.' The implication was

because of his connections. 'But you know that, don't you?' It was a rhetorical question.

Lunny fell silent, though his disappointed gaze spoke volumes. Moments later, he left.

Franklin stalked into the muster room and silenced Wells with a glare. He dropped onto his chair facing the wall. Fortunately, his desk was furthest from the little wanker.

The assorted paperwork that related to Christina van Hoeckel's property damage absorbed Franklin physically but didn't engage his mind. Wells's close proximity thwarted inquiries into the poison-pen case, which frustrated him. He was equally aggravated by Christina's ducking and weaving. Either she didn't trust him or she had another motive for holding back.

Was it to hide her wrongdoing? Protect an ex or current lover? Heed a threat?

She didn't know it yet, but she'd just red-flagged a bull.

———

She recalled their first encounter as clearly as today's breakfast: All-Bran, sliced banana and soymilk; a dashing man who lit the room with his baritone laughter.

Huddled by the punchbowl, she and her girlfriends sipped fruity cocktails. Their feet jiggled to the beat as they stole shy peeks at the young men. At one point she glanced down to adjust the nerine on her breast.

'May I have the pleasure of dancing with the most beautiful girl in this room?'

Startled, her eyes lifted to meet pale grey ones. They were soft clouds, mesmerising, mischievous and mirrors to the warmth in his voice. She returned his smile.

Their gaze still locked, she lifted a hand and rested it in his, her calloused fingers cloaked in white satin. She noticed short fingernails scrubbed yet stained and, when they twirled, blisters on his palms. She sensed the strength of his wiry body through the pressure on the small of her back.

They danced and danced, she fancied with the grace of Ginger Rogers and Fred Astaire. Finally stopping to sip punch and talk, they had eyes for nobody else. He charmed with tall stories and made her feel beautiful because that was how he saw her. She felt like the luckiest girl alive, particularly when they traded dreams and found them harmonised.

That very night she discovered her soul mate, and she had never doubted that.

SUNDAY 14 MARCH

CHAPTER SEVEN

'DON'T YOU *EVER* WAKE UP GRUMPY AS HELL?'

Some people were obnoxious first thing in the morning: cheerful, chatty, capable, chic. Everything Georgie was not; everything Bronwen Silvers epitomised. Yet despite their differences, they'd clicked during high school, been flatmates, backpackers and fruit-picking partners in their late teens and continued to be bosom buddies in their twenties.

Bron leaned against the windowsill. When she laughed, her carrot-red bobbed hair flashed in the morning sun. The silver flute she stroked contrasted with crimson fingernails, as did the rings on her fingers. Those fingers were never idle.

Georgie contemplated the hands wrapped around her coffee mug and bare fingernails in need of a file. She rarely wore nail polish, being prone to chip it before she left the house. The creativity that stemmed from her fingertips was limited to words and less lucrative than her friend's artwork.

She told strangers she was a writer and let them draw their own conclusions. But in reality, she edited tomes on square roots and fractions and wrote health and safety material. These cash cows paid reasonably, were dead boring and while in progress shut down her imagination. That meant zero, zilch, nil, *nada* fictional output in anyone's lingo. When she'd quit her job at the law firm to study, she'd imagined it leading to a glamorous writer's life. She'd dreamed of loyal fans, masses of published articles, generous cheques and a row of novels with Georgie Harvey on the spine. *Joke, right?* She'd received more rejection slips than cheques and settled for the odd byline without payment to broaden her portfolio.

Conversely, Bron's two solo exhibitions in the past twelve months alone had been sell-outs, and patrons were queuing up for commissions. She lived comfortably on the proceeds of her contemporary pastels. Georgie was proud and envious.

She waved to Joanna Holt, who dropped a kiss on her partner's cheek and rushed out, wearing Blundstone boots, jeans ripped at the knees and a grungy T-shirt. Wisps of grey and ash-blonde mottled hair already escaped the ponytail secured by an ordinary elastic band.

'She's chucking bricks today.' Bron said it with a *go-figure* gesture but Georgie knew what lay behind that bravado.

As Jo approached her fortieth birthday, a pap test had highlighted a low-grade lesion in her cervix. It scared the shit out of them all, not least Bron and Jo. The pre-cancer was excised and Jo's prognosis was excellent, but the experience had triggered a deep soul-search and respite from her high-flying accountancy career.

'You and Jo cruise along, don't you?'

'Unlike you and Adam, GG? I suppose we do. Though occasionally I pick a fight for fun.' Bron sniggered.

SANDI WALLACE

'Sometimes she drives me nuts, agreeing with everything I say, no matter how stupid.'

'I don't need to try to stir AJ. It happens by itself.'

'Is that why you're avoiding him today?'

Georgie wrinkled her nose. She'd escaped to Bron's for a stay on both the script and AJ. He'd been a dogged shadow last night, asking annoying questions. About the court case, where she'd been the previous evening and why she was pissed off with him.

'How much did you tell him about Daylesford?'

'He got the bare bones, that'll do,' Georgie replied. 'I'm a grown woman and don't have to report my every move.'

'All grown up. Intelligent and independent, huh, Georgie Girl?'

Georgie shrugged.

'And that's why you insisted on representing yourself in court. *And lost.* Instead of using one of Adam's associates... Because you're so intelligent.'

'No one likes a smart arse,' Georgie retorted with an eye roll. 'Okay, so stress *independent*. He'd frown on me going into Susan's house and freak out that I borrowed her stuff. He'd tell me I don't know what I'm doing and shouldn't get involved. And that'd make me all the more determined.'

———

Franklin placed hands on hips and winged his arms sideways to block the entrance to the TAB. Paul Wells tried to push through from behind him. Franklin bent his knees to reinforce his stance.

'I'll sort it. Let me through.'

Engrossed in the chaotic scene before him, Franklin snorted exasperated streams of air from his nostrils. Wells was an idiot and would charge right in without summing up first.

He inhaled to focus his mind and caught a whiff of cow dung and sweat. Now he pinpointed the mêlée culprits in the far-right pocket of the shop. High-pitched threats and blows flew between these two young males.

'Call yerself a mate! I'll kill you!'

'As if. You're too much of a pussy.'

Franklin frowned as the tall bloke rained blows on the shorter one's torso. He knew these jokers. They were thick as thieves normally.

Several bystanders cheered and egged the blokes on. They looked like kids in a schoolyard about to call *Fight! Fight! Fight!*

Leigh smacked at Ryan's fists. Ryan's punches grew wilder and faster. His face turned fiery red with exertion and fury.

'Imbecile,' Wells hissed just loud enough for his partner to hear.

Franklin itched to punch Wells but would never give him the satisfaction. He couldn't wait to be rid of the conceited, privileged cockhead who took up space at their station. The greenest of green probationary constables—as long as they didn't have connections to the brass—would be an asset by comparison.

'Let me through, Franklin.'

Franklin ignored Wells and continued his assessment of the betting agency. He needed to know what the brawl was about and sort it before someone copped a serious injury. He reckoned Ryan was the instigator of the fight and Leigh had seriously upset his mate.

A woman. It's gotta be about a woman.

Franklin couldn't imagine anything else getting between these two.

Inside the doorway to his left were Roger and Mick, the father-son team of farmers from Abergeldie. They debated the next race in loud ocker accents.

'Think we should put ten bucks on Nancy's Reign, Dad.'

'*You dumb prick –*' There was a world of hurt in Ryan's words.

'Each way or on the nose?'

Punters in front of the televisions shot angry glances at the fray between Ryan and Leigh and towards Mick and Roger, who'd lifted their voices over the ruckus. The blokes cursed, turned back to the screens and strained to hear their race. They'd be annoyed at a masked robber with a sawn-off shotgun if he interrupted their gambling fix.

Franklin didn't flag immediate risk to anyone but the two combatants. Yet things could swiftly escalate with a surge of testosterone and adrenaline. At Ryan's next taunt, he called to the two brawlers, 'Righto, you two. What's going on?'

Most of the punters craned their necks towards Franklin, but the Abergeldie farmers continued their deliberations. Metres in front, Ryan jabbed Leigh's face, left then right. To Franklin's relief and amusement, both skimmed the shorter bloke's jaw.

'Hey! Are you two thick or deaf?' Franklin raised his volume over the din and let three patrons exit. He saw why the manager had called the station. The fracas was costing the TAB business and could end up with the shop trashed or one of these blueing knuckleheads comatose. 'Cut it out,' he shouted.

Mick and Roger glanced at the policeman and nodded

together. He hadn't addressed them, so they resumed their debate. Leigh seemed to be more than protecting himself now. He threw an uppercut that would've been perfect if Ryan hadn't tripped. The Abergeldie farmers paused, chuckled and turned away.

Franklin stepped forward just as the brawling men fell into the cluster of customers near the televisions. As one, the gambling addicts pushed away the two young blokes like a battering ram.

Ryan and Leigh ricocheted across the room. The scene was almost comical, especially when Roger and Mick finally chose their next horse as if nothing else was going on.

Franklin nudged past the farmers. He eluded Leigh's elbow.

'Wasn't my fault. Your old lady was up for it!'

Spittle flew from Ryan's mouth as he countered, 'She's me wife, ya bastard. And yer s'posed to be me best mate.'

Franklin collared the aggrieved man in the midst of winding a fist. The mob chortled, then lost interest.

I was right. It's about a woman.

He nodded to himself.

Leigh's done the dirty deed with Ryan's wife.

He still restrained Ryan and gave Leigh a look that warned him not to try anything. He said to the TAB manager, 'These two cause any damage?'

The manager shook his head with a discreet smile.

'All right then. We're going to have coffee and shoot the breeze, boys.'

'Rather have a beer,' Ryan said.

His old mate grinned, seconded the motion, then scowled.

'We need to take this down to the station,' Wells said.

Franklin glared at him. 'No need for that, Constable. In

fact, you can tootle off. The boys and I are going for a cuppa.'

'Hey,' said Ryan. 'Why should I have a coffee with this bastard?'

'Because I said so,' Franklin replied, shooing Wells.

'You could have your coffee and we could have a beer at the Rush.'

Alcohol was the last thing these jokers needed. Their breath already reeked of it.

————

AJ was out when Georgie returned. Sort of relieved, she settled into the study, accompanied as usual by the cat and dog. She mulled Bron's advice on her love life and procrastinated with coffee and cigarette breaks while the clock ticked towards the script deadline. Eventually, she scratched a passable draft and orbited the document to David Ruddoch's computer.

Georgie checked her watch: *Made it.*

She clipped her notepad as she sprawled back in her chair. When she bent to retrieve it, the points jotted while driving to Daylesford caught her attention.

Most prominent on the page was Susan's telephone number.

Even before the first *burrup-burrup*, Georgie knew it would ring out. She visualised a frustrated Oscar, perched on the hall table, eyes fixed on the phone, as he waited for his mum to answer it. She imagined the cat's misery after the final ring echoed through the house and replaced the receiver.

————

Fortunately, after much complaint, Franklin got the blokes settled at the Pastry King Café.

'Righto, I gather you've had a falling out.'

Ryan's face flushed. *'He screwed my missus –'*

'She was asking for it!' Leigh shouted back.

Franklin's 'Keep it down!' went unheeded. A couple at another table were transfixed. The shop assistants shook their heads and leaned on the counter to watch.

'That's not the point –'

'What're ya s'posed to do if a sheila comes onto ya?'

'Okay, fellas.' Franklin held up his hand. 'Settle down. Ryan, what happened?'

One ear attuned, he did a quick scan. He'd selected a chair that faced the street to keep an eye on things while he sorted the feud. Through the window he saw a woman reverse from the centre island parking despite signs prohibiting it. She pulled her burgundy Camry into the path of a white Ford Econovan. The latter locked up, followed by a stream of cars behind it. All marginally avoided impact but let off frenzied horns. The Camry sailed away, and Franklin thanked his lucky stars that he didn't have to deal with a multi-car pile-up on Vincent Street.

Imagine explaining that to the district inspector.

He noted the men had toned down. 'Well, Leigh. What's your side?'

A flood of customers filled the shop, keeping the assistants busy. He still listened to the shorter bloke's version and the occasional outburst from the other while he helped a woman manoeuvre her pram through the throng. She ordered a cappuccino and squeezed onto a nearby chair.

'Okay. So what do you plan to do about it, boys?' Franklin asked.

'I dunno,' Leigh said.

Ryan shrugged.

'You've been mates forever.'

They grunted.

'So, why don't you,' Franklin nodded to Leigh, 'apologise to your buddy? And you,' he told Ryan, 'accept his apology?'

This suggestion triggered an uproar that silenced everyone else in the shop. The young mother sat taller to better observe. She unconsciously ran her finger around the rim of her cup.

Franklin raised his brows, satisfied the boys were close to a resolution.

'Look. I'm sorry, mate. Shouldn'ta done it.'

Ryan stared at his old friend, whose eyes were stuck on the tabletop. 'She's always been a bit of a tart, I s'pose,' he conceded. He scowled when his mate vigorously agreed, yet extended a hand and declared, 'Reckon we can both do better than her.'

Franklin thought, *Yes!*

Leigh's 'Wanna have a beer, mate?' left Franklin abandoned. He watched the men cross the street pulsing with day-trippers and locals. Ryan grabbed his buddy in a headlock, jabbed without contact. They laughed and headed for the Rush.

———

Within minutes of her email to Ruddoch, Georgie had morphed from triumphant to gloomy.

'Where are you, Susan?'

She remembered the woman's stuff was still in the Spider and jumped up, alarming her own cat. The tortoiseshell had been curled next to the laptop, accepting the occasional stroke over her ears as the computer warmed her belly. Phoebe hissed and stalked to her cat flap. Georgie beat her to the door.

Minutes later, she sat cross-legged on the floor, shoes off. The stash from the farm—the photographs, album and shoebox—surrounded her and would perhaps provide a clue to Susan Pentecoste's location.

She tossed the lid off the box originally containing size-eight beige court shoes and tipped out the letters. Georgie extracted one at random and unfolded the sheet of feint-ruled paper. She leaned against the retro, black velvet couch.

Dear Susan,

The old water tank has given way. No more dips on top of the tower on hot days! It seems everything, and nothing, changes. Rather like my letters. I sit beside the window, looking at the countryside but not seeing it. I gather my pen, full of thoughts of what I shall write to you and then the ideas disappear and the page has yet again only a few ramblings of a silly old man.

I wish my letters were on par with yours – newsy, cheerful and energetic.

Write soon.

Jack

The undated letter also lacked a return address. The handwriting was neat, rightward-slanted script with loops and connections which bore a strong resemblance to Grandma Harvey's style.

Intrigued whether Jack was Susan's lover, Georgie scooped up the pile, flipped it over and, with luck, back to its original order.

She plucked the topmost note, her posture a little more erect.

Dear Susan,

Little has changed since my last letter. Days are busy, albeit somewhat tedious. There is a lack of highlights in my life (self-inflicted, it is true), which is frightening. If it is already dull while I am active and able to drive, imagine when ageing gets the better of me.

I must say how sorry I am that Roly's fate remains a puzzle. It is without a doubt a barrier to moving on. Not that you have to, of course. One good thing about growing older is that nobody can tell us what to do!

I will leave this note here and hope to hear from you shortly.

Jack

'Well, hello.' Between the lines, it appeared that Jack was besotted with Susan but she wasn't ready for a relationship. But what did he mean by *Roly's fate*? A biblical reference?

Georgie stamped a cramp from her left calf and grabbed the next letter.

Dear Susan,

You must be careful. Although you feel a need to know what happened to Roly, it may be dangerous to pursue it. Let it rest, my dear, as difficult as it may be.

Jack

Georgie's pulse accelerated in pace with her fingers. The left hand dropped a note onto the read pile. The right took a fresh one.

Was medical negligence associated with Roly's death? But how could pursuit of that be dangerous?

Dear Susan,

It would be delightful to see you again. I shall

look forward to that. I fear that you will find me
a changed person now. From out of the blue,
after my 65ᵗʰ birthday, my hair turned white and
thin, like on a baby's crown. Yet underneath, I
am the same man. But can you empathise? I
suspect you'd have changed little, spring chicken
that you are.

Please take care. I hope your silence about Roly
means that you have let the matter rest?

Jack

Maybe Jack held the answer; not the Roly stuff. Perhaps
Susan was in bed with him right now. Where, though?
None of the letters had a sender's address. Clearly Jack was
old and wrinkled, but he could live in Tyabb or Tokyo for
all Georgie knew, although dips in the water tank hinted at
country Australia.

Dear Susan,

Have you changed your mind about visiting? Of
course, you are busy with Abergeldie and all
your other responsibilities. However, if you feel
inclined to visit, you know you are always
welcome.

I hope you have taken heed of my advice. By the

same token, I hope you have not taken offence at the interference of a silly old man. Your latest letter was so restrained, so out of character, that I fear I have upset you.

Take care and write soon. Oh, and by the way, I don't believe for a minute that you're looking old, too. A touch battle-scarred, yes.

Jack

Poor Jack; living in hope, waiting in vain? She read on.

Dear Susan,

Your letter came as a shock. You know I anticipate your notes, but your latest words frightened and saddened me. The truth does not always liberate but rather becomes a liability.

Please write again soon.

Jack

What the hell had Susan written that scared the guy? And really, how could truth become a liability?

After she'd scanned the rest of the letters, Georgie felt

more confused than enlightened and squashed them back in the box.

She stared at the newer photograph of the Pentecostes; the dashing chap in his cardie, his plainer wife in her suit. Jack wanted more than friendship, while Susan remained devoted to the man she'd married. Had Susan succumbed to Jack's charm, or was she still dealing with the manner of her husband's death?

Was either the cause of her disappearance?

Though it was hard to see Jack as a stalker who'd abducted Susan, Georgie added it to her list of possibilities. The old man couldn't be dismissed merely because he sounded civilised and lonesome.

Georgie picked up the ringing landline, frowning at the distraction.

'How's it going, GG?' Bron asked.

Georgie responded absently, her thoughts on Jack.

'What's wrong? Are you and Adam fighting again?'

'Nuh. It's Susan Pentecoste. I'm still clueless. And Ruby will expect an update today.' She filled her in on the letters.

'So mysterious Jack's either the key or a detour,' Bron said.

'I've already spent hours on this.'

'But you're a dog with a bone, aren't you, Georgie Girl?'

CHAPTER EIGHT

As Franklin rose to leave the café, the woman with the baby spoke. 'You sorted them out okay.' She smiled timidly.

He sensed she wanted to chat and relocated to her table. She sat on the edge of her chair and fiddled with her necklace. She slid the gold locket from side to side, shy and mute.

Franklin instigated introductions and small talk about the weather: it began fine but now held the whiff of a cool change and more rain. Cathy loosened up and soon perceived that a paternal streak lurked inside the blue monkey suit. She pushed her three-month-old, Tyson, into his arms. Franklin bounced him as he'd done for baby Kat, and the infant chuckled. Cathy clapped her hands to further excite the bub.

Yet, despite the fun and his attempts to draw out whatever was on her mind, she tucked Tyson into the pram and left.

'A dog with a bone,' Georgie said aloud, after Bron hung up. At the word *bone*, the golden retriever at her feet thumped her tail. 'Later, Moll.' She chuckled when the dog sighed and dropped her head. 'Shall we flick through Susan's album then?'

The first part contained photographs of Roland Pentecoste, with Susan, with mates or on his own. Many pictured him at work. He drove tractors, strained fences, drenched sheep, fixed machines, assisted calf births and bottle-fed lambs. In all, he looked robust and jovial. His wife's weathered face was also happy as she mucked in wearing identical overalls. They were two-of-a-kind characters.

Georgie eyed them wistfully. Would she and AJ be together when they were old and wrinkled? She'd wager that Susan hadn't had doubts.

Snippets from the local paper and a number of thank-you notes, discoloured with age, followed the photos. Roly had apparently spent a great part of his life helping the community.

Molly suddenly leapt up and ran to the back door, then rushed back and snuffled Georgie's hand.

'What's up?'

Molly nudged her, knocked the album from her lap.

'You can go outside if you want,' Georgie said. 'You go in and out that flap three thousand times a day.'

Molly did two full circles with nose bent to tail. She halted and gave her deep warning bark. She seldom used it.

'Okay, Moll. Let's see what's up.'

The dog shot out the door and bolted to the side fence. Georgie followed.

'Oh, please. Help!'

It was Michael Padley's voice. 'Adam, Georgie, are you there? Oh, dear. Anyone?'

Georgie scaled the fence and found Michael bent over the inert body of his wife, sobbing.

'Ruby, can you hear me? Squeeze my hands.' She waited, unconsciously holding her breath.

To her relief, she felt faint pressure. She exhaled.

Ruby too released a gasp.

'Michael, what happened? Have you called an ambulance?'

He shook his head.

Georgie assessed Ruby's pale, clammy skin, her irregular breaths, clenched neck and facial muscles and dashed inside.

'Paramedics are on their way,' the operator told her.

But that wasn't good enough; she needed them here *now*.

She numbed. In a blur, she heard the operator's questions, answered and followed instructions.

'Give the patient aspirin if it's on hand. You're on a cordless phone? Good. We'll stay on the line and talk you through it. Now, I need you to monitor her vital signs. Commence cardiopulmonary resuscitation if she goes into full cardiac arrest – if there's no breathing, no pulse. Treat for shock.'

Georgie and Michael were the ones in shock. They watched Ruby, hoping she wouldn't die.

Georgie sat the man down and folded his gnarled hand around his wife's. With luck that would help them both. She suppressed her own fear, acted calm and brushed a palm over Ruby's brow.

The older woman faded in and out of consciousness and didn't respond to Georgie's gentle voice, apart from a sporadic flutter of her eyelids. At times, the tendons in her neck went taut, then the pressure eased. Once, she moaned.

Ruby's eyes rolled and her body slumped just as the ambulance screamed into the one-way street.

Pandemonium followed. The ambos administered oxygen. They loaded their patient into the van as if she weighed fifty kilograms rather than at least one hundred and thirty. They rigged her to machines and slammed doors. The vehicle powered away.

The right indicator signalled and brake lights flickered. The ambulance hooked into Rowena Parade and vanished.

Georgie rubbed her arms. Had the day suddenly turned cold? No, the iciness was internal.

Deemed too frail to travel with his wife, Michael let Georgie bundle him and his walking stick into the Spider, and she raced to the Alfred Hospital.

CHAPTER NINE

THEY HELD HANDS, WAITED, OVERWHELMED BY THE controlled chaos. Fraught orderlies pushed trolleys. Doctors and nurses rushed past, avoiding anxious loved ones. The business of saving lives was set to constant noise and activity and the omnipresent odour of disinfectant.

They picked at sandwiches on a par with the cardboard pasta in the pub a few days earlier and drank foul coffee from paper cups.

'It's all the worry over Susan,' Michael told Georgie.

She squeezed his hand.

'I've never seen her so worked up. She's the happiest person I know. She lights up the room, like she used to light up the stage, doesn't she?'

'She sure does.' Georgie swallowed away the sting in her throat.

'She thinks something awful's happened to Susan. You will help, won't you, dear? You'll find Susan and set Ruby's mind at rest.'

Michael looked directly at her. A teardrop hovered on

each of his red eyelids. He clutched her fingers with physical strength she hadn't thought he had.

The sting became a spiky lump.

'Won't you?'

Georgie gulped.

Then, 'Of course,' fell from her mouth.

She mulled over that promise during the next few hours. While she smoked outside with nurses, visitors and patients accompanied by wheelie-drips and as she trawled the corridors for toilets and a cafeteria that might sell better food than the vending machine.

She hoped not to fail. If she believed in God, she would've prayed for Ruby to live to see her friend again.

Finally, a doctor introduced himself. He then crouched before Michael.

'Mr Padley, your wife is in intensive care in a serious but stable condition. She suffered a myocardial infarction. In layman's terms, she went into cardiac arrest as a result of a blockage in the coronary arteries.'

Michael bobbed his head, skin stretched over his face. He gripped Georgie's bicep, and she rubbed his knobbly hand to comfort them both.

'Your wife was unconscious, with no pulse or breathing during transport to the hospital,' Dr Wilson continued. 'The paramedics administered a controlled electric shock using a defibrillator machine to re-establish a normal rhythm in Mrs Padley's heart.' He paused. 'I'm trying to keep this simple. Do you follow me so far?'

Michael and Georgie both nodded. Ruby had died but came back following a jump-start.

'Good, good. Once we got Mrs Padley into intensive care, we were able to treat the symptoms and stabilise her. Over the next few days, we'll monitor and assess your wife's condition. In all probability, she will progressively recover and, with medication and rehabilitation, be home again soon.'

Georgie wasn't certain if the sob came from her or Michael. But they sagged together. Ruby would pull through.

'Mr Padley, you are welcome to sit with your wife.' The doctor added, 'But it's family only for the interim, I'm afraid.'

Georgie left the hospital after Michael vowed to call if Ruby's condition changed or if he needed anything. She slumped at the Spider's wheel, drained and lost. Then she recalled her pledge to Michael and found focus. She would help Ruby by tracking down Susan Pentecoste.

First, she'd finish her review of the album from Abergeldie.

———

Franklin stepped into the station. Wells seized his arm and propelled him to the truck, firing off a verbal report.

They approached the same ramshackle cottage they'd been called to way too many times. Franklin tensed with each kilometre, worried they'd walk into a bloody murder or murder-suicide. His worst nightmare involved the four kiddies.

But this instance came to little more than highly vocal push-and-shove. They took the husband with them, to go through the motions. No doubt, before the ink dried on the charge sheet and intervention order, the wife would say she didn't want to go ahead. Then she'd invite the prick back into the home. And so it would go, all over again.

Didn't she realise that the next fight could be fatal?

As soon as the husband left, a youngster with an overdue project on capital punishment bailed up Franklin at the front counter. Why things became urgent on a Sunday afternoon mystified him.

The kid's project: matters archaic. His mind leapt to the letters penned by Solomon and churned over the facts while he dealt with a steady stream of customers. He managed one clandestine phone call only to be stymied at the post. The Ballarat Base Hospital registrar wasn't available until next morning. His other idea couldn't be handled by phone and would have to wait too.

The shabby station suddenly seemed far too small amid an influx of burly blokes in uniform, with hefty equipment belts and loud voices. The twilight shift had arrived. Sundays were their sole seven-hourer, and it was unheard of for one of the team to stay on after changeover. If you were fortunate to be on day shift, at five o'clock you were out of there.

He shoved off and considered the pub versus a night in with Kat. Neither held appeal. Instead he tapped on a plate glass window and caught the eye of Lewis Davis.

The owner of The Springs Real Estate clutched a mobile in a meaty paw. He beamed and unlocked the front door, still in animated conversation on the phone. As Franklin checked out pics and blurbs for current offerings, amazed at the prices, another person entered.

'Jennifer.' His nod was curt.

'John, hi.' She hunted for a hole to disappear into.

As Jennifer McGuire pulled out her rent money, Franklin said, 'I read *On the Beat* this week.'

The journalist blushed. 'Oh?'

Before he could rip into her about the inaccurate article, Lewis waved him over.

Still furious, Franklin dropped into the visitor's chair and blurted out, 'I'm thinking about selling the house.'

'You finished the renos?'

'Don't think I'll ever be finished,' he admitted. 'Plus, I hate the kitchen.' That put it mildly. He wanted to vomit when he walked into the room.

'Didn't you and Donna do that up together?'

'That's why. It's Donna all over. Especially the pink walls.'

The older man gazed at him sympathetically. He tucked in his five chins and pursed soft red lips. Then he blinked. Whatever he was about to say made him uncomfortable.

'Is it really the pink walls, or is there more to this sudden interest in selling?'

Franklin snorted, pissed off and embarrassed. He disguised it with an awkward laugh. Had the other man sensed his desperate fucking struggle with fear of change and the need for it, while somehow surviving his daughter's teens?

———

Georgie flicked over the pages of the album. She imagined Susan clipping each piece. She pictured wrinkled hands, perhaps with the odd liver spot and slight tremble, as they aligned the entries under the album's plastic sleeves and smoothed out air bubbles.

Did she talk to her dead husband as she documented another fragment of their life?

Was it a therapeutic or torturous pastime?

Georgie found where she'd left off and continued. Unlike the earlier pages, the cuttings in this section hadn't yellowed. Their sources ranged from the *Advocate*—the local newspaper—to the Melbourne dailies.

She noted that the first article dated back six days short of five years. Handwritten in the margin was '*Herald Sun*. Monday 19th March.'

MAN MISSING AFTER FARM FIRE

Respected farmer and local personality Roland Pentecoste, aged 58, is missing after a suspicious fire engulfed his property on the outskirts of Hepburn last night.

His wife, Susan Pentecoste, aged 54, was airlifted to Alfred Hospital in Melbourne, suffering serious burns and smoke inhalation.

She remains comatose and in a critical condition.

Police and emergency services were called to the scene in central Victoria at around one o'clock this morning.

Crews struggled to control the blaze, believed to have started in the hay shed, with their efforts hampered by strong winds and perilously dry conditions.

Police have been unable to locate Mr Pentecoste; however, when arson squad detectives and chemists arrive at the scene later today, they will significantly extend the search.

A Country Fire Authority spokesperson stated that the incident is being treated as suspicious and a crime scene has been declared.
The inferno destroyed several outbuildings, along with vehicles and machinery.
The property's residence, its crops and livestock, all escaped major damage despite intense wind shifts.
Five CFA trucks, twenty-eight fire fighters and other volunteers from the townships of Daylesford and Hepburn Springs attended the scene, many of them friends and associates of Mr and Mrs Pentecoste, who are longstanding members of the small rural community.

'Bloody hell!' Georgie was gobsmacked. She reread the article as she recollected snippets of Ruby's voice and grew increasingly horrified.

Not even after the fire, she'd said. Then, *She's lived there alone since she lost Roly.* Her friend's dramatic breath, before saying, *You know, it really was such a –*

And when Georgie took the Daylesford turnoff, Ruby had tried to tell her something about Roly, too, but she'd missed the significance each time, with each interruption, and now she couldn't ask her friend about it.

But the successive headlines were a story in themselves:

WIFE REMAINS IN COMA. MAN'S BODY NOT RECOVERED

HUSBAND NOT ARSONIST, WIFE SAYS

'ROLY DID NOT TRY TO KILL ME' (Exclusive with wife in missing body mystery)

ROLAND PENTECOSTE STILL MISSING (Police have no leads)

COMMUNITY DIVIDED OVER ABERGELDIE INCIDENT

TOWN MEMORIAL: ANNIVERSARY OF ROLAND PENTECOSTE'S DISAPPEARANCE

REWARD FOR MISSING BODY MYSTERY

WHERE IS ROLAND PENTECOSTE? (Three years on) – This one had Matty's byline!

LET ME BURY MY HUSBAND (Wife pleads for information)

Georgie's fatigue had vanished. But tension coiled her muscles.

She jolted when her mobile rang. She jumped to numb feet and reached for her handbag. Her hands shook when she saw an unfamiliar number and feared the worst for Ruby.

Wrong number.

Georgie blew out a breath and flicked the mobile to silent but vibrating, sorely tempted to take the landline off its hook. But she couldn't in case Michael called. She picked up the album.

Much later, she pushed it aside and gazed into the middle distance. The lines above her nose deepened.

Letters from Jack alluded to danger associated with *what happened to Roly* and a potential lovelorn stalker situation.

And a series of articles featured AWOL Roly and his wife's near death.

How did these explain Susan's movements?

The apprehension that had washed over Georgie at the Wombat Arms two days ago struck again. And with it came a stab of guilt which made her gasp. She'd initially dodged Ruby's call to find Susan and then treated her as an annoyance.

It was partly her fault that her big-hearted neighbour lay in ICU.

———

Franklin pulled a photocopied page from his jeans pocket. He stared, laughed quietly.

Amazing what a ceasefire with the kid does for my attitude.

Maybe he didn't have all life's answers worked out yet, but he knew this case was under his skin. And while one part of him dutifully hoped it wouldn't spiral from sick notes into violence, the other wished it wouldn't fizzle out.

He processed what he knew so far.

Solomon was the author of poison-pen letters targeted

at two young mothers. Was Solomon the writer's real name or pseudonym? Surely, it had to be the second.

The women became friends after the birth of their children, on the same day, at the same hospital, four weeks ago. Was Ballarat Base Hospital the link?

Apart from the timing and location of the births, the Daylesford women were both unmarried, which formed another common denominator. Yet, Tayla lived with her parents, Lauren with her long-term de facto.

Franklin reread Tayla's letter for the umpteenth time.

Your illegitimate child has been Born outside the sanctity of marriage and against the Values of our society. Only virtuous women deserve children. The Bible says the LORD hates the ways of evil people. You and your bastard walk the Road of Death unless you beg His forgiveness and atone for your sins.

Solomon

The words were an island on the A4 sheet, large margins its sea. The irregular capitals screamed judgmentally. Everything about the letter seemed deliberate—from the precise word spacing and calligraphic script, to the single underline below the signature—and totally wacko.

What did Solomon imply about walking the road of death?

She had numerous acquaintances and a select group of good friends. They were those who stood by her no matter what, who even after a long interval picked up right where they'd left off, and who corresponded for years before meeting again only to nearly fall over backwards because their friend had changed. They'd grown old, lost their hair or developed a pot belly – or in her case, become more weather-beaten on top of the scars. Nonetheless, they were the same people under the skin and on paper; just the outer wrapping altered.

All that aside, she was pleased to have made a new friend. They'd met a few days ago but instantly connected; perhaps because they were very different, yet also alike in many ways. She longed to see her again and felt infused with a vigour that had been lacking in a while, along with less pain in her chest. Now, when she held her hands on a horizontal plane, they barely trembled.

She dropped her hands and looked into the horizon. Her lips puckered.

There was an era when she wouldn't have questioned her impression of a person. She would have trusted her instincts and believed the goodness in the smiling eyes and kind words.

But she was a different woman these days.

PART II

MONDAY 15 MARCH

CHAPTER TEN

GEORGIE LAY WITH HER HANDS BEHIND HER HEAD. A smile unfurled, then dropped. She chewed her bottom lip.

Fear for Ruby, curiosity about Roly, connection with Susan; these had merged into a primal need for the most basic comfort of sex. Indeed, amazing sex. Did that make her amoral? Did it matter?

Her hands slid under the doona and over her body, reviving the night before.

The front door banged. She met him in the hallway. An aura of cold air clung to his clothes and hair, along with tinges of beer and aftershave. He wound his footy scarf around her nape, drew her close. They melted into each other and kissed, their tongues probing. He pushed her against the wall, pinned her arms wide. Intense hazel eyes stripped her naked. Her hot nipples stood erect. Their breaths were ragged. Impatient fingers tore off clothing that dropped to the floor. His sweater, her black turtleneck, his blue jeans entangled with her moleskins. His sleeveless grey T-shirt pulled against his chest and hard biceps. As his fingers traced her belly, his cold bracelet shocked her skin. Her breasts swelled inside the lacy black bra. She almost came when his lips trapped a nipple; he nipped and teased. He lifted her by the arse so she straddled his hips. As her legs circled his back, he thrust inside. Like a first liaison, the sex was hard and fast and virtually wordless, though far from quiet. They moved instinctively. It was animal, orgasmic, perfect.

She moaned.

'Was it as good for you as it was for me?' AJ asked, in his Bogart–Casablanca voice from the doorway.

Georgie grinned. 'Maybe. But I vote we practise more.'

'Raincheck, kid.'

Sometimes he went too far with the Bogart thing.

'Some of us have to work.'

She bridled, as he'd intended. 'Writing *is* working.'

'Sure, sure. I bet you play all day instead of writing.'

'No, I don't,' she lied. It was only a little white lie.

He dug through the wardrobe. 'So what's on the agenda today?'

I was hoping you wouldn't ask.

Six years ago they'd had a fling at the law firm – literally at the firm. They'd been on-again, off-again since and had cohabited here in Richmond for the past three years. AJ then to now had become more responsible and oppressed by his parents' expectations and the conservative men's club of law. He'd be up in arms over her first search at Abergeldie and her borrowing of Susan's effects, let alone a return trip. Even her promise to Michael wouldn't count. AJ'd say it's black and white: none of her business.

Ruby and Michael filled the terrible gap left by her dad and Grandma Harvey, and she hated to think about their mortality. So if they were worried about Susan, it *was* her business.

Georgie frowned.

With her neighbour in intensive care, she couldn't ask the myriad pressing questions. What happened to Roly? Who was this secret admirer, Jack, and how did he fit in? Had Ruby recalled the names of friends or siblings? Could she elaborate on the disturbance that preceded Susan ringing off?

AJ tilted his head. 'What's wrong?'

'Just thinking about Ruby. And Michael.'

He nodded. Concern flooded his face as he stripped to shower. She liked what she saw.

'So what's on today?' he asked again.

Damn. Thought I'd side-tracked him.

She rolled over and mumbled, 'Oh, not much.' That wasn't a little white lie but a black one.

'Must be nice being a lady of leisure.'

Georgie exclaimed 'Huh' on rote. Yet, for all AJ's teasing, he sympathised with the pressures of sometimes unreasonable deadlines and the tedium of bread-and-butter work. He knew her writer's dreams and the challenges.

She flipped onto her back and stared at the ceiling. If all she'd amount to as a writer was scribe and editor of mind-numbing works, maybe they should try for another baby.

She squirmed, inside and out. The motherhood idea freaked Georgie and explained why the recent loss of their unplanned baby sparked confused reactions of relief and grief in her, whereas AJ grew more determined to get married and try again.

Qualms about the birth and not being blindly in love with her kid were small concerns compared with her real fears.

I drink, smoke, swear and speed too much. And like AJ says, I get one-track-minded about whatever I think's important at the time. What if I forgot all about my kid and didn't pick it up from day-care or something?

The picture was too vivid, and Georgie felt a wrench of guilt.

See, I'm not cut out for it. Ask me again in five or ten years.

Did they have five or ten years?

If they ditched all talk of weddings and nappies, would the old *Georgie and AJ* reappear? Would they fall back in sync? Could they regain the closeness they used to enjoy but lately she shared with Bron, Livia and even Matty? Might AJ shed his conformity and appreciate that her defiance, unpredictability and dedication to her current project were exactly what he used to admire in her?

Too many unknowns.

Georgie closed her eyes and resolved to pick up her game and make this the year she got noticed as a real writer.

'Already dreaming about your lazy day?' AJ chuckled. He snapped her legs with his towel.

She sighed in relief when he didn't press the point, forcing another lie. Instead, he donned suit and tie and joined other commuters in their rush to work, many afflicted by acute Mondayitis.

Under the shower, she reflected smugly. Despite its Big Dipper ride in emotion and income, freelancing ousted dread of the first day of the working week. Periodically, it *was* more akin to play than work. Not that she'd ever admit it to AJ.

———

Daylesford topped the day's agenda. But before that, Georgie made a call.

'*Mrs Padley is in a serious but stable condition.*' The ICU ward nurse was helpful but professional, saying the requisite minimum. '*I'm sorry, ma'am, but visits are limited to immediate family at this stage. Perhaps in a few days. Yes, I believe her husband is with her. Of course, you're more than welcome to call again.*'

While her fingers were in the mood, Georgie tried Abergeldie. As before, the call rang out.

She sat on the back step with coffee mug and cigarette and contemplated the complexity of life. Around her, Molly played solo soccer, Phoebe groomed herself in readiness for a cat nap, and a russet leaf fluttered down to soak in a puddle.

Clearly it was people who made life complicated: relationships, ambition, greed, even—or especially—sex. That was the crap that cluttered things.

She retrieved the Spider from next door and headed for Daylesford. Facts and images churned in Georgie's brain during the long drive.

Ruby's heart attack triggered by anxiety for her missing friend.

A community that turned on Roly after he vanished, with many of them believing him capable of assaulting his wife, of embezzlement, of a double life as a secret agent or bigamist.

Georgie's impression that he and Susan were kind-hearted souls.

Her growing angst for the missing woman.

Missing woman. When did I make that jump?

CHAPTER ELEVEN

FRANKLIN NICKED HIMSELF SHAVING, SWORE AND reached for a tissue to staunch the blood. He knocked Kat's uncapped lipstick into the vanity bowl, cursed again and used the tissue to swipe the wine-coloured goo.

Why can't she put her stuff away?

He drifted to the previous night and breakfast this morning. He and Kat had achieved a truce, yet he felt uneasy. Was this new makeup the spoils from a previous shoplifting dalliance? Wasn't she too young for warpaint anyway? She was pretty without it; didn't need to make herself look cheap. Although she would no doubt complain, *Oh, Dad. I don't want to be* pretty. *I want to look* hot.

A drop of blood splotched the basin. Hand lifted to rinse the bowl, he paused. The lipstick residue on the white porcelain resembled the substance on Christina van Hoeckel's bonnet. He rubbed, sniffed and even tasted it.

'Well, well, well,' he said, then smiled at the image of himself in an English Bobby's hat and rocking on his heels.

So lipstick had found its way onto Christina's damaged vehicle. But why would she conceal graffiti? Why be uncooperative? It indicated a motive more personal and difficult to fathom than bored youths.

As Franklin left the house, there was a bounce in his stride, and he stretched taller than his five-foot-eleven.

He had until four o'clock to revisit the van Hoeckels and progress the poison-pen case. He'd donned his spare uniform to disguise the informal nature of his inquiries. While he managed to keep it quiet from the detectives in the crime investigation unit located half an hour away at Bacchus Marsh, or even Lunny, he could work the cases his way and get a taste for being the detective he'd aspired to be but was stymied by circumstances.

Pumped, he hummed the *Rocky III* theme song, *Eye of the Tiger*. The overnight rain had cleared and roads dried. So far it was fine but not a stinker. It called for a spin on the Ninja.

———

Not surprisingly, by the time Georgie reached Daylesford the area had lost any illusion of charm. It closed in. It grew darker than the so-called mean streets of Melbourne. She drove with the convertible top up, cocooned in the Spider.

Abergeldie also oozed menace. This was where Roly had disappeared in the middle of the night. Where Susan had suffered smoke inhalation, head injuries and second-degree burns to forty per cent of her body and had been left to perish. Where, after rousing from her five-day coma, she'd returned to face horrific accusations against her husband and live in limbo.

Georgie realised that Ruby literally meant Susan had *lost* her husband. She shivered and entered the kitchen following a cursory knock.

'Bloody hell.'

The previously pristine floorboards were mud-smeared. Tomato-sauce-and-egg-encrusted plates filled the sink, along with cutlery and a frying pan. The aroma of fried bacon lingered in the air.

Excitedly, she called, 'Susan? Are you home?'

Silence.

She retraced her movements of two days before. The loo had been recently used – an odour clung in the closet-sized room. Dirty water spots lined the basin. A racing form guide lay next to the telephone in the hallway. Nothing else differed.

'Fuck!' She jumped and looked down.

Oscar had brushed his tail against her legs.

'Oh, you gave me a fright,' Georgie said, picking him up. To a melody of purrs, she gave him food and fresh water.

Pressing redial on the landline connected to the local betting agency. Georgie sat at Susan's desk, fiddled reflexively and contemplated. After a while, she admitted that she'd run out of ideas at the house. She checked the outbuildings on the way back to Grimwells Road. No sign of Susan or her Land Cruiser.

Despite her initial excitement over the disorderly kitchen, Georgie questioned whether Susan would leave it in such a mess. Added to a lonely feline, she guessed the older woman hadn't returned – although *someone* had.

———

Georgie babied the Spider along the rough surface of Grimwells Road and turned into the next property. Minutes later, she faced a woman on a tired verandah, both with a stoop that belied gravity. The old woman dried her hands on a floral apron with bright pink flounce. Her eyes creased against the sun. She glimpsed Georgie's outstretched hand and wiped her apron again.

Georgie dropped her hand and thought fast. The woman struck her as chary of strangers and doubtless would be more so of writers. It called for a family-friendly tack.

She explained that Ruby and Michael Padley were pals of Susan Pentecoste and they'd asked her to visit. So far the truth. The white lie was that the Padleys were her grandparents.

'Oh, well, Georgina –'

'Call me Georgie. Or George.' She softened the correction with a smile, while wondering how the woman made the jump from Georgie to her full name, when she could just as easily have assumed Georgia. She figured it was because Georgina was a name from the woman's generation.

'I'm Mrs Patterson. You'd better come in, Georgina.'

Georgie bit her tongue. The woman could call her what she liked if it meant her cooperation.

Mrs Patterson offered a cuppa while she chopped green tomatoes for chutney, but all through the introductions and beverage making her husband gawped at their visitor. He frowned when Georgie's grateful smile turned to a grimace after the first mouthful of coffee came with a syrupy hit. So much for *black with none*. She quickly planted on a smile.

'And how do your folks know Mrs Pentecoste?'

'Ruby, ah, Grandma and Susan grew up together. Grandma's been worried about her because Susan promised to call last Sunday and apparently hasn't been home since.'

She couldn't raise the dirty dishes in the homestead's kitchen without revealing her intrusions but expected Mrs Patterson would tell her if Susan had been home.

Mr Patterson pushed his battered hat high up a forehead beaded with sweat on a map of wrinkles. He clicked his false teeth decisively. 'Well, jeez,' he drawled. 'She did go away awful sudden-like. She asked you to collect her mail, didn't she?' he checked with his wife.

'Yes, that's right.'

Mr Patterson added, 'And she asked you to feed that cat o' hers. Said she was goin' away. For a couple a days. When would that have been, Mum?'

Georgie cringed. Pet hate: men who called their wives missus, mum or the old lady. Also impatient with slow thinkers, she sipped the awful coffee while Mrs Patterson dithered.

'Well, I guess. Hmm. It couldn't have been Satd'y because we always have the children here. We have five children, thirteen grandchildren and four great-grandchildren.'

She stopped, brandished the vegetable knife in mid-air and beamed at Georgie, who obliged with, 'You both must be very proud.'

Mrs Patterson bobbed her head and continued to dice and talk. 'It might have been Sund'y. Let's think.' She sucked her teeth. 'Must have been.'

The couple nodded in unison perfected over decades of marriage.

'Yes, Sund'y; around dinner time. You know, Mrs Pentecoste doesn't often get away. And not usually out of the blue. But I guess she can.' Mrs Patterson looked doubtful, then thought it through. 'Yes, I suppose what with young Roger and his son, Mick, running the farm these days, other than the mail and feeding the cat, everything else cares for itself.'

'Roger and Mick manage the place now?' Georgie

pretended to know the father and son.

'Yes, that's right. They laboured on Abergeldie for years and years. And then, was it two or three years after Roly went?'

The husband shrugged, and Georgie mulled over the way his wife referred to Susan formally but didn't for others. She supposed even she had quirks.

The wife went on, 'Well, there or thereabouts, Mrs Pentecoste handed over the reins via one of them leaseholds. She stayed on in the house, though.'

Georgie backtracked. 'So, she told you she'd be away a few days. Did she say where or why or who she'd be with?'

'Now that I come to think of it, Georgina, and correct me if I'm wrong, love,' Mrs Patterson glanced at her husband, 'but I don't actually think she said *where*. I assumed she was going to stay with her niece Margaret in Ballarat. Or that she and *Pam Stewart*,' she said the latter with a sour-taste contortion, 'might have been doing one of those little trips with the Community Centre. Oh, that Margaret is so good. She looks a lot like Roly, too. She comes down to stay with Mrs Pentecoste at least one weekend every month, she does.'

So, Margaret-the-niece occupied the other bedroom. 'And Pam is?'

'Oh, I'm s'prised you don't know – what with your grandparents being such good friends of Mrs Pentecoste.' She narrowed her gaze but explained, 'Pam Stewart is Mrs Pentecoste's closest friend. Though I don't know why. She's a floozy! And Mrs Pentecoste is such a respectable lady.'

'Mum,' Mr Patterson cut in. 'That's enough.'

'Well, she *is* a floozy. She lives on her own in Daylesford. Always has a bevy of men sniffing around. Another cuppa, dear?'

Over a second cup of coffee, this one without sugar, Georgie tried her last questions.

'So Susan doesn't get away much?'

The husband answered. 'Well, jeez, we reckon she stays close in case there's news on Roly.'

That was the perfect opportunity to coax more about Roly. Georgie discovered that they'd been initially drawn with the pendulum of public opinion over the violence at Abergeldie. But these days the old couple asserted that Roland Pentecoste was a great man and wouldn't hurt his wife physically or by voluntarily vanishing.

After all this talk, Georgie still had little to go on. She bummed out on her next two questions also; the Pattersons were clueless about Susan's state of mind the previous week and had no relevant phone numbers.

Just my bloody luck.

Georgie's ideas dried up shortly after and she made moves to leave. But halfway down the rickety front steps, a final query struck her. 'Do you know how to contact Susan's buddy, Jack?'

'Jack who?'

The million-dollar question. 'I'm not sure.'

'Oh, dear. Georgina, there's so many Jacks. Not to mention Johns, who're often known as Jack. There's Jack Rowe, Jack Greenwood –'

'Never mind.' Georgie held up her hand. 'If you think of a special Jack, please give me a call.'

The Pattersons nodded. They'd exchanged telephone numbers in case of news.

Georgie escaped with a headache and few useful facts.

———

Franklin fired up the Ninja and rode to West Street, the trip too short for the fury of the motorbike. Christina's damaged Corolla was conspicuous in its absence from the driveway, the glass also purged. The mother grudgingly admitted Franklin to her living room.

Bailey gurgled from the play mat as he performed frenzied pre-crawling break-dance movements. A man lounged in one of the blue velour armchairs. Expression unreadable, he massaged his chin using a pistol grip. Christina perched on the other chair and rubbed her arms. She didn't introduce the bloke, who left the room.

Franklin remained standing. He drilled his eyeballs into her and coerced eye contact.

'Christina, about your property damage.'

She swallowed but held his stare.

'Do you have further information?'

Her headshake was unconvincing.

'What about the lipstick on your bonnet?'

Her mouth slackened. She didn't speak.

'It *was* lipstick, wasn't it?' he pressed.

Christina said, 'How would I know? I just found... I just saw what you saw. Some dirty marks. Could've been lipstick, I guess.'

'Your friend in there.' Franklin jerked his head to the closed door. 'He the one you were with Saturday night?'

'No!' Her denial was shrill. 'And he's got nothing to do with what happened anyway.'

'Car at the repairer's?'

'Yes. A friend's helping out with the cost.' Her eyes slid to the doorway.

Must be some friend to foot the bill of all that glass replacement.

Franklin also wondered if the wife knew; he'd spotted a gold wedding band as the man rubbed his chin.

He persevered further, obstructed all the way. He left Christina's home muttering, 'Can't help those who won't help themselves.'

Even so, Franklin planned to identify the boyfriend and check whether his wife had retaliated against the affair. He'd also investigate Christina's ex-lovers.

In yesterday's door-to-door, a neighbour had named the man suspected of being Bailey's father. The fellow was of interest to police but only had form for theft. Unless spite was his motive, Franklin found it hard to fit him in the frame. Still, a lead is a lead.

The neighbours opposite Abergeldie weren't home, and after she knocked on the flywire door of the house on the other boundary, Georgie heard clicks and buzzes.

The crude sign on the front gate saying *Keep Out!* hadn't deterred her. But it unsettled her to be forced to converse through the heavy mesh on the screen door. She squinted and just made out an attractive woman in an electric wheelchair with a young boy perched on her knees.

'Haven't talked to them from over there in years' amounted to the extent of the neighbour's cooperation. Meanwhile, her little boy didn't speak or move.

His mother said, 'Got nothing more to say.'

As she manoeuvred the chair around the door to shut it, Georgie saw a painful shiner in a rainbow of black, blue and yellow. The woman silenced her with bloodshot eyes and slammed the door.

Some people have their own secrets and demons to battle.

CHAPTER TWELVE

Before Franklin wasted more energy on Christina van Hoeckel's half-arsed call for help, he would throw himself into the poison-pen case.

While the letters reeked of an unhinged religious element, he couldn't ignore the obvious common denominator for the young mothers: Ballarat Base Hospital. He rang the hospital registrar and after a few minutes on hold ran through the preliminaries with the woman. Her astute questions gave him a positive first impression.

He broadened the inquiry period to three months, noted details for the core maternity team and received a promise from the registrar to email the rota along with a list of admissions for that timeframe. Although the Birkley and Morris babies were four weeks old, a wider picture might reveal something pertinent.

She provided names of the medical staff on the ward when Tayla and Lauren went into labour but hastened to add, *'Of course, you can't forget the volunteers, cleaners and personnel that move between the wards. We're a public hospital – we don't have the luxury of St John's. My staff has to multitask, doing quite a bit outside the official job description.'*

Franklin mentally tacked on paramedics, specialists, administrators, catering crew and orderlies. In all, he faced an extensive suspect base from this line of inquiry alone.

Added to his pet theory, and if he also considered family and friends of the two women, he would be resource-challenged, yet a thrill tickled his spine.

That's what I'm talking about!

He panged with guilt. Lauren and Tayla's privacy had been violated, and they'd been intimidated. More than that, Solomon's letters arguably constituted threats to kill. It was vital that he narrow the list of suspects, then apprehend the perpetrator before those threats escalated into actuality.

Franklin wrapped up with questions for the registrar to put to her midwifery team.

'I'll do my best to get back to you soon, but it'll depend on how busy the mums keep us!'

He had to be content with that for now.

———

Luckily, that was just Franklin's warm-up.

Next he caught a few envious looks as the blue-over-white Kawasaki chewed the Midland Highway. He hugged the curves of the bushed area on Daylesford's outskirts and full-throttled through the open plains of the spud and crop country that followed. He smirked as he always did when he passed the Swiss Mountain Hotel in Blampied. Whoever named it must've had a great imagination. The humble weatherboard pub with its one ute parked outside couldn't be further from a chalet hotel on a lofty mountain.

Not far past the pub, he hooked left onto the Blampied–

Mollongghip Road. After the long straight and three more left turns, he reached Dingley Dell Road. Then, his destination: a bush block and its rutted single track in lieu of a driveway.

On arrival, he reflected wryly that the upside to his slow battle with hair loss was no worries about helmet-hair. He ruffled the fuzz on top and approached the weatherboard cottage.

Cottage? Franklin corrected himself to house. That ugly square box without eaves or verandahs and in constant darkness from the thicket of trees that overhung it couldn't be called a cottage or a home.

At this point, he realised his brain had gone into overdrive.

He admitted to the keyed-up sensation he got when in pursuit of a strong lead.

The hospital angle was necessary to check and could only be eliminated once he'd exhausted it – unless Solomon was just metres away, inside that bleak house.

Franklin was so tense he jumped when his mobile rang. 'Shit.' He fumbled through the pockets of his leather jacket.

When he answered, the hospital registrar leapt straight in. *'I managed to speak to three of the girls who had contact with both your mums and none are aware of threats to patients or staff, then or now. Or nasty letters...'*

'And did they recall anything unusual on or about the ninth of February?' He'd asked her to question her staff specifically about the day of Tayla and Lauren's births. 'Odd or upset visitors? Commotion between the mums?'

'No, nothing.'

'Did they remember Tayla Birkley and Lauren Morris?'

'Oh, yes, especially Tayla. The girls said she was a rowdy one! She added a few words to their vocabulary that day, and

that's hard to do in our job.' The registrar laughed, then seemed to hold the receiver closer to her mouth. *'Can you tell me more about the case?'*

'I'm sorry, not at this stage.'

He heard her sigh. She must have enjoyed something out of the ordinary.

'I'll talk to other staff—confidentially—and get back to you if we come up with anything. And I'll email that info you asked for later today.'

He thanked her and pocketed his phone as he rapped on the flywire door. Flakes of paint dropped off with the vibration and fluttered to the ground.

Franklin banged again. A kookaburra laughed, mocking him, but the place was otherwise hushed.

The front door had opaque glass panels and the house was raised on brick footings with just a few miserly windows up high, so he couldn't see inside.

Just the same, instincts told him that Arthur Hammer wasn't home.

He moved to the back door, the one sunny part of the property.

The fetid smell of a corpse hit him and he recoiled.

How could he forget?

Art had two potted plants, one each side of the doorstep. Two fucking ugly cacti with flowers the colour of the rotten meat they smelled like.

He blocked his nose and knocked but knew it would go unanswered.

Art's bicycle was also absent from its hanger outside the back door, so he might be in town for supplies or on one of his regular rounds of nearby pubs, preaching to the unconverted.

Franklin lost track of time as he traversed the local area.

He checked the obvious places; no sign of Art or his ancient racer. His last loop past the man's Mollongghip property meant he had to push the Ninja to make it back for change of shift at four. Fortunately he hadn't passed a radar. That would've taken a fancy tap-dance. Or he would've copped a hefty fine, demerit points and a stern lecture about setting an example for the rest of the community: speed kills, even police officers.

————

'Don't get too comfortable,' Scott Hart said.

One foot inside the station, Franklin replied wryly, 'Hi, honey, I missed you, too.'

'We're going to Meeshan's farm. The wife wants to hand in hubby's unlicensed Winchester. She's sick of him waving it around when he's pissed – although she's more worried he'll shoot himself in the foot than anything. At any rate, she wants it out of the house while he's in Shepp today.'

'Keys,' Franklin said and thrust out his hand.

————

Through her commercial litigation past life, Georgie had discovered it paid to approach inquiries with a veneer of pleasantness and a core of persistence. Generally that opened the vault of data – some useless, some priceless. And so with relative ease she obtained information from the local and Ballarat-based hospitals and medical centres. Good news–bad news: Susan Pentecoste had not been hospitalised or recently under the care of her doctor, who was Dr Ibrahams in Daylesford.

Similarly, the local shopkeepers knew Mrs Pentecoste from Hepburn but hadn't seen her since at least the weekend before last, which corresponded with Ruby's aborted telephone conversation with her old friend and the Pattersons' story.

Georgie took a break in Daylesford to digest information gathered so far. Mid-afternoon on a Monday; back to sleepy-mode in the town. Most of the cars and people she picked as locals. There was abundant parking and a relaxed pace, even down at the lake.

Yet, as she sat on the deck of the Boathouse café and looked over the sparkling water, she almost ached with frustration and angst. In her legal job, she'd skip-traced, coaxed information, negotiated deals and even bullied the other side. That experience had been a debatable asset in court three days ago and she felt out of her depth now. Face it, commercial litigation revolved around deals gone wrong with money at the hub, not a woman's safety.

CHAPTER THIRTEEN

Much to Georgie's chagrin, it'd come time to enlist the help of professional investigators, so she located the local cop shop in Camp Street.

It was a plain brick-veneer building situated high above the road. Garage on the ground floor; concrete steps to the entrance.

The locked entrance.

Georgie tapped on the screen, then the side window. She checked her watch.

It's four-thirty in the bloody afternoon – there should be a cop about.

She skirted the building, couldn't see alternative access and returned to the front. There she knocked louder. Still no response. She cursed.

There's always a cop lurking if you're a bit over the speed limit but not when you need one.

———

'Who's the babe?' Harty asked as they pulled into the station's driveway.

With barely a glance at the woman on the stairs, Franklin shrugged. 'She's probably lost her keys. You can handle it. I'll secure this.' He indicated the confiscated shotgun.

'Oh, I think that will be my pleasure, mate,' Harty replied, rubbing his hands.

Franklin laughed and brushed past the visitor. He locked the gun in the storeroom and headed for the kitchen, intent on a cuppa in lieu of lunch. If Harty's babe kept him busy long enough, he'd make some calls on the poison-pen case.

Jar of Nescafé in hand, he suddenly craved Lunny's espresso and snuck into the sarge's office. In the boss's chair, he riffled through the desk drawers and jumped when the telephone rang.

'John Franklin, Daylesford Police.'

'Ah, Detective Franklin, I was hoping to reach you. My name's Renee Archer...'

She ran out of steam, so Franklin explained, 'We don't have detectives at the station here, Renee, just uniforms. My rank's Senior Constable, but John will do.' Maybe highlighting this would put her at ease.

As Renee sniggered, he prompted, 'Tell me, how can I help?'

He swivelled towards the window between Lunny's office and the front office. Through the striped one-way glass, Harty's visitor couldn't see him, but he enjoyed a clear view.

'Um, could I come and see you?' Renee said.

'Of course. Unless it's something I can help with over

the phone?' he suggested. Chances were it was a trivial matter.

———

The younger cop towered over Georgie's five-foot-seven, taller even than AJ who checked in at six feet. His long neck jutted forward in turtle fashion, and thick black hair and sideburns framed his square face.

'Scott Hart, ma'am,' he said with a smile. They shook as Georgie introduced herself.

She scanned the station, unsure how to start. The interior matched the outside, tired and unremarkable. The front room was compact but neat, with brochures aligned on the counter, posters relatively plumb on the walls, things in their place. It was less austere than the cop shops she'd unfortunately encountered before. The lingering aroma of hot dogs and male bodies wafted with warm air, and a police radio squawked. An unseen male with a sexy bass tone talked in another room. Testosterone saturated the place.

She spotted Hart's rank on his badge. He looked at least late twenties, mature for a constable. She guessed he was one of the university graduates favoured by the more PC and corporate style of today's police. She hoped he'd improve upon the chauvinist pigs she'd clashed with before.

'Ah, I'd like to report a missing person,' she blurted out.

Hart's grin dropped. He pulled a form from the filing cabinet and plucked a pen from his top pocket.

———

As Renee wavered on the phone, Franklin heard the bird at the front counter say to Hart, 'I'd like to report a missing person.'

He straightened in Lunny's chair.

'*No, I can't do this over the phone,*' Renee finally said. '*I need to speak to you face to face.*'

'No problem,' Franklin replied while he strained to hear Harty's conversation. 'We'll be out and about later, so soon would be good.'

His caller hesitated. He heard Harty ask preliminary questions and wondered how the woman was *possibly* missing since Saturday March 6. Either she was or wasn't. Then, to top that off, the woman admitted she didn't even know the missing person.

'Renee?' Franklin prompted his caller, thinking Harty's babe was making a false report to get attention.

'*Okay,*' Renee agreed. '*I'll be there in a quarter of an hour.*'

'She's my neighbour's friend,' the crank explained to Harty. 'The two women were chatting two Saturdays ago, and the one who's gone missing disconnected suddenly. She was supposed to ring back and hasn't.'

Franklin approached the counter. 'Are you telling me that you're making a missing person's report on the basis of a forgotten telephone call?'

'Well, yes –'

'On the basis of what your neighbour said?'

'Yes, but –'

Franklin thought it seemed a bit far-fetched.

She glared at him.

It's a fair question.

He asked, 'And you're from Melbourne, I take it? A tourist?' He didn't peg her as one of the real locals. She was either a day-tripper or one of the Melbourne capitalists who acquired property for their investment portfolio.

'Yes, I'm from Melbourne. But no, I'm not a tourist,' she snapped. 'I'm here to report a missing person.'

'All right, Hart. I'll take over this one.'

The constable motioned and retreated.

'Your name?' Franklin tapped his pen on the counter. 'Address? Occupation?'

She told him, then fired back, '*Your* name, address, rank?'

Surprised, he said, 'Senior Constable John Franklin. My address is none of your business.'

They glowered at each other.

'Perhaps we got off on the wrong foot,' he admitted, but the woman seemed intent on rubbing him up the wrong way because she answered, 'You think?'

He held the gaze of her unnerving brown eyes. It bugged him that she seemed familiar. From where, though? Doing what?

Ah, I remember you. You're that bird from the Wombat.

He assessed her head-to-toe. Definitely the same pool ace that'd perked up the pub with her sultry looks and throaty laugh.

He snapped back to the present, raised his eyebrows and said, '*Writer*, eh? Is that your interest in this MISPER?'

Harvey said, 'No, I told you what my interest is.'

He ignored her. 'Can't stand journalists. You lot beat up a story. Twist things. It's all sensationalism and ratings. You and scumbag lawyers are as bad as each other. If you've come from Melbourne to stir up trouble and concoct a story –'

'I'm not here as a writer.' She waved a hand. 'Can I please make this report and go?'

He leaned forward to rest an elbow on the counter. Then he narrowed his eyes, straightened and asked the necessary questions. What's the welfare concern? The victim's state of mind? Has she taken drugs? Got reason to be away, money troubles, been arguing with anyone? Has she done it before? Are there obligations—apart from this *supposed* telephone call—that she's missed? What was she wearing, driving? Is she on medication? Has she been in contact with family? Is she suicidal?

Lastly, he backtracked to a blank at the top. 'Victim's name?'

'Susan Pentecoste. From Abergeldie on Grimwells Road, Hepburn.'

Franklin's stomach tightened. He pictured Susan Pentecoste. A stalwart of the local community. Warm and generous, stoical and deeply religious, all of which had been tested in the wake of her husband's disappearance. Had the strain ultimately pushed her over the edge?

No way. She'd survived the fire, media frenzy and public speculation. She wouldn't suicide now.

He mentally thumped his forehead. This wacko from Melbourne had him overreacting. Susan was on holiday.

He completed the balance of the report, gave Harvey the duplicate copy and said, 'It's quite clear that Mrs Pentecoste made arrangements with her neighbours to collect her mail and feed her pet after planning a holiday. There's absolutely no reason to be afraid for her welfare, *Ms* Writer.'

She blushed.

Franklin concealed his amusement. 'Look, keep in touch. If she's away for an extended period, we may upscale it.'

'Can't you make your inquiries now?'

'On the basis of what? A *writer's* overactive imagination?'

'Whatever. You just sit on your hands then, and I'll find her,' she said sarcastically and left the station.

At the same time as Harvey slammed the front door, Franklin had the last word: 'Go back to Melbourne, *Ms* Writer. There's no need to worry your pretty little head.'

Harty joined him at the window and they watched her climb into her swanky convertible. He said, 'Bit of a stunner, isn't she?'

Franklin gave him a quizzical glance. 'Not my type of woman.'

His mate slapped him on the shoulder and said, 'Sure there?'

He dodged Franklin's backhander and retreated to the muster room.

———

'That went well. *Not*,' Georgie said inside the Spider. The cops were useless, so she'd have to keep bumbling away until the pieces of the puzzle dropped into place. Then she'd make Franklin eat humble pie.

'Shit!' She realised that she'd monumentally fucked up. She'd overlooked a potential lead.

She immediately checked the online White Pages via her mobile for a Margaret Pentecoste in Ballarat. From her conversation with the Pattersons, she knew spinster Margaret had to be on Roly's side of the family, considering the said resemblance to her uncle. That being the case, she must have a silent telephone number because there were no M Pentecostes—in fact, zero Pentecostes—listed for Ballarat.

Fortunately, Georgie enjoyed better success with a second search, and minutes later she arrived at Rose Cottage on Bridport Street.

She pulled the Spider onto a gravel embankment and paused to admire the garden. Lavender and old-fashioned rose bushes were in abundance, and a rambling variety entwined the picket fence and curled up the posts of the miner's cottage. At the front door, she heard strains of Louis Armstrong's gravelly *Hello Dolly* and inhaled the floral scents.

The woman who opened the three-panelled door was slim, tall and dressed in an outfit more suited to a night on the town than a Monday afternoon at home: a black short-sleeved sweater with beaded red roses, teamed with a pleated black skirt. Bluebell coloured irises glittered at Georgie, accentuated by fluffy white hair and sparkly black daisy-shaped earrings.

After introductions and reference to the Pattersons, Pam Stewart invited her in, swishing her skirt in an unconscious pirouette. The silk pleats flared and Georgie glimpsed burnished red stilettos.

That's My Desire replaced *Hello Dolly*. Georgie adjusted her stride to the slant of the floors and ducked the doorways, copying Pam in her perfumed wake of sandalwood, jasmine and musk. They travelled through two tiny living areas and passed two bedrooms to the left. They entered a large room with a carved honey-coloured pine overmantel topping the fireplace. Furniture pressed against the walls and framed a dance square in the middle.

Pam introduced the tubby gentleman aged in his mid-to-late seventies simply as Harry. He wore a black dinner suit, bow tie in the exact shade of Pam's beaded roses, and polished leather shoes. He seized Pam's hand. As they twirled, fingernails trailed up and down Georgie's spine with every nuance of Armstrong's voice and every lift and swell of the band. They separated. Harry bent in a deep bow. Perspiration glimmered on his brow, yet Pam appeared as fresh as her daisy earrings. She flicked off the compact disc player, and her man left.

'My dear,' Pam said in a melodious tone. 'Sit. I'll be back in a jiffy.'

She re-emerged with tall glasses of orange juice. After a gulp, Georgie was smacked with a generous tequila shot. She instantly admired this energetic and unpredictable Pam Stewart. And began to see why the staid Mrs Patterson would label her a floozy: *envy*. On the basis that choice of friends gave a good indication of character, her estimate of Susan Pentecoste rose.

Georgie launched with the phone call owed from Susan to Ruby. Pam's questions and comments helped the story unfold, albeit convolutedly, while her face reflected a collage of emotions. They digressed into Ruby's hospitalisation, Georgie's promise to Michael and all manner of things in between. She stammered to a halt. Beguiled by the quirky warmth of the older woman, she'd revealed too much of herself and AJ.

Pam clucked, then plied her with another spiked drink.

Georgie took a few mouthfuls and a relaxed fuzz settled over her. She sighed. Then the fuzzy feeling reminded her of a nickname used for police when she was a kid, *the fuzz* and in turn, the missing part of her story.

Pam giggled during Georgie's recount of her visit to the police station. 'Oh, John Franklin's a teddy bear once you get to know him. He's rather protective of our little community, which can give the wrong impression.'

Teddy bear?

Georgie snorted. 'He made writer and tourist sound worse than leprosy.'

Pam's lips quivered.

'There I was thinking, "It's cops like you that deserve to be called pigs" when I realised I'd seen him at the Wombat Arms a few nights ago. And, can you believe, I considered spending time with the arsehole?'

Over Pam's laughter, Georgie added, 'He made me feel like an idiot. But I know something's seriously wrong.'

'Perhaps he went in a bit heavy. But I tend to agree with him. Although it's a bit peculiar that Susan took off in such a hurry, it does seem that she planned to be away –'

'Yeah, for a few days.'

'I'm sure there isn't cause for alarm.'

All well and good, except for the tremor in Pam's hands which Georgie couldn't help but stare at.

She roused herself and asked, 'Did you know she was going away?'

She sat out the pause.

At length, Pam conceded, 'No, and I was surprised that I couldn't reach her by the end of last week, but we're grown women.'

'The Pattersons said Susan doesn't go away very often.'

'Well, no. She prefers to stay at home. In all the years I've known her, the longest time she's been away, except for when she was in hospital after the fire at the farm, was a week. And then, that was with Margaret. Aside from that, we go on the odd short trip through the Community Centre or church. My money's on Margaret.'

Pam withdrew and brought back an address book, which she thrust at Georgie, tapping an entry with a cerise fingernail.

Georgie obligingly dialled Margaret Pentecoste's number. She rolled her eyes as it rang out.

Story of my bloody life.

She saved Margaret's number and address on her mobile.

'Susan's always said she'll only leave in a wooden box,' Pam mused.

Georgie almost laughed. That's what Grandma Harvey used to say, and she lived in the family home right up to the end.

Stubborn biddies.

'That won't be for a long time,' Pam went on, 'because she's strong as an ox. Oh, handling the farm on her own got too much, so she let Roger and Mick have most of it. But she'll never willingly leave her and Roly's home.'

'Do you think her trip connects to Roly?'

'I don't see how. He's been missing for so long.'

Big blue eyes turned on Georgie. 'She believes he was murdered, you realise?'

CHAPTER FOURTEEN

Espresso poised for first sip, its aroma flaring his nostrils, the front door buzzed. Franklin peered sideways. Hart was on the telephone. He sighed, hitched the service belt above the bony points of his hips and steeled for a potential rerun with the crackpot from Melbourne.

It wasn't the writer but another bloody female. In the past few days, the balance of Franklin's male to female customers tipped towards the latter. In her early thirties, this one wore strawberry-blonde hair that coiled in spirals to her narrow shoulders, red-framed glasses and a black T-shirt under a rainbow-coloured body-hugging dress in turn worn over faded blue jeans. An infant snuggled her chest. It sported a tri-coloured beanie, purple jumper with white teddy bears at the waist and blue track pants.

As he thawed in the wake of another paternal surge, the woman said, 'John Franklin?' and, at his nod, added, 'I'm Renee Archer.'

'And what's his name?' Franklin asked.

Renee tilted her chin high and laughed huskily, like a blues singer. '*Her* name is Alex. But thank you.'

He raised his eyebrows.

'For confirming I'm not pigeonholing Alex. I'm trying to avoid the pink, girlie stuff. I don't want Alex driven into the subservient little girl role, playing with Barbie and makeup. Not unless she wants to, of course. But if she'd rather play with mud pies, climb trees and become a dan in karate, well great!'

'Even if she breaks a leg?'

'*Especially* if she does.'

'What does your hubby think?'

In tandem with his question, Franklin noticed she wasn't wearing a wedding band and groaned.

She wiggled her bare left ring finger and laughed again. 'Oh, I am married, although I don't wear a ring and kept my surname. I don't approve of the whole chattel thing. You know, being branded a married woman. Carl's fine with it, he's used to me being independent. He's so preoccupied with changing the world anyway.'

Her tone was neither resentful nor regretful. In fact, she acted poles apart from the hesitant caller earlier.

Renee seemed to perceive his thoughts. She explained, 'Sorry about before – on the phone. I nearly backed out. If Carl knew I was coming here...' After a beat, she added, 'But now that we've met and with what Tayla and Lauren said –'

———

Georgie's heartbeat quickened. She raised an eyebrow.

Murdered?

'Believes he was murdered? They still don't know what happened to him?'

'Oh, there are plenty of theories, but I don't think we'll ever be certain. Not after this long.'

Pam suddenly looked very sad, frail even. She clamped her mouth and refused to elaborate.

Eventually Georgie stopped flogging that point.

'Do you have contacts for Susan's other family and friends?'

'Oh, a few.' Pam picked up the address book. 'She's a little funny like that. She has loads of friends but keeps us... I don't know how else to put it but compartmentalised from each other. Her friends from here, from Melbourne, Nhill, Wychitella and so on, we're all separate groups.'

'Do you think that's because a lot of people turned on Roly after the fire?'

'Possibly, dear.' Pam drummed her fingernails as she said, 'I can help you with local friends, although I doubt that would do you much good. There's no one closer to Susan than me.'

Out of ideas, Georgie finally confessed she'd poked around at Abergeldie and Pam chuckled over the encounters with feline Oscar.

'The kitchen was pristine on my first visit but filthy when I went back. Do you think –'

'Oh, that would have been Roger and Mick,' Pam cut in. 'Susan lets them have free rein of the place. Housework's not their forte.'

'What about this Jack guy. Know who he is?'

Pam shook her head and wrote something in elegant script. 'Here's the phone number for her sister. They were close until Ann moved to Sydney. She has four children, and now that her children have their own children, the girls don't see each other very often. Ralph and Norma are years older than Susan, who's the youngest of the four. They never married and live together in Maryborough. I wouldn't bother contacting them, they're pretty much hermits. On Roly's side, there's only Irwin, his brother. But he's loopy.'

At Georgie's surprised laugh, Pam said, 'I'm a lot older than you, so I can get away with saying it! He *is* loopy, with advanced Alzheimer's, poor thing. And his wife, Thelma, died giving birth to Margaret's sister, which left poor Margaret and Irwin alone.'

More dead ends than leads, it seemed. But one lead might be all she needed.

'I don't have a phone number for Mick and Roger. They're easiest to catch at Abergeldie... Or the TAB.' Pam added the betting agency with a grin.

Before she left Rose Cottage, Georgie tried Susan and Margaret's telephone numbers. She then contacted Ann Campbell in Sydney. Pam listened, rapt. Georgie spun the story so as not to unduly concern Susan's sister and drew a dead end.

Why was she unsurprised?

———

'Ah, you're friends then?' Franklin pictured the mums, Tayla and Lauren.

Renee smiled and interpreted, 'What you mean is: "Ah, so you've received a letter too?"'

Her mood was infectious; Franklin chuckled and mocked a bow. 'I promised discretion.'

'Well, you've done fine.' She touched his forearm, which was a bit familiar, but he didn't mind.

Franklin let Renee settle into the interview room, fixed two fresh espressos and grabbed the poison-pen dossier.

He skimmed her letter. She sipped the brew and adjusted Alex's position.

'When did you receive it?'

He arranged all three poison-pen letters on the desk.

'Ten days after Alex was born,' Renee replied. She handed an envelope to Franklin. 'I kept this and all. See, it's postmarked 1 February.'

Franklin plucked the envelope by a corner and positioned it fourth in line.

Large margins isolated the text on both Renee's A4 page and the ordinary DL-sized envelope. It struck him again that it could symbolise that the words and their writer were surrounded by an impenetrable sea.

The content also matched.

He squinted to compare the calligraphic script. Although mere weeks separated Renee's letter from the other two, he noticed a minor deterioration in the penmanship: a wavy baseline and irregular capitals. He bagged the evidence, wishing he knew an expert who could interpret the handwriting, and gulped his tepid coffee in one go.

'Ideas on the sender?'

Renee lifted her palms. 'I wish.'

Franklin drew eye contact. 'You mentioned Carl's reaction to you coming here. And cut yourself off.' He gently pressed, 'What's the story?'

'Carl makes his living—and I'm not complaining; we live very well—out of controversy. He's a lobbyist and gallivants all over the place. Unfortunately, it's the type of job that makes enemies, and so he tries to keep his two lives separate. Home and work – two different worlds.'

Franklin chewed over the word *enemies* as Renee continued.

'We used to live in Melbourne, but twelve weeks into my pregnancy with Alex, I was mugged. In the car park of Chadstone shopping centre, would you believe?'

'One of Carl's enemies?'

'No, it seemed unrelated to Carl's work, but he still thought I should have a bodyguard and live in a fortress, but I put my foot down. I've no intention of living a half-life, always fixated on what might happen. I'm a glass-half-full type, if you hadn't gathered...'

She faltered. Franklin nodded and inched nearer.

'Okay, let me back up a little. Alex was fine. But I wasn't going to take chances with my bub after the mugging, so I decided we'd move to the country. Daylesford would be an ideal place to bring up kids, plus there'd be a network for my poetry. To keep the peace with Carl, I agreed to his security precautions at the house. I take my own little protective measures while he's travelling but I never dreamed Daylesford would be anything other than safe. Well, I was shocked when the letter arrived.'

'Do you think there's a connection to Carl's work?'

'No.' Her reply was firm. 'If it were just me that got a letter, maybe, but with the other two...no, there's a bigger picture here. Someone with a vendetta against unwed mums.'

'The writer assumed you're an unmarried mother.'

'And I guess that's my own fault. No ring, going by Ms Archer, phone listing under my name – that's because I baulked at a silent number. And I guess I don't talk about Carl much. It's one of my protective measures. If I don't say too much, I won't let it slip when he's travelling. He was away for Alex's birth.'

'That's a real shame,' Franklin commiserated.

'No, that's life in our house.' Renee chuckled.

'Seriously, I'm used to it. At least we never go past the honeymoon stage. Each time he comes home...'

Franklin blushed.

Too much information.

'How do you know Tayla and Lauren?'

'The maternity centre first. Then we met properly at mothers' group and hit it off straight away.'

'Has there been contact from Solomon since the letter?'

She paused, but he got the impression she'd already thought it through.

'I've had a few hang-ups on the phone. I pick up, the line's open but no one speaks. Could be Solomon, I guess.'

'No follow-up letters?'

She shook her head.

'Have other mothers received letters?'

'Don't know.' Renee grimaced. 'The three of us met for coffee this morning. Lauren doesn't want all this to get out and end up the hot topic of gossip. She only let Tayla quiz me because we're friends and we three don't fit the mould. I mean, the others are married and wear big rocks to advertise it. It's patent that this Solomon is targeting unmarried mums and got it totally wrong with me.'

'Sure did,' Franklin agreed, then asked, 'Where did you have the birth?'

'Same as the other two: Ballarat Base. Carl wanted me to go back to Melbourne and have Alex at Cabrini or at least St John's in Ballarat. But I'm no snob. I don't need a private hospital. I'd rather be in a ward than stuck in my own little room with no one to talk to.'

They chatted further, then Renee departed, and Franklin returned to the stark interview room to ponder developments.

He updated his daybook, concluding with:

Solomon seems to have made a mistake in sending a letter to a married woman.

Lack of research? Made assumption regarding Renee?

Alternatives: letters are random and/or sent to all new mothers. Or Solomon does realise Renee is married but is judging her alternative lifestyle.

Common denominators: babies under three months old and born at Ballarat Base. Part of same mothers' group. All visit local maternal health centre and live/shop here.

Check: if share medical clinic, general practitioner, obstetrician, etc.

———

Harty entered as Franklin was stroking his chin. 'All good in here?'

Franklin closed his book and gave a thumbs-up.

'The inspector wants us to drop Meeshan's firearm into Bacchus Marsh, then go across to Ballarat to pick up a brief and some internal mail. After that, he wants us to do a radar patrol on the Midland. He and Lunny have copped hoon complaints.'

One of those hoons was the rider of a blue-over-white Kawasaki Ninja and definitely knew better. Franklin jumped to his feet.

The front door buzzed. As Harty moved to answer it, he said, 'Leave in five or ten?'

'No probs.'

Franklin reckoned that'd give him enough of a window to check his emails. It took ten minutes to log off his partner and get back into the system, thanks to the antiquated server. He seldom gave out his email address and there were just three messages despite it being almost a week since he'd checked the inbox. The most recent had been sent by the registrar of Ballarat Base Hospital. He printed the message and exited the system.

Harty returned. 'My turn to drive.' He jangled keys and grinned.

'Okay.' Franklin's reply left his mate open-mouthed, but being the passenger allowed him to scan the maternity ward roster and admission details for the last quarter. No surprises that Tayla, Lauren and Renee were all listed.

Another name sprang off the page. Cathy Jones who'd had a son named Tyson on 16 December. Not being a fan of coincidence, Franklin pictured the mother at the bakery yesterday. Her behaviour and the equivalent age of her son – it all corresponded.

He made a note to visit Cathy Jones and added at the bottom of his to-do list: *Visit Abergeldie to check on Susan Pentecoste.*

Franklin gazed out his side window, and his eyes flicked as the car whizzed past telegraph poles. His mind wasn't on what he saw, though. He vowed to sort out the irrational writer from Melbourne and solve the poison-pen and van Hoeckel cases before Wells or the Ds in Bacchus Marsh caught wind.

———

Georgie declined another drink, then asked, 'It's been well over a week since Susan left Abergeldie. Do you *really* think she's fine?'

She might have backed off if Pam's vivid eyes hadn't clouded to grey-blue. That launched the pop song *What You Waiting For?* into her psyche, and she visualised an oversized clock.

The clock's ticks increased in volume and speed during her return to Richmond.

It diminished during her domesticated evening with AJ; pizza and red wine before the television. This was the sort of night that reminded her how good she and AJ could be together. Theirs hadn't become a relationship of convenience, had it? Maybe their problems stemmed from being too alike. Both headstrong, certain their way was the right way.

She shut down her fluctuating feelings about AJ.

And her mind soon oscillated back to Susan.

What You Waiting For? haunted her again. The stupid song made her toss right through the night.

————

Their life echoed their last night together, perfect in its ordinariness to the great part, topped by a special dinner in celebration of nothing but a happy union. Afterwards, they pushed away the velvet chairs and miner's couch, rolled back the heirloom floor rugs and danced until breathless in their drawing room, especially ardent when he placed *That's My Desire* under the needle.

It wasn't a case of wearing rose-coloured glasses. Oh, no, they'd fought – about things worth arguing over and those that weren't.

And they'd experienced their share of misfortune. What farmers didn't taste fire, drought, flood or infestation over the years, along with pressure from banks? They'd

overcome illness, dealt with the heartbreak of remaining childless and lost loved ones. But they'd done it together, and that's what made the difference.

He said they had the trifecta: lover, best friend and business partner. They had somebody to share everything, good and bad. Warts and all, a permanent fixture, rather like meat and three veg, the essence of a simple but good life.

He'd lifted his glass that last evening and toasted, 'To us. To the woman who is still the most beautiful girl in the room.

'To the best being yet to come.'

TUESDAY 16 MARCH

CHAPTER FIFTEEN

'*And it's back to summer weather for Melbourne, with an expected top of thirty. The high will remain with us until at least the weekend, but there's more rain on the outlook. The Bureau warns that this will be the wettest autumn on recent record and —*'

Georgie flipped a hand sideways, smacked the radio's snooze button and killed the overly cheerful voice. She prised open one eye, then the other. First to admit she wasn't a morning person, Georgie gazed at the ceiling, procrastinating. Eventually she swung to sit up, and her stomach heaved. She dropped back to the mattress. Her temples thumped waves of pain, and her left eyelid twitched with the incessant beat of a heavy rap.

The music in her head switched from rap to pop. Three lines of the song *What You Waiting For?* had replayed all night, along with the tick of the oversized clock. She craved more sleep, decent sleep, without those annoying lyrics. Instead, she pushed back the sheet and emerged.

'Aargh!' AJ said with mock fright.

She squinted at the bathroom mirror. Rat's-nest hair,

mascara-clogged lashes, smudged rings under bloodshot eyeballs, all prominent against pale skin. She resembled a morning-after-binge vision but had actually drunk very little.

Georgie laughed. It'd be a worry if you never laughed at yourself.

'I spoke to Michael, George.'

She sucked in a breath and held it.

'Ruby's doing well.'

The air whooshed out. 'Yes!'

'The doctor's going to check on her this afternoon. Hopefully, she'll be out of intensive care and up to visitors later today.'

'That's so good.' Her legs turned to jelly with relief. 'I was psyching myself up to ring the hospital.'

She tucked her forehead into AJ's mid-back and wrapped his bare torso with her arms. Her headache eased several notches. He reached behind and patted her butt, saying, 'You think too much.'

'Probably,' Georgie admitted.

People to see, things to do.

She pulled away, headed for the shower.

Last night, her brain had certainly been hyperactive. Images of Pam Stewart merged with worst-case-scenarios for both Susan Pentecoste and Ruby Padley. Added to the 3D flying slideshow were newspaper headlines, disabled women sporting black eyes, an arrogant country cop and Pedantic Percy, the magistrate who'd almost snatched her licence. The imagery pulsated to what she now considered the most irritating pop song ever in the charts.

———

'Oh, it's you,' Cathy Jones said.

'Were you expecting someone else?' Franklin asked. He anticipated a negative.

She blinked and widened her eyes. Her left one was lazy and sleep-encrusted. Tangled hair completed the crazy-just-awake-woman image. 'No,' she mumbled through a yawn.

She flapped the sides of her dressing gown, crossed them snugly and secured the waist tie. He caught a glimpse of a camisole and French knickers set in black cotton with ivory trim. Three months post-partum, she had a great figure; a gently rounded belly and swollen breasts but trim thighs. Donna would have hated her. She'd never recovered her pre-baby shape. Not before she took off.

'Cathy, can I come in?'

Her fingers sought a gold locket under the dressing gown and slid it along the chain.

'I need to talk to you, and I don't suppose it's crash hot having a copper on your doorstep at eight in the morning.'

She scanned the street for nosy neighbours and stepped aside.

'You're here now, so I guess you'd better come in.'

'Do you know why I've come?'

The corners of her mouth twitched and her shoulders lifted.

————

The door banged behind AJ as he left. Georgie dialled two numbers, from memory now, but neither Susan nor Margaret Pentecoste answered. Then she forced herself to sit at the desk and go through the workday motions. Foremost were her computer inbox and phone messages.

David Ruddoch had left several – each with a rising inflection. Texts demanded she phone in relation to the first-aid script. His latest voicemail gave a deadline of twelve o'clock today for her call. Despite the implied threat, she'd finish her message check before she rang him.

The emailed feeler for an editing job failed to entice. Clients driven by the hip pocket often had unrealistic expectations and they preferred talks at arm's length until rates and terms were established. That could wait at least another day. She added a yellow sticky note to the row on the wall.

The next two phone messages were pleasure, not business. The first was Bron, who chased an update on all matters from AJ to Susan Pentecoste. The second, her mum, Livia, who just wanted a chat.

Georgie obliged both as she stroked the scarred edge of the blackwood desk salvaged from a hard-rubbish collection. The desk was the first piece to grace her writer's office, and she'd rubbed beeswax over the nicks and initials carved into its top to capture its history rather than over-restore it. She swivelled in the black chair, a gift from AJ, its fresh-leather aroma more subtle now. Thick planks of oiled jarrah on stacks of red bricks formed a three-tiered bookcase and flanked the desk. Slimline laptop here, antique lamp there, somehow the old and the new fit perfectly.

Next, a virtually maxed-out credit card gained grace on various bills. Smug with the results, Georgie picked up the ringing telephone.

'*Georgina.*'

It was the unmistakable voice of AJ's mother. Her stomach dropped.

Stupid, stupid idiot. Should have let the machine pick up.

She mumbled and waited for the inevitable, counting *Four, three, two...*

'*I expected you to be at work,*' Jane Gunnerson said.

The woman never let her down.

'I am. I. Work. From. Home.' Georgie's teeth were gritted.

'*Oh, well, yes, I suppose you do. Although you ought to have resumed your legal career by now.*'

Yeah, right. She'd been a glorified personal assistant, not a lawyer. Highlight of the job: doing Jane Gunnerson's son on the head partner's mahogany desk.

'*Look at how well our Adam is doing, Georgina.*'

Georgie grunted. She tolerated *Georgina* from few people and cringed if Livia said it, as it signified trouble. From Jane Gunnerson—too high and mighty to allow her son's girlfriend to call her anything less than Mrs Gunnerson (and thus Georgie called her nothing)—it was torturous.

Besides, the statement didn't deserve a reply. They would replay twists on this conversation to hell and back. No wonder she shied from AJ's marriage proposal. She'd also be hitched to his pomp-arse parents.

'*Geoffrey would like Adam to join us for luncheon on Sunday. It is high time for the next step in his career. If he is to make Silk by the age his father did, he must sit for the Bar.*'

Georgie tuned out. AJ had to decide for himself. His buddies at Berkowitz Clark Oxford, along with his father's well-connected cronies, were guaranteed to throw him briefs, which would make his transition from solicitor to barrister smoother than most. The rise from Junior to Queen's Counsel (aka a Silk after the silk court gowns these barristers wore) would follow. If he told his folks to stick it because he'd rather build furniture, Georgie would be far more impressed.

'...Adam could arrive at twelve, for twelve-thirty?'

'Huh?' Georgie said.

'For luncheon on Sunday. Oh, and you're welcome to join us. If you wish.'

It would almost be worth accepting the reluctant tacked-on invitation to spite Jane Gunnerson. But Georgie said they'd check their diaries. While AJ's mother spluttered, she hung up with a flourish that rivalled her bewigged perhaps-one-day-father-in-law's best effort.

Two minutes later, she answered her mobile to, 'Have you been terrorising my mother again, George?' Fortunately, AJ laughed as he said it.

'Didn't take her long.'

'Never does. Not keen on lunch?'

'We could get a better offer.'

'True. We'll think on it, then,' he said. They hung up.

She decided one of the best things about AJ was his acceptance that she and his mother would never be mates.

Mates.

Pam and Ruby.

Invisible threads to Susan.

Georgie shook her head. She turned back to the computer and tried to concentrate.

Fuck.

She wanted to focus on other responsibilities. But Pam Stewart's obvious distress for Susan Pentecoste and Ruby laid up in hospital for the same reason distracted her. The agonist-antagonist contest wouldn't stop for a lame assignment, regardless of David Ruddoch's fury. It pushed her back to Daylesford; to hell with everything else.

———

They hovered awkwardly in the hallway.

Franklin started, 'Want to tell me about it? What you wanted to talk over in the bakery?'

'Okay, but let me get changed first.' As she padded down the hallway, Cathy called, 'Take a seat.'

She soon re-emerged in a long sundress and sandals. 'I'll make coffee.'

A few minutes later he took a sip from his mug as Cathy curled up with her own in the armchair opposite.

'Tyson sleeping?' Franklin asked.

She nodded, and he said conversationally, 'He a good sleeper then?'

His first sergeant had told him one way to get a witness to cooperate is to talk about their kids, pets or whatever it is they have a passion for.

'Uh-huh.' Her face lit up. 'I've been lucky. He's been a great sleeper ever since I brought him home. Other mums are lucky to get two hours between naps. Want to see my photos?'

They pored over her brag book, so similar to Kat's chronicle at home. Copy of the ultrasound; first cuddle and first bath pics; clipping from the local newspaper; poster-paint imprint of Tyson's miniature hands and feet. All the usual, with one jarring absence, but he'd hold that subject until she relaxed more.

Cathy suddenly fixed on him. 'I've had a letter from a crank. Two actually. One straight after Tyson was born and the second letter last week.'

Franklin straightened.

She fetched papers from the hall table. 'Here's the first one.'

He perused it and asked, 'Do you know Tayla Birkley, Lauren Morris and Renee Archer?'

'Vaguely. I've bumped into them at the health centre. We don't socialise.'

He pulled out the other three letters in their baggies and confirmed the wording, overall style and formation of the calligraphic script. 'They have a match for yours.'

Cathy shivered. 'My second one runs along the same line. Except it gets nastier.' She passed it over.

Shit. Already an escalation? How much time do I have before this wacko wants more action than letter writing?

He read it twice.

You must lie only with your husband and be tempted not to the door of a stranger, or tempt a stranger to your door. Children should only be borne to Virtuous women, Righteous women, or as bastards be damned to follow their whore-mother's steps down to death. You must beg His forgiveness and atone for your sins. Or your end will be Bitter.

<u>Solomon</u>

Franklin considered *nasty* a bit soft. Unhinged was more like it. He easily arranged the five letters in chronological order, as the author's handwriting declined with their mental state over the three-month period.

'Has Solomon been in touch in other ways?'

'No,' Cathy bit her lower lip. 'Oh, a couple of times the phone's rung, but when I've answered it, no one's spoken. After a few seconds, they hang up. And once or twice, I've felt like someone's watching me. That could be my imagination, though.'

'Do you know who Solomon is?'

'No, I wish I did.' She suddenly switched from apologetic to angry. 'What right has this person got to send disgusting letters? And make threats? How do they get off judging a stranger, without knowing their situation?'

Cathy's eyes blazed when she looked at him. Then they filled and tears flooded her cheeks.

———

Georgie swerved from the Daylesford off-ramp at the last moment. Instead, she continued along Western Freeway.

Margaret Pentecoste held the key. Pam believed that Susan was with her niece in Ballarat or, if not, the woman would know her whereabouts. Easy enough to loop back to Hepburn later if necessary.

At Ballarat, she parked and pulled up a map on her phone. She worked it out and found herself in a street a short distance away, in the old part of town. Not among the trendiest addresses adjacent to Lake Wendouree but a short stroll from it and Sturt Street's shopping and business district, in Ascot Street South. Nestled amid period homes, Margaret's property was one peg down from *location, location, location*.

Georgie stepped through the low picket fence and followed a no-nonsense pathway carving straight through low-maintenance gardens to the verandah. Rendered brick above weatherboards clad the Californian bungalow. Its ivory and tan trims offset butter walls and at least three red brick chimneys topped the galvanised iron roof. On first impressions: immaculate to the point of sterile.

Georgie banged the brass knocker twice and waited. Overcome with déjà vu, she called Margaret's name and rapped on the glazed panel.

After a minute, she pulled out her mobile and dialled.

Rings echoed between her phone and the house.

The call rang out, unanswered by even a machine, and ghosted away.

CHAPTER SIXTEEN

FRANKLIN FOUND A BOX OF TISSUES AND CROUCHED, offering it to Cathy. His knees cracked, thanks to past footy injuries, making her giggle. She alternated between laughter, tears and hiccups for the next few minutes, then wiped her face with the bottom of her dress.

'Are you right to go on?'

'Yeah.'

'I'm wearing my policeman's hat, not being a nosy parker, okay? I need to ask several questions so I can piece this together.'

She bobbed her head.

'Tyson's father? I noticed he doesn't feature in your brag book.'

Franklin had a terrible gut feeling.

'Oh, yeah. Tyson's father. Well, he was a nice guy – or so I thought, until I went out with him. Unfortunately for me, he thought buying a girl dinner gave him prerogative to have his way with her. And he didn't stop at no. So, he wasn't a nice guy after all... Tyson and me, well, we're on our own and likely to stay that way. Not that I'd change it. It just wasn't how I'd planned to have a family.'

Franklin's skin burned in a rush of anger. He was pissed off but not at Cathy.

'You didn't report him?'

'No.' She anticipated his next question. 'And I still won't. We used to work together, and everyone knew I had a huge crush on him. So maybe I did ask for it.'

'Cathy –'

'Maybe I sent the wrong signals. Gave him the impression I'm easy and would *put out*.' She hooked her fingers.

'You're the victim. He's a criminal. Date rape is as serious as other types of sexual assault. You have to realise that.'

Franklin leaned across and took her hands. She gave a half-smile.

'You've got to report it.'

'No.'

'You need to, if only to protect other women from this predator.'

'I get what you're saying. But it's a small town and everyone would gossip. Plenty of people would point their finger and blame me – and some of them would be my friends. I wouldn't care so much if it affected just me. But Tyson's my number-one priority. I won't have him growing up with the stigma... I won't let him think he wasn't wanted!'

Franklin couldn't argue. As a parent, he sympathised. Kids were about the only true innocents and deserved to be protected.

Cathy stonewalled further discussion about the rape, so he reverted to the poison-pen missives.

'You have no idea who this Solomon is?'

She shook her head.

'You had Tyson at Ballarat Base on December 16th. Did anything odd happen while you were there? Incidents with staff members or other patients? No one strike you as obsessive or judgmental?'

'Nothing.' She sighed.

'Do you belong to a mothers' group?'

'No, I expected there'd be awkwardness over Tyson's dad.'

Next, he jotted down details of her doctor, medical clinic and maternal health centre. He'd map the links between the victims, hoping that not all roads would lead to the hospital, which contained too many possible but not altogether probable suspects. In any event, he still had local angles to investigate.

'The staff at the health centre? Anyone there a potential Solomon?'

She hesitated, then shrugged.

Franklin scrutinised her face while he finally asked, 'Have you ever come across a bloke by the name of Art Hammer? Arthur Hammer.'

Cathy thought for a moment. 'I don't think so.'

'Ever been to one of the local pubs and seen an old man on his soapbox about women?'

She looked perplexed. 'What do you mean?'

'He actually stands on whatever's to hand outside the pub and rants about women taking babies into pubs or breastfeeding in public. Or, one of my favourites, condemning them for going to the pub without a suitable male chaperone.' Franklin snorted, and Cathy looked stunned. 'He rotates around places here and outside town too.'

'You're kidding.'

'Nope.'

'I'm not keen on pubs and haven't been near one since before I fell pregnant.'

He nodded.

'So you think this Arthur Hammer is Solomon?'

Franklin lifted a palm. 'No, it's just a line of inquiry. Don't read anything into my questions, okay?'

'Sorry.'

'No need to apologise.' Franklin rubbed his chin and contemplated other common denominators between the mums and the letters.

He slowly reread Cathy's two letters.

An idea struck. He lifted his eyebrows. 'Are you religious?'

'No. Well, I'm Christian but don't go to church. Haven't done since my teens, except for weddings and funerals.' After a small pause, she voiced what he'd thought, 'It sounds straight out of the Bible, doesn't it?'

'It does,' he agreed. 'If you were to label yourself— Catholic, C of E, Uniting—what would it be?'

'Presbyterian.'

'Oh.' Franklin was disappointed. Lauren had considered speaking to a priest. He knew that Roman Catholics had priests, whereas Presbyterians referred to their preachers as ministers. The women didn't even have a mutual lapsed faith.

The hospital's odds shortened.

———

Georgie picked around the house, checked each window. Thick white lace draped all but the fanlight over the back door. She climbed on top of Margaret's wheelie-bin and peered into a spotless kitchen. The younger Pentecoste woman belonged to the Proud Housekeeper league with her aunt.

Unfortunately, the niece was less naïve than Susan. Both external doors were locked.

Foiled, Georgie scanned the back garden and spied a garage tucked at the bottom. Like their rental in Richmond, vehicular access was a rear laneway. She jogged down and circled the windowless, coloured steel construction. One access door to the garden was padlocked. She let the lock drop against the door.

Did the shed hold Margaret's car? Susan's Land Cruiser?

She wished she knew.

So far, the detour had proved to be another time waster. Georgie pushed a note and her business card underneath the front door and backtracked towards the Alfa.

'Yoo-hoo!'

She pivoted.

'Hello there,' a woman with a cherubic face called. She waved a dimpled arm over the paling boundary fence. 'Are you looking for Margaret?'

Georgie managed a 'Yes' before the other woman talked on.

'She's not home.' Aqua eyes shone inquisitively, then flicked towards a honking car. 'Oops, I have to run!'

The chubby woman trotted to the vehicle. As she hopped into the back, Georgie heard a gaggle of excited female voices. They sped towards Sturt Street.

Pained by anticlimax, she counted on the note working when Margaret returned.

Meanwhile, it wouldn't hurt to dig elsewhere.

———

Where the Western Highway had earlier dissected Sunshine to Ballarat in its bland, anonymous motorway manner in around seventy minutes, Midland Highway meandered from the regional gold town to Daylesford in about thirty-five.

Despite it being a weekday, Georgie couldn't shake free a couple of cars. Every time she pulled the Spider away, either the white Nissan Skyline or the black Ford F-150 would leapfrog the other and sit on her tail.

At a tiny town called Newlyn, she veered onto the gravel shoulder outside a church-come-antiques store to dig out her ringing phone. The cars passed. No doubt mates having a bit of fun. She checked the mobile's screen as she slid it into the cradle.

Then flicked to her watch and swore, 'Fuck. The bloody deadline!'

She thumbed the connect switch. 'David!'

'It's past twelve –'

'Yes, I'm –'

'You need to take this seriously.'

'I am. Just –'

'We need to meet.'

'Oh?' Her stomach dropped.

'Your script needs severe editing, and, well, we need to meet. All of us, to get this thing back on track. How are you for tomorrow?'

Georgie hated to admit it, but she needed payment for the project to cover her imminent credit card bill and rent share. They agreed to gather at Miller Street at ten the next morning.

She swiped sweat from her brow and shifted on the

leather seat. High twenties already; the sun held a vicious kick. Tempted to stop at Daylesford's ice cream parlour, she instead gravitated towards Abergeldie. It had to hold a clue to Susan's absence.

———

Simultaneous with an empty-stomach growl, Georgie strode into Susan's kitchen. As she did, she experienced something she'd often sensed at Bron's. The house wrapped her into a hug and welcomed her to come and go. She did a quick walk-through.

First disappointment: Oscar didn't materialise, even when she called.

She inhaled stale air. Saw no change since yesterday, right down to the crusty plates piled in the sink.

Bigger let-down: Susan hadn't returned.

Georgie's energy waned. She was sapped by the anticlimactic start, clueless about what to do next and needed to refuel her body. She attacked a packet of chocolate chip biscuits and necked the coke lurking in the back of the fridge. Flat but cold, it hit the spot.

She re-paced the house, searched more thoroughly. Even so, she knew it was time wasted, that second-guessing her instincts and the Patterson-Stewart network would result in the same answer.

Back in the kitchen, she kicked out a chair and slumped onto it, elbows on the table. She munched on a biscuit, brain-strained, still clueless but determined to make a breakthrough.

She returned to Susan's bedroom, ran a hand over the bed and under the mattress. Found nothing.

'Where are you, Roly?' Georgie addressed the musty

men's clothes in the left wardrobe. Glancing at the barren pillows, she added, 'Where are you both?'

In the study, she swivelled in the desk chair until the sofa, bookcases and filing cabinets swirled. She grabbed the edge of the desk. Drummed her fingernails. Focused on one bookcase. Narrowed in on the mate to the album she had borrowed on Saturday and reached for it.

Consistent with the one back in Richmond, it contained newspaper clippings. Or rather, photocopies and printouts of archived stories at the beginning, followed by cuttings of more recent articles.

Subject matter for all: John Schlicht.

———

Franklin couldn't throw off his dark mood. And he couldn't say if it related more to Cathy's rape, Solomon's threats or Art Hammer's vanishing act.

Okay, that was probably a bit Kat at her Drama Queen best. But while the old man normally turned up like a bad smell and had fairly predictable habits, now when Franklin wanted to find him, he couldn't.

A drag past Art's Mollongghip property and checks with the publicans at Burke's and the Rush Hotel all bombed. Rather than spend the next hour trawling the other nearby pubs to come up with more nothing, he decided on a new tack.

———

'Why the hell would you have a scrapbook on Schlicht?'

Georgie flicked through Susan's book, frequently shaking her head. She remembered stories about Schlicht and his thugs and the notorious Honoured Society, Melbourne's so-called Mafia. A curious kid, Georgie had curled at the feet of Grandma Harvey, enraptured, yet also suspicious that the accounts amounted to urban myth.

Susan's articles tracked allegations against Schlicht and his counterparts. That they used the vegetable markets to conceal drug activities and launder the proceeds, while extorting a fortune from other merchants. They produced, imported, transported and distributed cannabis, heroin, cocaine and amphetamines. Sex, drugs, violence. Deadly reprisals from rival gangs. The police impotent or in the pocket. All there in the articles, some journalists more gloves-off in their approach than others.

Urban myth or fact, it sold newspapers and generated big bucks for the commercial TV stations currently cashing in on one sleazy underworld show after another.

Her recollection hazy, Georgie knew that Schlicht had somehow lost his stake in the markets and dropped away from the underbelly of organised crime. She hadn't seen his photograph for several years and the bushy grey brows, frigid grey-blue stare on a long, bony face that earned Schlicht the nickname 'the Iceman' spooked her.

Not the type of guy you'd want to meet in a dark alley.

Nor was he an obvious subject for a scrapbook.

Intrigued but time-poor, Georgie tossed the album onto the Spider's passenger seat for later and headed away from the homestead.

CHAPTER SEVENTEEN

A white Toyota utility came up the driveway as she drove down. There wasn't enough room to pass, and the other driver didn't pull over.

Georgie waited for him to reverse and found herself in a standoff. Two men glowered through their windscreen.

They alighted but didn't approach. Georgie sighed and hopped out. A blue heeler barrelled up and landed heavy paws on her chest. She collapsed onto her butt. She eyeballed the dog, pinned more by his snappy jaw and freaky one-blue-one-brown-eyed glare than his weight.

'Trigger,' one of the men commanded. 'Off.'

The dog snapped again, extracted his paws and retreated to his master's side. The older man shuffled forward and stretched a hand to Georgie. He pulled her upright, squashing her fingers.

Hand still trapped, she scanned up to his face. Tight mouth. Cold stare. Weather-beaten skin, florid and veined. He had a build to match the dog, only very tall, squeezed into khaki overalls and topped with close-cut grey hair.

'Help you?' He belatedly released his grip.

Georgie fed him the story she'd told the Pattersons. The man's expression transformed to a beam.

'Thought you was from the bank.'

Georgie pictured her thongs, jeans and tank and suppressed a grin.

This guy's not too sharp.

'Roger.' The older guy pointed a thumb to his chest. 'And this here's me son, Mick.'

Abergeldie's lessees.

They each pumped a handshake, and Georgie winced at duplicate hand-crushes then brushed off her butt. Trigger snoozed in the shade of the Spider, and the men lolled against their ute.

'Mrs P took off las' weekend. She told me and me boy, Mick here, that she'd be away a couple a days. Expected her back before now. Not like her to go off for more than a day or two. She likes it here.' Roger waved a vague hand at the property.

Mick agreed, drawing Georgie's attention to him. She noted an uncanny resemblance between the father and son, including drinker's complexions and strong ocker accents.

'Still, it's up to her,' Roger continued. 'Not for us to say anythink. Pretty lonely for her since Mr P went.'

'Do you know how I can contact Susan's friend, Jack? It's possible she's staying with him – if she's not with Margaret.'

'I dunno which Jack Mrs P would be vistin'. Don't seem proper. She's married to Mr P.' Roger's eyes hardened.

Georgie suggested, 'Perhaps he's a relative?'

Both men shrugged. But the father continued to be the spokesman. 'Don't ring any bells with me.'

Great. Will my next question be a dud too?

'Do you think her being away has anything to do with Roly?'

Suddenly, the men's thick necks retracted. Dour lines replaced all trace of the farmers' grins. She frowned, confused and intrigued.

'What ya mean?' Roger asked.

'Well, Roly goes missing, and then almost to the day five years later, Susan takes off. More than coincidence, do you think?'

Roger lifted his shoulders. Mick scratched his scalp with long, jagged fingernails.

Why have they gone shifty?

Her writer's instincts fired, as did her questions.

'What do you think happened to Roly?'

'I dunno,' Roger muttered.

'Do you think he's dead?'

The man yelled, 'I said, I dunno!'

Trigger growled. Mick put a hand on his collar.

Georgie felt a trickle of fear but persisted. 'Why do you think Roly disappeared?'

Mick bent forward, yanking the dog, and stuck his nose close. So close that she could smell beer and bad breath. He jabbed a finger into her collarbone. Pounded at the same spot until her eyes smarted and heart thudded.

Show no fear. Don't back down.

'Dad said he dunno. We can't tell you nothin'. Stop being a nosy bitch and get out of here.'

She battled an impulse to fight back. There were times and places to take on adversaries. This wasn't one of them. The farm was secluded, and she was outnumbered by two giants and their mongrel.

To Georgie's relief, Mick stepped back. She moved to

the Spider with faux calm. Roger reversed the ute until she had room to pass.

Grateful to leave Abergeldie behind, she wiped damp palms on her jeans and turned onto Howlong Road. When the tyres gripped tarmac, she accelerated and tried to persuade herself that she'd imagined the farmers' violent response.

She failed.

And grew even more convinced that Roly's demise drove Susan's actions.

———

Franklin zipped past the cop shop hoping none of his workmates spotted him. He parked the bike on the low side of Camp Street and well off the road, next to a vintage Suzuki GT750. Each time he saw the glossy teal duco offset by masses of chrome it almost tempted him to trade the Ninja for an old classic.

But he'd never do it.

'Pastor?' Franklin stepped through the arched entrance and into the foyer of the former Baptist Church.

Music, together with the clatter of crockery, drew him through to the kitchen. A funky song about Jesus played loudly. The pastor sang along even louder and washed coffee cups. Franklin called out again rather than spring a surprise.

'Frankie!' Pastor Danni pivoted to face him. Her cheeks popped out with her broad smile, making the million freckles on her face more prominent. She looked about Kat's age but actually fell closer to his own.

She gave him a hug that squeezed the air from his lungs and brought on an attack of guilt. He and Danni could be good friends if he made an effort. They had plenty in common—from motorbikes to their football team—and didn't have to worry about that traditional male-female impossibility of a platonic friendship.

Danni wasn't just one of the very few female church clergy in the country. She and the other lesbian pastors could probably be counted on one hand.

'Coffee, Frankie?'

'Can I pick your brain too?'

She tilted her head and punched his arm lightly. Then the pastor brightened his day with another hundred-watt smile.

———

'Afternoon. Can I get you a cuppa?'

Georgie surveyed Lewis Davis across the desk. Dressed in a cheap suit, he could have passed for a farmer on church day. His manner was effusive and assessing, yet amiable too. The real estate manager possessed an X Factor beyond Pam Stewart's character reference and the fact that he was one of Roly Pentecoste's best mates.

Georgie accepted and rested elbows on the desk while she waited. Her head felt heavy with sudden fatigue.

So much driving. So much thinking. My brain hurts. Is it all a waste of time?

She watched Davis weave through the overcrowded office, two mugs hooked on one hand, packet of biscuits in the other, amazed by the large man's graceful gait.

'Interest you in a bickie?'

He proffered a packet of Tim Tams. Georgie shook her head, appetite depleted by the biscuits from Susan's kitchen and the croissant Pam Stewart had pressed on her as she recapped the morning.

'So you're a friend of Pam's?' Davis asked. Crumbs fell from the side of his mouth and sprinkled his suit with cookie dandruff.

'Kind of. Yes.'

She explained how they'd met and the purpose of her visit now.

Davis's smile stretched his face but no longer reached his eyes. They became dead fish eyes. 'You said yourself that Susan made arrangements with her neighbours and told Mick and Roger she was going away. And that there's every chance she's with her niece.'

'Well, yes.'

'So, what are you *really* doing here?'

He sounded tired. She didn't know what to say.

'What do you hope to gain by dredging up the past?' His voice took a harsh edge that made his smile creepy.

'I just thought –'

'No,' he said, leaning forward. The façade of a smile dropped. 'That's the problem. I don't think you've thought about this at all.'

'Aren't you worried about Susan?' Georgie asked incredulously.

'Not from what you've told me, no. But if you're going to set things off again and she's going to come back to, well, the whole Roly thing all over again, then yes. And I'll hold you personally responsible.'

Davis stood and snatched her half-full mug. He stalked into the back office.

Georgie felt the curious gaze of the receptionist as she left.

———

'I'm after some scuttlebutt.'

'Well, I knew you weren't here for Bible studies.'

They sipped coffee, chewed biscuits and shared a smile.

Franklin said, 'I'm working a case with a religious element in a series of poison-pen letters – threats, really. The language is old-fashioned and sounds like it's out of a Bible.'

'Maybe you need Bible studies after all?'

He tipped forward on his chair. 'No, what I need is any inside knowledge on religious nutters in our area.'

'You've thought of old Art Hammer, of course?'

'Yep. He's a definite possibility, but I can't track him down.'

'I haven't seen him in a while either...but I was away for that clerical conference in Sydney last month—remember? —and just this week had a course on in Melbourne.' Pastor Danni scratched the side of her mouth. 'Are you going to eat that last bickie?'

'And here I was thinking you were about to break my case.'

'Chocolate helps me think.'

He passed the plate. 'Confidentially, the letters are nut jobs against unmarried mums. I reckon an old bloke's behind them. Someone deeply religious who thinks women should be kept in their place. It's real old-school stuff, so maybe you've had trouble with him too.'

'Because I'm female, lesbian or a pastor of the Community Church?'

'All three?' Franklin admitted. 'Our fellow's a traditionalist, and I can't see him here.' He waved at the coffee urn but broadly meant the progressive religion and

Danni's congregation. 'But he might have let you know he doesn't like the way your church does things.'

The pastor nodded. 'I see what you mean.' She stood. The leather of her biker boots creaked. 'And I may be able to help.'

———

It had been a fucked day, so far. No joy with the niece. A bunch of reading material on Victoria's underworld. A whole lot of aggro from Mick and Roger. And now Georgie had upset one of Roly's best mates.

What if he was right? What if Susan returned from a sojourn with her niece to find *the whole Roly thing*, as Davis put it, back on the agenda, along with her own life under scrutiny?

Georgie knocked a cigarette from the packet. She leaned against the shop window and smoked two in succession, but it was mechanical rather than enjoyable. She took the last drag and crushed the butt with her heel. Throughout, she'd focused on a two-storey Tudor-style red-brick building opposite The Springs Real Estate.

I'm right. There's plenty to be worried about.

The banking chamber held one customer and three staff members in air-hostess uniforms. The customer and teller joked and chatted. The other two bank officers spoke in hushed tones under the swinging Information sign. Georgie approached and waited.

Goosebumps pricked her skin. The temperature and an ambient odour reminded her of the inside of a fridge.

The staff still ignored her. She cleared her throat and the younger woman glanced over.

'Oh, hello? Sorry, we didn't see you there. How can I

help?'

'Douglas Macdougall, please.'

'Do you have an appointment?' the woman asked, rising.

'No, I'm sorry.'

'Oh, I'm sure the manager will see you. Back in a tick.'

It wasn't easy to kill time in a bank. Unlike in a doctor's surgery, there weren't even back-issue magazines to flick through. The hairs on Georgie's arms stood to attention from the cold now and she spent a minute in contemplation of those fine strands before she sought other distractions.

She was spinning a brochure carousel when a telephone buzzed.

'Welcome to ANZ Bank, this is Carol,' the woman who had thus far ignored Georgie said. 'Oh, it's you! Hang on, I'll ask. Excuse me, miss. Can I have your name?'

'Georgie Harvey.'

Carol repeated it into the receiver and paused. 'Oh. Yeah.' She hung up.

Georgie arched a brow, but the banker ducked her head.

The other officer returned and regarded Georgie awkwardly. She jiggled on the spot and said, 'I'm sorry, Ms Harvey. Mr Macdougall isn't in the office.'

Bullshit.

Georgie frowned.

'If you leave your number, I'm sure he'll give you a call. When, um, when he comes in.'

On the steps outside the building, Georgie decided that Macdougall wouldn't call. She contemplated his avoidance and could only think that his good mate Lewis Davis had seen her head for the bank and warned him.

Why?

What are they hiding?

CHAPTER EIGHTEEN

FRANKLIN MOUNTED HIS MOTORBIKE AND RODE TO THE top of Wombat Hill. Throughout the short trip he churned over the morning's meeting with Cathy Jones. It couldn't compensate for her rape, but he vowed to catch the sadist Solomon before the sicko destroyed her self-esteem.

One step at a time.

He sat at a picnic table with notepad ready. How to handle Pastor Danni's information hadn't solidified yet. He'd chew that over while he made his first call from the mobile.

The registrar cross-referenced staff on the ward while Renee and Cathy were at Ballarat Base with the original list for Tayla and Lauren's stay. There were a handful of common names on the nursing team. The three she'd spoken to yesterday, along with four other midwives – one who'd retired at the end of February and another whose round-the-world long service leave jaunt began in March.

That left two nurses with realistic opportunity.

On top of this he had a list of doctors and aides to the maternity ward.

But what was the motive for any of these?

Forget motive for now, begin with the means.

So the list grew. Unfortunately, just two were rostered on and the registrar's talks with them were in fits and starts around a difficult labour and an anxious mother-to-be with Braxton Hicks contractions. Both seemed to be non-starters.

No further enlightened, Franklin feared subsequent inquiries at the hospital would prove equally time consuming and fruitless.

Right, time for the new and improved theory.

The next number he dialled was a local one: the Blue family from Goo Goo Road. His day of frustrations continued when he reached an answering machine. He left a carefully worded message that requested Earl Blue or his parents return his call.

Franklin toyed with the photo Pastor Danni had given him. An unsmiling pasty-faced youth in a wanker gangster hat, unbuttoned collared shirt over T-shirt. This was not the portrait he'd expected of Solomon.

And Danni had said, 'He doesn't fit your profile exactly. He's much younger than what you're thinking, only seventeen. But he could be your poison-pen writer.'

Sceptical, Franklin's eyebrows had risen.

She'd passed the photo and pointed at the kid in the forefront. 'Earl Blue joined us early last year. He came across as wonderful at first – friendly, helpful, kind, and we actually thought he'd make a great pastor. But after he ingratiated himself into the church and leadership group, he started to flex his muscles just a little too much in the youth group.'

'How so?'

'He started spouting some Old Testament scripture. His behaviour became more and more zealous. He told the girls to dress less provocatively – and these girls don't show a bra strap or singlet, let alone cleavage. Then he got angry, scary angry, when things didn't go his way or people disagreed with him. By that stage, we realised he'd come into the church to disrupt and maybe destroy it from within.'

So despite his young age, Earl Blue matched most of Franklin's profile. But he'd hit another snag; his two red-hot suspects were both AWOL, and he was left in a holding pattern.

———

Franklin arrived at the station with minutes to spare. He was rostered on two-up with Scott Hart, who agreed to kick off their four-to-midnight stint playing catch-up on their respective portfolios. In addition to general duties and handling files for other branches or the Bacchus Marsh detectives, each officer held an area of responsibility to take the strain off Lunny. Franklin looked after Youth Liaison—which included organising community events like Blue Light discos, camps and outings—and the social club. Harty had the Station Portfolio, which roped in bail reports, station cameras and logs, but because he was young and keen, he often worked on the rosters and cleaned the police vehicles as well. *Vehicles* suggested a larger fleet than their one permanent four-wheel drive, any loaners they were lucky to have from another station, and a bunch of pushbikes. The joys of a sixteen-hour country station.

As Harty checked the bail records in the watch-house, Franklin called Lauren Morris. He detailed developments with Renee Archer and Cathy Jones, except for Cathy's sexual assault.

After reciting Solomon's latest letter, he said, 'It struck

Cathy and me that the letters could be quotes from the Bible.'

'For sure. Read the newest back slowly. I want to write it down.'

She considered the script and commented, *'This one's extreme, isn't it?'* There was another pause, then she added, *'It's even more old-fashioned than ours. Do you think they're quotes from the Old Testament?'*

That tallied with his thoughts. And equally fit both Art Hammer's impromptu sermon style and Earl Blue, according to Pastor Danni.

'Why don't Tayla and I see what we can come up with?'

Franklin grinned, happy to shift responsibility. His idea of fun wasn't poring over a Bible. He scrawled notes into the daybook, then noticed the last thing on his to-do list. It made his stomach flip.

'Hoy, Harty,' he called down the short corridor.

His buddy appeared in the doorway seconds later. 'Yo?'

'Let's take a ride out to Abergeldie to check on Susan Pentecoste.'

'Uh-huh. Following up your girlfriend's report, are we?'

Franklin hurled his Akubra-style police hat.

Harty ducked. 'That's a bit disrespectful, isn't it?' He retrieved the hat and brushed it off.

'They're the stupidest things they've brought out,' Franklin replied as they jostled down the hallway.

'Just as well they've issued us with caps then. Gotta keep grumpy old farts like you happy.' Harty didn't have a chance to dodge Franklin's backhander to the gut.

Lunny entered the station. 'I could have you on report for that,' he said with mock severity.

'Nice get-up, boss.' Franklin gestured towards Lunny's navy tracksuit and white runners.

'Pretend I'm not here,' was the airy reply. 'Couple of matters to clear up...'

'Maeve's sister isn't down again, by chance?' Harty asked.

Lunny's blush confirmed his least favourite sister-in-law was in residence at the station house next door. Luckily, her visits were as brief as they were frequent.

'Hmm. Are we still on for fishing tomorrow, John?'

The sarge's voice held a note of panic. Tempted to stir him by saying he'd swapped his rest day with one of the other blokes, Franklin took pity and nodded.

'I'm driving,' he told Harty, snagging the keys from the board.

———

'Dam's full,' Harty commented as they pulled up the farm's driveway.

'It's strange to have so much rain and see everything green in autumn, isn't it?'

'Yeah, but good strange.'

Franklin nodded at the distinction. 'Easter's only a couple of weeks away, yes?'

His mate agreed.

'It's funny, isn't it, that we've got so used to drought and Easters when the fire season's still in force that we've forgotten other years when it rained all long-weekend and was cold enough to freeze your balls off. It's still bloody hot now, though.'

Mick and Roger waved as they drove past. The farmers wore sweat-soaked khaki overalls over bare torsos as they strained fencing wire on the top paddock.

The cops slipped through the white picket fence up at

the house and sighed. The shade of the cypress windbreak gave welcome relief.

'These look a bit sick.' On the verandah, Harty crumbled dry soil from a potted plant between his fingers. He touched a rose leaf, which crackled before falling off. 'They need a drink.'

'You're not wrong,' Franklin said. It was uncharacteristic of green-thumbed Susan Pentecoste to neglect her plants. Even after Roly's disappearance, she'd overseen the care of all plants on Abergeldie's house block, along with the stock and crops, until she recovered enough to personally tend them. He remembered calling here with his former sergeant, Bill Noonan, after Susan's release from hospital. They'd found her with watering can in hand, fussing over foliage not half as withered as these rose bushes. Surely she'd have arranged for someone to water the plants if she'd planned this holiday? Perhaps she'd left in haste or never expected to stay away so long.

The two men matched strides to the kitchen door and entered, calling, 'Susan?'

No response.

Harty gestured with a head twitch and Franklin nodded; words were unnecessary. They did a swift inspection.

In the study, Harty said, 'Who's been a bit creative here?'

He threw a notepad from the desk to Franklin, who examined the doodles. There were spirals and three-dimensional cubes and grim faces. Among the artwork were random words – several in block letters, others in a thready, rightward-slanted script, but all similar enough to belong to one writer.

'"Susan? Niece? Roly-Susan link. JACK. Holiday?

WHERE?"' he read aloud. 'Gotta be the work of that Georgie Harvey bird, don't you think?'

His partner played devil's advocate. 'Not necessarily.'

'Bit cheeky, walking in and making herself at home.'

'What? A bit like us, you mean?'

Franklin grimaced. 'We're cops on a welfare check, and she's a civvy who shouldn't have just waltzed in. Not the same thing.' He motioned to the pad. 'I don't suppose she meant to leave this behind.'

'She mightn't have noticed she'd done it. I got into a bad habit at uni and doodle all the time. It's not until later that I realise what I've done.'

'I wouldn't know about that.' Franklin swatted his mate. 'Some of us are ordinary working-class coppers, not brainy upstarts.'

'Hardy, ha, ha. Hey, do you reckon that's weird?'

Harty pointed to the bookcase. Franklin noted the perfect alignment of the books on six of the seven shelves. They were in ascending order according to height, each spine plumb. The bottom shelf held the tallest volumes and replicated the order above until midway along. There, several books collapsed across a gap corresponding to a couple of absent ones.

'Notice a few big books lying around? Yea high.' He spread his hands a foot apart.

'Nothing in here,' Harty said.

'Check the bedrooms. I'll take the other rooms.'

They regrouped minutes later.

'Anything?'

'No, and I wouldn't be surprised if Harvey's taken something from Susan's bedside table. There's not much dust on the surfaces, considering the gravel road and all, but what's there's been stirred up.'

'Harvey's pissing me off,' Franklin complained.

'Hmm. It's one thing letting yourself in to have a quick look-see, but filching Susan's gear is pretty rich,' his friend agreed. Then he added, 'It's always possible that Susan took the books with her.'

'I suppose,' Franklin conceded. 'Get Mick and Roger in here for a chat.'

While his partner summoned the farmers, Franklin pulled out his ringing mobile.

'Constable Franklin?'

Senior Constable, but he let it go. A couple more words and he'd identify the caller with her very familiar voice.

Don't tell me.

She said, *'It's Christina van Hoeckel here.'*

Damn. I was so close.

'I'm ringing about the, um, incident with my car the other day.'

'Oh?' Franklin said, intrigued.

'I want to drop it.'

He let the silence sit, then asked, 'Why's that?'

'Oh, it's just kids.' Her attempt at casual fell short. *'Their parents will sort them out. No need to get them in trouble with police.'*

'Is that right? Well, it's gone too far now. Even if you were to withdraw your complaint.' It hadn't; he just wanted to gauge her reaction.

'You can't do that,' she shouted. Then added softly, *'Can you?'*

'I'm not sure, Christina. I'll have to get back to you.'

He called off, chuckling. Let her sweat for a few days, then he'd pop over and see if she was ready to come clean. He intended to find out why she'd lied.

———

Franklin was still grinning when he greeted Mick and Roger with handshakes and backslaps. Trigger trotted behind them and collapsed with a sigh onto the mat by the stove.

'We was tellin' Scott here,' Roger pointed at Harty, 'that we had a sheila nosin' about today. Didn't we, Mick?'

His son bobbed his head.

'Get her name, did you, Roger?' Franklin asked.

'Georgie somethink.'

'Harvey?'

'Yep.' The older man clicked his fingers. 'Anyhow, she had a cock-and-bull story about Mrs P. But we reckon she was really casin' the joint.'

'How's that?'

Mick puffed out his cheeks but let his dad speak.

'Well, it's not like Mrs P to go away for more than a couple a days, like. But it's up to her, isn't it? Not like she's had many holid'ys, 'specially since Mr P went.'

'Susan told you she was going on a holiday?'

Father and son nodded.

'Where was she going?'

'Dunno.'

'Say when she was coming back?'

'Nup.'

'You worried about her?'

'Nup.'

'This Georgie Harvey – what do you think she was up to?'

'You know, casin' the joint. That's what they call it, isn't it? Checkin' it out before they rip the place off.'

Franklin shot a glance at Harty, who raised an eyebrow

and gave a slight headshake. He hadn't mentioned the possible theft.

'You'd better have a look then and see if anything's missing. Take your time.'

He rued his words as Mick and Roger took an age to check each room. Their voices became excited in the main bedroom. The officers joined them.

'Mrs P's photos are gone.'

Harty took down details and trailed his partner and the farmers into the study.

'That don't seem right,' Mick said to his father. He pointed to the bottom of the bookcase.

Roger knelt, knees groaning. He thrust away Trigger's snout and pushed up the leaning books. He considered the thickness of the gap; measured it with his thumb and fingers. With a scratch to his chin, he said, 'There's somethink missin'. Mrs P has these special books with real nice leather covers. Thick ones they are. That right, Mick?'

'Um. Ah...'

'C'mon, stop ditherin'. Think!'

'Oh, Dad.'

'By jeez, Mick.' Roger rose. 'Her books are missin'. No doubt about it. She always has 'em on the shelf there or on the desk here. Nowhere else. That sheila's stolen Mrs P's things, hasn't she?'

Harty excused himself and left the room.

Franklin held up a hand to diffuse Roger's anger.

'Leave it with us, we'll check it out. What else did you discuss with Georgie Harvey?'

'Nothin',' the father said quickly.

'Did she give you an idea where she was going after here?'

'Nope,' Mick replied.

SANDI WALLACE

'Mate,' Harty interrupted. 'We've got an urgent job.'

———

Franklin was poised to jump into the police truck when his mobile rang again. He threw the keys to his partner and answered the call while buckling into the passenger seat.

Lauren Morris sounded excited.

Hart flicked on strobe lights and siren. He negotiated the gravel driveway. Turned onto Grimwells Road and white-knuckled the steering wheel.

Franklin gritted his teeth as the four-wheel drive bumped over corrugations. He listened to Lauren.

'It depends on which version of the Bible you use. I dug up an old one and found sections in the book of Proverbs that sound a lot like Solomon.

'Chapter five, verses three to four say: "For the lips of a strange woman drop as an honeycomb, and her mouth is smoother than oil: But her end is bitter as wormwood, sharp as a two-edged sword."

'Don't you think that's similar to Solomon saying, "your end will be Bitter"?'

He agreed, and she continued. *'Verse five says: "Her feet go down to death; her steps take hold on hell."*

'Remember, Solomon said, "be damned to follow their whore-mother's steps down to death" in the latest letter; and "you and your bastard walk the Road of Death" in the one we got? Verse eight –'

They hit a pothole. Franklin's head bumped the side window. He cursed, righted himself and his daybook. 'Sorry. Go on, Lauren.'

'Eight says: "Remove thy way far from her, and come not nigh the door of her house."

'Very close to Solomon's "be tempted not to the door of a stranger, or tempt a stranger to your door."

'Then fifteen is: "Drink waters out of thine own cistern, and running waters out of thine own well."

'That makes me think of drinking out of a toilet cistern. Yuck. But it's all sounding a bit familiar, isn't it?'

'We're not far away,' Hart interjected. Despite the blind corner ahead, they could see a plume of smoke.

'Sorry, Lauren. We're on our way to an emergency. Can you give me the rest quickly?'

'Okay.' She sped up. 'Eighteen to twenty: "Let thy fountain be blessed: and rejoice with the wife of thy youth. Let her be as the loving hind and pleasant roe; let her breasts satisfy thee at all times; and be thou ravished always with her love. And why wilt thou, my son, be ravished with a strange woman, and embrace the bosom of a stranger?"

'That ties with "You must lie only with your husband" and the whole stranger reference in Solomon's letter to Cathy.'

Franklin could hear a distant wail, even above their siren, radio and Hart's occasional exclamation. An ambulance or fire truck was on its way to the collision too.

Lauren continued, 'Chapter Six of Proverbs says: "These six things doth the Lord hate: yea, seven are an abomination unto him." One of those being, "To keep thee from the evil woman, from the flattery of the tongue of a strange woman."

'Pretty similar to Solomon's "the LORD hates the ways of evil people"?'

'Proverbs goes on and on about adultery and prostitution, but I think Solomon's twisting the words to suit their own agenda and roping in whatever they consider being contrary to a righteous or virtuous woman. I mean, all they've got against us is that we're unmarried mums – except Renee, *who is married. I don't think any of us are cheating on our partners with another guy, married or not. We wouldn't have the energy, for starters.*

'Anyway, *I could find dozens of references in Proverbs alone that have strong links to Solomon's letters. These are just a few examples. And there's also a lot of weird capitalisation in the Bible – whole words or the first letter of words that are midsentence and don't need a capital.*'

'It all ties together,' Franklin agreed.

He felt Hart tense.

He did likewise.

They were a few kilometres from the crash scene, but an approaching clearance would give them a glimpse. The person who'd called in the accident had done so anonymously before fleeing, which meant they were ignorant as to the number of casualties and extent of injuries or fatalities. Merely that it was serious and *there's blood everywhere.*

'*So, basically Solomon seems to be using an oldish version of the Bible as a source for the letters,*' Lauren said. '*Or their memory, I guess. Could be a priest, a parishioner or anyone familiar with the Bible, active churchgoer or not. All we know is that they're religious, fanatical even, and Christian.*' Her excitement diminished. '*I suppose we haven't narrowed it down at all.*'

Although her research did only endorse current theories, Franklin reassured her.

———

Franklin viewed the destruction ahead with clenched guts.

A minivan on its side. Engulfed in flames. It had

sparked a grassfire that seared a stripe through the adjacent paddock.

Nearby, a sedan with a piano-accordion front end. It must have flipped, judging by its battered bonnet and roof.

Debris scattered in every direction.

No sign of life.

CHAPTER NINETEEN

GEORGIE'S PULSE QUICKENED WHEN THE *BUMBLEBEE* sang. She dug out the mobile but didn't recognise the number. No Ballarat or Daylesford prefix; probably not Margaret Pentecoste or good news on Susan.

'Hello?'

'Georgie?'

It was Michael Padley. His voice sounded strained; there was lots of background noise.

'Michael, is everything all right?'

'No. It's Ruby.'

Georgie sucked in a breath. Felt afraid to ask.

'She's...'

Please, fuck, don't let it be the worst.

'She had another turn.' He sounded a thousand miles away.

Had?

Georgie squeezed her eyes, blinking back pools. A lump jammed her throat.

Death had touched Georgie before. She'd found the body of her first cat. Bloodied and broken; killed by a careless driver. Heartbroken and naïve, she'd believed she'd never recover, nor experience worse.

'Georgie, are you there?'

She couldn't speak, now lost in the time of her grandmother's passing, expected and peaceful yet still painful.

Her memories darkened further. She was holding her dad's hand, overwhelmed when she felt a weak squeeze. She watched him try to speak, then heard the death rattle. A bittersweet moment: at last, release from the tentacles of the brain tumour, while that final goodbye twisted her heart into a corkscrew.

'Can you come, please?' Michael's voice was tiny, bewildered, so sad.

The corkscrew skewered again. Ruby and Michael were quasi-grandparents. Neglected but brimming with unconditional love. Ruby couldn't be dead. Last week she'd been excited about a play her friends were about to open and had dyed her hair Siren Red.

Don't ask me to see Ruby's body. I'll scream – right here, on the main street of Daylesford.

He said, *'Are you there?'*

'Yes,' she whispered. She verged on puking, exacerbated by a billow of black diesel fumes from a light truck as it passed.

'Can you come straight away?'

'Of course, but I'm...' She stopped before naming her location, the trigger for Ruby's heart failure. 'It will take me a while.'

'Oh.' Michael sounded hurt. *'Ruby will –'*

'You mean she's –'

'Back in intensive care. I'm so worried. They won't let me see her.'

Georgie nearly laughed. Intensive care meant alive. Not well but still kicking.

She sprinted for the Spider, assuring Michael she'd be there soon. But she cringed at the lie. Her return to Melbourne could take up to two hours if she clashed with commuters.

———

Georgie rummaged for her keys. She upended her bag on the pavement, scattered the contents. Key wedged into ignition, mobile into cradle, she shifted into reverse and noticed a flyer stuffed under her windscreen wiper.

'Damn it.'

She jumped out, pulled the flyer, dumped it on the passenger seat and gunned the engine.

Take two. She pressed a speed-dial number, reversed, almost collided with a car behind.

The call was answered, and Georgie announced herself. *Fuck*, she went into a queue.

'Come on, come on.'

She cursed the operatic on-hold music. Tapped her steering wheel. Floored the car.

'*I think Adam's finishing off his call,*' his PA said cheerfully. '*Care to hold a little longer, Georgie?*'

'Yes.' She ground her teeth.

'*George?*'

Finally.

'AJ, I might lose you. Reception's not great here.'

She filled him in on Michael's call. 'I can't get there for an hour or so.'

She hit a rut at 130 kph. The steering wheel jolted.

'*Where are you?*' he yelled over her curses.

'Just out of Daylesford.'

'Again? Why?'

'Not now!'

Three seconds on, she cut his aggrieved silence. 'AJ, save the bullshit for later. Can you take care of Michael until I get there?'

He promised.

She disconnected. Honked at a slow-moving tractor. She pulled out and passed, narrowly missing an oncoming station wagon. Rammed the accelerator. Demanded that any god listening keep her safe from cops and radars.

Time stretched.

Her hands ached from death-gripping the wheel. Eyeballs stung. Stomach churned.

Still a long way to go.

She raced to the hospital. Every risk worth it. Every minute a waste.

———

Georgie circled and swooped on a parking space. She dropped her keys while locking the Spider and tripped at the entrance to the Alfred. She located AJ and Michael, her eyes bugging to stop tears.

'No news,' AJ said. He hugged her tight.

'That's something,' she replied as they clung together for a moment.

She sat next to Michael. She clasped his gnarled, shaking hand. AJ perched on an identical hard plastic seat on the old man's other side.

Michael shrank as the minutes ticked. The pain in Georgie's chest ballooned.

Hours passed.

———

At 9.05pm, a white-coated woman approached.

'Mr Padley, I'm Dr Quinter.'

After quick handshakes and introductions all round, the doctor told Michael, 'Your wife will have to undergo more tests, but she's stable and out of immediate danger.'

They cheered. Quinter crouched before Michael and took his hands.

'You're not going to be much use to Ruby unless you take care of yourself. Why don't you go home and rest? She'll sleep through the night and you can see her in the morning.'

Michael argued but eventually allowed Georgie and AJ to lead him from the hospital. They tucked him into their sofa bed and saw him fall into an exhausted, uneasy slumber.

Sleep wouldn't come to Georgie. She sat by Michael's bedside until dawn cracked.

———

The angst returned. The tightness in her chest, the shake in her hands and, of course, the tears, all back.

In reflection, there was no mystery to why she felt poorly. It came down to The Day looming on the calendar, yet not signifying an end. This onset of frailty was simply a symptom of her sadness. Not just sadness but signs too of her loneliness, anger and, yes, pure unchristian rage at the unknown, although not

for retribution. A greater being would delve out justice in due course.

She pushed her hands onto her knees to stop the trembles. Young ones favoured the term *closure* these days. At first, she'd baulked. Why shut the door on the best part of her life? But lately, she'd tried the word out, when alone or talking to God.

She had an idea how to find closure. It was worth trying, for what else could she do?

What did she have to lose?

WEDNESDAY 17 MARCH

CHAPTER TWENTY

'I CAN'T BELIEVE YOU LIED TO ME.'

'I didn't lie.'

'George, it's a lie by omission and we both know it.'

'AJ –'

'Don't try to wheedle back into my good books.'

'Keep it down. Michael will be back in a minute.' Their neighbour had gone home to bathe where he had the safety features of grab rails and step-less shower.

'You should have told me what you were up to.' AJ's voice was quiet but sharp.

'All I've done is check out a few things for Ruby to try to find her friend.'

'It's the way you've gone about it. I mean, for fuck's sake, you broke into this woman's house and stole stuff from her.'

'I didn't break in.'

'Only on a technicality.'

Their volume had cranked up again.

'And I didn't steal anything. I *borrowed* a few items. I'm sure Susan wouldn't object.'

'What if this Lewis Davis is right? What if she comes back from a holiday to find you've been nosing around, asking a whole lot of people a whole lot of questions and dredging up all this history involving her husband? For fuck's sake,' he swore again, something AJ wasn't prone to. 'Didn't you stop to think?'

'Yes. I *did* stop and think.'

AJ's mouth flapped, but she overrode him.

'I stopped to think about everything they've,' she tossed her head in the direction of the Padley's home, 'done for us. I thought about how worried Ruby was and how that's completely out of character. I tried to reach Susan Pentecoste on the phone. Couldn't. Thought, what should I do next? So I drove to bloody Hepburn and checked things out. And I ended up with, as you said, a whole lot of questions.'

'Which you're not equipped to handle.'

Georgie snarled at him before she continued. 'Then Ruby had a bloody heart attack because she's so frantic and I promised her—through Michael—that I'd see this through. Thinking Ruby'll get better faster if I prove her mate's okay. And don't forget I went to the cops. Is it my fault they're dickheads?'

She glared. He returned it.

'Yes but –'

She cut him off. 'So then I contacted a few of Susan's acquaintances, tried to see her niece. I've thought *long and fucking hard* about everything I've done over the past few days.'

Georgie's chest heaved. They still faced off.

Several minutes elapsed. AJ grew less irate, and Georgie experienced a sense of disassociation. She disconnected from her body. Her hearing dulled.

He asked something. His lips moved like a bad soundtrack dub, out of time with his voice.

'What?'

She focused, and the numbness ebbed.

'What else haven't you told me?'

Georgie crossed her fingers. 'Nothing.'

This was not the right juncture to discuss fears for their future. He'd be shattered that she'd shared intimacies of their relationship with Pam.

AJ's posture relaxed. She exhaled.

He said, 'Maybe I overreacted. Tell me everything again from the beginning.'

They perched on the end of the bed that Georgie had barely slept in overnight. Her story stammered at first. Once it flowed, even with AJ twice interrupting to probe facts, she strayed little.

'What now?' he queried when she fell silent.

'Well, today I'm going to ring Susan and her niece until my fingers fall off or I reach one of them. I've got a meeting with David Ruddoch et al. to workshop that script I've been struggling over, then a re-write, I'd say. After that, if I'm lucky, I'll skim over the latest stuff I *borrowed* from Susan Pentecoste. And then I'll work on a plan for tomorrow.'

AJ nodded.

'I suspect that'll include another trip to Hicksville and more digging. It's bloody frustrating that I can't do much today.'

'You know I can't take time off,' he started.

Georgie did a hand-flap. 'It's not a two-man job.'

'It was one thing yesterday.'

'But a different thing altogether today. I get it. Don't worry.' She knocked his knee. 'I can take care of myself. A couple of pushy farmers don't scare me. Me, big tough woman.' She did a Tarzan-beat to her chest.

They both spat out a laugh.

The front door closed, and Michael's walking stick tap-shuffle signalled his return.

'We'll keep this quiet,' she whispered. 'Michael has enough to cope with.'

AJ kissed her. 'You're stressed about Susan, aren't you?'

'Yep. Not quite as much as I am for Ruby, but,' Georgie paused, assailed by emotion, 'this isn't a half-arsed effort to find a distant mate of Ruby's anymore. There's Pam too; she's gorgeous, and we're talking about her best pal. Besides —and this might be hard to understand because I only know her second-hand—Susan's grown on me. It may sound corny, but she's become like an old family friend.'

———

Breakfast was coffee and a cigarette for Georgie, toast and cereal for the men. Neither objected to her smoking at the open window above the sink, although normally they would.

Each coped with their anxiety uniquely: Michael chattered like a five-year-old who'd drunk too much red cordial, Georgie retreated into herself, and AJ acted the overattentive host.

———

He moved towards the wreckage. The heat and intensity of the flames engulfing the minivan almost drove him back. Dreading what he would find, he approached with a raised hand, palm forward, shielding his face. Locked in a vacuum, nothing but his own breathing penetrated his psyche.

As his stride became a jog, he emerged from the void. He could hear Hart on the portable radio, close to his heels. In his peripheral vision, he noted the simultaneous arrival of an ambulance and fire truck. Then he realised he was yelling at the mangled and burning masses. Urging any survivors to respond.

Torn between which vehicle to check, he saw the firies and ambos rush to the minivan. He swallowed hard and tried to force the driver's door of the sedan. A man turned towards him. Blood poured from a gash on his forehead. His deathly white face contorted.

A quick glance told him the front end had rammed into the car's cockpit. The dash and steering column pinned the man's legs. He pulled again on the door, eyes fixed on the strained face. It didn't budge. He pressed his hand against the glass of the driver's window. Felt helpless.

The man gasped and his breaths turned to rapid pants. He thrashed and sobbed words but didn't make sense. His ghostly skin highlighted the dilated brown pupils and bloodshot whites of his eyes. Tears streaked his cheeks and ran into his open blue lips.

The driver writhed and gestured with a bloodied hand into the distance.

He released an ear-piercing scream merged with two comprehensible words—'My son!'—and dropped unconscious.

Franklin woke before he had to relive the rest of yesterday's nightmare smash. Sweat matted his chest hairs and, despite the warm morning, his bones ached with a pervasive chill. He clenched his eyes and shook his head to purge the devastating images.

The man died in transit to Melbourne after the State Emergency Services crew freed him with the Jaws of Life. They tended to his fifteen-year-old son. Not wearing a seatbelt, on impact he'd catapulted through the Commodore's windscreen and landed on a fence post several metres from the wreck. It lethally impaled him through the spine and propelled his intestines through a massive cavity in his gut. The driver had been a local widower, the sole parent of two children, and now his daughter was orphaned at thirteen.

It cut Franklin to the core that at only a few years younger than Kat she had lost her world. She'd need all the support of the community to survive this catastrophe.

The passengers in the minibus fared better. Physically, at least. They were a group of adults with intellectual disability returning to Ballarat from a day trip at Hepburn Spa. The van flipped onto its side, fortunately its right face. A quick-thinking carer forced open the sliding door on the left and cleared his charges before the vehicle ignited. They then crouched in the shallows of the nearby dam, petrified by the grassfire. That they'd worn seatbelts saved their lives. They would soon recover from their contusions and abrasions, broken ribs and dislocations. The repercussion on their mental health was a question for the long haul.

The bus driver wouldn't have to worry about emotional consequences: he died on impact, which might be a small comfort to his de facto wife over the weeks and months ahead.

Franklin knew the crash would leave him with permanent scars. You can't help remove a kid staked to a fence post and be the same man you were before. Nor can you forget terrified adults huddled together and drenched in blood, their shrieks and moans inhuman. He'd worked casually at the abattoirs for extra income when Donna went on maternity leave. What he'd witnessed yesterday reminded him of the panic of animals at slaughter.

Shortly after Franklin and Hart's arrival, backup police units swarmed from Trentham, Ballan, Creswick and Ballarat, along with additional fire trucks and ambulances and several SES vehicles. Lunny materialised with a fluorescent police vest thrown over his tracksuit in haste. Much later, the three Daylesford policemen handed over the reins to the major collision investigation mob. Yet they knew the accident would spark a chain reaction that they would deal with long beyond the specialists leaving the scene.

The skid marks at the crash site most distressed the cops. The MCI crew reckoned the anonymous witness had probably caused the tragedy, and that the bus driver, his passengers and the Wombat Flat family were all innocent victims. When the Daylesford boys left, the experts had only scratched the surface of the case. But if their preliminary call was substantiated, no one would rest until the bastard got his just desserts.

―――――

'Dad?' Kat nudged the bedroom door. 'You awake?'

'Yeah, come in.'

She entered with vegemite-smeared toast and freshly plunged coffee. She placed the tray on his knees, perched on the side of the bed and scrutinised him. Father and daughter had exchanged roles of carer and charge. If the circumstances weren't so tragic, it'd be funny.

'I'm all right, Kat.'

'You were talking in your sleep. I think you were crying, Dad.'

'Come here.' He opened his arms and they hugged, somehow not upturning the breakfast tray.

A tear trailed Kat's nose. Franklin brushed it away with his thumb. He again said, 'I'm all right. It was horrible out there but –'

'It's all part of the job?'

'Yeah, something like that. Aren't you going to be late for school?'

'I thought you'd want company on your day off.'

'Nice try.' He slapped her arm lightly. 'You're going to school. I'm going fishing with Lunny, so you don't need to worry.' He tensed his abs and pummelled them. 'See, tough as nails.'

'Yeah, *right*.'

'Oh, good. We're back to normal. Teenage daughter is embarrassed by her father and giving cheek.'

She rose, laughing, and wiggled her fingers from the doorway.

Kat departed and Franklin practised his customary coping mechanism: keeping busy. He tuned the radio to a golden oldies station, volume to the max. He sang along loudly, showered and dressed. It wasn't pretty, as he couldn't hit the top notes and tended to make up the lyrics, but tension dripped away.

———

Who doesn't have a mobile or answering machine these days?

Georgie dressed and paced. Smoked and paced. Dialled and paced. Drank black coffee and paced.

She flicked her wrist. Calculated AJ'd dropped Michael at the hospital by now.

She dialled Susan and Margaret again. She cursed. Drank more scalding coffee and studied the wall clock. AJ would have reached his office on Lonsdale Street, right in the heart of the legal precinct.

At 9.35am, Michael rang as arranged and reported good news: a marked improvement in his wife. He still sounded like he was running on red cordial but quoted Dr Quinter, saying *She'll be fine.* Then he admitted Ruby might need a bypass operation but hastily added that Quinter inclined towards betablocker medication, rehab and radical lifestyle changes at this stage.

After that, Michael returned to Ruby's bedside and Georgie resumed pacing.

———

Something brushed Franklin's shoulder blade. 'Shit!'

He pivoted towards a sheepish Tim Lunny.

'Sorry,' the sarge yelled over the music. 'I rang the doorbell.' He dropped to speaking tone as Franklin turned down the radio. 'But you didn't hear me. Can I give you a word of advice?'

Franklin raised a brow.

'Don't give up your day job.'

Lunny chuckled as they climbed into his Monaro coupe. Franklin stretched out his long legs and settled into the sculpted bucket seat. He inhaled the scents of leather cleaner and carpet deodoriser and reflected that the Monaro was one of the few cars in which he enjoyed being a passenger. Although, *driving* the sporty V8 far surpassed passenger thrills, particularly through the curves of the little-used roads out Vaughan way. It matched in power and handling the unmarked Ford FPV-GT a detective buddy let him sample. Awesome.

'Can't get over you lashing out on a swanky car at your age,' he commented, as he'd done periodically since Lunny bought the coupe. It'd been his own celebration gift when he was promoted to sarge at Daylesford. Not that he was happy to see Bill Noonan go; none of them were.

'Ah, yes. One of the upsides to ageing is that you can treat yourself instead of the kids. Once the kids leave home, that is.'

'Hmm. Well, I guess I have about five years to go then.'

Lunny snorted. 'Guess again. We didn't get rid of the last one until she turned twenty-nine. These days they often stay until their forties.'

They drove without speaking through Hepburn Springs and snaked along the Hepburn–Newstead Road with the Monaro in its element. They powered past Breakneck Gorge. Near the turnoff for Howlong Road, Franklin wondered if Susan Pentecoste had returned to Abergeldie. He dialled the farm.

The call rang out. He tapped the mobile on his knee.

'Are you okay, John? You want to see a counsellor?' Lunny had misread his mood.

Franklin cringed. The accident had been a shocker, but he'd cope; he couldn't imagine a scenario bad enough that he'd sit in a stuffy office, sharing his feelings with a shrink. 'Nuh. I'm fine. Harty might be a different story. Yesterday's smash would be his worst.'

'Melissa's going back to Melbourne tonight.' Lunny referred to Hart's girlfriend, who commuted between Castlemaine and the city during her final year at university. 'If it's going to hit him, that'd be when.'

They brooded. Eventually, the sarge asked, 'How about a debrief over a few snags and beers later, then?'

A bunch of mates, an excess of beer and plenty of dark humour? No blots on service records or shit stirring about seeing a shrink by cockheads like Wells?

Definitely a better idea.

'Whatever,' Franklin borrowed Kat's favourite phrase and shrugged. 'I was actually chewing over Susan Pentecoste and that bird from Melbourne. Don't suppose there's any need to worry, though.'

Lunny agreed.

They fell silent again and wound past a derelict cottage. Rusted iron peeled away from a verandah supported by leaning posts, and its deep-set rot somehow reflected Franklin's unease.

CHAPTER TWENTY-ONE

Soon, they approached Cricket Willow in Shepherds Flat. The birthplace of the Australian cricket bat, its oval was an oasis nourished by purified sewage water. They pulled over moments later. Lunny was reluctant to drive his Monaro off-road, even across the privately owned paddock adjacent to their favourite fishing spot on the Jim Crow. So they took their gear and secured the car before hoofing the last 500 metres.

Lunny adjusted his grip on the esky and asked, 'Have you ever regretted joining the cops?'

Surprised, Franklin glanced at his boss. 'Nope. You?'

'Mmm. If I'd been a boilermaker, as my dad wanted, I wouldn't have baggage from cases like yesterday's crash. Hard to switch off, isn't it?'

Franklin nodded and they trudged a few metres, inspecting the creek for a deep pool and the bank for a suitable clearing. They found the perfect place and grunted together.

'You wouldn't have enjoyed being a boilermaker.'

'Probably true. What would you have done instead?'

'I can't imagine doing anything else.'

'No regrets, then?'

After a hesitation, Franklin admitted, 'A few. Donna for one. I don't think we should've got married so young. She hadn't tasted life enough and was never going to be happy being a copper's wife in a small town for long. And Kat tied her down. She wasn't ready for the whole deal.'

Lunny cast and settled onto the bank, with his back against a knotted gumtree. 'What else?'

'Nuh. Your turn.'

Lunny was quiet for several minutes, then sighed. 'I wish I'd travelled when I was young.'

'You still can. You're not that old.' Franklin grinned to take off the sting, especially on top of his earlier crack about the Monaro.

'Maeve and I are considering a cruise next year. Fiji, Noumea...' Lunny flicked his line and reeled it in. His bait had vanished, so he replenished the hook and recast.

He said, 'You must be sick of Daylesford. Few of us can work in the same station as long as you have. Six or seven years and we generally get twitchy. Although, I must say, I'm in no hurry to leave, and I'm coming up for eight years. More to the point, Maeve'd have my guts for garters if I put in for a transfer.' He chuckled, then glanced at Franklin. 'Sixteen years, though.' He shook his head. 'Why don't you go for your sarge's stripes, mate?'

Franklin's line jolted. He pulled up. The rod arched away from the rigid line. He jerked. The line cleared the water.

'Catch of the day.' Lunny chuckled again.

Franklin jiggled his brows and removed a snagged stick.

'How about it?' the older cop persisted. 'I'll put your name forward.'

'If I was going for a promotion, it'd be for the suits,' Franklin replied, then wished he'd kept his mouth shut. He'd never verbalised his ambition.

'A detective, huh? Well, why not? I'll put your name up.'

Franklin looked away. He watched the water trickle over pebbles and submerged branches.

'I think I've got a bite,' Lunny said excitedly. He gave the rod a few twitches, checked his bait. 'Nuh, false alarm.'

He reached into the esky and threw a beer to Franklin before popping one. 'What do you reckon? Will I have a chat with the district inspector and get it rolling?'

'I can't leave Kat to do the course. And afterwards, I'd be posted who-knows-where to start with and then have to wait for a vacancy in Ballarat or Bacchus Marsh to get back to the area. And even they're too far away. It's ideal living and working here – I'm on the spot if Kat needs me.'

'I get that it's hard being a single parent, John,' Lunny interrupted. 'But you need a life too.'

'I can't leave Kat, and it wouldn't be fair to uproot her. All her buddies are here, and it'd be a big mistake to move her in her senior years of school. It could stuff up her whole life.'

Lunny sighed. 'Can't talk you into it?'

Franklin shook his head, miserable.

The sarge switched subjects. 'Yesterday the worst you've been to?'

'Accident?' On Lunny's nod, Franklin replied decisively, 'No. The worst was a mate from the footy club who decided to take himself out; it would've been a couple of years before you transferred in. Smitty strapped himself and his three kids into his station wagon, then didn't steer or brake at the first bend with a decent drop. They crashed through the guard rail and shot over the edge. They reckon he flipped twice before smashing into a massive gum. *That* was bad. Those little kiddies didn't fucking deserve to die like that.'

It hit him afresh. The stench of petrol and blood overlaid by eucalyptus.

'They didn't deserve to die *at all*.' Lunny violently swatted a fly.

A few minutes passed before the sarge spoke again. 'My worst was out at Box Hill. My first posting out of the academy and I was downright green. In my second month, I had three horrific weeks. In the first week, a man stepped in front of a train. It wasn't a suicide, but it was pretty gruesome. Then my partner and I copped a shotgun suicide. A young Turkish girl. The parents didn't have much English, which made the whole thing worse. The mother was distraught, and I couldn't find a way to make it any better. So I patted her back and left fast. The next bloomin' weekend, a little old lady got bumped crossing Maroondah Highway. Jesus, that was messy. The driver had a nervous breakdown, even though it wasn't his fault.'

'The little old lady's time was up.'

'He couldn't see it that way.'

'Imagine how hard he'd have taken it if he'd been drunk or speeding.'

'I tell you what,' Lunny said loudly. 'It's lucky I had Maeve to talk to. I very nearly left the force, thinking if this is what it's going to be like, I won't be able to cope. Ah, but you find your ways, don't you?'

'Sure. You have to deal with it or get out. You're no good to anyone, least of all yourself, if you drag yourself in every day stressing over what's going to happen or carrying a chip on your shoulder.'

'That goes for life generally, doesn't it?'

'Yeah, and thank God most people wouldn't, *couldn't* do what Smitty did. Put it this way, it was pretty rough when Donna left, but I got over it for Kat. And because life's too short.'

They fished quietly. Franklin sensed that Lunny was more upset than he was willing to admit by yesterday's accident and in reliving the Box Hill horror too.

'Keep an eye on my line, John,' the sarge said.

Franklin watched him retreat to the car.

He returned composed and buoyant. 'Righto, my place for a barbie and drinks later. Harty will be back from Melissa's by change of shift, when Slam and Kong will be coming off. Irvy and Wellsey are on arvo shift, so we'll divert the phones to the portables and then everyone except Bert will be there.'

'Sounds like a plan,' Franklin approved, clunking his upraised can against his friend's.

As he took a sip, his mobile rang. He moved out of earshot.

———

It was Cathy Jones. Distraught, she babbled, *'I really think someone's watching my place. It's freaking me out.'*

Franklin demanded details. It boiled down to Cathy's suspicions. He told her he'd come right away and listened to a long silence.

She hiccupped and heaved a breath. *'No, don't worry. I'll go to my sister's place in Gordon. She runs an artists' commune and it's always crowded.'* In a steely voice, she added, *'Solomon won't follow us there.'*

Franklin wondered if her restored confidence was real

or feigned. She was adamant. They debated. She won, the compromise being that she'd contact him the next day. He returned to his rod as its tip bowed and the line stretched.

———

Shortly before her meeting, Georgie ran out to the Spider to retrieve Susan's album, her notepad and the paraphernalia she'd dumped on the passenger seat in her haste to get to the hospital.

She sorted and set up priorities for later, momentarily confused by an unfamiliar sheet of paper. Then she recalled pulling the junk mail off her windscreen yesterday.

However, when she unfolded the page and read the text, she realised it was definitely unwanted but not random or innocuous.

At that instant, the full complement of the health and safety committee arrived at the door. Still rattled, Georgie went into auto-mode to meet, greet and settle them at her dining table.

She forced herself to focus on the director's catalogue of faults in the script. After a lengthy spiel, David halted. Georgie heaved an internal sigh, re-affixed her professional face and retaliated with her own list. Top issue: the vagueness of the brief.

Her spine straightened so quickly it cracked. She'd recognised a parallel to the Hepburn quandary.

All questions, no answers. No idea where to go from here.

She pushed her mind to the present, and under David's pedantic command, they workshopped.

Despite itching to dial the Pentecoste women throughout the exhaustive meeting, the script began to crawl. By mid-afternoon, the OH&S threesome departed, confident Georgie could add the spit and polish.

She immediately rang the Ballarat and Hepburn numbers burnt into her brain. No joy.

On her desk, the folded sheet seemed to glow, beckoning her to pick it up. She slammed her hand down on the letter and stuffed it into her top drawer.

No one would make Georgie Harvey a victim or scare her off.

She took Susan's second album to the sunny courtyard, along with her pack of Benson & Hedges and a brimming glass of cabernet sauvignon.

Soon neither cigarettes nor alcohol could compete.

———

THE ICEMAN INTERVIEWED IN FARMER'S DISAPPEARANCE

Sources revealed to the *Herald Sun* yesterday that John Schlicht, 57, purportedly masterminded the disappearance of Hepburn farmer Roland Pentecoste, 58.

Schlicht, aka the Iceman, has been a person of interest to police for numerous years, with suspected connections to Melbourne's organised crime ring.

As this paper recently reported, Schlicht has been implicated in the transportation and distribution of illicit drugs and

strong-arm tactics at the fruit markets for four decades.

On more than one occasion, the question has been asked: 'Why have charges never been proven against this alleged crime boss?'

Asked but not answered.

While accusations of police protection flourish, Schlicht's activities may finally come under long-overdue scrutiny.

An informant has apparently disclosed to police a connection between Schlicht and Mr Pentecoste's vanishing.

Mr Pentecoste has not been seen since the early hours of Monday 19 March, after he and his wife, Susan, 54, were separated during their attempts to contain a mysterious blaze at their grazing property.

Mrs Pentecoste suffered severe head trauma, second-degree burns to much of her body and smoke inhalation.

Fortunately, CFA volunteers discovered the unconscious woman and emergency aid was administered until she was airlifted to the Alfred Hospital.

In the following days, it was revealed that Mrs Pentecoste had been attacked with a blunt instrument by an unknown assailant and she was lucky to survive her ordeal.

Nearly a week after the assault, she emerged from a coma and began the slow road to recovery.

Meanwhile, there was no trace of her husband, and contention regarding his involvement in the events of 19 March abounded.

The local community in Victoria's mineral springs region became divided over this debate, and in the six months since the arson attack, police have had few leads until an associate of Schlicht turned informer yesterday.

———

ICEMAN INFORMER SUICIDES IN BIZZARE: 'MISING BODY MYSTERY' TWIST

In a shocking twist, the informer who two days ago made allegations to police that career criminal John Schlicht murdered missing Victorian farmer Roland Pentecoste has apparently suicided in a Fitzroy flat overnight.

Police were called to the Johnston Street apartment at 12.20am, following a report of a disturbance at the address.

They discovered the body of Angelo Sartori, aged 36, who is understood to have taken his own life by hanging.

Sartori had previous convictions for the production and distribution of amphetamines, sexual assault and numerous driving offences, including reckless driving causing serious injury.

It is believed that he claimed to have witnessed the payback murder of an associate of Schlicht, in addition to the attempted murder and murder of Susan Pentecoste and her husband, Roland, respectively.

———

PRESS ACCUSED OF KANGAROO COURT

Prominent criminal lawyer Benjamin Footman, acting for John Schlicht, 57, yesterday lashed out at police and the media with claims of bias and defamation.

At a press conference outside his Camberwell office yesterday morning, Mr Footman said, 'It's trial by media. My client has not been charged with anything whatsoever connected to the distressing disappearance of Mr Roland Pentecoste, and yet the press has him convicted by its kangaroo court.'

Mr Pentecoste went missing contemporaneously with an attack upon his wife and arson at his farming property in Hepburn seven months ago.

This paper revealed an associate of Schlicht, Angelo Sartori, had claimed involvement in these events by his then employer, Schlicht; however, Sartori committed suicide several days after approaching police with these claims.

According to Inspector Rick Uris of the homicide squad, 'We haven't a witness or sufficient evidence to charge Mr Schlicht with involvement in the attempted murder of Mrs Pentecoste. Nor are we in a position to lay charges in relation to Mr Pentecoste's disappearance, although we are exploring several leads.'

Meanwhile, Footman yesterday continued his attack upon the media, saying, 'This is an obscene breach of Mr Schlicht's civil liberties. If there is insufficient evidence to charge my client with any crime—as there obviously is, because he is innocent of every claim—then the police, press and public have a duty to respect the presumption of innocence.'

He concluded the press conference with a warning that 'Any defamation of my client's character will be vigorously condemned and civil proceedings immediately brought to recompense Mr Schlicht.

'He is entitled to fair and reasonable compensation for the pain, suffering and financial impact on his business affairs caused by such outrageous and unjust behaviour.'

LET ME HAVE HIS BODY: WIFE BEGS

The wife of central Victorian farmer Roland Pentecoste has sent an open letter to *The Age* pleading for information relating to her husband, who has been missing since 19 March last year.

In that letter, Mrs Susan Pentecoste states:

'Over the past year, I've had too much time to think about where my husband is.

'In my heart I realise there is no other explanation but that he is dead and has been all along.

'We had thirty-five years of good marriage. I would like to know what happened and why, but giving Roly a proper Christian burial is by far the most important thing.

'If it was you who saw my husband last, Mr Schlicht, as some people have said, please tell me where to find Roly, so I can give him the send-off he deserves. I promise to never tell a soul whatever else you say to me, if that's what you want.

'If you had a wife and the tables were turned, wouldn't she do the same?'

CHAPTER TWENTY-TWO

'Hello, I think you've got yourself a live one!' Lunny's eyes shone.

He helped Franklin land a fat carp that would have been terrific on the barbecue if it weren't for the river grubber's muddy flavour. However, they'd had a good fishing day and bagged a brown trout and redfin between them, both of legal size, and headed for the station house.

They reached Howlong Road.

'Pull off here. Let's check the Pentecoste place,' Franklin directed.

Although he grumbled about stone chips and dust, Lunny did as instructed. Franklin could've walked faster. At Abergeldie, there was no sign of Mick and Roger, and the off-duty policemen entered the homestead as Hart and Franklin had a day earlier.

After prowling through, Franklin dropped onto a kitchen chair. He drummed his fingertips while the sarge observed.

'In theory, I can blow apart Georgie Harvey's worries,

but what if there's some substance to them?' Franklin remarked. 'This doesn't feel right at all.'

'How's that, mate?'

'It's out of character for Susan. Her number-one priority,' he unconsciously echoed the phrase Cathy Jones used yesterday concerning Tyson, 'is always this place. Even though Mick and Roger run the farm, she never leaves it for more than a few days. Besides that, she's transparent. She says it as it is, no matter what. You always know where you stand.'

'Ah, but do you really? How well do you *really* know Susan?'

'Well enough,' Franklin said. 'Remember, while you were on that secondment down in Melbourne, Bill Noonan and I were heavily involved with the arson investigation and whatnot when her hubby disappeared.'

'But how well do you really know anyone?' Lunny pressed. 'Only as far as they want you to, right? Everyone has secrets – little ones or otherwise. Things they keep private.'

'Yeah but –'

'C'mon. As you said earlier, Susan's gone on an impromptu holiday, that's all. Let's go; we've got beer getting warm and a barbie to crank up. Tomorrow's soon enough for you to put on your shining armour and hunt up Susan Pentecoste.'

Franklin's guts twisted as he wondered if Lunny was right.

———

'Hello?' Pam Stewart answered. Laughter echoed in the background.

Georgie gave mental thanks for at least one old duck having a mobile phone. 'Where are you? Can you speak?'

'Well, I just got out of the pool. Aqua aerobics is such fun, dear. You must try it.'

'Aerobics isn't my thing,' Georgie said dryly. 'I'm uncoordinated.'

'That's the beauty of doing it in the water! No one can see exactly what your feet are doing, and it's impossible to trip up.'

Georgie chuckled at the image of herself in some ridiculous water aerobics pose.

A sudden commotion of laughter and splashing snapped her out of the daydream.

'Pam, can you please ring me when you get home?'

'Of course. I won't be too long.'

While she waited, Georgie skolled her neglected wine and chain-smoked.

A quarter of an hour later, the landline rang. On speakerphone, Georgie updated Pam with Ruby's condition and her unsuccessful attempts to contact Susan and Margaret Pentecoste. She omitted mention of the letter under her wiper but described in detail Susan's second album.

Pam listened, making shocked noises. At the end, she said, *'I never knew.'* She sounded ten years older.

'What do you mean?'

'Oh, I read the articles in the newspapers. I even helped Susan write her letter to the paper. But I never knew she'd been collecting those clippings all along. I thought she was coping quite well. Considering.'

'Outwardly calm but falling apart inside?'

'It would seem so, dear. Oh, no.' She moaned. *'I've let her down all these years.'*

'If she wanted to talk about it, she would have. And you would have listened.'

'*Naturally.*'

'So you can't blame yourself that she bottled it up. Besides, you said she keeps her friends separated. Perhaps someone else is her Roly-counsellor.' Georgie changed tack. 'What about this Schlicht angle? I gather the police were light-on for suspects and at one stage the Iceman was their prime candidate. Then it just fizzled out.'

'*You have that right, dear,*' Pam murmured. She sighed, then explained, '*It was a very trying period for everyone. Neighbours pitted against each other, the town divided. But people took sides without thinking it through. Why would Roly want to set fire to his own farm? Why would he try to kill Susan? The idea's absurd. You've never met a couple so devoted.*

'*Without doubt, it made more sense for this Schlicht man to have been behind it. He's a thug and drug dealer, after all. But why would he hurt Roly? We never understood. There were all sorts of stories bandying to and fro, but they didn't make sense.*'

Georgie cut in, 'Because Sartori killed himself before he made an official statement?'

'*Yes, that and because he was a convicted felon himself. Could anybody trust him?*'

'True. Not the ideal witness.'

'*What we heard about Angelo Sartori was so vague. That he witnessed John Schlicht kill this other chap and was part of the gang that set fire to Abergeldie. He alluded to them killing Roly but then killed himself before he explained everything, including why they had to kill our friend.*' Pam broke off. Her sighs stabbed at Georgie, who didn't know what to say.

Neither spoke for a minute, then Pam said, *'Oh, I'm not stupid. I do realise criminals don't have to use logic like the rest of us or play by normal rules. It could have been as daft as Roly looking at the wrong person the wrong way, I guess.'*

'Hmm. Money for nothing, sex without strings and punishment without police or court.'

'What, dear?'

'Something I read once. Along the lines that criminals go for instant gratification, with no concern about right and wrong or the things that constrain the rest of us.'

'What else are you thinking?' Pam asked a moment later.

'Makes you wonder if Sartori killed himself or if somebody did it for him.'

Pam sucked in a breath. *'It does, indeed.'*

They contemplated that twist in silence. Georgie didn't know what her friend was mulling over, but she pictured the threatening note left on her car and started to sweat on its sender.

———

Georgie turned her focus back to the Pentecostes. 'What else can you tell me?'

'I don't know,' Pam's voice trilled. *'My memory's not as good as it used to be.'*

'Not so's you'd notice.'

'If you knew me ten years ago, you'd think differently. I'm not as quick to recall details or think laterally as I was.'

'Okay. I'll give you a specific...' Georgie realised that what she said next would wound.

Necessary evil.

'Tell me about the day of the fire.'

She heard Pam take several juddering breaths, and her

heartbeat accelerated as she waited. After a long gap, she wondered if Pam would answer at all. She shifted the phone to make room for her notepad on the desk as Pam sighed.

She traced random doodles into the margin and stilled her impatience. Certain things can't be rushed, like brewing a good beer. She knew if she pressed Pam too hard, she might push her away.

Finally, Pam said, *'Well, we had lunch together, the three of us, at Abergeldie. As you know, I don't drive and Roly, as usual, was busy around the farm with Mick and Roger. So, Susan picked me up in her four-wheel drive.'*

'That's good, keep going,' Georgie urged.

'I remember that Roly's tea went cold because Jenny McGuire from the Advocate *arrived.'*

'A journo from the local rag?'

'Yes. She was writing a story on Roly. He'd gone to the aid of an accident the previous evening. Her idea was to tie this into a piece on his achievements and active involvement in the community, that type of thing. When they finished, we all had afternoon tea. That's right, we baked scones!' Pam laughed, recalling the trivial detail.

Georgie grounded her. 'And then what happened?'

'Well, Susan and Roly were going to dinner –'

'What was the occasion?'

'None. They were taking up a special at Windows on Vincent.'

Georgie vaguely remembered the restaurant but couldn't picture it in the context of her recent excursions. 'Is it still there?'

'It became a pancake place and changed again since. Oh, I am enjoying this detective work!' Pam sobered. Perhaps it

struck her that she verged upon the last time Roland Pentecoste was seen alive. *'Oh, that's not appropriate, is it?'*

'It's okay. Better to laugh than cry, usually.'

'Yes, well. In any event, Roly and Susan dropped me home on their way to the restaurant. They had booked an early sitting. It must have been between six and six-thirty.'

'And then?' Georgie prompted.

'Well, that's all I know firsthand. From what Susan told me, they had a wonderful evening. It was just as well, as it turned out. One last special night...' Pam cleared her throat and continued, *'They returned home and went to bed after checking all the usual things.'*

'Go on.'

She sighed deeply. *'In the middle of the night—well, not long past midnight—Roly woke suddenly. He shook Susan awake and they went outside in their pyjamas with jumpers over the top. They found the sheds alight, and Roly jumped into fighting the flames while Susan phoned the CFA.'*

Georgie visualised. It morphed into real-time: *Shivering in my PJs.*

Pam said, *'She phoned the captain, Phil Isaacs. Then she pulled on a pair of work boots and went back outside. The strong wind that night made matters worse. It made it harder to see through the smoke and stirred up the flames.'*

Georgie was surrounded by a dark night sky. Orange aura near the sheds. Horrific noises. Cracking, roaring, snapping.

'But she made out that the fire had almost taken the hay shed and other buildings were under threat or on fire. She struggled against the noxious smoke. Her eyes watered so much she could barely see.'

Pam paused.

Georgie couldn't see properly. Fumes burning her lungs. Coughing, gasping.

'Susan called and called but she couldn't hear a thing above the roar, and the animals going berserk. Her throat hurt from the smoke and from screaming for Roly. She couldn't find him.'

Georgie teared up.

'She did what she could with blankets and buckets of water,' Pam continued, 'praying the fire fighters would arrive before the whole place went up. She doesn't recall what happened next. There's a big blank until she woke up in hospital days later.'

In a high-strung tone, she said, 'They left her for dead. That was the plan: to knock her out and let the fire finish her off. Chances are they hoped to frame Roly for it. Or banked on everyone assuming there were two bodies.'

Pam sobbed. A prick of pain responded in Georgie. She searched for reassurance, a positive. 'Well, Susan survived their horrible plan. Whoever they were. She must be a very gutsy lady.'

'Oh, she is. That's why I have to believe she's safe and well.'

'Yes, you do. There's no point thinking otherwise.'

'I pray for her safety.'

Pray hard to your god, Pam. Pray hard.

———

**KEEP YOUR NOSE OUT OF THINGS
THAT ARE NONE OF YOUR BUSINESS
YOU WILL ONLY GET ONE WARNING!**

Ordinary copy paper. One run-on sentence. Printed in Arial font. In landscape orientation. All uppercase. Approximately 50 point and bold type with the word *one* underlined.

Georgie had an enemy.

Who?

It had to be connected with Susan; she couldn't imagine being warned off the first-aid job. That made a nervous laugh pop out.

At least I've still got my sense of humour.

Back to business. Who had she pissed off? Who had she stirred up over the past few days?

Top of the list: Roger and Mick, the farmers from Abergeldie. And she had a bruise to prove it.

Next: Lewis Davis from The Springs Real Estate. He definitely regretted sharing his Tim Tams with her.

Lewis's buddy Douglas Macdougall, even though she'd yet to meet him.

Surely not Susan's neighbours, the Pattersons?

What about Pam? That lovely old duck could not be behind the threat. Scratch Pam.

She couldn't forget John Franklin but doubted he'd bother with a note. The sexist local cop would take a direct approach.

AJ – it was so wrong on so many levels to even add him to the list that she cringed, but he did try to be overprotective. Fortunately, he'd been busy in his office when she called alerting him to Ruby's second heart attack and hadn't even known she'd returned to Daylesford. She crossed him off again.

Georgie reread the note twice more.

Nobody but Pam knew she'd stumbled on the Schlicht angle, right?

She puckered her lips. Make that Pam and Bron. On a long shot, the farmers and the cops might have an inkling too. And with every extra person came the chance of something said, overheard, slipping...

She gulped a finger of scotch.

I am not scared, and I am not giving up until I've found Susan.

———

She felt like one of Enid Blyton's Famous Five on an adventure. You could call it *Five Go to Castlemaine* or *Five Find the Truth*, except she didn't have anybody with her. So perhaps it should be *One on a Quest*.

She giggled a trifle shrilly.

Years earlier, a friend had said you reach a point where you don't become older in your mind, even though your body ages. Up until a few years ago, she'd agreed. Her mind stayed around mid-twenties: old enough to have some sense, young enough to be optimistic and resilient. Since then, both mind and body had started to crack up. But today...today she took on a mission.

She donned slacks and sensible shoes and packed a synthetic shopping bag. Food, water, torch, map and directions. She pulled her niece's sunhat over wiry hair. If she'd been at her own home, she would have taken a host of other things.

Her smile faded. She settled on adding a carving knife from the kitchen drawer and the tyre lever from her toolbox.

No good pretending this was a *Girl's Own* escapade.

THURSDAY 18 MARCH

CHAPTER TWENTY-THREE

'THAT'S NOT YOUR GIRLFRIEND'S ALFA, IS IT, MATE?'

Franklin followed Mick Sprague's finger to a black convertible. He ignored the jibe about the wacko Melburnian being his girlfriend.

Slam went on, 'Course, I didn't meet her the other day. But seeing as we don't get many of the old Alfas around here, I'm guessing...'

The number plate matched.

'It's no coincidence. It's Harvey's all right.'

'Can't wait to meet her. Harty reckons she's hot.'

'Are you still going on, Slam?' Franklin feigned surprise. He accelerated. The gear spread over his partner's lap tumbled everywhere.

They navigated the Burke Square roundabout while Slam groused.

'Let's hover near the school crossing and scare 'em into doing forty clicks,' Franklin suggested. 'Lunny's had complaints from the lollipop lady again.'

His mate cocked his head, so Franklin added, 'We all

know the old girl's pretty easy-going, so when she says she's "sick to the eyeballs of hoons" it must be bad.'

'It's the mums doing the school-drop that are the worst offenders.'

Franklin nodded. 'Speeding, double parking –'

Slam clicked his fingers. 'That's it! You wanna do the school patrol so you can pick up a yummy-mummy. You dirty bastard. And what would your girlfriend from Melbourne think?'

That deserved a backhander.

Custom was slow. By 9.45am, the partners had cautioned a couple of harried mums and were on their way back to the station. They received an urgent callout to a West Street address familiar to Franklin. Unaware if the offender lurked, they flicked on lights and siren and tore away.

———

The police truck screeched to a stop outside the humble brick veneer and the two cops alighted. A woman and baby wailed inside the house. Slam and Franklin exchanged glances. Franklin extracted his baton but held it in his off-hand and close to his thigh. Both rested a hand on holstered weapon.

A man shouted, also inside the building. The cries halted. Then the child howled louder, while the woman yelled something unintelligible.

Dread balled in Franklin's gut. He swallowed and bellowed, 'POLICE! Open up!'

The baby quietened.

Wait or force entry? Franklin considered the risks.

The decision was made for him. Christina van Hoeckel threw open the door.

She glared. Her face was red, puffy and wet with tears. A pink singlet stretched over her huge bosoms. Yellow slimed her front. Red specks stained the slime.

'About bloody time,' she bitched before doing a double take of the baton in his hand. She registered their gun-draw stances and snapped, 'You won't need your fucking guns.'

Franklin slipped the baton onto his duty belt and relaxed.

Out of Christina's line of sight, Slam lifted his eyebrows and swivelled his eyes towards her and downwards. At first, Franklin thought his mate was ogling her boobs. Then he noticed her hands.

The shakes weren't remarkable.

The fresh nicks were.

'She's all yours.'

The speaker dripped sarcasm, added a lip-curl and a soft snort.

Franklin recognised the man from his previous visit and held up a hand. 'Wait here. We'll have some questions.'

'It's got nothing to do with me.'

'That right, Christina?'

Distractedly, she flapped a hand. 'No, he didn't do anything.'

Franklin let him go for now.

The bloke pushed past and tossed Christina another contemptuous glance. He strode to a car parked in front of the neighbour's house and slammed the door.

Franklin wondered if it signified the end to their love affair.

Christina watched her boyfriend speed away and then she resumed her wails. When she stamped her feet in a toddler's tantrum, Franklin wanted to shake or slap her. He did neither.

Slam cleared his throat.

Franklin introduced his offsider, then prompted, 'You reported an attack, Christina?'

Still hysterical, she led them down the short hallway to a bedroom. There, her baby shrieked between hiccups. His face was beet red. Shards of glass lay at the foot of his cot. The ragged curtain over his window fluttered.

Christina's breaths shuddered. She worked to compose herself.

'Look at this.' She picked up a large honeycomb rock. Fragments and blood flecked its surface. 'It just missed poor little Bails!'

Curiously, she didn't go to her child. Franklin lifted him from the cot. Bailey gazed with saucer eyes, then snuffled into the blue shirt. Franklin stroked the boy's back.

'He doesn't seem to be hurt.'

'The arsehole just missed him. Poor little Bails.' Christina dropped the rock, missing her toes by centimetres. She wrapped arms across her chest and chafed her hands.

'You want a coffee, Christina?'

She nodded a yes to Slam. Then stared at where he'd stood while he clattered nearby.

In an eerie monotone, she said, 'I was in the kitchen and heard this big crash. At first, I thought something'd exploded. Then I realised it sounded like glass breaking. Bailey howled and I spilt his food all over me.' She gestured at the goo on her top. 'A bit went on the floor. I was glued to the spot. Then I snapped out of it and went to go to Bailey's room, but I slipped over on the stuff I'd spilt. Dazza came running out of the shower and we got to Bailey's room at the same time. I saw the torn curtain, glass everywhere and a hole in the window. I couldn't look at Bailey's cot. I was so worried what I'd see.'

She faced Franklin. 'Do you get what I mean?'

He pictured the recent car and minibus accident. The way he'd switched to autopilot to face the carnage, although it didn't stop him being sickened by what he'd witnessed. 'Yeah, I do.'

The baby rubbed a fist into his eye. Franklin thought he'd soon be asleep.

'I screamed and picked up bits of glass with my hands. I got all these cuts and that freaked me out even more, so I flicked the blood off my fingers. It went everywhere. Darren slapped me. And yelled at me to shut up. He told me to shut Bailey up too. I peeked at Bails then. And I saw he wasn't hurt. I nearly wet myself. Relief. You know?'

She waited for his nod.

'Coffee's ready,' Slam called.

Franklin turned to the doorway. Christina's sudden grip startled him. She gestured towards Bailey. She took him and smothered her child's crown in kisses. She sniffed his downy hair and wet it with fresh tears.

'It's not fair. He could have hurt my baby.'

'*Who*, Christina? You know who's responsible, don't you.' He said it as a statement, not a query. 'It's not kids, like you said on Tuesday, is it?'

She tightened her arms around Bailey and brushed past. In the lounge room Slam had arranged mugs and biscuits. The two cops sipped coffee and watched Christina rock her baby.

She murmured a non-stop mantra. Incoherently.

Then she fixed on Franklin. 'I'll talk to you but not him.' She pointed at his offsider.

Franklin tried to reason with her. It was useless. He lifted his palms to Slam.

———

Once Slam had retreated to the truck, Christina said, 'I don't know who did it exactly. All I know is that he calls himself Solomon.'

Franklin choked on biscuit crumbs.

'I've had letters from this creep. He wrapped one around the rock today too.'

Christina placed Bailey on his play mat and disappeared.

She returned with a bundle of crumpled notes, the topmost dirt- and blood-stained and more wrinkled than the rest.

Before Franklin read the letter, she said, 'I wanted to tell you on Saturday. When he wrote on my car bonnet "Atone Whore" with lipstick and then broke all the windows. And he wrecked Bailey's capsule. Why would he do that?'

She waited for Franklin's reply. He shrugged, for lack of a good answer.

'But then I got scared and all mixed up,' she continued. 'What if going to the cops made him even angrier and he did something worse? So I rang to tell you to back off. But at the same time, I kinda didn't want you to listen. I wanted you to keep going and catch the creep. But I didn't think he'd go further than smashing up my car. I never expected he'd do this. You know, actually attack me or Bailey. Dazza's jack of it. He reckons I'm too much of a liability with a sicko stalking me and Bails.'

She broke off, crying. Franklin scanned the letter.

Whore, you are evil. You sicken good Christians, are a home-wrecker and besmirch our Society. You are not a clean or worthy woman and you do not live virtuously. Every day you live is in Sin. I am ANGRY that you have not responded to my letters. You have not changed your ways. I told you to Atone, Whore, but you have ignored me. Adulterous women shall be punished. You will pay for your Sins. You and your bastard.

Solomon

'Some Christian.' Christina sniffed. 'This guy must live in the dark ages.'

'How's that?'

'I'm only doing what most women would.'

Franklin forced his brows not to rise.

'So I like men.'

'And don't mind if they're married.'

'So? Dazza's wife doesn't satisfy him, and I can. No strings.'

'Perfect relationship,' Franklin said dryly. Even as he said it, he acknowledged he had no right to judge Christina. Not for being an unwed mother, promiscuous or sleeping with a married man. Not for anything at all, unless she broke the law.

Pity Solomon's worldview was so skewed that he didn't realise the same thing. As such a devout Christian, why didn't he leave it to God to sort out Christina? Why target the baby? And, more importantly, did the rock miss Bailey's cot by luck or design?

Solomon had raised the stakes. Why? What had pushed him beyond his nasty little letters? And how close was he to the edge of the abyss?

What would he do next? Would he kill?

Worries and pieces of the riddle preoccupied Franklin after he and Slam left the van Hoeckel residence, even while they interviewed the few neighbours who were home.

'Well, are you going to tell me what else is going on?' Slam asked.

'Huh?'

'Don't act the innocent, mate. There's more to this story than a random rock through the window, isn't there?'

'Hmm.' Franklin dodged with, 'Bloody typical that nobody saw or heard a thing. It always amazes me.'

'Hear no evil. See no evil. Speak to no cops, except about what's common knowledge.'

'Oh, well, that means less to write up.'

'Yeah, that's true.' Slam brightened, then reverted to his earlier train of thought. 'What were you scribbling in that daybook of yours?'

Franklin ignored his buddy. He tuned out the police radio.

Trees flicked by, their leaves browning and dropping.

CHAPTER TWENTY-FOUR

He had too many questions and too few answers; meanwhile Solomon's actions had taken an ominous twist.

Franklin had hoped for a break in the case. A tie between the women other than the Ballarat Base Hospital and that they were single mums in Daylesford. As yet to run it by three of the mums, he only had a fifty per cent strike rate on Art Hammer so far: Cathy had never met the bloke; Christina had been harassed by him at various pubs but thought he was all talk and no action. As for Earl Blue and his odd-bod behaviour at the Daylesford Community Church, Christina didn't recognise him from the photo, and she had no connection with the church. The bugger hadn't phoned him back either. He needed to follow up with Blue and check back with the other mums on both local wackos soon.

Okay, so what *did* he have right now?

Bailey van Hoeckel: aged five months, born at the Trentham Bush Nursing Hospital.

Significance: Solomon's games dated back to at least

October, and the hospital link was demoted to tenuous at best, unless a staffer worked at both Ballarat and Trentham. The person could be an agency nurse or aide.

Shit, that could mean more hospitals and more victims.

Franklin jotted a reminder to check the agency angle.

The letter-wrapped rock was the work of a psycho who'd scrutinised Christina subsequent to sending his initial letters. Who'd witnessed her relationship with a married father of two, along with, as the latest gossip had it, another couple of local blokes. That someone *apparently* blended in so well that no one on West Street noticed him that morning, either before or after hurling the rock.

Presumably a local, could even be a neighbour.

Franklin added the idea to his book and rechecked his interview notes.

Christina wasn't part of a mothers' group and went to a different medical clinic to the others, whereas the women all visited the maternal health centre and a number of the same local businesses.

But what if Solomon lacked official association with any of these? How would Franklin narrow in on him?

And what if Solomon was a woman? Not much would surprise him in this perplexing case.

He debated whether it was time to get the suits involved or share his inquiries with the Daylesford team. Franklin was loath to do either. Christina had begged him not to divulge the Solomon-stalker aspect of the case. Brazen she may be, but she didn't fancy being dubbed *the whore who copped a rock through the window,* particularly as she hoped to talk Darren back into her bed.

Franklin ticked off a mental list to justify keeping quiet. He figured Christina, Tayla and Lauren could fend off gossipmongers if it came to it, but he'd protect Cathy Jones's privacy wherever possible. Besides, the crime investigation unit was perpetually busy and under-resourced, so they would handball it back to the local uniforms. This would mean more meaningless paperwork and delays as they battled interdepartmental, bureaucratic bullshit.

What could the CIU detectives or his workmates do that he wasn't already onto? He still had Blue and Hammer to chase and the mums to re-question. It wasn't serious enough—yet—to necessitate upscaling the investigation. He and Slam went through the usual motions in a criminal damage case. They hadn't done any less than required due to Franklin's omission.

On a personal level, the case was big and exciting. Chilling. But exciting. Franklin resolved to hang onto it a little longer and see if he could crack it. Then he'd establish if he possessed aptitude for CI work. And if he did, what then? Well, it might not be too late to apply for the suits in his forties, when Kat grew more independent or left home.

The certainties in life were death and taxes. And change. You always needed to be ready for change. Donna had taught him that one early on. Maybe he should give her a call and thank her. One day.

———

Jenny McGuire reminded Georgie of a horse. She wore a chestnut ponytail drawn back from a long face. Her laugh was a bray crossed with a neigh and seemed more to do with a nervous disposition than a happy one. She'd pulled up outside the *Hepburn Shire Advocate* in an older-model Ford Telstar sedan, its gold-brown duco faded and patchy.

That Georgie had waited outside her office at 9.00am

had visibly thrown the journalist; she'd probably anticipated an uneventful Thursday morning in sleepy Daylesford.

Georgie considered Daylesford anything but sleepy and uneventful. She didn't personally know people in Melbourne with underworld connections, yet they were behind every fence post here.

'You want to see our archives?' McGuire repeated, incredulous.

'Aren't they computerised?'

The journo's mouth twitched. 'Depends. These days, yes. A few years back, not so much. What period are you looking at?'

'Five years ago.'

McGuire gave a shrug.

'Paper archives then.' Georgie added, 'Unless you have a copy of the local-hero article you wrote on Roland Pentecoste handy?'

A blush spread over McGuire's face and neck in ugly blotches. It resembled red ink diffusing on tissue and fascinated Georgie.

But when she didn't answer, Georgie acted off-hand. 'Doesn't matter. I'll have a peek at the copy around that time and find it. I guess the Pentecostes cropped up in the paper a lot back then.'

'What do you expect to find?'

Georgie blew out a breath. 'I'll know when I see it.'

'What's it to you? Are you doing a story on it?' McGuire fingered Georgie's business card. She reread: *freelance writer and editor*.

'Not sure.' Georgie again replied candidly. There could be a story in it. Perhaps she'd toss out the novel-in-progress taking up her bottom drawer and adapt this real-life drama.

Resigned, McGuire grabbed a set of keys and jerked her

thumb. Georgie tracked behind down a corridor and into a dungeon-like room that smelled musty despite the newness of the *Advocate* building. McGuire indicated the approximate starting point and stomped away.

Georgie faced an array of boxes and sighed. Then she set to work. Several of the boxes were incompletely labelled, which made a tedious task torturous. But she eventually located the relevant carton and carried it to the tiny laminate-topped desk on metal legs flanked by a low-backed, hard plastic chair.

Rather than jumping to D-day, Georgie selected a pile of papers within a three-month period—from one month before the fire at Abergeldie—in order to picture the township. No mean feat as she had to arrange the papers chronologically first.

Finally, the newspapers were organised, yet she procrastinated. She considered McGuire's question. She asked herself what she expected to find. Her honest answer was nothing. Stuff all. But she needed to go through the motions and hoped to stumble across a clue that would piece together the jigsaw. It appeared that stumbling on information could be her forte.

For a non-local, the contents ranged from unremarkable to laughable, with a few in the totally cringeworthy category. A substantial percentage of each weekly edition comprised real-estate adverts and trade classifieds. Tourism matters rated of crucial importance and often covered opening pages. A host of local organisations advised on events, issues and projects. The police reported crime statistics, prevention and other community topics.

Hot news tended to be the wins of local identities – from record sales at the stockyards to a debutante making good at the trots. The local births, deaths and marriages section contained unflattering photographs, humdrum stories and complex pedigrees. Free legal advice, a television guide and gardening column were regulars towards the back. Public notices outnumbered the negligible employment opportunities. Predominantly male sport commandeered the rear spread.

The personal ads engrossed her the most.

Seeking same sex, swingers and a Sagittarius. Whatever turns you on.

Among the drivel, Georgie discovered various mentions of the Pentecostes in the context of their farming and community involvement. No hint of entanglement in scandal, controversy or legal dispute.

She reached for the edition around the date of Roly Pentecoste's disappearance and coincidently his interview with McGuire. Her temples ached and she massaged them. Maybe her eyesight was affected because she had to scan the paper again.

———

Franklin tapped his fingernails impatiently. Each ring made him more certain he'd be unlucky yet again. But as he was about to hang up, he heard, *'Blue residence. Hello?'*

He identified himself and asked for Earl Blue.

The woman hesitated. *'What's this in relation to?'*

'I'd like to speak with Earl – he's your son, yes?'

'Yes.' She sounded even cagier now.

'So I'd like to speak with your son about some incidents in town.'

'Have those radicals from the Community Church stirred up new trouble for him?'

'This is not in relation to the Community Church. Why would you think it might be?'

'They caused him trouble last year.'

Other way around, as Pastor Danni told it. And he knew who he trusted.

'But whatever they're saying about him now, it isn't true.'

'How can you be certain until you know what it's about?' He felt baffled.

'Has this got anything to do with White Lake, Wisconsin?'

'Wisconsin in America?'

What the fuck is she on about?

Franklin didn't have control of this conversation. And he reckoned that Earl Blue inherited his nutter genes from his mother.

Mrs Blue laughed a brittle, high chortle. *'My Earl is at a Christian camp in Wisconsin in the good ol' US of A. And before that, he was at a conference retreat in Ohio, and before that he was doing some schooling over there.'*

Franklin wondered *Is she setting up her son's alibi here?* Casually, he asked, 'When was he at home last?'

He crossed his fingers, kind of wanted Earl Blue to be his crook at this stage.

'Just after that pastor,' she spat the word, *'from the so-called Community Church kicked him out.'* She paused, then added, *'End of September last year.'*

Franklin screwed up his mouth. If Mrs Blue's claims were corroborated, Earl Blue could not be Solomon: he could not have tossed the rock through Christina van Hoeckel's window or trashed her car from America, and the letters were postmarked locally, so he couldn't have sent them either.

Earl Blue might be off the hook, but at least Franklin still had his prime suspect: Art Hammer.

———

Three checks confirmed her eyesight wasn't faulty.

Although the fire broke out on Sunday evening and the *Advocate* went to print on Monday, the paper had managed to feature the event at Abergeldie on page one. An image of frantic efforts to contain the blaze covered three quarters of the page, while the editor's text embellished the scanty details available.

Ironically, a short article on page three reported the huge success of a Rotary Club meeting and dinner on the Saturday night before the fire. An accompanying photograph depicted Roland Pentecoste, his arms slung around the shoulders of Lewis Davis and a Bill Noonan. Doug Macdougall linked to the human chain via his mate Davis.

Georgie noticed the *second and final week* dinner package at Windows on Vincent that Susan and Roly took up on the fateful Sunday evening.

What was omitted interested her more. McGuire's local hero piece on Roly had presumably been postponed in the reshuffle.

One other article caught her attention. It had McGuire's byline.

LOCAL MAN KILLED IN HIT AND RUN

A twenty-eight-year-old local man was the victim of a fatal hit and run on lower

Raglan Street, Daylesford at approximately 9.40pm on Saturday evening.
A male witness attended to the victim while waiting for the ambulance; however, the man lost his life before reaching hospital.
Police are appealing to the driver to come forward or for anyone with information to contact officers at the Daylesford station or telephone Crime Stoppers. Callers can remain anonymous.
The man who arrived at the scene shortly after the accident is not currently available for further questioning.

Georgie heard an echo of Pam Stewart's words: that Roly had *gone to the aid of an accident* the evening before the fire. She supposed he was the unnamed witness.

Vexed at time wasted on reading instead of action, she flipped through the successive editions. She found articles Susan had clipped; and a follow-up piece on the hit and run that named the victim as Joseph Bigagli of no fixed address, whose mother lived in nearby Creswick.

After re-filing the papers, she exited the dungeon. A surly youth with numerous piercings manned the reception desk. Georgie interpreted through hand signals and shoulder shrugs that McGuire was on a mission, probably avoiding her and the question: why did the *Advocate* dump the feature on Roly Pentecoste? Such a story would have been timely while debate about the local personality thrived.

But more urgent questions screwed Georgie's brain. Why the journalist didn't name the accident witness. What she knew about Joseph Bigagli. Whether the culpable driver was ever arrested. And what she thought of the allegations against John Schlicht, aka the Iceman, in particular about his part in Roly's supposed murder.

She planned to interrogate McGuire face to face. Her fiery blush and body language were liable to reveal more than she articulated.

———

Georgie leaned against the *Advocate*'s exterior and noticed a police wagon whiz past.

She speed-dialled a number and lit a cigarette.

First, they exchanged greetings. Next, she put her request to Matt Gunnerson. 'Matty, I need a favour.'

'Burst my bubble, why don't you? I thought you longed to hear my sexy voice.'

She visualised his eyebrow wiggle.

'Oh, if I didn't live with your brother. Anyway, much as it's always fun to talk to you, this is serious.'

'Fire away, Gee. What you got?'

'Something right up the alley of an intrepid crime reporter.'

Georgie gave details of the hit and run. Although it could prove irrelevant, the timing and vagueness of the *Advocate*'s report intrigued her.

She could almost hear Matty's back crack as he sat taller, hooked. He promised to research the tabloids.

'What else can I do?'

She grinned. He was just a little too eager. It would be a race to see who wrote the story first at this rate.

After thinking on it, Georgie also solicited whatever Matty could rake up on Jenny McGuire. The local journo made her antennae twitch.

CHAPTER TWENTY-FIVE

'FUCKING HELL. WHAT'S SHE UP TO NOW?'

Franklin pulled a U-turn at the roundabout and headed to the Coles car park. He zoomed into an empty space near the *Advocate* and slammed his door before Mick Sprague closed his folder.

'Hoy, Harvey. I've got a bone to pick with you.'

The writer dropped her cigarette and ground it with a sandalled heel. Her eyes bored into Franklin's. They were deep brown pools that may as well have been steel shutters. He couldn't fathom her thoughts.

'Yeah? I planned to drop by today. You saved me the trouble.'

Cocky bitch.

'You could face charges for your little efforts at Abergeldie the other day, *Ms* Harvey.'

'*What?*'

'Break and enter. Unlawful entry. Theft.'

'You've got to be kidding.' She looked shifty saying it.

'C'mon, guys,' Slam murmured. 'Calm down, will you?'

'So, what have *you* done about Susan?' Harvey demanded. 'Found her yet?'

'There's no reason whatsoever to be concerned for Susan Pentecoste.' The moment he said it, Franklin felt a tad hypocritical. Only yesterday he'd told Lunny things weren't kosher at Abergeldie. Incensed, though, he couldn't backtrack.

'Thought as much. Done nothing. Right?' She dropped her voice but not the exasperated tone and proceeded to update him on what she'd learned so far.

Franklin shook his head. He caught a glimpse of Slam watching them both with a grin. He'd no doubt be on the blower to Harty as soon as this was over.

'So,' Harvey challenged, 'am I the only one that realises Susan's behaviour is connected to her husband's murder?'

'*What?*' He repeated Georgie's earlier exclamation.

She spouted her far-fetched theories, then asked from left field, 'How can I get in touch with Bill Noonan?'

'Why, so you can harass him too?' Franklin exploded. 'What's my old boss got to do with your crack-pot ideas?'

'Crack-pot ideas, my –'

'Calm down, you two.' Slam tried to pull Franklin away. 'Everyone's watching you make dickheads of yourselves.'

Franklin scanned the area and saw he wasn't exaggerating. Blood rushed to his face. He swallowed his retort and signalled a truce. 'Agree to disagree?' he suggested.

She fixed him with those sphinx-like eyes. Without severing scrutiny, she tapped a cigarette from its packet, lifted it to her lips and cupped one hand as she flicked her lighter. Her pupils reflected the flame. She drew back, the tip of her tongue pointed between her teeth. Puckered lips blew a stream of smoke in his direction.

She'd no doubt intended to be insolent. Yet for some strange reason, Franklin found the gesture immeasurably sexy.

And that made Georgie-bloody-Harvey even more infuriating.

———

Even if she hadn't recognised Douglas Macdougall from the *Advocate's* photograph of the four middle-aged Rotarians, Georgie would have been tipped off by his prominent Scottish brogue. She accosted him in the banking chamber as he conferred with Banker Two. Cornered, he agreed to an interview.

Though a reluctant host, he was a gracious one. Of course, that could simply be the country way. And would account for the thicker waistlines on country folk than their city opposites sported. In any event, Macdougall plied his visitor with coffee and jam tarts before they got serious.

Lewis Davis may have warned his pal about Georgie but that didn't mean Macdougall was prepared for her questions.

'Can you describe the last time you saw Roly?'

The banker's nose turned pulse red. *Oh, fuck*, he started to bawl. Men weren't supposed to bawl; Georgie would have coped better with anger. She averted her gaze.

'He's dead. It's not fair. The bastards. They murdered him.'

His accent grew stronger and harder to decipher.

Georgie passed a box of tissues from his desk and wriggled her toes as a distraction while the Scotsman recovered.

Eventually he took a hiccupping breath and lifted his head.

'Who murdered him?' She scanned his reactions. 'Schlicht and his gang?'

Macdougall's face blanched, then flushed. He exploded into another bout of sobs. 'I don't know,' he replied.

He seemed sincere; there were no evasive or guilty tells that Georgie could distinguish, so she steered him back to the day before Roly disappeared.

'If I'd known. Ach, we had a grand night. Lewis, Billy, Roly-boy and me. We had our meeting, the Rotary meeting. And later on, we went to the pub and downed a few ales. It were about nine o'clock when we got there. We spent the next hour or so together and Roly left about ten or a wee bit earlier.'

'You're certain of the times?'

He squirmed and confessed, 'As best I can be sure. We have our usual habits and I cannot recall it being different, so I think it's a fair estimate.'

'Douglas, do you know what Roly did after he left the pub?'

'Aye. He had to park on the lower end of Raglan because the street were packed when we got there for the meeting. On his way back, he came across a man who'd been run over.'

Georgie's spine tingled. 'Joey Bigagli?'

Macdougall considered the name and nodded. 'Aye.'

She urged him on.

He explained that Roly had stayed with the inert Bigagli until the ambulance arrived. Bill Noonan was the Daylesford police sergeant back then and a friend of the Pentecostes, plus a fellow Rotarian. When Roly called him directly after reporting the accident, Bill rushed to the scene. Later, Roly had gone home to Susan and bed.

'Do you think this accident involving Bigagli sparked what occurred at Abergeldie the next night?'

Macdougall raised his palms, then dropped them on the desk.

Georgie tested an alternative motive. 'Can you think of anything controversial involving Roly—or even Susan—at that stage? Say, anyone they were feuding with?'

'No. He were well respected. Everyone liked them both.'

'Did you see him on the Sunday? The day he went missing.'

'No. We had a wee talk on the phone, chewing over this poor Joey Bigagli fellow. Mind, everyone were talking about it in town. We woulda caught up on Wednesday, like usual. We always met at my place on a Wednesday to play a few hands of cards and for a wee drop of single-malt.' He smiled at the memory of a happier era. Then the corners of his mouth drooped. 'What's the relevance?'

'Not sure yet,' Georgie admitted. 'But things are beginning to click. There has to be a connection between this hit and run, what happened to Roly and whatever Susan is up to.'

Macdougall reacted by bursting into tears again.

Georgie mumbled that Susan was bound to be fine and left.

Fortunately for Macdougall, the vertical blinds afforded privacy to his office.

On the downside, the man's breakdown prevented her questioning Lewis Davis's hostility. And why Douglas Macdougall had avoided her previous visit.

———

Heat whacked Georgie's face as she left the frigid bank; it had to be the hottest day in ages. Something else whacked her: she'd not asked Macdougall how to contact Bill Noonan. She'd made yet another bloody stupid mistake. Should she return to find out? Georgie winced and climbed inside the Spider, determined to find an easier way to locate the retired policeman.

No more man-tears today, please.

A loop past the *Advocate* confirmed McGuire remained AWOL, so she took a pit stop.

'Any news, dear?'

Georgie slipped through the cottage's entrance with a headshake. She fumbled inside her handbag to dodge the changes in Pam Stewart.

Susan's friend was as immaculately dressed and coiffed as usual. She still moved with the elegance of a dancer. But she seemed smaller and fragile.

'Nothing your end, then?'

The older woman answered with a grimace.

As she loaded Georgie with food, Pam bombarded her with questions. Georgie began her update and soon lost her appetite. She pushed the club sandwich aside.

Throughout the account, Pam's expressions oscillated between wide-eyed disbelief, laughing delight and tearful despair. It exhausted Georgie to watch. Clearly her report had been information overload for the older woman.

Or that was how she justified her omission of the threat left on the Spider's windscreen.

'Bill Noonan? The ex-policeman? I wish I could help.' Pam tugged at her elegant blouse. Its sequinned waistband skewed to the side. 'Really, Bill and I and his wife, Gabby, we've little more than a passing acquaintanceship. I can't recall whether they live here in Daylesford or nearby. I have never needed to phone them myself. Bill and Roly, on the other hand, they were like this.' She held up crossed fore- and mid-fingers.

Soon, they digressed, as they generally did.

'You and Adam, dear. How are things at home?'

'Confusing. Good. Better, overall. I guess I haven't told him much regarding this Schlicht angle, yet.'

'Much?'

'Nothing,' Georgie confessed. 'He wasn't too happy about my run-in with Roger and Mick. He'd spit it at a whiff of organised crime and might try something stupid like telling me to leave it alone. And *that* could be the snapping point in our relationship.'

Pam patted her hand and clucked.

Why do we tell strangers things we scarcely admit to ourselves?

Georgie tore off a crust and chewed without tasting.

Screw that, Pam's not a stranger.

She rose. 'Things to do, people to see.'

She refused a bed for the night. She preferred the anonymity of a motel where her irregular comings and goings wouldn't disturb anyone. Besides, she couldn't function without nicotine, the single vice they differed on to date.

'Blast Margaret,' Pam exclaimed as they walked towards Georgie's car. 'If only she'd pick up the phone. She must have seen your note.'

'You'd think so. And that one phone call could solve this whole thing.'

'I wish Susan had told me what she planned to do.'

'Or kept in touch while she's away.'

'We must keep trying them both, dear. Let's ring them at every chance. We'll strike it lucky sooner or later. Look at the progress you've made already.'

Hell, yeah, great progress. One step forward, two steps back. Damn shame it wasn't the other way round.

———

Franklin ducked out when Slam was busy. He'd logged a phone call to the camp where Earl Blue supposedly lodged but at around 11.00pm last night in Wisconsin time, and he didn't expect progress on that for a while.

Something about Mrs Blue's eagerness to supply itinerary and relevant contact details for her son convinced him she was telling the truth, but he'd go through the motions to exhaust the line of inquiry.

Right now though, he visited Roz at the Wombat Arms.

'Beer, Franklin?'

'Nah, thanks. Still on duty.'

She leaned across the counter and brushed strands of her auburn bob behind her ear. 'What can I do you for, then?'

'Art Hammer.'

Her facial expression changed but he couldn't interpret it. 'Seen him lately? Some of the other local publicans haven't.'

'You don't know?' Roz pivoted her head to check the patrons. All were happy for now.

'Know what?' He didn't like where this conversation seemed headed.

'Poor Art died.'

'You're kidding?'

TELL ME WHY: WHAT WILL THEY RISK FOR ANSWERS?

'Heart attack while he was giving them heaps at the Radio Springs.'

'Shit, poor bugger.'

Roz nodded. The man may have been a pest, but she clearly had sympathy for him. 'They took him to hospital, but he didn't make it.'

Franklin's mind jumped. 'He rode out as far as Lyonville on his pushbike?'

'Apparently so.' Roz straightened. She crossed her arms. 'The man got about.'

'Shit,' Franklin repeated, still stunned. 'When did this happen?'

How did I miss it?

'About three weeks ago.'

A punter called for a drink. Roz turned to serve him.

Meanwhile, Franklin calculated back three weeks. It tallied with Kat's suspension from school. He'd obviously taken his ear off the ground while preoccupied on the home front – if he'd been told, he hadn't taken it in. And that was right when Pastor Danni had been interstate.

If he'd kept his mind on the job better, he wouldn't have wasted all that effort trying to find a dead man.

And he may have nabbed the real Solomon by now.

———

Cow dung, sweet hay and sweaty armpits – despite standing a good three metres from Mick and Roger, the combined odours were heady. She had seen the men notice her car draw up the gravel driveway and likewise caught their glance as she entered the paddock via a large gate that squealed on its hinges. Yet, now they ignored her. It pissed Georgie off.

Mind you, she reckoned it was a cumulative bad mood, chiefly caused by her earlier clash with Senior Dickhead John Franklin and the man-tears encounter with Douglas Macdougall.

Or had she turned anti-male? No. She was confident that Matty would come through with his promise to fax his finds to the awful but cheap motel where she would again kip for the night and ring with more information that evening. So she wasn't about to spurn anyone based on what swung between their legs.

'Hey, Mick, Roger. Could we have another chat?'

At the sound of her voice, Trigger lifted his head and stared.

Mick scowled and muttered. Roger removed his battered hat and scratched his scalp. Neither of the men looked her way.

'Susan hasn't shown up, has she?' Georgie persisted.

'Nup,' was Roger's sparse reply. He fiddled with the windmill parts strewn over the ground.

Okay, time for Plan B.

Georgie retrieved a bag from the Spider's passenger seat and returned.

'Look, I've got nice cold cokes here. Why don't we call a truce and I shout you for info?'

Roger and Mick ogled the cans and traded glances before nodding. They sat on the open tailgate of the ute and sipped the soft drinks. Father and son appeared relaxed, but Georgie positioned herself ready for a quick getaway and furthest from the vigilant blue heeler.

'What can you tell me about Roly?'

Too open-ended, her question dangled. She tried again.

'I gather he was a nice guy and everyone got on well with him – as they do with Susan?' Georgie cringed at her reference to Roly in past tense. She hoped for once to be wrong.

'Yeah, Mr P was a great bloke,' said Roger.

'A great bloke,' Mick echoed.

Those few words suggested that they (added to her, Pam and Macdougall) thought of Roly in past tense. Already more information than she'd gleaned from the farmers two days ago.

Unsure if they would remain cooperative, Georgie repeated the question causative of a fifty-cent sized bruise over her collarbone. 'What do you think happened to him?'

'Dunno.'

'Did he have dealings with John Schlicht?'

She thought Mick flinched but couldn't be sure.

'Can you think of a reason why this so-called Iceman from Melbourne might have harmed Roly?'

'Nup.'

Frustrated, Georgie tried a wild card. 'Was Roly mixed up in something even a little bit dodgy?'

Roger pulled his mouth into a straight line and scraped the toe of his right boot into the dry ground. He dug a small hollow.

His son wiped a bead of sweat off his nose.

Georgie swore silently and persevered. 'Was he involved in a business deal at the time of the fire?'

The veneer of cooperation dropped. Roger bristled and Mick glared at his father, as if to say, *I told you so*. Georgie brushed aside the question with a sweep of her hand, vowing to tack back later.

She gave them an easy one to calm the strained atmosphere.

'I know that Roly went to the Rotary dinner on

Saturday night and on his way home he came across Joey Bigagli, who'd been in a car accident. Right?'

Roger's shoulders loosened. 'Yep.'

As he felt the tension leave his master, Trigger's chin dropped onto outstretched paws.

'So what did Roly get up to on the Sunday? Anything out of the ordinary?'

'Nuh, don't think so. I think we all did the usual round here. Don't ya reckon, Mick?'

His son signalled agreement.

The dog sighed. Georgie's peripheral vision caught his eyelids drooping.

'So, you guys were working the farm back then?' She knew this but wanted the men to stay chilled.

'Yeah, but then we was labourin' for the Ps. Mr P did all the work with us, but. These days we run the place, kinda.'

Georgie pressed on. 'You took over with a leasehold a few years after the fire. Had you planned this with Roly? I mean, did he plan to hand over the run of the place when he and Susan retired?'

Mick nodded emphatically. Trigger groaned in his sleep.

Roger hesitated and said, 'Not exactly.'

'Dad!'

'Son, it was bound to come out. Thought it would've been before now.'

Georgie frowned to conceal her excitement. She sifted her previous questions and the farmers' reactions. She hazarded, 'Were you working on a business deal with Roly?'

'Sort of.'

Mick drained his can and squeezed it into an aluminium wad.

Not a happy chappie.

'What was the deal?'

Roger scratched his scalp again, examined his fingernails and flicked gunk from under them. He faced Georgie. She was intrigued to literally see his forehead smooth. With relief?

'My old lady cleaned us out when she upped and left us, and our little farm was all we had. Was small, but it had a little house – nothin' fancy, but it did us. And the bank was gunna fore...forec...you know.'

'Foreclose?'

'That's it.'

Georgie guessed, 'So Roly helped you out with a loan or gift that would get the bank off your back?'

'Yup. He gave us twenty grand. That kept the bank sweet, and we got to keep our place. We'd still help here, but. We'd never not want to work here.' He gazed at the emerald landscape fondly. 'We hadn't worked out how we'd repay Mr P. He said he didn't care. Then the fire happened and...'

Georgie tried to understand their motive. 'And you haven't mentioned the loan, or gift, or whatever you want to call it, because the police might've treated you as suspects in what happened to Roly? Or were you worried that Susan would ask you to repay it?'

After a long pause, Roger said, 'I dunno. We couldn't pay it back and didn't wanna talk about it, I s'pose. Was embarrassin' havin' to take Mr P's money in the first place. It wasn't just that my old lady took off; we'd got in trouble on the geegees too.'

'You nearly lost your farm because of horse gambling?'

Maybe her voiced pitched, because Mick interjected, 'We don't take a bet much anymore.'

Yeah right, mate.

Mick's deep flush matched his father's, whether because of the fib or their secret.

Georgie shrugged. Everyone has their demons. Hell, she didn't expect a nomination for sainthood in this lifetime.

'We felt bad when Mrs P asked us to take over the farm. It's a bit like double-dippin'. We had nothin' to buy in with, so we lease it. She don't want much rent, just a cut of whatever we pull in. And we've never told her about the twenty-G.'

Roger hunched, ashamed.

'Okay, that's all out in the open.' Georgie brushed her hands together. 'Done and dusted for now. *But*...you owe me. What happened to Roly and what Susan's up to – I think they're connected.'

She scrutinised their faces.

'Are you still holding back something that might shed light on all this?'

'Nup. But if we did know somethink, we'd tell ya.'

From Mick, this was a breakthrough.

'And the hit and run? Is there a link, do you reckon?'

Unfortunately, Georgie struck out.

'Can't see how,' replied Roger.

'Can't see how,' echoed his son.

———

The motel manager matched negativity with obesity. He wore filthy clothes that didn't flatter his bulk and grunted with the effort of rising from his chair. When he had to refill the paper in the fax machine, he moaned. Then he blatantly read her message as it slowly printed and held it for ransom.

'Four bucks a page.'

A rip-off but she needed that information.

They exchanged cash for the crumpled sheets that'd absorbed his skin oils. He slapped the key to unit ten on the counter.

'You have to get your breakfast menu back here by six-thirty tonight.'

A whole sixteen minutes and crap choices. She'd skip brekkie or go into town.

The thought of food tempted her to the Wombat, to down a hearty steak and a few beers. Instead, she kicked off her sandals and sprawled on the bed. Its shiny purple eiderdown, complete with stains and holes, rivalled its burnt orange counterpart in unit six. She smoothed out the wrinkles and rued the oil patches but managed to read Matty's fax.

It was an extract from the *Herald Sun*.

POLICE WARN DRUGS, FATIGUE AND SPEED ARE TAKING TOLL

It has been a horror start to the weekend on Victoria's roads.
In two separate incidents, two lives were lost, and three teenagers remain in critical condition.
A dangerous joy ride in Frankston resulted in a fatal collision involving a freeway overpass last night.
The unlicensed driver, aged 16, was not wearing a seat belt at the time of the accident and died instantly.
His three young female companions,

aged between 14 and 16, sustained grave injuries and are in critical condition at Alfred Hospital.

Police are also investigating the death of 28-year-old pedestrian Mr Joseph Bigagli of Creswick, who was struck by a vehicle in Daylesford at 9.40pm yesterday.

According to Mr Roland Pentecoste of Hepburn, who was a witness to Mr Bigagli's accident, the victim lost consciousness when emergency service personnel arrived.

Mr Bigagli died before reaching hospital. Anyone with information in relation to the Daylesford incident should contact police immediately.

The road toll now stands at 71, which is 11 more than the same time last year.

A police spokesperson has expressed alarm at this increasing trend and urged Victorians to reduce their speed, not drive if under the influence of drugs or alcohol or when fatigued and warned against using mobile telephones while operating vehicles.

It is probable that one or more of these factors contributed to yesterday's tragic fatalities.

'*Very* interesting.'

The *Herald Sun* had published more information about the fatality in Daylesford on the morning following the incident than the local rag managed by Monday.

That seemed significant. It all did. She just didn't know how it fit together yet.

With more questions than answers plaguing her mind, Georgie quit the motel.

CHAPTER TWENTY-SIX

MUCH LATER, GEORGIE AWOKE. DISORIENTATED. Confused as to what roused her. It took a moment to recall where she was.

Back at the crummy motel.

Georgie sat upright on the double bed. She strained to listen and see. Her eyes grew accustomed to the dim light penetrating the flimsy curtains and the clock radio that glowed 11.59pm.

A bad dream? What if it wasn't?

Goosebumps pricked her skin.

Although situated on one of the main drags into town, the motel had minimal passing traffic at night, and the units were set back. It was doubtful that road noise had stirred her.

As far as she knew, only hers, the manager's residence and one other unit were occupied. She pulled back the curtain. Unit one, non-smoking section: in darkness. Ditto the fat manager's house and the rooms between. The car park contained her Spider and a Volvo outside the first unit.

If the manager had a carport or garage, it must be attached to the other side of his place.

Georgie dropped the curtain.

It's nothing. Go back to bed.

She snuggled under the bedcovers and squeezed her eyes, willing sleep.

Fuck.

There was something out there. Or someone.

Footsteps?

She lay rigid as her pulse thudded in her ears.

She told herself to calm down. Blamed a stray dog for the crunch of gravel and forced life into her frozen limbs. She tiptoed to the front door, but each step sounded too loud.

Georgie slipped the security chain in place. The snick of the chain resounded through the unit. Her breaths turned shallow and fast and audible.

She checked the button on the front door. Locked.

She couldn't remember if the bathroom window was shut. It was even darker in there, so she crept with hands outstretched. She misjudged the layout, bashed her shin against the toilet and stifled a curse. She eased down the lid, stood on it, reached for the window. As she wound it in, she heard a new noise.

Georgie stilled before cranking faster until the window shut firm, then snuck to the bedroom. She pushed the sole armchair against the door. It was a slow, terrifying manoeuvre. The heavy chair grazed the industrial carpet. The scrapes were a shrill beacon that announced her location to the intruder.

Georgie reached for her phone.

The front awning rattled.

She fumbled the mobile and it fell to the floor. 'Shit,' she whispered, dropping to her knees to grope for it.

More footsteps in the gravel. A pause. Then a metallic scrape. A key—or pick—inserted the throat of the door lock, wiggled and withdrew.

Her fingers struck and then wrapped around the mobile.

Another key twisted in the lock.

She remembered with horror. Matty rang after she'd returned from the pub. The phone beeped and disconnected. She'd stupidly let her battery go flat and come to Daylesford without the charger.

She dropped the useless handset.

Georgie heard a muffled cuss and the jangle of keys.

She cursed choosing a motel so cheap that the unit didn't have a landline. Not that it made much difference. The part-time cop shop on Camp Street would be as empty as the room next door. When help arrived from Ballarat or Castlemaine or wherever, she would be dead or have dealt with it alone.

Well, I opt for the latter, thanks.

Despite her brave internal dialogue, with each of the intruder's moves, Georgie grew more scared. She grabbed the home brand fly spray and Bible. Motel room trusties; practical weapons.

She heard a rough male voice. Her nerves screamed. She held her breath again until her lips numbed.

Breathe. Be quiet.

Another man replied. She strained. Did she recognise the speakers? Impossible to tell. They seemed to be arguing outside her window but quietly, so as not to rouse the occupant: her. She couldn't decipher what they said.

The men's voices became fainter. There was a cuss and scuffle in the gravel.

And shortly after...the distant sound of an engine.

Then, quietness. Blissful fucking silence. Except for the pounding in Georgie's veins. She sank onto the floor and hugged knees to her chest. Her entire body jittered.

You will only get one warning.

Was she on borrowed time?

Eventually, her eyes fluttered. She jolted upright, sucked in a breath and listened. Her smokes lay on the bedside table. A short distance away but two attempts to work her jelly legs failed. She gave up.

Soon, her chin dropped. She vowed to stay awake. Then caught herself coming out of the next doze.

PART III

FRIDAY 19 MARCH

CHAPTER TWENTY-SEVEN

THIS WASN'T A TIME FOR REGRETS. REGRETS SERVED little purpose in any event.

But one thing kept rolling inside her mind.

If only she hadn't involved her niece.

With her sharp sparrow features and sometimes intolerant attitude, many didn't see the woman beyond her niece's outer crust. They didn't know the kind, generous person so like a sister to her.

That bond swelled and tugged when pressures of past weeks threatened to burst. At her niece's home, she'd been nurtured, humoured, cajoled, nagged and loved.

But that doubled her predicament, not halved it. Contrary to popular opinion, a burden shared is not lessened in its load.

There are always consequences.

———

The Barina's bonnet felt cool. Check points: late-model buzz box, immaculate conservative navy blue duco, matching interior. Exactly the type of car Georgie expected Margaret Pentecoste to own, but simply that it was parked outside her house didn't mean it was hers. Her car might be in the rear garage.

Georgie wondered at the woman's silence to the note stuffed under the door on Tuesday. Maybe she was too tight to make a phone call. Or she'd tried Georgie's mobile since its battery went flat. Both were improbable. She searched for alternative explanations and tried to talk herself out of bad omens.

A male voice made her jump. Loath to admit it, she'd been rattled by the motel disturbance. It had her flinching at shadows...and the postman's cheery hello on his early round of Ascot Street South. She smiled to the fluoro-vested man. He leaned over the scooter's handlebars with a small bundle of mail.

After he'd whizzed away, she flicked through the letters. All addressed to Miss M Pentecoste and from banks and superannuation funds, nothing juicy. Georgie debated. Drop them in the box or hand them to Margaret when she answered the door? She decided on the former. If her bone knickers in the spare room at Abergeldie were any indication of character, Margaret would take offence at Georgie handling her mail.

She banged the brass doorknocker several times.

'Yoo-hoo!'

The neighbour.

'You back then?' the woman called. Her boobs bounced as she jogged into the yard. Before Georgie replied, she rushed on, 'Did you catch up with Margaret the other day?'

'No –'

'Oh, what a shame! I told her that a girl—*you*—came calling before lunch on Tuesday. But I didn't have your name. So silly of me.'

They did belated introductions and Georgie asked, 'Do you know if she's home now, Megan?'

'*Well*, that's her car there.'

Megan Frawley pointed to the Barina.

'So I'd say so,' the neighbour continued. 'Although she quite often walks up the street instead of driving. She hardly ever works on Fridays, so I'd expect her to be in this early. She isn't answering?'

Georgie barely said 'No' before Frawley elbowed past. She rapped on the door and hollered, 'Yoo-hoo! Margaret! Are you there?'

Her ears ringing, Georgie commented, 'Is she deaf?'

Too gullible to read her dry undertone, the woman replied seriously, 'No.' Then said, 'Well, she could be at work, after all. The accounting firm, you know.'

She waved towards Sturt Street, maintaining the fast flow of verbal diarrhoea. 'She goes in Monday, Tuesday and Thursday, although she does change the days occasionally, and she's also on Council, and that keeps her going left, right and centre. Of course, she could be gadding about with Aunty Susan.'

Adrenaline coursed through Georgie.

Aunty Susan?

But Frawley continued without pause. 'But if they're out together, they'd have to be in Susan's car, I guess. Although Margaret much prefers to drive herself.' Frawley laughed. 'She moans about climbing into her aunty's truck.'

Accountant. Buzz box owner. Sensible undie wearer. Yep, she'd bitch about travelling in a four-wheel drive.

Frawley recaptured her attention. 'Mind, I haven't seen Susan since the night before last, when we had our usual predinner sherry.'

Georgie tried to dot-point the information suddenly coming thick and fast.

'She wasn't there last night, but she's been staying with Margaret for…oh, the past week or so. It's such a treat for Susan to stay so long. She normally stops a day or two and then, *whoosh*, off she goes, back home.' Frawley added, 'I guess she's gone back now.'

Georgie shook her head. Without an operational mobile, she'd resorted to a payphone to check with AJ, the Pattersons and Pam Stewart for updates on Ruby and Susan. Ruby had improved overnight but there was zilch news on Susan.

'Oh?' Frawley reeled. 'Well, perhaps she stayed with Margaret again after all. You know,' she said, leaning in. 'I thought I heard Susan's truck last night. Outside Margaret's here.' She gestured to the space behind the Barina. 'Quite late it was, too. It rumbled there for a while, and I peeked out the window, but it wasn't Susan's. It was a utility, not like hers one bit.'

The rumbling ute troubled Georgie, although she wasn't sure why.

Frawley puffed her chest and flanked her belly with both hands. 'Bully for them if she stayed again! They must have patched things up.'

Georgie lifted a brow. 'Oh?'

'I think they had a tiff,' the neighbour confided. 'Night before last, they swung between a little touchy and too polite. I recall thinking they must have had a barney or were bone tired from all their gadding about. They've been out more than they've been in this week!'

This explained why it'd been impossible to reach Margaret. But her disregard of Georgie's note still grated.

'You know,' Frawley repeated, 'the other day they went away for a night – on the spur of the moment, it seemed to me. I fed Topsy and turned the lights on and off for Margaret. We do that for each other.'

Georgie perked up. 'You have a spare key?'

Frawley nodded.

'You should pop inside Margaret's, to check she's okay.'

The neighbour screwed her nose.

'Well, you think Margaret's home but she's not answering, right? So, what if she's fallen over, broken her leg and can't move? Wouldn't she want you to check in case of emergency?'

Frawley's blue-green gaze lost some lustre. She was torn.

'What would it hurt?' Georgie urged. 'A quick look. If she's not there, she needn't ever know. If she is, she'll appreciate your concern.'

She couldn't pinpoint why it felt crucial to convince Megan Frawley.

Still debating the right course of action, the woman returned to her house. A few minutes later, she shut her front door.

Her movements plunged into slow-mo.

Frawley hesitated at Margaret's gate. She examined the key in her right hand. Then walked up the short pathway and thrust the key into the lock.

She extracted it and turned to Georgie, saying, 'I'm not sure.' She bit her lip.

Georgie took her hand and guided it to the lock. She

nodded encouragingly. Wanted to scream, 'Open it.' Instead whispered, 'It's the right thing to do. Go on.'

The neighbour rolled her eyes. Up, down, sideways in both directions.

———

Georgie did a mental fist pump when Frawley finally unlocked the door. But her excitement waned as she stepped onto the polished pine floorboards and called, 'Margaret.'

No answer.

The women quickly eliminated the front two rooms. They moved down the hallway and exchanged a glance. Frawley pegged her nose. Their footsteps faltered. Cold sweat dotted Georgie's lip. Dread settled like a brick in her gut.

The next door on the right sat ajar.

'I'm not going in there,' Frawley said. Yet, she shadowed Georgie as she pushed the door with her toe. It swung open.

Frawley screamed. And Georgie recoiled.

A beige shoe lay on its own near the doorway. And its pair sat a few feet away – still attached.

'*Margaret*,' the other woman shrieked.

At least it wasn't Susan Pentecoste.

Georgie looked at the body. Then away. Shocked. She gulped bile. Fascinated and appalled, her eyes crept back to Margaret's waxy, slightly bluish skin. Vacant stare, milky glaze, like cataracts. She reached towards Margaret's neck to check for the carotid pulse that wouldn't be there.

Frawley followed Georgie's fingertips which trembled on the verge of contact, arrested by jagged abrasions and deep bruising. The blood drained from her face. She reached horror-saturation point.

Georgie led her to the bench on the verandah, loosened her blouse and rubbed her back. She waited until the crisis elapsed, swallowed back another rush of bile and re-entered the house to dial the police.

Fucking idiot for letting the mobile run out of juice.

The bloody operator wouldn't let her tell the story. They followed their stupid script while she tore at her hair.

But then she decelerated. Poor Margaret was beyond urgency.

As she spoke more slowly and clearly, she noticed a doormat inside the entrance. After eventually hanging up, she lifted the mat and sighed.

On the honey floorboards were one business card and note to Margaret. Well, that was a minor mystery explained. Margaret had never seen Georgie's message. Now irrelevant, she pocketed them.

Georgie sat next to Frawley, who'd heaved her breakfast onto the lawn but now appeared more composed. Questions begged answers and the clock ticked until the cops flocked.

'Did you see the driver of the ute that stopped here last night?'

'No.'

'Could you tell if it was a male or female driving?'

Frawley did a mute headshake.

'Were there passengers?'

'You think that the driver was Margaret's killer?'

It was pointless mincing words. 'Potentially.'

'And I didn't do anything. I let them drive away!' Frawley paled to eggshell and wailed, 'No!'

Sympathy would reduce the woman to a useless puddle.

So Georgie pressed on. 'Can you describe the ute? Its make and colour?'

'Not really.'

'Try harder.'

The neighbour screwed her face. 'It might have been a Ford, but it could've even been a Chevy or Dodge. Not new but not ancient. I'm hopeless with cars. I think it might've been black...but it was dark, so it could've been deep blue or even red, I suppose. I didn't have my specs on. I'm a little bit night blind.'

Meaning you could have seen a Bigfoot 4x4 Monster Truck and be clueless?

Frawley became too distraught for continued questioning, and Georgie couldn't trust herself to speak without grilling. So, they waited in silence.

CHAPTER TWENTY-EIGHT

THE FIRST COPS ON THE SCENE SEPARATED FRAWLEY and Georgie. Then, as the area swarmed with uniforms and officious plain-clothed personnel, they were whisked to the nearby police station.

There, Georgie waited and waited. Was interviewed and her every phrase probed, then forced to wait further. Eventually, a two-finger typist who couldn't spell words with more than double syllables prepared her statement. The detective took her through it. She signed and escaped.

Georgie was exhausted. Thanks to fuck all sleep, dealing with Mr Plod and being a witness in a homicide.

Outside the cop shop she considered her battle plan. Her head pounded and her stomach growled. Her car was about a kilometre away, outside what used to be Margaret Pentecoste's home but was currently a crime scene.

It had been a fucking awful day so far.

She hated the country. She wanted to return to the city and immerse herself in normality. But this thing wasn't over. Susan Pentecoste was still missing, out there somewhere, along with her Land Cruiser. It wasn't over until the proverbial fat lady sang.

'How's *Ms* Writer then?'

She cringed at the familiar voice yet noted the inflection on Ms was less pronounced than before. Reluctantly, she met the stare of the arrogant cop from Daylesford. John Franklin.

In jeans and T-shirt but definitely not a figment of her overwrought imagination.

Her fucking awful day had gotten worse.

———

When Franklin spoke again, he surprised her.

'I heard on the grapevine what went down at Margaret Pentecoste's. Your name came up. I thought we should sit down, have a *calm* chat and exchange info. What do you reckon?'

She couldn't reply, literally too dumbfounded and drained.

He rested his hand on her shoulder blade and propelled her several blocks.

They'd missed the lunch crowd and took an outdoor table. A lone woman sat inside the café amid shopping bags, sucking up a milkshake in a tall silver cup. Franklin ordered while Georgie contemplated his shift in attitude. Minutes later, fat sausage rolls, yoyo biscuits and steaming coffee arrived.

They didn't speak while they devoured the food. Plates emptied, Georgie fumbled her lighter and Franklin leaned across. He lit her cigarette, then his own. She inhaled the distinctive aroma of his Marlboro and drifted to long summer days at Mentone Beach, when her dad was alive. Memories flickered through her mind. Golden Gaytime ice creams, hot golden sand, coconut-fragranced sunscreen. One final dip in the warm salty water amid shrieks of laughter; the panorama tinted by a fiery sunset. Suddenly, Franklin climbed a notch on her approval rating, to hover above total arsehole. A bit of sustenance, smoking her dad's favourite tobacco and an offer to share information only went so far.

He had a lot of redeeming to do.

He shut up and listened to her story—on the whole— which earned him extra points. Every so often he lit a Marlboro or rubbed his hand over his hair. Sporadically, he interrupted with a question. And once, he patted her knee. She didn't know how to take that. Was it a come-on, a put-down or his attempt at kindness? She liked to be in control when it came to men. This one left her alternately stumped and exasperated.

At the end of her narration, Franklin remained silent with a finger hooked under his nose and thumb propping his chin. After some moments, he massaged his temples and said, 'We should talk to Bill Noonan.'

Just yesterday he'd refused to help her contact the former police sergeant.

She replied sarcastically, 'Really? I would never have thought of that.' And he smiled wryly.

———

Franklin stalked ahead, leading her in the direction of the cop shop. Then he veered towards a white SS Commodore, an older model still in good nick.

As he drove Georgie to collect her car, he said, 'Bill took early retirement three and a bit years ago 'cause Gabby—his wife—gave him an ultimatum. Let it go, retire and have a life, or she was going to have to move on.' He grunted softly. 'It takes a lot for a copper's wife to do that. Either your marriage stuffs up near the beginning or it stays solid. Gabby's one of the best, so if she couldn't hack it after twenty-odd years, that tells you how bad Bill got.'

Georgie suspected he'd just shared on a personal level. She wanted to probe his cop-marriage but instead asked, 'What was Bill obsessed with?'

Franklin parked outside the cordoned-off scene on Ascot Street South. He faced her and answered, 'Vindicating his good mate Roly. Proving he had nothing to do with the fire or attack on Susan. And finding Roly's killer.'

'Could Schlicht have done it?'

'Yes. Ah, Georgie...'

It was the first occasion he'd used her name in a non-adversarial tone. She kind of liked the way his bass voice played with it.

'At least the Iceman finally copped a stretch in jail.'

'To do with –'

'No, worse luck,' Franklin interrupted with a headshake. 'Unconnected. He went down eighteen months after Roly vanished. He's at the new Castlemaine jail now. When they're coming up for release, they ease them out of the system by sending them close to home. His time's up soon.'

'So he can't be behind Margaret's death? Or Susan's disappearance?'

Franklin snorted. 'Never say never. Anything's possible.

He couldn't have physically killed Margaret, but that doesn't mean he didn't orchestrate it.'

Georgie realised he hadn't contradicted her assumption that Margaret's murder and Susan's absence were connected. And he'd silently agreed that these events linked to Roly's much earlier apparent murder.

She didn't know whether to crow or shit herself.

CHAPTER TWENTY-NINE

GEORGIE TAILED FRANKLIN TO MUSK VALE, A LITTLE place on the Ballan–Daylesford Road. They convoyed up a short gravel driveway to a white-weatherboard and red-tin-roofed farmhouse. Various roof pitches were evidence of a series of extensions. Its homeliness appealed to her.

She stepped out of the Spider and scanned the farm. Precise rows of lavender in rich, red soil filled a large paddock adjacent to the house block. Further afield, black and white cows munched and viewed the newcomers. On the right, a couple of horses ran, graceful and free-spirited. As she watched them, Georgie breathed the fresh air deeply, letting it relax her. It smelled like more rain on the way.

A woman called, 'Hello!' She approached in blue jeans and a black T-shirt with a long-faded logo. She held a white plastic bucket of feed in one hand, flattish cane basket with a layer of eggs in the other. Franklin broke into an affectionate grin as he lifted his hand. She juggled the bucket to wave back, her face splitting into a beam.

Georgie's first impression of Gabby Noonan was a good one.

Second impression: brilliant. A generous measure of neat scotch was what Georgie needed. Not to have to ask for it, a bonus.

A freshly scrubbed Bill Noonan joined them shortly. Franklin's ex-boss was stocky with a balding crown. Saddlebags under his eyes and a ploughed field for a forehead were no doubt baggage from his years on the force. Yet, his face crinkled with good humour, accentuated by upward-reaching crow's feet.

Gabby pottered in the kitchen that adjoined the living room. She listened but said little. Bill perched, both hands on his knees as if ready to spring. Franklin sank into the deep couch, one leg crossed over the opposite knee, hands behind his head. Although he'd already heard Georgie's story, he listened attentively but poker-faced.

She again omitted the threatening note and motel disturbance and glossed over her discovery of Margaret Pentecoste's body. Gabby gave her a shrewd smile, but Georgie thought she'd pulled off a level of nonchalance with the men. Otherwise, she told it straight, with Franklin adding his ten cent's worth at the end.

———

Bill leaned back. He rubbed a hand across his chin, its silvery-white growth rasped in synchronisation with his wife's rhythmic chopping of vegetables. Georgie applied herself to re-emptying her scotch glass. Mellowed by the whisky, her eyelids drooped.

'Roly was a good man.'

Bill's voice startled Georgie from her trance.

'He was a good chap with not a bad bone in his body. It devastated Susan to come out of the coma to find him gone. But worse than that, that the court of public opinion held him as prime suspect for the arson and her narrow escape.'

Riveted, Georgie put down her glass despite the tawny mouthful left in the bottom.

'Utter rubbish, of course. Any person who'd ever met Roly could see that. Fair call that us coppers are the worst for assuming anyone's capable of anything.'

Franklin nodded and Gabby snickered.

'But that's a hazard of the job. You have to be cynical, and you have to trust your gut. Some people are rotten to the core, while others will cross the line occasionally or have the capacity to. Then there's the last, smallest group. The ones who are good right the way through. Roly is one of those – absolutely and unequivocally.'

Georgie noticed Bill's tense switch: past to present. Confused about Roly or in denial?

He tugged the corner of his eye with his right index finger.

'We—the Daylesford team—tried to convince the hierarchy that they'd got the wrong end of the stick and to look at the evidence more carefully. Unquestionably, Susan was meant to die in the fire. It didn't take *us* long to realise that Roly had probably been knocked off. We expected his body to turn up in due course. But it was bloody impossible to get the Ds to focus the right way.'

'The defectives,' Franklin interjected. He glimpsed Georgie's nose twitch and corrected, 'The *detectives* wasted too much time and effort suspecting Roly and then,' he finger-snapped, 'their resources dried up.'

'Too bloody right,' Bill agreed, picking up the story. 'So I started doing a lot of unpaid overtime, trying to work it out myself. Eventually, I was asked if I wished to consider a transfer to South Gippsland. A place in the sticks. Perhaps Fish Creek.'

'You've got to be kidding,' Georgie exclaimed.

'You'd better believe it,' Gabby replied, and Franklin smiled crookedly.

'Our life's here,' Bill continued. 'Gabby's family is a stone's throw away, and our kids have settled between here and Melbourne. I'd worked a few stations, but the majority of my time as a copper—the best bits overall—was at Daylesford.'

He puckered his lips. 'And so, I took the hint and quietened down. Didn't give up but tried to be more discreet. Still, Gabby here gave me an ultimatum. And rightly so because in hindsight, I came this close,' he held gnarled thumb and index finger millimetres apart, 'to losing it. I would have done practically anything to solve Roly's case, except have to hit the singles scene in my late fifties.'

A tea towel struck his ear. Bill glanced at his wife, who laughed at his weak joke. It broke the tension before he launched back into the story.

'Susan's been to see me quite often since Roly disappeared. Wanting updates, reassurance that something's happening. Over and over, she's said, "All I want is to bury him. Give him a proper send-off." It's enough to break your heart. She became so desperate that she wrote a letter to the paper and later tried to see Schlicht in jail. When he refused to see her, she wrote to him direct. Five letters, I think.'

Gabby's knife clattered. 'William Noonan! You never told me that.'

Georgie pictured the Iceman. She tried to imagine

writing to him or wanting to visit him in prison. Ugly thought.

'Yeah, well.' Bill shrugged off his wife's comment. 'Anyway, she pleaded with Schlicht to tell her the location of Roly's body. Promised to keep whatever he told her in confidence. She would have kept her word, too. But he never answered her letters.'

Georgie chewed her nail and skimmed from Bill to Franklin. Unreadable faces, except for the cold anger in their eyes.

Bill continued, 'Once, much earlier on, I found a chink in his armour.'

'Hah!' Gabby hacked into a pumpkin.

He lifted his palms to the ceiling. 'I couldn't help it. I got so frustrated that I leaked a little information to the *Advocate*.' He repeated the thumb and finger gesture. 'Then the media had a field day, and so did Schlicht's soly.'

Georgie nodded, recalling Susan's clippings: one reported accusations from Schlicht's pompous solicitor of trial by media, and if she remembered rightly, in the same article the head of the homicide squad admitted they'd stalled in the Pentecoste case. She watched Bill's face flame. Her stomach knotted in sympathy.

The retired cop said, 'The Iceman de-iced himself enough to say how distressed he and his friends were at this so-called discrimination and the abuse of his privacy. He proclaimed his innocence and that we, the police, wanted to fit him up, no matter what or how.'

'Yeah, right,' Gabby retorted.

Georgie studied the three faces. Relative strangers, from a different world, and her path only crossed theirs through Susan's story. She didn't know them well enough to be sure Bill or Franklin wouldn't fit someone up – especially if that someone was the Iceman and especially to vindicate a mate. She fixed on Gabby's disgusted expression and reckoned she trusted the woman's judgment.

Franklin took up the narration. 'The police commissioner at the time had a political agenda. All this bad publicity wasn't doing him favours. He did a quickstep to placate the civil libertarians and told us hands off Schlicht and his associates. He also put a plan in place that was supposed to show off a squeaky-clean force. Funnily enough, it backfired when a bunch of corrupt big knobs were uncovered, who in turn ratted out a number of others on their way down. End of the day, Schlicht copped minor drug charges as a token conviction –'

'And he's due for release any day,' Bill added, slamming his hand on the chair arm. 'But mark my words, I'll see him go down for what he did to Roly. And I hope Susan is there to see it happen.'

'Right,' his wife interrupted.

Georgie looked at Gabby squarely and made out the faded logo across her chest: *Be reasonable – do it my way*. She squinted to read the next line of smaller, cracked embossing. *For women who take no crap*. She clicked with Gabby even more for that T-shirt and wondered where she could buy one.

The woman grinned, as if she'd read Georgie's mind. She said, 'No more talk until we've had dinner. Bill, take these kids for a walk while I finish up.'

Nobody argued. Maybe they'd read her T-shirt too.

Georgie gulped fresh air and half-listened to the men as they strolled around the farm, but her mind bulged with information overload.

They knocked back two bottles of red wine with a veritable feast of organic stuff from the Noonans' property. Franklin talked about the daughter he was raising single-handedly. It showed another side to his character, and Georgie covertly scrutinised him. His face animated, his laughter deep and natural, he described Kat's scrapes and monumental, often instantaneous, mood swings. She sounded like a normal fifteen-going-on-twenty-five girl: wild hormones, constant testing of the boundaries, mouthy smart aleck one minute, her nice self the next.

Georgie was the first to admit she'd been a bitch at fifteen. She couldn't rewrite history but tried to be a better daughter to Livia these days.

Franklin glided up a notch on her approval scale, though his rating was still tenuous.

They tidied up, then retired to the living room. Georgie broached the question that had been on her lips since they'd arrived at the Noonan farm. 'Do you think Susan's okay, Bill?'

He rubbed his chin. 'It doesn't look good.'

Franklin agreed. Everyone brooded.

Georgie sucked in a breath and took the plunge. She finally fessed up about the note and previous night's disturbance at the Daylesford motel.

'Righto,' Franklin yelled over exclamations from their hosts. 'You're backing off right now. Okay?'

He leaned into her personal space. His breath was warm and held tangs of wine, onion and coffee. It disturbed the wisps on her forehead.

His agreeability rating nosedived.

Bill paled to match his thatch of white hair and said, 'I'd have to agree, Georgie. You're dealing with violent scum here, and if they're onto you poking around, it –'

'It doesn't bear thinking about,' Gabby finished his sentence.

Georgie was furious and embarrassed.

Breathe. Ten, nine...

Counting down to one, she then asked Bill, 'When did you last see Susan?'

Her change of tack flummoxed the men. It was Gabby who replied. 'A couple of weeks ago, wasn't it, darl? She stayed for dinner and then kept you up chatting for half the night. I ended up going to bed.'

'Two weeks ago tomorrow?' Bill hazarded.

His wife agreed. 'I'd say so.'

'She's keen to have another go at seeing Schlicht in jail,' the old cop recalled. 'The anniversary of Roly's disappearance is coming up, and it always makes her toey. John here keeps me in the loop on developments, but there's been none in ages. Basically, Susan and I rehashed old ground.'

'More than a coincidence, then,' Georgie mused. 'The very next day she goes to Margaret's, stays a few days, then drops off the radar. Meanwhile, Margaret is...'

'Margaret is murdered,' Franklin snarled. 'Get it, kiddo. This is serious shit. You're better off not knowing more. I offered to share info, to see what you had, but that's it.'

'Oh, so your idea of *sharing* was a one-sided deal. I'd tell you everything, you'd tell me as little as possible, then I'd crawl back to Melbourne, huh? Fat chance.'

'This isn't a game, a chance for you to mount your high horse... Butt out and leave it to the experts.' Franklin stalked outside, slamming the door.

'I'm involved, whether I like it or not,' Georgie said under her breath. She refocused on Bill. 'You sure you only rehashed old stuff?'

He thought back. The creases in his face rumpled more.

'Well, for the most part. You'd have come across Schlicht's girlfriend, Ariane Marques, in Susan's scrapbook? Young, mad, French and crazy for him. She has a list of form yea-long,' he gestured, 'but all small-scale stuff going way back. Streetwalking, possession, that sort of thing. Years ago, she was in the frame for a vicious attack on an old bird. Snatch and grab with a bit extra. But the victim couldn't ID her, so Marques got away with it. Then, once she hooked up with Schlicht, she got cannier and inherited his protection. Mind, there won't be much of an empire left for the Iceman when he gets out. One crim goes to the slammer, another steps up. He'll have to claw back his piece of the pie.'

Bill frowned, as if trying to remember the point. He bobbed his head and said, 'Anyway, Schlicht and Marques were shacked up together, living between their millionaire's palace in Melbourne and Schlicht's Castlemaine country house. Whenever Schlicht got pulled in for an interview, Marques came along. Whoever she buttonholed copped an earful. Must be the frog in her. Look, I've digressed. The point is that I *did* mention something that caught Susan's attention.'

Georgie jerked straight. 'Yeah?'

'Schlicht has an estranged wife, Helena. Many moons ago she reverted to her maiden name, Watkowska, and moved with their son to a place near Trafalgar, but they've never divorced. He mentioned her in a couple of interviews. I got the impression that it was a half-arsed split; certainly not acrimonious at his end. And I don't think the girlfriend knew about the wife. Not back then.'

'That's it?' Georgie deflated, perplexed as to the significance of Schlicht's wife.

Bill sighed and they dropped into silence.

After a gap, she asked, 'Going back to your investigation into Roly's disappearance-slash-murder. Why did you suspect Schlicht?'

'Because we knew *that* he did it. We even knew why and how. But we couldn't prove a bloody thing!'

Gabby placed a hand on Bill's arm.

'How's that?' Georgie demanded.

'Schlicht was the driver in a hit-run fatality the night before the fire. The victim was Joey Bigagli, the son of one of his closest associates. Schlicht trusted Bigagli – or Little Joey, as they called him in the trade. He treated him as his own kin. At any rate, Bigagli set up in competition, and the daft bastard even tried to recruit a few of his previous boss's henchmen.'

'What an idiot.'

'Yep. So Schlicht decided to make an example of Bigagli's disloyalty.'

Confused, Georgie said, 'But how does that link to Roly?'

'Roly arrived first on the scene of Bigagli's accident,' Bill explained. 'Bigagli didn't die immediately, and Schlicht had broken the golden rule by dealing with it personally.'

'Go on,' she urged.

'Roly was a *risk*, you see. Bigagli might have told him what'd happened, or Roly could have seen the hit-run. Schlicht owned a XJ6 Jag-Daimler with pearl-white paint. Jags are a rarity hereabouts, and that one stuck out like dog's balls. If Roly saw it, he would have described it to a T.'

Georgie's eyes narrowed. 'So Schlicht removed Roly as insurance?'

'Yep. And the fire at Abergeldie was supposed to obscure everything. Hopefully, we'd think Roly'd incinerated or, if that failed, that he was the perp. All the better if Susan died in the fire because of the chance Roly had given her information implicating Schlicht. But by miracle, she survived.'

Gabby made a strange noise.

Bill rubbed his wife's knee and said, 'Angelo Sartori confessed everything. *Off* the record. Apparently, Schlicht's gang—Sartori being one of them—set fire to the place, knocked out Susan and scooted the moment they heard sirens.'

Georgie murmured, 'And Roly?'

'They took him back to Schlicht's Castlemaine property, interrogated him repeatedly and, finally satisfied that he knew jack shit about Bigagli's murder, snapped his neck.'

Sickened, Georgie said, 'You had everything. Why couldn't you nail him?'

'Why?' Bill eye-rolled. 'Because before Sartori made it official, he topped himself. Or persons unknown did it for him. And our detectives were out at Bacchus Marsh: not local and overworked, lazy or crooked, take your pick. Maybe they were under pressure to let things lie. Maybe they'd been offered a transfer too.'

'To Fish Creek or another fucked place?'

Bill grunted. 'Whatever the reason, I had nothing to back me up. All I needed was a bloody warrant for Schlicht's car and his property, but the commissioner personally knocked me back. Whether he was on the take...' He lifted his palms. 'With our star witness dead and some of our evidence having mysteriously vanished from what should've been secure storage, he reckoned I didn't have probable cause.'

'That sucks.'

'It sure does,' Gabby agreed.

'Worse still, the hierarchy accused me of having a breakdown or at least a warped perspective because Roly's a close mate. Even when the press picked up the scent, my crew couldn't get the help we needed. Nobody would touch it with a ten-foot pole. Once I'd been offered the transfer, everyone became too shit-scared to openly pursue it. Even John and my other mates stepped back.'

———

They'd fallen quiet for a while. Georgie was processing what she'd learned.

'So, have you come to your senses and decided to back off?'

She swivelled, startled by Franklin's voice. He'd slipped into the room and propped against the wall behind her seat.

He rubbed his temple and added, 'Or do you reckon you can solve it alone now?'

His tone lacked the earlier sting, and she didn't bother answering – mainly because she was clueless what to say. Her mind reeled with too much information, the reverse of a few days ago. How did it all fit together?

What was Susan up to, and where was she?

Why had Margaret been killed? By who?

Was the aborted break-in at the motel connected? And were that and the written threat linked? If not, then Georgie had more than one foe.

'You'll be staying overnight.' Gabby broke into her thoughts. She stood. 'You can't go back to the motel. Whoever it was last night may well return.'

Georgie couldn't face another sleepless night in the motel or driving back to Melbourne in the pitch black of the country. She didn't even fake a protest.

She followed Gabby to a spare bedroom filled with toys, posters and general grandkid-clutter and found herself with a cordless telephone and her host's blessing to call whoever she needed. She ticked off a mental list—Pam Stewart, Bron, AJ and the Pattersons—and heard Franklin's car fire.

She dismissed the resulting mix of relief and disappointment and dialled.

———

It was cold and dark. At first, she'd thought it was quiet too. But there were many sounds when she grew accustomed to her solitude. Birds, frogs, crickets – all soothing, and listening to them helped pass time. Rodents, possums and feral dogs made frightening noises and she tried to block them.

She couldn't read her watch in the blackness or see day turn to night. But she sensed it was The Day. Coincidence or fate? It didn't matter, but it was fitting. Perhaps God would grant her wish in a roundabout way.

She sighed. It turned to a gasp. Pain gripped her chest, shoulder and temple. She drifted in and out of consciousness, had bleak dreams and another turn.

She awoke, fought the urge to urinate, then gave in. The first time had been the worst. Now, she knew there was no alternative, and decorum flooded to the heavens.

SATURDAY 20 MARCH

CHAPTER THIRTY

No offence to the Noonans, but Georgie couldn't wait to escape Daylesford. Bigots and criminals, secrets and innuendo, the air here was oppressive. Thick with odious matters she shouldn't have become embroiled in.

So, as she watched her hosts shrink in the rear-view mirror, her breathing eased. Nightmares had seen her sleep-deprived for the second night running, worse for unrelieved sexual tension. Not to mention she felt damn lost without her mobile and emails. It all made for a hell of a cranky Georgie; a jack-in-the-box ready to explode.

She cleared the intimidating avenue of giant cypress trees and glimpsed pastures through tall gums. These would open to paddocks, like some clichéd Australian landscape painting, then she'd reach the highway on-ramp and be Melbourne-bound.

The car ahead braked inexplicably. She almost rear-ended it. She blasted her horn and gunned past. Fuck the solid white line. She grinned into the mirror and left the other driver for dead.

Bad word choice.

The Spider suddenly vibrated. She freaked.

Had a tyre blown? The gearbox packed up? The judders continued. She jerked to the right. The ride smoothed. Georgie spotted corrugations on the verge, designed to alert dozy drivers.

She laughed. Yet her fingers clenched the steering wheel.

After some minutes, her grip relaxed but tension knotted her shoulders. Music sometimes helped; singing loudly and badly, even more so.

She fiddled with the radio. Still out of range for her favourite station. She killed the static and heard a truck gear down.

'What the hell?' She glared into the rear-view mirror at a massive chrome-toothed grill. She watched it pull back. Then the truck accelerated. Backed off at the last moment.

Fear, fury and pigheadedness kicked in simultaneously.

'If you arseholes think you scare me off,' Georgie yelled, 'think again.'

The driver increased the gap between her convertible and his truck. A bizarre pursuit vehicle, if that's what it was.

She crushed the accelerator. The Alfa shot forward. The truck followed. It nosed to within inches from her bumper.

Her heart pounded. Cold sweat pooled her armpits. Outrun or outwit?

Think. Quickly.

The Spider handled to around 175 kph but not on this mediocre road. Georgie yanked the wheel and hit the gravel edge without braking. The little car fishtailed. She righted it. The logging truck roared past with a blast of air-horns.

'Oh, that'd be right,' she protested. 'Just a truckie in a hurry.'

She cursed until she laughed; laughed until she hiccupped. Then pulled back onto the road, in front of the car she'd overtaken earlier.

Her stomach ached from the fit of laughter. Soon the hysteria gave way to blinding pain in her temple.

Georgie stopped at the next lay-by, switched off the engine and rested her forehead on the steering wheel. She groped in the glovebox, struck a packet of paracetamol, the one swiped from Abergeldie. She dry-swallowed three tablets with her eyes squeezed shut, not intending to doze on the roadside but soon drifting off.

She lifted her head, gazed at her reflection in the mirror and thumbed away smudged mascara. She felt no better for the kip.

'Harden up, Harvey.'

Georgie turned over the ignition and listened to the Spider's purr.

'Home, baby,' she said, slipping onto the roadway.

Home. AJ. Responsibilities other than the Pentecostes. It sounded good.

―――

Fortunately, the rest of the trip was uneventful. The headache retreated as the distance between her and Daylesford expanded.

Back in her Richmond study, Georgie checked her emails, the answering machine, the small pile of snail mail AJ had placed beside the keyboard. She put her mobile on charge, impatient to check its messages. And then opened the OH&S document David Ruddoch wanted yesterday.

Georgie stared at the screen. The words jumbled.

This time yesterday, she and Megan Frawley hadn't discovered Margaret Pentecoste's body. She'd virtually written off the motel disturbance and its implied threat; ditto for the windscreen note. She was yet to meet the Noonans and ignorant of Schlicht's motive for Roly's disposal. And she hadn't seen another side to Franklin, merely to have her original (low) opinion reinstated.

And this time yesterday she was only half as fearful for Susan.

Georgie swallowed bile. She tapped out a string of words, deleted a block of text and undid the deletion. The ringing landline made a welcome distraction.

'Ms Harvey?'

'Yes,' Georgie confirmed guardedly.

'Detective Kyriakos from the homicide squad,' the caller rattled machine-gun style. Before Georgie could reply, Kyriakos continued, 'My team's investigating Margaret Pentecoste's murder.'

Georgie managed, 'Oh?'

'Unfortunately, we didn't get to see you in Ballarat yesterday. However, I understand the local CIU interviewed you. In fact,' Georgie heard paper shuffling, 'I have a copy of your statement right in front of me.'

Georgie's heart thudded. She felt guilty of something.

'We'd appreciate you coming in this morning to resolve one or two discrepancies, if you would.'

It was a polite command.

Georgie had anticipated a breather from the Pentecoste mess, but that was already kaput. Her headache not fully gone and she was up to her nostrils in crap again. Kyriakos's summons amounted to helping the police with their *inquiries.* Did that mean they considered her a suspect? And *what* discrepancies?

Oddly, the detective's call spurred an adrenaline rush. Shortly afterwards, Georgie dispatched her redrafted OH&S script to Ruddoch and flicked on her mobile, juiced enough to check her messages. She always joked that her mobile was an appendage, but the backlog after a day and a bit off-air astounded her. Georgie retrieved several text and voice messages from Matty Gunnerson and one 'Important but not urgent, please call' request from John Franklin date-stamped earlier today.

Stroppy Franklin could wait, unlike Matty's belated update. She dialled him from the car, and they agreed to catch-up at the Royce, a hotel opposite the homicide building. If Matty could trace his AWOL brother, AJ would join them.

———

Georgie's energy waned. As she approached the St Kilda Road Police Complex, she wished for a traffic jam—hell, anything—that would delay the unavoidable. No joy. She even found a four-hour parking space immediately.

'Here goes nothing,' she murmured, dragging her feet towards the base of Victoria's murder squad.

The dirty-mushroom-rendered walls with tinted windows towered ahead. She gazed up and wondered which floor Kyriakos occupied.

'Whoops,' a man said as they collided. He juggled his pie.

Georgie apologised; he grinned before taking off. She noted the piece bulging under his jacket. Cop.

Three guys chuffed on fags in the smokers' nook. She

guessed they were coppers, too, because they openly examined her. One was a honey, which distracted Georgie from official matters for a minute.

Who'd want to get involved with a cop? No way.

A classy silver motorbike parked on the grassed nature strip turned her head.

But I could handle that hot and throbbing between my legs.

Her smirk faltered at the murky-beige steps before the automatic doors. She aimed at blasé but blew it wiping sweaty palms on her jeans.

She obeyed the sign directing all non-official personnel to reception, but the uniformed officer there ignored her. Her eyes bored into his shaved skull while he yakked on the phone; tried to force his attention. He whinged about lack of parking near the courts for over five minutes, during which she shifted her weight, sighed and drummed fingers on the counter. He hung up, then took two calls in succession.

'Ahh, PSO,' she said, as if struck by a revelation.

Receiver glued to his ear, he looked at her. Georgie glanced at the emblem on his blue uniform and thought he caught the implication: *Protective Services Officer – not a real cop.*

Screw manners. She interrupted. 'Georgie Harvey, to see Detective Kyriakos in homicide.'

The PSO shoved across a clip-on visitor's pass bearing her name and pointed to a black vinyl bench. She perched in front of a display case and faced a menacing balaclava-clad skull. And there waited further while road noise and wind pummelled the glazed wall behind her.

———

Finally, a young female in civilian dress beckoned. She swiped an ID card at the elevators. The talking lift announced the ninth floor in a tinny voice. Georgie trailed her guide to the anteroom of another secure zone. She sat on a bright blue sofa and checked out an honours board. The buzz of voices and frequent trill of telephones reassured her that people were on the other side of the partition.

As she waited again, impatience battled apprehension. She disguised the trembles in her hand by drumming her fingernails on the sofa arm. Soon, she forgot both emotions.

AJ filled her imagination. He'd left home before she returned, leaving the animals to be her welcoming committee and source of much-needed hugs. She drifted into picturing him naked to the waist, muscles pumped.

'Ms Harvey?' startled her out of the daydream.

Kyriakos in the flesh matched Georgie's mental image. Late-thirties, medium-sized, she wore wedged court shoes and a black suit. The outfit too heavy for Indian summer, it screamed efficiency and authority. Likewise the blunt hairdo framing carob irises implied intelligence and a no-nonsense demeanour.

The detective motioned Georgie to follow. They weaved around civilians at their desks who typed furiously and talked on the phone at equal rate. Then they passed a cabinet of busts and other exhibits.

Kyriakos reached a room a few metres square and waved her inside. Large windows fronted a cityscape shrouded in sunlight despite looming black clouds. Five maroon desk chairs clashed with the predominantly beige, black and blue décor of the police complex. A workstation and computer dominated dead centre of the room (both beige, of course). The artwork consisted of a small Monet print hung too high to appreciate.

We're here to concentrate seemed to hum from the computer.

Although the room wasn't as officious as she'd expected, Kyriakos was. Georgie sat where pointed to and tried not to fidget.

The detective shuffled papers without eye contact. The air-conditioning recycled the warm computer, stuffy room and tinge of perspiration smell peculiar to sealed offices. Despite the balmy atmosphere, Georgie shivered and clenched her jaw to stop her teeth chattering.

'Right,' Kyriakos said, leaning back. 'You can expect to return to see the team handling the inquiry into Susan Pentecoste's potential disappearance. In the meantime, we have issues to iron out, haven't we?'

Georgie shifted.

'There is a fundamental discrepancy between your statement,' Kyriakos pointed to the copy before her, 'and that of Megan Frawley. Do you know what I'm referring to?'

With a shake of her head, Georgie sat on her hands so the detective wouldn't see them quiver and misinterpret nerves for guilt.

'Hmm. I wonder.'

The computer hummed while Kyriakos's words hung.

'Would you care to explain your interference with the crime scene?'

Georgie's mouth flopped.

What interference?

'What did you remove from my scene?'

Bewildered by the detective's aggression and the question, Georgie spluttered, 'What?'

'Here's my predicament. Ms Frawley observed you

remove an item from the deceased's residence after discovering the body. Care to enlighten me?'

Georgie's eyes bugged. She repeated, 'What?'

'An item from under the deceased's doormat. Does this jog your memory?'

Georgie's guts plummeted. She hastily explained the note she'd left for Margaret and her retraction of it and her card.

Kyriakos scrutinised and listened. She scratched an efficient record. 'I find it remarkable that you mentioned your purpose for being at Ms Pentecoste's home to the Ballarat detectives but not your note.'

'I honestly didn't think about it,' Georgie protested. 'I was standing there, looking at this mat inside the hallway and it occurred to me that my note might be caught underneath. Sure enough, it was. So I pocketed it. I didn't consider it important.'

'Ms Harvey. You understand that your actions and misleading statement have compromised your integrity as a witness? What else have you lied about?'

'Nothing. Nothing!'

Georgie muddled through another account of her actions before and after stepping into the cottage on Ascot Street South – minus all emotion and suppositions, as instructed. Kyriakos prepared a supplementary witness statement. She maintained her poker face.

'Am I a suspect?' Georgie asked, anxious.

Kyriakos hitched a caterpillar brow. 'No, it would have been all business in that case.'

If this is your nice side, I'd hate to meet your alter ego.

Just then, a tall, rugged guy, ten or fifteen years Kyriakos's senior, tapped and entered the interview room.

'Inspector Brian Mitchell.' He extended his hand in a firm, dry handshake. 'This is my show.'

Huh! So much for Kyriakos calling it my *scene.*

'Helen, you all done in here? We've got to get moving.'

Kyriakos nodded. 'I was explaining what'd differ if we considered Ms Harvey a suspect in Margaret Pentecoste's murder.'

Embarrassed, Georgie said, 'I'm a writer, what can I say? Inquisitive by nature.'

'See this room?' Mitchell fixed her with an amber stare. He cocked his head and said, 'This is a *witness* room. Compact, non-distracting, also considerably non-threatening. Agree? This is where members of the public are generally brought for discussions regarding a homicide. The victim's family, neighbours, witnesses and so on. Now, on our way out, I'll show you where you'd be interviewed if you were a suspect in one of our murders.'

He crooked his finger.

Intrigued, Georgie followed the inspector through more clusters of desks filled with coffee cups, files and notes. By whiteboards overlaid with masses of neat notations. Near cloak stands resembling phantom-people, sheathed in suit jackets, ties, spare pants – all pressed, impregnated with dry-cleaning fluid and ready to grab on the way to a crime scene, airport or court.

Kyriakos clip-clopped behind with a precise, determined stride. Despite his seniority and stature, Mitchell moved lithely in rubber-soled shoes. They filed into a chamber with an illuminable Interview in Progress panel above it. Kyriakos slammed the soundproof door.

'If you were a suspect, Georgie, this is what would have gone down.' Mitchell paused. 'I would have sent two armed officers to collect you from your home. The officers would have driven into the secure basement and escorted you directly into this interview room. We would have offered you the services of a duty solicitor or the opportunity to access your own legal advisor. By the time I finished, you would have been charged or arrested.'

Georgie blushed. Educated via TV crime and novels as per most of her generation, she ought to have realised Kyriakos took the soft road.

The tiny room had a suspended ceiling. Bare fluorescent tubes were hot and cruelly bright. A one-way window faced the door. Three basic chairs bordered the square table pushed to the side wall. No visible audio and video-recording gear and nothing to comfort, entertain, distract or use as a weapon.

Her visual tour stopped at the inspector's face. He hooted; Kyriakos joined in. Georgie relaxed and she laughed too.

The officers escorted her to the foyer. During the lift's descent, she quizzed them on the case.

Mitchell's ironic reply: 'No comment.'

They shook hands and Georgie unclipped her visitor's ID.

She suddenly remembered something the policewoman mentioned earlier. 'You said I'll have to come back in relation to Susan's *potential* disappearance. Surely now it's a missing person's case?'

The detectives exchanged a glance.

Mitchell answered cryptically, 'A different team is looking into Susan's whereabouts.'

'As a missing person or a dead person?' Georgie demanded.

Two inscrutable faces.

Georgie had been dragged into this mess, only to be

excluded. That sucked, and she wouldn't leave the building until she received assurances about Susan – until convinced the police were tracking her, urgently.

Mitchell sensed her anger and stubbornness. He said, 'Don't worry, Georgie. We're onto it. Let us do our jobs.'

'Do we have your undertaking to keep out of it?' his partner added. 'To stay in Melbourne until the matter's resolved?'

Fat chance.

'No comment.'

In contrast with the detectives' genuine mirth inside the interview room, this time their chuckles didn't reach their eyes. Georgie surrendered her ID and wondered if she'd see them again.

She also wondered why she felt so sad.

CHAPTER THIRTY-ONE

Mid-morning and the minutes whipped by. Franklin drummed a pen on the dining table. Strewn over the pine tabletop were Solomon's poison-pen letters, Franklin's daybook, Kat's *Good News Bible* (which he suspected she hadn't opened since her last religious education class in primary school) and a roll of Christmas wrapping paper. On the latter's plain side, he'd map out everything he knew about Solomon and note the gaps. Plot the links between the victims. Visualise the big picture.

He checked his watch. With a glance at the still-blank paper, he took a mouthful of strong coffee.

'C'mon. Wake up.'

After dinner with the Noonans, he'd picked up the remainder of the late shift, running through to after 2.00am and then *on availability* until the day crew came on at morning tea. No complaints; Lunny did well to swing the switch with no notice. Franklin spent most of the slow night shift agonising over Susan Pentecoste's absence, her niece's murder and all the dire shit he and Georgie Harvey dredged up yesterday. His brain already in overdrive, the pre-dawn hours on alert to emergency calls further contributed to an exhausted insomnia. He'd eventually given up on sleep and traded bed for reviewing the Solomon case.

Cotton-wool brain meant it'd all too soon be 6.oopm and time to clock on, with nothing gained.

He drained his mug and slammed it down. He rubbed his chin. And reread Solomon's letters. Something bothered him.

Franklin listened and realised it was so quiet he could hear the clock tick.

In a knee-jerk reaction to Kat's shoplifting escapade he'd grounded her indefinitely. Scarcely a few days later and he'd backflipped after she volunteered to keep well clear of troublemaker Narelle King. Thus, with his daughter at Lisa Cantrell's, the house was free of distractions. No radio, nerve-stretching teenage-girl talk on the phone or histrionics.

Yet the wrapping paper remained blank. And Franklin's mind drifted.

A piece of work, that Georgie Harvey.

Admittedly, he admired her tenacity and commitment to a promise. But that promise had intersected with homicide and personal risk, and she should back off. She'd achieved her aim in getting the MISPER file upgraded.

Yes, but too late for Margaret.

The nagging inner voice imitated Donna. He shut it down, reverted to Harvey.

If she had more sense than mulish guts, he wouldn't have to worry about hand-holding the unpredictable writer from Melbourne whenever she developed a harebrained theory. She was a liability.

In more ways than one.

The blank sheet glared at him.

———

'Stop fucking around,' Franklin muttered after more time had sped away.

He picked up a black marker. Crude flowcharts and text soon covered the wrapping paper. He shook out writer's cramp and mulled over his handiwork.

'Better.'

He rose and stretched. Moved to the kitchen to boil the kettle and tapped his foot as he waited.

A watched kettle never boils. A watched-for woman stays missing.

The mental jump to Susan Pentecoste surprised him. What was she up to? Was she safe?

He rubbed eyes gritty with exhaustion. His shoulders slumped. Susan was a sensible woman, a strong woman, but even now he was finding out how much she hid behind a brave face. To get inside her mind was akin to cracking the Rubik's Cube: lots of twists and immense frustration. Her continued absence, especially in light of her niece's murder, worried the heck out of him.

With a shot of steam and a shrill whistle, the kettle interrupted.

Franklin poured water over coffee granules and made another leap.

Cause: the anniversary of Roly's disappearance. His murder. Effect: Susan goes AWOL.

There's a reason for everything and a trigger for all events. Now he had to apply that logic to the Solomon case.

He sat down and studied his notes until they blurred. He squinted. What was the objective of Solomon's fanatical letters? No, not just his *letters*; Solomon had progressed to violence. So, what drove him?

Cause equals X.

Effect, or Y, equals the threats, stalking and assault.

Bloody algebra had never been Franklin's strong point and it failed to help here.

To maintain momentum, he recorded the dead ends next. Art Hammer: literally dead and had died prior to Solomon's attacks at Christina's home, so he couldn't be the crook. Earl Blue: alibi confirmed by reliable sources; he, too, couldn't be Franklin's man – unless Blue worked with an accomplice here in Daylesford. Franklin shook his head. Solomon's outrage at Christina's behaviour was first-hand and personal, not orchestrated from the other side of the world.

He pulled out a red marker. In thick chisel-point strokes, he made a new section entitled 'The six motives'. The key motives for murder had been drummed into his head during his rookie days. Franklin still remembered one of the instructors had barked, *Memorise them because the reasons people kill translate to other crimes against persons too.*

'GAIN. ELIMINATION. LUST. REVENGE. CONVICTION. JEALOUSY.'

The first three he put in reserve. Although the case contained a sexual element, he didn't think Solomon lusted after his victims, and he hadn't demanded money. Equally, revenge seemed remote with the range of targets involved.

A warped ethical and religious conviction motivated Solomon, which translated to a desire to punish. That in itself presented a wide field to analyse.

Franklin pondered the final motive.

Did jealousy also drive him?

Click the Rubik's Cube, infiltrate the mind – Solomon's

mind now, rather than Susan Pentecoste's. Franklin scrawled more notes.

'What's Solomon jealous of? The attention the mothers receive (from men and/or the community)? Can't he attract a partner?'

Makes sense. He's totally wacko.

Franklin rubbed his chin and wrote, 'Because they have a child and Solomon can't? Is he sterile? Or, single and therefore can't have kids. (NB See link to target: single mothers.)' Appended, 'Could be gay.'

Pause. He scratched the paper again with, 'Maybe he had a bad childhood. Only child of single parent and crap upbringing? Anti all single mums?'

Lots of maybes and not much headway.

'Cockhead. Don't forget Solomon could be female.' Franklin's voice jarred in the hushed house. 'Male/female doesn't change things though. The motive could be the same. *She* could be jealous on the same grounds. That's *if* jealousy has anything to do with it.'

Frustrated, he stabbed the marker into the paper. He snagged the word 'CONVICTION'. Apt.

Georgie Harvey leapt into his brain. 'Dammit, why hasn't she called?' Pissed off with her ignoring his earlier text message, he painstakingly keyed another and hit send.

———

Franklin scowled at Solomon's letters. 'C'mon, tell me what's going on here!'

He shoved everything aside except a clean segment of wrapping paper. In block letters, he wrote: 'HOW DOES SOLOMON KNOW ABOUT THE BIRTHS?'

'Ah, that's the key,' he breathed, then paced the floor awhile.

He lit a cigarette, took a pull and blew a string of smoke rings out the open window.

'If he doesn't work in the hospitals, how does he discover the pregnancies and/or births?'

Franklin thought back to Donna's pregnancy and groaned. She'd bought a pregnancy test, and everyone knew within five minutes.

Small-town joys.

Break it down.

First to guess: the pharmacy assistant who'd sold Donna the test kit. First to be sure: doctor, medical receptionist. Next: her friends, him (yes, in that order), their families and colleagues. No obstetrician for them, not on a copper's wage, just the GP all the way through, with the help of midwives. First to see the baby: hospital staff, him, family. Then Kat became hot town property and earned gooey oohs and ahs wherever they went.

'Pharmacy staff' got noted under suspects but without gusto. These days you could buy pregnancy tests from supermarkets. Was he going to add checkout chicks to the list too?

Besides awareness of the births, Solomon also believed the mothers were unwed. What source would reveal both?

Franklin paced again. He reflected on the victims. Each one individual, of different strokes. He centred on Cathy and Tyson. Cute kid, nice mum. She was so proud of her brag book.

That's why they call 'em brag books.

Donna had stuffed full an Our Baby album. Proof of how fucked up and selfish she was: she'd walked out on her kid when she walked out on their marriage, and she'd left behind Kat's baby album.

He pulled it off the bookshelf and leafed through the pages.

Blood test: positive for pregnancy. Photos of Donna and her ballooning belly and one with them cuddling, his hand on her bump, both tired and excited. The clipped birth notice from their local rag. A few special *congratulations* cards immortalised behind plastic sleeves. Photocopy of Kat's birth certificate. Photos of every first event.

Franklin shut the album softly. He ran his hand over the cover, wistful.

Back in work mode, he mentally compared Kat's album to Tyson's. What did they have in common? Apart from the absence of a dad, Tyson's book mirrored his daughter's.

How did it help? Not a bloody lot.

Not everyone needed early blood tests, but ultrasounds were the norm. He jotted 'ultrasound/radiology/pathology staff' under the suspect list. Department and camera stores were popular for printing photos when Kat arrived, but today people could do their own at home. So that angle wasn't much chop.

'What about...?'

Franklin snatched a copy of the *Advocate* and flicked through. He pumped a fist to the roof. 'Yes!'

———

'Let's see. "Porter-Walters. Colin and Arnica of Daylesford are pleased to announce the safe arrival of their new baby boy, Darren Oliver, born on 11 March. Brother to Jessica." Beau-ti-ful!'

As expected, the births column provided bub's

particulars and a photograph of mother and child, along with enough family information for Solomon to draw conclusions, *rightly or wrongly*.

He squeezed his eyes and imagined birth notices for the five young mothers Solomon targeted.

Five. Five that I know of.

His stomach clenched. With Daylesford's virtual population explosion of late, how many additional mothers were victims of the malicious writer? Were there other switches from threats and stalking to actual violence as yet unknown to him? If he flunked out again today, he'd need to analyse the hospital records and newspaper archives and personally interview all relevant mums. Too time-consuming and Solomon might escalate again in the meantime. It was imperative he crack the case before Solomon snapped.

So assume five for now.

He fixed on the Porters' announcement and contemplated what Solomon would have learned of his five victims from the local paper.

Renee Archer's announcement of daughter Alex's birth would not have mentioned her political lobbyist husband, which led Solomon to conclude an unwed status.

Similarly, lapsed Catholic Lauren Morris had probably succumbed to family pressure and avoided attention to her de facto relationship with the father of Millie and Aiden.

As Solomon would have, he'd spotted straight up that Cathy Jones hadn't mentioned Tyson's father in his birth notice. The last thing on earth she'd do was ID her rapist.

For little Tayla Birkley, unashamed of being a single parent and proud of son Callum, no interpretation would've been required.

Lastly, as gossip went, Christina van Hoeckel had never

clarified which of her numerous lovers fathered Bailey, and naming a dad could have been libellous without a paternity test. She was a sure-fire tainted woman for Solomon.

He seized his ringing mobile, anticipating Georgie Harvey.

'Franklin.'

Lunny. And he sounded pissed off.

'Yeah, boss?'

'Get your arse in here. Pronto.'

———

Within minutes, Franklin stood before his angry friend and superior.

'You know you've got good mates in Hart and Sprague, don't you? Pretty much whatever you tell them, they treat like gospel. True? If you say jump, they say "How high, mate?" You ask them to keep something mum, they'd do it. Hell, even if you don't *tell* them to keep quiet, if they *gather* that's what you want, they respect it. Unless one of them, usually Sprague, accidentally opens his big mouth. Right?'

Franklin shifted. He shrugged.

'Sprague let slip about this van Hoeckel case out on West Street. He mentioned, "the sneaky bugger's running his own book" and then clammed up. I presume he's referring to you, Franklin, and that means you're keeping back from this investigation.'

Lunny drilled him with a livid stare. Franklin chewed the inside of his cheek and shook his head.

'Wasn't it less than a week ago that Wells made identical allegations? And I warned you that you're required to be a team player. We have to work together,

Franklin. There's no room for egotism or machismo in this station.'

'Understood, boss.'

'Is it? I wonder.' Lunny viewed him shrewdly.

'We're following all leads in the van Hoeckel matter. If I knew who the crook was, I'd have him in here straight away.'

That much held true.

'You're not running your own crusade?'

'No.' Franklin maintained eye contact but squirmed inside.

'Why aren't you resting anyway?' Lunny asked unexpectedly. 'You look like shit. This can wait. You're on at six, go get some shut-eye.'

Weariness swamped Franklin anew. He found himself nodding and promised to rest before shift start. Back home, he pushed the Solomon paperwork into the sideboard, away from stickybeak Kat.

He dialled a number.

'Bloody hell.' The mobile was out of range or switched off.

CHAPTER THIRTY-TWO

'So, what's the goss on Jenny McGuire?' Georgie asked between mouthfuls of vegetarian ravioli. She chased the flavours of olive oil, mushrooms, green olives and semi-sundried tomatoes with a draught of Corona.

Matt Gunnerson swallowed. 'Hold your horses, Gee. Let me eat first.'

'Oh, come on, bro,' AJ demanded.

'Yeah, I told you everything. It's your turn.' Georgie gave Matty's arm a light punch.

'Okay, okay. Apparently, she showed great aptitude at uni. But despite her tutors' high expectations, they didn't think she was as good as she was capable of being when she graduated. Her stint at the *Advocate* was supposed to give her practical experience in a rural environment, to give her writing extra insight and edge.'

Matty paused to slug bourbon and coke. 'What's really strange is that she's content to stay a hack reporter in the sticks. One of her previous colleagues—a journo I work with—reckons that McGuire's pathetic. She's too scared to push people's buttons, to work the boundaries, let alone cross them.' The crime reporter sniffed.

'So, was she paid off or frightened off?' Georgie mused.

'She would have panicked once she connected Roly's disappearance with Joey Bigagli's death. Sorry, Bigagli's *murder*,' AJ commented.

'And back then it would have been easy enough to link Bigagli and Schlicht –'

'When you asked me to check into Bigagli's hit and run the other day, Gee,' Matty interrupted, 'I didn't click until later in the day. I planned to fill you in on that, plus the goss on McGuire, except you went incommunicado.'

She joined the dots. 'So it's on good odds that McGuire dumped her local hero piece on Roly because she was scared? Worried Schlicht might take out more insurance – just in case Roly passed on something incriminating to McGuire during her interview.'

'Complicated,' AJ remarked.

'That's an understatement. This whole thing is more than complicated. It's outrageous that Roly died for no reason. And Susan...'

Georgie's unfinished sentence led to an uneasy silence, thankfully broken by a text beep. She checked her mobile.

'Ring me pls. Franklin.'

She hit delete and shouted another round of drinks.

———

'Too many people love the sound of their own voices at these gigs,' AJ muttered.

They scanned the foyer filled with conservative art patrons, along with a handful of eccentric artists and regular people.

'Yeah, your mum would fit right in.'

'George, I realise you and Mum are completely different. Can't you try to get along though?'

'Hmm.'

'So, lunch at my parents' tomorrow?'

'Can't make it.' She grinned. 'I've got a lead to check out.'

'Jesus. Why can't you leave it to the police?'

Georgie bristled. She bit back a retort and instead walked away. AJ tagged along.

'You don't know where Bron's masterpiece is?' he asked.

'Nuh. We'll find it, don't worry – it'll stand out. Most of this stuff is... Hang on, this one's pretty good.'

'You reckon?'

'*Karma*,' Georgie read the title. 'Suits it.'

The woman next to her pulled her lips into a tight line as the *Bumblebee* tune erupted in Georgie's handbag.

'*Where are you?*' demanded Jo Holt, Bron's partner.

'The foyer.'

'*Well, get here quickly.*' Jo gave directions and rang off.

Georgie grabbed AJ's hand.

'You never answered me, George,' he said, as she elbowed through the throng, pulling him along.

'What?' she snapped.

'My parents. Lunch. Your plans. Why you can't leave it to the cops,' he spelled out.

'Why?' She stopped.

AJ crashed into her.

A list of reasons hovered on her lips. Blunt was best, so she said, 'For Ruby, mainly. C'mon, I won't do anything heroic or stupid. Okay? Trust me.'

Georgie took off.

AJ caught her hand, halting her. 'I'm not a doormat, George.'

She gazed at him, troubled by his intensity. 'AJ, you know how much this means to me.'

He puffed out his cheeks.

She continued, 'Our visit to Ruby just before... There she is, lying in her hospital bed, so frail and opposite to her normal self. Then she grabs my hand and squashes it. Why? Because she's worried sick for her friend Susan. Literally worried sick. What happens to Ruby matters to me, AJ, and the only way I can help her is to find Susan. And you know what else? I care what happens to Susan too. She's out there,' she waved, 'and I'm scared for her.'

'Yeah but that's all the more reason –'

'If I promise to be careful, can't we leave it at that? I've got to check out the few points that're bugging me. Okay?'

He wavered.

'Okay, AJ? Are *we* okay?'

What a weird turnaround to be the one asking that question.

Before he responded, Georgie saw Jo on the stage with Bron behind her. She pulled him up the stairs.

Bron's green eyes shone. Excitement bubbled from her pores. Jo danced a jig and blocked their view until they were front and centre.

'Adam and Georgina,' Jo said with faux formality. 'I present to you the work of eminent artist, *Bron-wen Silvers*.'

'Wow.' AJ gave a low wolf-whistle.

Georgie spotted the red sticker. 'You've sold it on opening day!' She smacked a kiss on Bron's cheek.

They sobered, mesmerised by their friend's monochrome oil-on-wood. Its style more artistic and sinuous than realism, it whispered emotion. She'd captured late-night Melbourne in shades of grey. The famous frontage of Flinders Street Station, the streets of the cross-intersection greasy, cars and pedestrians united in a quest to escape sheets of rain. Despite the deluge, a few youths hunched on the station steps with plastic bags over their heads or blowing on frozen fingers. In the background, yet focal to the painting, a girl—tiny, fragile, malnourished—huddled against a pillar of the arching station mouth. Juxtaposed were her prematurely world-weary expression and her childish thumb-sucking while she clutched the paw of a battered teddy in the other hand. In this portion of the painting, Bron introduced a smudge of rust-red. The girl's T-shirt, the teddy's breast, both bloodstained. Instead of being safe and warm with family, the youth epitomised the heart-rending poverty, aloneness and despair of kids living rough on the streets. Too easy to ignore; too important not to.

It resonated deeply with Georgie and ramped up her fears for Susan Pentecoste.

She forced down a lump in her throat. To allay the atmosphere, she squeezed AJ's hand, whacked Bron's back and aped an art critic. 'The artist impresses upon us the importance of art in educating society, not merely in producing fluff to adorn our walls. In *Caught in the Crossfire,* she superbly expresses her anger at the victim's pain –'

She broke off to answer her mobile.

'Franklin here.'

Georgie's mood soured. She stepped away.

'You get home safely?'

'Well, obviously,' she replied sarcastically, perplexed by his tone.

A brief pause, then Franklin reverted to his customary cocksure self. *'Bill Noonan filled me in on the information he'd given you about Schlicht's wife. Are you thinking of paying her a visit?'*

Georgie played innocent. 'What?'

'I figured you'd be planning to continue your gung-ho amateur sleuth tactics, instead of leaving it to the experts.'

'What's it to you?'

'Well, if you must stay involved, I could take you along when I visit Helena Watkowska. It'd have to be my next rest day.'

She pretended to consider his suggestion. 'Oh, when would that be?'

'At some point this week, but I need to check the new roster.'

'Sure, get back to me,' Georgie said ambiguously. She disconnected and smirked. She hadn't agreed to wait.

———

Even before yesterday, sleep had been elusive, and any snatches came at a cost.

It had nothing to do with the joys of shiftwork.

Since the car and minibus accident earlier in the week, with slumber came nightmares. In a cyclic re-enactment of the horror smash, Franklin moved towards the teenaged body pierced to the fence post. As he lifted the victim's head, the short-cropped blonde hair transformed. It became long, crimped tresses, framing Kat's ashen, lifeless face. He screamed in the dream and jolted awake. Then lay stiff, deafened by his heartbeat. He was torn between a desperate need for sleep and dread of it.

Now, despite Lunny's reprimand, the imminence of a

break in the Solomon case and thoughts filled with Harvey, fatigue prevailed.

He slept deeply and dreamlessly for the remaining afternoon.

His intention to call McGuire was forgotten.

SUNDAY 21 MARCH

CHAPTER THIRTY-THREE

Until this point, the hunt for Helena Watkowska had been a challenge—a fun use of Georgie's old law office skills—though also frustrating. Bill Noonan had mentioned that Watkowska lived outside of a town called Trafalgar, but an electronic White Pages search came up blank for a phone listing. Georgie had widened it to the Gippsland area and still hit a wall. Ditto for Schlicht.

She'd then tried a google search for the woman under her maiden name, but that'd bombed too. A land title search for both surnames in Trafalgar had similar bad luck. But she wasn't surprised. Discretion would rate highly for the estranged wife of the Iceman; she wouldn't make it too easy by listing her phone number publicly or purchasing property—assuming she had some—in her own name. Georgie supposed she'd hide behind a company or trust if she were Watkowska, and she decided not to waste more time on that avenue.

She'd considered other means of finding Schlicht's ex, growing increasingly anxious. The *Warragul Citizen* seemed to cover the Trafalgar area. Georgie wasn't hopeful that a newspaper based that far away would have the local knowledge needed to track Watkowska. An answering machine picked up when she tried the reception number. Then the direct line for the reporters rang out, so she'd scratched that idea.

By now, she was itching for action and figured trying the personal approach couldn't be less successful than the hour she'd just wasted in her office. So she jumped in the Spider and aimed its nose away from the city, in the opposite direction to Daylesford.

———

Despite shit-all sleep after being on the job until nearly 3.30am, Franklin was sharper than possum teeth by 8.00am. Ready to tear apart Solomon's sordid hobby, tame Georgie Harvey and her wild ideas and rip into the Pentecoste case.

He grabbed the phone.

She owes me; it's time to settle up.

He second-guessed his hunch and hung up. So far, the link to the *Advocate* boiled down to someone with enough gumption to obtain addresses from the phone directory after picking out victims through the new bubs column.

Franklin didn't know its circulation figures but the free paper served Daylesford, Creswick, Clunes, Trentham and surrounds. That meant it was easily available to a hefty catchment. Broaden that further if they put the announcements online these days too.

He scratched his chin, shoulders slumped.

'Come on. Think! Is it just a psycho reader? Or is this cockhead connected to the paper?'

The pendulum of confidence returned. The

breakthrough was there. On the Christmas wrap. The level of obsession, wacked-out conviction, information tainted by assumptions. It all made for a gut feeling that Solomon had personal access to his victims. They'd met but superficially.

A sleepy female answered his call. *'Hello?'*

'Jennifer? John Franklin. I've a few questions.'

That got her attention. *'What about?'*

'I'm working a case and can't elaborate at this point. But it could involve an employee of the *Advocate.*'

'Who, me?'

He eye-rolled. 'No, I'm not implying you. The party I'm interested in could be on the fringe of the paper. In the classifieds, photography or printing side of things, maybe. Can you help me out?'

The journalist reluctantly agreed to meet at the newspaper office within the hour. Franklin disconnected and immediately dialled the number of another woman with attitude.

'John Franklin here,' he said into the receiver.

At her frosty response, his pulse bounded.

'You didn't give me a chance to finish last night. I heard you visited the hommie squad yesterday.'

'Yep, you heard right.'

'Did it go okay?' He wondered why he cared.

'Sure, bloody fantastic. The best day of my life.' Georgie burst into laughter. It rang true, not bitter.

'Have you run into any more trouble?'

She retorted, *'Run into?'*

He sighed softly. Conversation with Georgie Harvey was not a tiptoe-through-the-tulips affair. It was like navigating a mine field.

'No more threats, break-ins...?'

'Course not,' she shot back but then conceded, *'No, but*

to tell you the truth, I was with other people all of yesterday after seeing the homicide detectives.'

He sighed again but with relief rather than frustration.

'Are you leaving it up to us now?' he ventured.

'Hmm,' she said vaguely. *'Have we finished our little chat?'*

He hesitated, torn. His cop instincts told him not to go there, not to ask her along and encourage her meddling. On the other hand, he knew she'd butt in regardless, so he may as well keep tabs on her. Besides, company on the long drive to Trafalgar could be good.

Even while he debated the sanity of including her, he heard himself say, 'I'm getting back to you on Helena Watkowska. I expect to see her Tuesday. You want to come along?'

'Hmm.'

Suspicious, he said, 'I don't want you going without me.'

Georgie's reply could have been a snigger or a snort.

'Look, you've no idea where this Watkowska woman fits in or how to handle the inquiry.'

'Oh, puh-lease,' she said sarcastically. *'Talking to someone isn't rocket science.'*

Franklin stiffened. He controlled his comeback. 'It might be dangerous. Consider who we're dealing with here.'

A marginal pause was followed by Georgie's deliberate words, *'I appreciate your concern, but I'll be fine.'*

Fucking bull-headed females. Who needs them?

Aloud Franklin said, 'Oh, man! I should've known you wouldn't listen to reason –'

'Reason –'

'Just call me later then.'

He hung up and glared at the receiver. Obviously

Harvey planned to see Watkowska. She could be on the road right now.

His conscience hoped Harvey was right and there'd be no harm in her visit to John Schlicht's ex-missus. Yet, his darker side suggested a hostile reception may be what she needed. It might force respect for him and his uniform.

Hah! So much for taming Harvey and her wild ideas.

———

As the Spider coasted towards Trafalgar, Georgie shrugged off the call from John Franklin and his suggestion they visit Watkowska on Tuesday. And she tried not to overthink her so-far-wasted morning and what that might mean for Susan's safety.

———

Still shaking his head over Georgie Harvey, Franklin picked up the phone again.

'Hey, Heddo. Franklin here.'

'Hey, long time, no hear!' his mate replied facetiously. They'd last spoken on Friday, when the CI bloke tipped him off that Georgie Harvey was at Ballarat station.

The detective yelled something incomprehensible to someone at his end.

Once Franklin held Heddo's attention, he asked, 'What've you got on the Margaret Pentecoste murder?'

'Mate, can't talk. We've got the hommies crawling up our arses here. I'll give you a buzz later today, providing things've quietened down. Okey-dokey?'

'Sure, no probs.'

Franklin realised Heddo had replaced the receiver. He drummed his fingers and jumped when the telephone rang.

'We've had a possible sighting of Susan Pentecoste's Land Cruiser.' It was Mick Sprague. No overtures.

'What? Fantastic. Where?'

'On the Ballan road. Saw her there three-quarts of an hour ago.'

'Who? And why the delay?'

'There's the thing. It was an anonymous report. A male caller rang from a public phone in town.'

'Crank?'

'Possibly. Anyhow, you wanna take a ride out to Susan's place and check if she's there, while we do a whiz around and try to pick up her trail?'

Franklin flicked his wrist to check the time, although he'd already decided to push back his meeting with McGuire if it came to it. 'Sure, Slam. Stay in the loop.'

It was premature to feel elated based on a vague and unsubstantiated sighting of Susan Pentecoste. The report could be the fallacy of a well-meaning local or a deception designed to mislead and misappropriate police resources for any number of reasons. The grimmest scenario: Susan's abductor covering his tracks.

CHAPTER THIRTY-FOUR

ALTHOUGH HE RECOGNISED THE LEAD COULD FIZZ OUT, Franklin felt excited as he retrieved his car from the garage. He sensed a resolution to the poison-pen case and that they'd see Susan home by sundown.

If he were a betting man, he'd back it on the nose.

This could be the best day in a piss-poor week.

He tensed at the wheel of his Commodore and scanned the landscape while flat-footing the accelerator. Time distorted: on the one hand, he seemed to arrive at Abergeldie quickly, while on the other, it took too long.

Out of the car, silence struck Franklin. His earlier optimism shrank to a marble in his throat. The farm exuded emptiness and melancholy. Dread stroked his nape.

His mobile provided a timely diversion.

'Yeah,' he answered Slam's call.

'Anything out your way?'

Franklin's stomach hollowed with disappointment. 'Not yet. I just got here, though. I take it you've had no luck?'

'Bugger it, no. We're going to keep zigzagging through town. I'll let you know if we find her. Speak later.'

After a moment, Franklin reached through the Commodore's window. He sounded the horn for two minutes.

A mob of white cockatoos took flight, their raspy screams abrasive. The sheep bleated and bolted along the fence line.

But there were no human reactions.

He yelled, 'Susan! You here?'

His words fragmented with a gust of wind and burst of rain.

It didn't matter. As he verified via a short sharp search, there was no one at Abergeldie to hear him. On the bright side, he found nothing to justify his earlier fear either.

Minuscule consolation.

———

This sleepy town in Gippsland had once cost Georgie a speeding ticket and a few precious demerit points, so as she entered Trafalgar she slowed and scanned for coppers.

Georgie considered the options and decided on Shirley's Hair – For Men & Women. Everybody knows hairdressers are a fount of fact and gossip. This salon held a captive audience of blue-rinse seventy-plus ladies, along with Shirley herself, who modelled a kaleidoscopic pompom hairdo, garish makeup and much-weathered skin.

'You're lucky to find us here on a Sunday,' Shirley told her. 'We're all off to the wedding of the year this afternoon!'

The ladies let Georgie go through her spiel, including the scanty description she had from Bill Noonan, then Blue-Rinse 1 said, 'Oh, yes, we know who you mean.'

B-R 2 nodded. 'You're talking about that gangster's wife.'

B-R3 said she thought Watkowska lived out near Willow Grove or Vesper, and the others agreed.

Georgie suspected they knew exactly where the woman lived, but she couldn't get more information from them.

———

May your news be good news had been the catchphrase of one of Victoria's iconic newsreaders. The newsman had perished with his wife during the previous year's horrific bushfires, yet Franklin repeated it for luck as he drove into Daylesford.

He'd turned the music off in case Slam called. In the unusual quietness, the soft squeak of the brake pedal and springs mocked him. *Nothing's going to happen. You're not going to find her. It was a shonky report,* they chanted.

'No news is good news,' he insisted, shaking away the pessimistic voices.

He pulled up outside the *Advocate* and caught a weird look from Jennifer McGuire. She'd seen him talking to himself.

Franklin grimaced. 'Let's get on with this.' It sounded more abrupt than he'd intended.

'Fine.' Huffy, she led him to the office. 'We won't worry about niceties then, like coffee.'

He'd deserved that. Franklin laughed. 'Sorry. You go ahead if you want, Jen. But I'm keen to get underway.'

McGuire dropped onto a chair. 'I have to admit, you've got me curious.' She'd thawed already. 'Can't you tell me what this is about?'

'Not yet.'

'Will you give me an exclusive then, when you can?'

McGuire blushed, as if scoops were outside her journalistic realm.

Franklin covered his arse. 'If I can.'

She sighed and passed him a page. 'Here's what you wanted. I've listed everyone directly linked to the paper's production. I haven't gone into distribution at this stage...'

Franklin scanned the names and job descriptions. No one jumped off the page as a would-be Solomon, reputed for aggressive behaviour.

'Harry Notman, dogsbody?'

'A hundred years old, as crooked as a builder's level and no more dangerous than mashed potato.'

Franklin chuckled. 'Rebekka Kirk, then? Classifieds and receptionist.'

'I don't know her too well. Bek's been with us for yonks but keeps to herself a bit. Friendly, though. Well liked. I can't imagine her doing something untoward. Unless it involved splurging on the pokies.'

Introvert, responsible for the classifieds and a gambler; Franklin gave Kirk a mental question mark.

Franklin ran his fingertip to the next name. 'Valerie Blyte, photographer.'

'Nuh. I can't see Valerie, well, cutting loose enough to get in trouble.'

'How's that?'

'She's a bit uptight, that's all.'

Although Solomon was dangerously fanatical rather than uptight, he gave Blyte a question mark, too, then moved on.

'Your boss, Mike Jones?'

'You know Mike, John. You've known him for years.'

'I know most of the people in this town.'

'But you know *Mike*. If it meant a juicy story, he'd potentially cross the line, but otherwise he's pretty straight.'

'*Pretty* straight?'

'Well, if he found a hundred bucks on the street, he wouldn't rush to the police station to hand it in. But he's kept me and the others in a job, the paper running and done heaps for the community. He can't be your man.'

She sat back and crossed her arms.

'Never say can't,' Franklin cautioned. 'Who does typesetting, copy editing, that type of thing?'

She laughed. 'You've got no idea about newspapers, have you? Mike does all the editing, I do most of the writing, with him doing the occasional piece, and we outsource the printing and distribution these days.'

'So this is it?' He flicked the page.

'Pretty much,' McGuire said. 'There's Mike's youngest, Brodie, who helps out. Though, help is being generous. And leading up to a special edition, everyone pitches in –'

'But nobody else is a regular?'

'A few others do columns or feed us sports updates and so on, but they write their rough draft and email it to Mike, who polishes it. They generally don't come into the office.'

Franklin pondered. He reckoned Solomon had met each of the victims, at least briefly. It had to be one of the *Advocate*'s core workers. Unless his theory sucked, which'd mean he'd be back to square one: the medical angle.

'I'll need addresses and phone numbers for Harry, Rebekka and Valerie.'

As McGuire scrawled the details, Franklin examined her handwriting. He couldn't imagine anything more poles apart with Solomon's calligraphic compositions. Where the poison-pen writer left a large margin around his rigid words, the journalist covered all available space in a scrawling script littered with crossings-out, i's without dots and t-bars that drifted to the right.

Just as he'd thought, she wasn't the crook.

Thus, it was *what* she wrote, not how, that made him jump from his chair, saying, 'Thanks, Jen. You've been a help.'

He left her spluttering.

———

Because of the immediate dividends at Shirley's Hair, Georgie cursed herself for not heading straight to Trafalgar that morning, instead of plugging useless searches into her computer. Then she drove until she found a pub several kilometres before Willow Grove.

Plonked in no-man's land with a bunch of sad-looking vehicles outside, it was surrounded by large landholdings with no visible housing. But Georgie backed herself. The second-best source of inside information in country towns, after the hairdresser, was always the pub.

She plumped her cleavage and courage and entered the building. She walked into a thick fug of body odour and alcohol fumes. Georgie ignored the pong and bawdy comments and propped herself at the bar.

It wasn't hard to catch the bartender's attention; he was drooling along with his patrons.

Guess they don't get too many women here.

She ordered a pot with her best coy smile.

From there, the publican melted to putty. She launched into her inquiry, he clueless to being played. He knew Helena Watkowska and Georgie wheedled the address and directions from him. Admittedly, she'd insinuated she'd revisit for a drink.

He'd get over the disappointment.

———

The bloody mobile rang. Franklin fumbled for it without slowing his stride.

It was Heddo from Ballarat's CIU. *'Got a tick? You want an update on this Pentecoste thing?'*

Raindrops fell thick and heavy in a fresh downpour. The temperature had plummeted. Franklin eased into the Commodore and cranked the engine and wipers.

'Hang on, mate,' Heddo said.

There were muffled sounds as his buddy covered the mouthpiece. While Franklin waited, he noticed that the inclement weather caught out tourists in short sleeves and flimsy pants or skirts. They scurried for shelter shooting livid glances skyward. He chuckled.

'First sign of madness, Franklin.'

'Huh?'

'Talking to yourself; or laughing at your own jokes.' Heddo barked a laugh. *'Righty oh. Let's keep this fair. What're you offering in exchange for my info?'*

'I don't have time to play games,' Franklin complained.

'Who does?' Heddo retorted. *'C'mon, I'll give you an update if you tell me what the go is with this Georgie?'*

'I really don't have time,' Franklin said. 'We'll keep that for a beer soon, okay?'

The detective sighed. *'I suppose.'*

He sounded like Kat. Drama Queen.

'Mate.' Heddo's tone was serious now. *'We've had these hommies in our face for days. It's driving us barmy. They don't tell us plebs much at all, you know how it is. What I do*

have as fact is that one Tony Scott and his pal Les Broadbent left their dabs all over Margaret's house.'

'Holy shit.' Franklin squeezed his eyes against an instant headache. Fingerprints don't get inside a person's home by themselves.

'Recognise the names?'

'I'll say. Cronies of Schlicht.'

'Got it in one. Besides that, it's bare-bones stuff. Margaret's death is estimated at midnight, give or take four hours.'

'So, even as early as eight on Wednesday night?'

'Yep, although everything's leaning more towards midnight or so. Cause of death was as guessed: strangulation with heavy-duty picture wire or similar. Nasty way to go and right up the alley of Scott and Broadbent. It looks like they picked the lock on the back door and took Margaret by surprise. She didn't put up much of a struggle, but then these guys would've easily overpowered her. The hommies're hoping for more forensics to seal the deal against Schlicht's buddies but reckon they'll piece it together either way. Of course, the perps aren't to be seen.'

Heddo flicked through a notebook or file, then continued, *'Oh, one of the other neighbours confirmed Megan Frawley's report of a vehicle outside Margaret's home sometime around midnight to one-ish, and although she was equally vague, it will help make our case. Broadbent drives an F-150, which tallies with reports of a big ute rumbling like a truck. Apart from all that, there's not much else for you.'*

'Any headway on Susan at your end?'

'Nope. I heard there've been a couple of possible sightings that've turned out to be nothing. I guess you know the hot shots from Melbourne have taken that over too? Yep,

well, I'll keep my eyes and ears peeled and give you a buzz if I hear something around the traps. Okey-dokey?'

'Sure. I owe you a beer.'

'Nuh. You owe me two,' his mate said and laughed.

———

Georgie took a left at *the really big tree*, a quick right at a bunch of roadside mailboxes, the best being the arse of a pink pig. After a hairpin bend, she steered to the right of the road's Y and travelled for *about two minutes*, wondering whether to time it on her speed or *Driving Miss Daisy*'s. Similar cryptic instructions brought her to a substantial but plain brick home bordered by three-foot-deep garden beds. Amazingly, it matched the bartender's description.

———

Franklin stared out the windscreen. Heddo's news rocked him.

Broadbent and Scott's connection to Margaret's murder scared him shitless for Susan's welfare. It seemed that her obsessive pursuit for truth about her husband had somehow triggered her niece's demise. Worse, Susan could go the same way as Roly and Margaret. He rejected the addendum *if she hasn't already* and substituted *if I don't find her first*.

As the rain ceased, he gained a second wind. He drove the few short blocks to Camp Street and past the police station.

On the same stretch was the manse belonging to the declining Presbyterian Church. The original manse, that is; it had been converted into a swanky boutique hotel when Daylesford became Victoria's short-stay capital. When the novelty of running the B&B had worn off and real estate skyrocketed, the owners then split the grand building into expensive apartments and on-sold.

Within a stroll of that and the church was the new manse, a humble miner's cottage notable for a garden that provided a riot of colour and fragrance year round. Out the front, Franklin yanked on the handbrake and jumped from his car.

———

As Georgie hit the doorbell, Franklin's warning echoed. She was empty-handed at the door of the Iceman's estranged wife. She had left her bag, including her mobile phone, in the Spider and told no one her destination or expected return time. Worse still, so concentrated on finding Watkowska, Georgie hadn't prepared a script.

The thrill of adventure shifted to angst.

CHAPTER THIRTY-FIVE

THE DOORBELL DREW NO RESPONSE; LIKEWISE Franklin's bangs on the front door. Exasperated, he fought his way through a dense garden bed and had to extract rose thorns from his jeans. He peered through the living room window and bombed out. The front bedroom window yielded nothing either. He rapped on the rear door and tried its handle, then swore in immense frustration.

Every time he made progress, something got in the way.

———

Georgie focused on Pam Stewart, Ruby Padley and Susan Pentecoste. Three warm, extraordinary women, all very different – she owed it to them to persevere.

A swipe of clammy palms on jeans, then she wrapped arms across her chest against the sudden autumn chill and the more invasive one inside.

She inhaled.

Right, I'm ready. Bring it on.

———

Franklin jogged to the church, up the steep, curved steps and into the shadows of the gothic building. The heavy timber door sat ajar. He squeezed through it, suddenly doubting the intelligence of his bull-in-a-china-shop approach.

He scanned the empty pews, the choir stalls, the mute organ. Rich timberwork glowed with beeswax. Pungent blooms filled old-fashioned vases. A book lay open on the altar.

'You're either a little too late or much too early.'

The voice startled him. He glanced towards the pulpit and saw a smiling bloke with a shiny billiard-ball crown.

'I'm sorry if I gave you a scare.' The fellow descended the small stairway.

Franklin took in the dog collar and ebony smock over pants of a similar hue. 'Not at all, sir, ah, Reverend.'

'Malcolm will do fine,' the minister said and reached out to shake hands.

In his civvies, unsure whether to make this official, he merely said, 'John Franklin.'

'So, John, did you miss this morning's service, or are you early for next Sunday's? Hmm, perhaps you've come for private counsel?'

'None of the above,' Franklin admitted, a tad sheepish. 'Are you on your own here?'

'Yes, there's just me at present. I rather enjoy this time alone on a Sunday. Just me and the Big Man.'

'Sorry for the intrusion, sir...Malcolm.'

'No, don't misunderstand. As the old saying goes, my door is always open. If it weren't for my parishioners and the community, I wouldn't have my role to play and this beautiful church would go the way of many and be sold for redevelopment.'

'Like the old manse?'

'Yes,' Malcolm agreed. A frown tugged his brow. 'So, you haven't yet told me how I can be of help.'

'Well, I hoped to find your housekeeper here.'

'Why?' His tone was sharp. 'No trouble I trust.'

'Why would you say that?' Adrenaline flooded through Franklin.

Yes, I'm on the right track!

When he'd scanned McGuire's list and spotted Valerie Blyte's address as the manse, the jump seemed obvious. They sought a religious nut, where better to find one? He could well have proved Lunny right that *to assume was to make an ass of u and me*. But instead of humiliating himself, he seemed to have hit pay dirt after all.

The minister cut across his thoughts. 'You are a policeman aren't you, John?'

'How'd you know that?'

Malcolm tapped his right nostril and smiled. 'Experience, intuition – and I've seen you in the newspaper and about town in your uniform often enough over the past years. Even here for the odd wedding and funeral.'

The men laughed, then the minister sobered. 'Can you tell me what the trouble is?'

'Not at this stage, sir. Any idea of where to look?'

'You've tried the manse and garden, I take it? Well, then, no such luck, I'm afraid. Valerie and I generally come together for early tea, but the time after service is our own.'

The minister took a few steps, tidied a stack of flyers and said, 'I'm done for the present. I'll see you out.'

They walked to the front door.

A brief slash of lightning illuminated the granite

horizon. Lost in thought, Franklin flinched when Malcolm gripped his forearm.

'Have you any news on Susan, John?'

So, the town knew that Susan Pentecoste was officially missing. Surely too, then, they were aware of her niece's murder.

Franklin shook his head and dodged the minister's distressed gaze. He felt guilty. He'd failed Susan and, with that, the community. If only he'd paid proper attention to Georgie Harvey first up.

'We prayed for her safe return this morning. She and Roly were part of our congregation since the day they moved to Hepburn, long before I came. Since Roly's... passing, Susan's seldom missed a service. Even throughout that most trying period, when I'll admit *my* faith wavered, she remained steadfast.'

He stopped. His stare magnetised Franklin until their eyes met. 'There's nothing that any one of my flock wouldn't do for Susan. Bring her home safe, John.'

I can't make that promise.

'I'll try. Of course, we're all doing our best.'

It sounded trite, even to him.

'But is our best as ordinary people good enough?' the minister commented, more cynically than Franklin expected – or thought appropriate.

'I couldn't say,' Franklin replied, although the question had been rhetorical.

———

Georgie heard fast-approaching footsteps. No chance to retreat now.

A woman opened the main door and peered through the security screen.

'Hello?'

'Hi there,' Georgie said with false brightness. 'Are you Helena Watkowska?'

'Yes,' the woman replied. She tilted her head sideways.

'Uh, can I come in? I'd like a chat.'

'You're not the media or here to sell me a thing I do not need?'

Georgie raised her hands. 'No. It's a personal matter.'

Helena wavered.

'Please.'

The woman must have sensed sincerity. She admitted Georgie, although with an uncertain smile.

Inside the hallway, they shook hands, with Helena returning a firm grip. She was large, more solid and sturdy than fat, and topped Georgie by three or so inches. Apart from a white apron, she wore a leopard-print blouse and black crepe pants with black low-heeled shoes. A thin gold chain with a crucifix circled her neck. Wavy brown hair with wisps of grey hugged a strongly featured face devoid of makeup.

Georgie thought handsome described Helena, and she judged her non-threatening, despite her powerful physique. With a mental slap she reserved judgment. Old-school dress style and cross hanging on her neck didn't mean much. She needed to be wary of Helena Watkowska.

'I was putting a cake in the oven. Would you mind?'

Georgie followed Helena into the kitchen. Oddly not out of place among the blond wood, stone and stainless steel sat an old pine rocking chair in one corner, to which Helena signalled her.

'What would you wish to drink? I can offer tea, coffee,

lemonade, fruit juice...or something stronger, perhaps?' Though she spoke excellent English, it was thick with a European accent and formality foreign to most Australians.

Careful. This ain't no Pam Stewart.

Georgie accepted lemonade.

She watched Helena scrape the cake mixture into a tin, which stirred childhood memories. She and her sister, Erin, used to fight over who licked the beaters or the mixing bowl, especially if they were baking a chocolate cake or lemon meringue pie. That was long ago, when time stretched to infinity, before the days and years went on fast-forward.

Time, fast-forward; the current-day race against the clock.

Georgie glanced sharply at Helena, who pulled up a stool beside her.

Drops of rain struck the large kitchen window.

'It is not the most beautiful day for a drive, is it?' The woman tented her fingers. 'I am sure you have not driven all this way to share lemonade with me.'

'No,' Georgie admitted. 'Look. I don't know how to put this.' She hesitated.

Her host lifted her palms. The gesture implied *Just say it*.

'I'm trying to locate Susan Pentecoste for her girlfriends Ruby and Pam and wondered if she's been in contact with you recently.'

'*Locate* Susan?' Helena echoed.

Not: Who is Susan Pentecoste!

'So you do know who I'm talking about?'

'Yes.'

'Has she been in touch?'

'Susan has telephoned on a number of occasions and also came to see me. Twice, as a matter of fact. She found me through a friend of a friend. It is remarkable how the country grapevine works, yes?'

Georgie said excitedly, 'Go on.'

'Well, on the first visit she came with her niece, Margaret.' Helena halted, then queried, 'You know Margaret?'

Only in death didn't seem appropriate. Georgie shook her head.

'Well, Margaret and I did not get along. She is...bossy, a bit strong? She would not let Susan and I talk freely. We found it very frustrating. It is that way with some people, is it not?'

Helena sighed. 'Susan, on the other hand, she is a very nice lady. We get along very well.'

Get: present tense. Good sign.

Georgie nodded encouragingly and stuffed a biscuit into her mouth. The buttery shortbread melted on her tongue.

'So, you see, Susan returned without Margaret. And we had a very good talk. We are already good friends. If I may say, she is quite like you, Georgie. A person with a nice... feeling around them.'

Georgie had heard plenty of adjectives describing her. A *nice feeling* about her didn't top the list. Sassy, fiery and unpredictable closely followed moody on what AJ called the Harvey Scale and all preceded the more complimentary categories of sexy and smart.

Was the woman bullshitting her? Why?

She ignored the personal tangent. 'You were saying about Susan...?'

Helena's expression hardened. She demanded, 'Why do you ask all this?'

Georgie scrutinised her, still uncertain. 'Just trying to

get in touch with Susan.'

'Oh?' Helena wasn't satisfied.

'Can you remember when she came to see you?'

'Yes, of course. The first time, when they came together...ah, Thursday week ago. We only had part of the day and a little the next morning because of Margaret's business commitments, and they were attending a dance on Friday evening.'

'And?'

'On the Saturday, my son Michael and his girlfriend were coming to dinner. I offered to change my plans or was more than happy for Susan to join us, but she was unhappy to impose. So, she returned late Sunday morning and stayed overnight. We enjoyed much of Monday together also. She promised to call me soon, to invite me to visit her home. I am looking forward to it...' Helena broke off.

Georgie watched emotion cloud her host's eyes.

Helena's next words were tremulous. 'She is missing?'

Georgie ducked the question, by asking her own. 'Did she mention her plans?'

'Not in detail. Margaret could tell you where Susan is.'

Georgie cleared her throat. 'That isn't possible.'

'Why not?'

Georgie puffed her cheeks. She stammered, 'Margaret, well, I found Margaret... The thing is, she's been murdered.'

'Pardon?' Helena's face drained.

'We—her neighbour and I, that is—found her two days ago. She was strangled, with...' Georgie shuddered, reliving the discovery. 'It happened around midnight on—' She stared at her host. 'Are you okay? Helena?'

Georgie jumped off her stool as the woman's eyes rolled and her lips tinged blue-purple. 'Helena!'

She grabbed her hand. Icy. She felt a feeble answering

squeeze and lowered the woman to the floor. She pushed a cushion under Helena's legs, loosened her blouse, placed her own jacket over Helena's torso and talked in a monotone.

Those dreary OH&S materials Georgie had written had exposed her to basic first-aid skills she'd never wanted to put into practice. Two near-faints in three days didn't bode well.

———

Franklin pondered the minister's words as he sat inside the Commodore. He battled the opposing forces of worry for Susan Pentecoste and obligation to apprehend Solomon. Both cases involved dangerous obsessions. One was a waiting game until they struck a lead. The other he could action without delay.

He turned the ignition and tried to visualise himself as Solomon. Where would she go?

Franklin dialled Christina van Hoeckel. No developments.

Next: Tayla Birkley. She, too, was fine, spending a quiet Sunday with her parents.

He figured Solomon had already realised her mistake in targeting Lauren Morris and Renee Archer, both in long-term relationships with their babies' fathers.

That left Cathy Jones.

———

Colour seeped back into Helena's skin. After a few minutes, she sat up.

'If you would help me off the ground please, Georgie,'

Helena said, her tone revealing she despised weakness in herself.

She brushed away Georgie's fuss, saying, 'So, then you are in truth here to ask why Susan came to see me? To see how that relates to poor Margaret. But I suspect that you have an inkling or you would not be here, yes?' She nodded at her own assumption. 'Likewise, I do not think you are very interested in all the little things that we talked about. The recipes we exchanged, gardening tips...'

Georgie opened her mouth.

Helena held up a finger. 'Susan and I have much in common. We have both lived without our husbands at length and become accustomed to our own company. Oh, my son does his duty, but he rarely has time for me these days, except for Saturday dinner.

'I am sure you know that my husband is...the *infamous* John Schlicht, yes? But before he became that man, we were childhood sweethearts back home, in Germany.'

That explained the accent.

'My parents wouldn't let us marry until I turned twenty-five, and a few years later, we migrated to Australia. Little Michael soon arrived, and we were happy for those early years.'

Helena broke off. She gazed through the window.

The rain fell harder.

Georgie let the silence hang.

———

Franklin checked his notebook and plugged Cathy's landline number into his phone. There was a small pause, then it started to ring. Five rings became ten. After a few more, it turned to pips as the call rang out.

Which meant nothing in itself. She and Tyson could be out for the day. Or they could have fled back to her sister's commune in Gordon. When they'd touched base yesterday, Cathy had been home in Daylesford and apparently cast off her stalker suspicions. Maybe her uncertainty returned.

Franklin dialled her mobile.

On the seventh ring, he could've sworn the call was answered, yet no one spoke. The line stayed open for a few seconds, then disconnected.

He redialled. It went straight to message bank, so he left an urgent request for Cathy to call. Drummed his fingers on the steering wheel.

He gunned the car and pulled the wheel, accelerating too hard for the wet conditions. The Commodore fishtailed, but Franklin scarcely noticed.

CHAPTER THIRTY-SIX

Eventually, Helena spoke again. 'The hardest thing I have ever done was ask John to leave us.'

The hardest thing?

Helena missed Georgie's incredulous expression and continued, 'You see, I have never stopped loving him. He was a good husband and father with just us. But I could not condone his business side. I could not have my baby grow up near his associates. They were bad men, and the man John is while he is with them...he is a stranger to me.'

'So, you think of him as a Jekyll and Hyde?' Georgie couldn't control her sarcasm.

'It is hard for you young women of today to understand.'

'Well, yeah. I do find it hard to get my head around.'

He's a fucking murderer for openers.

'No offence to you, Helena, but I don't see any redeeming features in your husband.'

'That's because you do not know him and perhaps because you don't have the same expectations of marriage, children...caring for the family home. You have careers, choices. My generation, particularly those with conservative parents and from very traditional towns, which was my upbringing, we were raised to be good wives and mothers.

'John too was...' she clicked her fingers, searching for the right phrase, 'hard-working in providing for his family. It is unfortunate how he chose to do that – that's why I had to distance Michael and me from it all.'

This time Georgie hesitated, weighing the duty to speak her mind versus social conventions.

Then she exploded, '*Unfortunate* is not a word I'd use either. Becoming a major player in Melbourne's underworld isn't comparable to settling for mowing lawns despite wanting to be a landscape gardener.'

'He's not a bad man –'

Helena's cheeks were red-spotted.

'We must have different dictionaries.'

Georgie felt flushed too.

They stared at each other. Georgie refused to apologise for being blunt.

The woman clasped her hands and held them to her lips. Praying? Or controlling her anger? Whichever, it was intense enough that her knuckles turned white.

'Excuse me.' She left the room.

———

Georgie stiffened. Helena was passionate and powerfully built for her age. She'd be no pushover, particularly if she came back armed.

The scent of baking cake rose from the oven. Normally it would make Georgie's mouth water. Now, it made her stomach acids churn.

She didn't know what to do. Should she stand with the

island bar between them? Wood and granite, that thing wouldn't move in a hurry and could be a good safety barrier.

'I'm sorry.'

Helena spoke softly, but in her tense state, Georgie jumped.

The older woman hovered in the doorway. Her eyes were puffy, and she sounded tired or sad or both.

'I cannot expect you to understand, but I will always love my husband.'

'We'll agree to disagree then,' Georgie paused. She heard those words echo in the voice of John Franklin. When did he say them? Two or three days ago?

She pulled her mind to the present as Helena dropped onto the other seat. 'So you're separated but not divorced, and you still love him.'

She tried not to sound judgmental but wasn't sure she succeeded.

'Yes, that is correct. Yes, we keep in touch. Regularly. And yes, once he is released from jail, he will visit with us here. I will not see him in jail, and I do not go to his home. That is our rule. He comes to us, Michael and me.'

'Why?'

Helena shrugged. 'He is a different man with just us. I told you that.' Her tone was sharp.

Unease washed over Georgie anew. 'Sorry, go on.'

'Susan wanted to know more about my John, too. She thinks he was responsible for Roland's...disappearance. I told her I do not read about or get involved in my husband's business affairs –'

'Business affairs,' Georgie mocked, then wished she'd held her tongue.

'Yes! His business affairs. That is how I think of it. I told

Susan I will not question him on her behalf, as much as I'm fond of her. She was disappointed but gracious.'

'What did Susan gain from talking to you?'

Helena flinched, insulted.

'I didn't mean it that way,' Georgie apologised. 'What I meant was, did you help her directly? Did she become reconciled regarding Roly, or did you...' She trailed off.

'I see what you mean, but I am not convinced I helped her.'

'Oh?'

'We talked about John and the very little I know of his other life. When he is freed, I believe he will revert to his property in Castlemaine. He does much of his business in Melbourne, but he prefers the country lifestyle for the solitude, the privacy. We both prefer the country.'

'Yet you live on the opposite side of Victoria.'

'Yes, I needed distance.'

'What else did you tell Susan?' Georgie prompted.

'She left me calm, but I do not think she has given up on finding what happened to Roland. She needs to bury him, farewell him. And I quite understand.' Helena felt the crucifix at her throat.

Georgie eyed the pendant. Religion had never helped her. She'd tried it after her dad's diagnosis; he'd still died. And it hadn't made his death any easier to sit in a damn church and pray.

She worried that Helena would start Bible-thumping. Instead, the woman remained silent.

Is this going to be yet another wasted day?

Georgie asked, 'Did Susan mention where she was going after she left here Monday?'

'She was returning to Margaret's.' Helena's eyes stretched with horror. 'Perhaps...'

'Perhaps, what?' Georgie urged.

'Perhaps she intends to go to John's property.'

'In Castlemaine?'

'*Near* Castlemaine. You see, it was as though she was gathering all the little pieces I shared of John and filing them away. She showed interest in where he lived. I told her where it is – well, best I could, as I have never been there myself. I do know it's on Rampage Road. I didn't think anything of it at that point. But reflecting back, she was keen to hear more.'

'It wouldn't be too difficult to find,' Georgie mused. 'We both found you easily enough, and this time she had the street name from the start.' Struck by a thought, she clenched her jaw.

Helena watched her.

'I really hope she hasn't gone to Schlicht's.'

'But he is in jail,' Helena protested.

'Yeah, but is the place empty? Did he live there alone?' Georgie blurted out.

Helena recoiled. 'I have no right to ask.'

'Well, I didn't specifically mean did he live with another woman. But now that you mention it...'

Georgie visualised the French woman with a vicious streak Bill Noonan described. She was curious whether Schlicht's lover was another taboo subject for his wife.

Her lips pursed, Helena stayed silent.

Eventually she said, 'I suspect he would have company. He is very much a man, with a man's needs.'

'I'm sorry to offend you. But if we're going to help Susan, we have to get inside her head.'

Helena nodded.

'We have to work out what she's gotten herself involved in.'

Georgie's statement hung.

Helena fidgeted her worn gold wedding band.

Georgie paced the length of the kitchen.

When their eyes met, Helena's fear seared Georgie's sockets. For a woman who determinedly thought the best of her husband and tried to ignore his business associates and activities, Helena appeared mighty worried for her new pal.

For Georgie, the discovery of Margaret Pentecoste's body and attempted break-in at her motel unit were too fresh, Bill Noonan's information too scary, even John Franklin's warning that morning to consider who they dealt with too apt for the idea of a lone middle-aged woman snooping around Schlicht's property to be agreeable.

Though the Iceman was behind bars, his associates loomed large.

———

'Cathy!' Franklin thumped the front door.

He tested the handle. Locked.

Drapes covered the windows. Franklin pressed his ear to the glass. He couldn't discern sound or movement.

He ran next door and raised his fist to bang the metal screen. It immediately opened to a white-haired woman, as short as she was plump.

'Yes, John?' she said.

Franklin recognised the lollipop lady who regulated traffic at the primary school crossing. 'Marnie, do you know if Cathy Jones is home?'

'Why, you've missed her by a few moments.'

'Was she alone?'

'With Tyson, of course. She wouldn't –'

Franklin interrupted. 'Anyone else with them?'

'Yes, as a matter of fact. Valerie – you know, Valerie Blyte from the op shop and Presy Church? She was carrying young Tyson. He must have a terrible cold, the poor mite.'

'Why's that?' Franklin frowned.

'Well, he was bundled up in layer upon layer of bunny rugs, but I caught a glimpse of his face. Crying his poor little lungs out and turning more beetroot by the second.'

He felt chilled. 'What was Cathy doing?'

'She followed Valerie to her car, talking very...' She gesticulated in lieu of finishing the sentence. 'I don't *think* they were arguing. Valerie seemed to be ignoring Cathy, focusing everything on the little tacker. Oh, I shouldn't tell you this, being a policeman and all, I wouldn't want Valerie to get in trouble.'

She's potentially done that herself.

'Go on.'

'She made Cathy drive. Valerie got in the back with the baby – behind Cathy.'

'And?' he pressed.

'You see, I don't think they put their seatbelts on. And Valerie doesn't have a baby seat in her car, so Tyson wasn't restrained properly.'

Almost laughable. If failure to restrain a child was Valerie Blyte's worst offence, he'd be a happy man.

'Which way'd they go, Marnie?'

She chewed her thumbnail. 'I'm not sure. Towards the church?'

Not for the first time, Franklin silently cursed the public's ineptitude for observation.

He turned to leave, but Marnie was saying, 'Well, she wouldn't have a car seat. She's been on her own for ages. Longer than me. Hold on, in actual fact, I wouldn't be

363

surprised if she does have a kiddie seat. I think she keeps all her old baby things in Mr Malcolm's shed.'

His gut reacted with a flip.

Baby things. In the minister's shed.

'Have her children left home?'

'What? Oh, no. She never had a child of her own. Wanted one desperately but she and Edward were never blessed – if blessed is the right word for youngsters these days.'

Oh, shit.

One of his theories fit: Solomon couldn't have a child.

'When you said *on her own –*'

'I meant widowed. Edward passed away well over ten years ago.'

Married woman desperate for a kid. Since widowed and too old to have one. Sees unmarried women having what she craves. And a religious nut on top of all that.

Marnie leaned in. Her face crinkled. She loved to gossip. 'Do you remember Edward?'

He gave a headshake as his mind raced.

Jealousy and conviction: motive. Position with the Advocate: *opportunity.*

'He killed himself.' She straightened theatrically. 'Well, *rumour* has it that he did. He drowned in the Hepburn Dam.'

Now Franklin recalled the case. Edward's death was ruled an accidental drowning, but many held their suspicions, among them Bill Noonan, who'd handled the local end. Edward had been an introspective man and suffered mild anxiety but wasn't on suicide watch, according to his doctor. His wife, Valerie, contested allegations of suicide, and the Coroner agreed – or lacked sufficient evidence to find otherwise.

'She never remarried?' Franklin asked Marnie, anxious to leave but morbidly fascinated by the way things clicked together.

'No and never will. She's as good as a nun these days. If she didn't need the income, she wouldn't take happy snaps for the *Advocate*. She'd rather spend all her life wrapped in the cotton wool of the church. She hasn't glanced at another man since Edward's passing. Not in *that* way.'

'And they were desperate for kids?'

'More fool them, but yes,' Marnie said good-naturedly; it was public knowledge that she didn't operate the school crossing for pocket money alone and was the proud matriarch of a substantial clan.

No time to waste.

'What does Valerie drive?'

'A white compact. I'm not sure what type.'

'I've gotta fly, but you've been a great help,' Franklin yelled, sprinting.

'Will you let me –'

The growl of the Commodore as Franklin floored it for Camp Street drowned the rest of Marnie's sentence.

CHAPTER THIRTY-SEVEN

GEORGIE DROVE WITH HER MIND PREOCCUPIED WITH calculations.

It was fifteen days since Susan Pentecoste's aborted telephone conversation with Ruby Padley that Saturday and about as long since she'd spoken to Bill and Gabby Noonan and the Pattersons next door.

After her court hearing the following Friday, Georgie—reluctantly at first—had answered Ruby's cry for help. Only nine days ago. It seemed much longer. With each minute, she became more wound up.

———

Franklin registered a small white Toyota parked outside the church.

Valerie Blyte's.

Empty.

He jogged to the front door. His hand unconsciously dropped hip-side to the phantom gun holster. AWOL along with his capsicum spray and baton, he was about to enter the worst type of incident—a volatile situation involving an infant—unarmed and without backup. Foolhardy.

But every second could save a life. Or lose one.

'...my baby,' Franklin heard Cathy say.

He crouched and eased the door until it was wide enough to squeeze through.

'You don't deserve a child,' another female said, presumably Valerie Blyte. 'People like you,' she dripped disdain, 'don't deserve children.'

Franklin held his breath. Counted to five and moved through the doorway. He dropped behind the last pew on the left.

'Please, give me my baby,' Cathy said, speaking low.

Franklin realised she'd instinctively modulated her tone to decelerate Blyte's aggression. He peered down the aisle towards the altar. The book had been moved, but it was otherwise as he'd last seen it.

He ducked.

———

At Trafalgar, Georgie nosed the Spider towards Melbourne. A ute trailed too closely. She tapped the brakes, forcing him to pull back, and returned her thoughts to Susan.

Last Monday, Georgie reported Susan's disappearance to John Franklin, the arrogant cop at Daylesford. On that same day, Helena Watkowska farewelled her new friend, who was ostensibly about to return to Margaret's home in Ballarat.

Two days later, Megan Frawley had sherry with Susan. That made her the last living person to see Susan before she vanished – that Georgie knew of.

Before Susan was abducted? Murdered?

———

'No! What makes you think you deserve this child? You aren't virtuous, a righteous woman. You're a slut, a whore. You had this child out of wedlock, you suck the community dry.'

'It's not like that. I'm not like that. You've got it wrong. Why are you doing this to us?'

Franklin heard footsteps while Cathy talked, and her voice changed direction. He peeked over the top of the pew and stooped again. He'd seen enough. Cathy stood next to the pulpit and looked up at Valerie Blyte, who held the howling baby over the lectern. Not as Franklin expected her to hold a fragile life but as though she would catapult Tyson at any moment.

She also brandished a knife.

He needed to get closer. The pews were open-base style; he could tunnel under them. It was imperative not to alert Blyte to his approach. Whatever had pushed her to this point, she still hovered between words and actions.

His presence could push her into the abyss and cost Tyson's life.

———

Vanished, abducted, murdered; the words stung Georgie. She drove numbly until she checked her rear-view mirror.

'Get off my tail, you moron.'

The ute continued to tailgate, a mere foot or so from the Spider's bumper. Georgie was pissed off but determined not to overreact as she had to yesterday's logging truck episode, and her anxiety for Susan absorbed her again.

She noticed the prematurely dark sky. Drizzle would

soon intensify into another storm. The driver behind flicked on his headlights. High beam or set wrong? White spheres blinded Georgie.

She looked away, fixed her eyes forward and her mind on Susan's plans and whereabouts. As to the four-day gap that followed Megan's last meeting with Susan, her best mate Pam Stewart was clueless, her niece Margaret's lips were sealed, and new acquaintance Helena either didn't know or pretended not to.

———

'Please, tell me why you're like this.'

Dead air.

Cathy altered tack. 'What's your real name – it's obviously not Solomon.'

Good girl, Cathy. Keep her talking. Keep her calm.

'Mrs Edward Blyte.'

'What's *your* name, Mrs Blyte? Not your husband's.'

Franklin fancied Cathy had edged forward but dared not check.

'That's what's wrong with you people. You don't respect marriage today. I respect my husband and my marriage.'

'How long have you and Edward been married?' Cathy's higher-than-normal pitch revealed her strain.

'We would have been married twenty-four years this September. But I lost my Edward twelve years ago.'

'I'm so sorry, Mrs Blyte.' After a pause, Cathy said, 'You've been a widow as long as you were a wife. That must be very difficult for you and your family. Your children –'

'Hah. We couldn't have children. Not like you people. You procreate like mice, yet Christians like Edward and I, who could give children a good home, were not blessed.'

'Tyson has a good home with me, Mrs Blyte. I'm not promiscuous, I do believe in marriage and kids having role models.'

'Then why aren't you married?' Blyte demanded.

Franklin halted, struck by Cathy's pain.

At length, she said, 'I've only told one other person in this town, Mrs Blyte. I was date-raped.'

'That's simply a fancy word for leading a man on and changing your mind.'

'No!' Cathy's one word held so much emotion. 'No, it's not like that.' Her tone dropped. She pleaded, 'I'm a good mum. Tyson's happy.'

'...not fair.'

Blyte's muffled reply barely reached Franklin as he burrowed through the pews. Could her hands be over her face? Or one hand, as she gripped the baby with the other?

He wondered about the knife.

'What's not fair, Mrs Blyte?'

'I was a good wife, a good Christian. I've done everything right. You don't see me cavorting with other men. I still love my husband – almost equally to God.'

Her words hung, then Blyte continued, 'I wanted children very much. I used to picture them with Edward and me, us all holding hands on our way to service. It was so real. I could feel their cuddles...and so much love. But then I was punished. First by taking my children, then my Edward. And I don't understand *why*.'

'Do you blame God?'

'No. I don't know. I'm confused. Stop talking. What's that?'

Franklin froze. He'd knocked a hymn book to the floor.

Georgie couldn't shake off doubt about Helena's reliability. Their meeting felt too easy; Helena had answered her questions with little resistance.

It troubled Georgie that she lived like an ostrich, with her head stuck in the sand about her criminal husband. How far would her loyalty go? Would she lie for him? Would she kill for him? Had she killed Susan and lied to Georgie from go to whoa?

———

'Mrs Blyte, please put it down! Point it away from Tyson. *Please.*'

Franklin's heart thudded. Should he break cover?

Then, Cathy spoke again, more calmly. 'You took a photo of us in hospital, didn't you? Have you always enjoyed photography?'

'My husband gave me a camera as a wedding present. It was my hobby. When he died, I had to go to work. I'd never worked outside the home before. My job had been to provide a good home for my husband, and then suddenly I needed an income. Apart from cleaning and photography, what else could I do?

'I clean the manse and church for the minister in exchange for my room and board. These days, I don't take photographs for pleasure. My photography pays for my essentials and fits in around working at the opportunity shop and helping with meals on wheels.'

'If your religion means so much to you, why are you doing this then? Why are you persecuting single mums? Me and Tyson?'

'Because you people won't listen.' Blyte's voice rose. 'I

warned you all, but you haven't changed your ways. That Christina is a rat, having sex willy-nilly.'

'But that's Christina, not me, or the rest of us,' Cathy corrected gently.

Franklin reached the third row from the front. He approached from the opposite side of Cathy and hoped she locked Valerie's attention.

'I warned her. Then the next thing, she is seeing yet another man and strutting with her breasts on display like a prostitute. She's fooling with *married* men. She's a home-wrecker.'

'So, what were you doing when you threw a rock through her window?'

'How do you –'

'Were you symbolically stoning the adulterous woman?' Cathy overrode Blyte. 'I don't get it... How can you justify what you've done?'

Cathy, back off. Don't make her angry again.

In the ominous silence Franklin hunkered at the front row. Before him stood a three-foot-high wall of panelling. He must break cover in order to reach the pulpit. If Blyte turned away from Cathy, she would see him.

———

'Fucking hell.' Georgie belted the Spider's dashboard. 'Who can I trust? What the hell's going on? Where is Susan?'

Tight hands gripped the steering wheel. And Georgie drove oblivious to the cars around her, the landscape that whizzed past, even the hail that pelted the soft-top and windscreen.

———

'No!' Cathy yelled.

Franklin was drenched in sweat. It sounded as though Blyte had upped the ante. If he showed himself, it could push her into the murderous chasm. On the other hand, the longer he delayed, the longer it left Tyson at incalculable risk.

'*Please*. Give me my baby. No matter what you think of me, Tyson hasn't done anything wrong.'

'He's on the road to death, as are the rest of the bastards.'

'No, he's not. Give…him…to…me,' Cathy commanded.

Franklin rose, vaulted the panel. He saw Cathy snatch Tyson. She kicked Blyte, her eyes fixed on her antagonist's.

'POLICE!' Franklin yelled. 'Valerie Blyte, stop! Cathy, move away.'

Blyte hunched, dropped the knife, clasped her groin with both hands.

She turned to Franklin, didn't see Cathy heave her knee. The woman's nose smashed with a crack and spray of vivid blood.

Cathy clutched Tyson to her left side and slammed her heel into the bridge of Blyte's foot. Once, twice…

Franklin kicked away the weapon and restrained Cathy. She struggled while he watched Blyte writhe. Tyson had been stunned into silence but now roared. Cathy hushed him and slumped into Franklin. He held her and dialled for help.

Blyte cupped her hands to the flow from her nose. She gazed at them, pleading.

Franklin snorted, revolted. This so-called good Christian may well have lost her husband under sad circumstances and been devastated by her childlessness, but it was impossible to empathise.

She'd intended to inflict grievous harm upon young Tyson – if not murder him. To take out life's disappointments on babies was depraved. As unchristian as you could get.

He heard a police siren and wrapped Cathy and Tyson into his chest. This wasn't how he'd envisaged the arrest going down.

Nevertheless, they'd got the right result.

MONDAY 22 MARCH

CHAPTER THIRTY-EIGHT

THEIR TONGUES MET. HE THRUST HARDER AND Georgie arched, riding the synchronised sensations of pleasure and pain. He caressed her pointy nipples. She almost orgasmed.

Almost but not quite.

Body on the brink of exquisite release, her brain took a lateral leap. She pictured Pam Stewart in the arms of her dance partner, then she shrivelled into an image of doubt and worry – for Susan.

'George,' AJ panted. 'Are you nearly there?'

She bit his earlobe, trailed her tongue along his jaw, nipped his chin. Warm excitement rebuilt as their bodies meshed.

Susan Pentecoste flashed into Georgie's consciousness. She was trying to tell her something.

What?

Georgie gripped AJ's shoulder. They flipped over, him on top and deeper. His breathing ragged, he contained his orgasm.

She squeezed her eyes and willed herself to come.

Imprinted on the inside of her eyelids was Margaret Pentecoste with jagged bruises around her neck. Georgie saw herself lean in and touch the semi-rigid body.

'Don't wait, AJ,' she urged, concealing her disappointment.

Moments later, he shuddered and sighed. They lay with sweat sandwiched between them until the clock radio sounded. AJ hit the off-switch and made to move.

Georgie tugged him back. Centimetres apart, still joined by his flaccid cock, she said, 'You know I love you, AJ?'

He replied, 'Same, babe.' Laid-back, yet his puzzlement showed.

'I'm close,' she whispered. 'Real close.'

Baffled, AJ frowned.

Even quieter, she said, 'To saying what you want to hear.'

He laughed. 'Aw, George. What's the big difference anyway? We already live together.' He stroked her nose and whispered, 'You don't have to become Mrs Gunnerson. It wouldn't bother me being married to Ms Harvey – I just want us to be *married*.'

Georgie rolled from under him. She'd said what smouldered for days. Now there were people to see and places to go in order to regain her sanity – and sex life.

———

First, she shuttled Michael to Ruby's bedside at the Alfred and paid another visit herself.

Georgie was relieved to see colour in Ruby's cheeks and the easy banter between the old couple. It boded well for an imminent release according to the coronary specialist.

After she'd flicked her eyes to the clock once too often, Ruby caught the tension and told her to go wherever it was she needed to be.

Georgie nodded. But she lingered to clasp Ruby's hand and kiss her. She pressed her cheek to the older woman's softer one for a long moment in silent apology for treating Susan as a wild-goose chase when Ruby had been right to worry.

Then Georgie left.

———

The place was naturally Daylesford. The time: mid-morning due to the mercy mission at the hospital en route. The person: Jennifer McGuire.

The *Advocate* reporter stood behind the reception desk. She faced Georgie, her discomfort palpable.

'Did you pull the human-interest story on Roly Pentecoste because of links to the Bigagli hit and run?' Georgie repeated.

McGuire's skin did the ink-on-litmus-paper thing, flushing from neck to cheeks in seconds.

Fascinated, Georgie said, 'You're going red.'

McGuire's skin blazed brighter. 'Golly, thanks. I wouldn't have realised if you hadn't pointed that out.'

'You also haven't answered my question.'

The journo thrust hands into her pockets and stared mutely.

'Did you pull the story because you were threatened? Or because you made the connection and shied away so you didn't draw attention to yourself?'

Flat-line mouth and cold eyes were McGuire's reply.

Georgie wanted to shake her.

'Come on. Give me something here.'

She forced her lips shut and waited for twenty beats. Frustrated by the reporter's non-response, she pressed harder.

'Did you make a connection between Schlicht and Bigagli, then Roly's so-called disappearance?'

McGuire said nothing. She lifted her shoulders, pivoted and left the room.

Georgie pondered her reaction as she drove the short distance to Bridport Street.

———

Pam Stewart wore a silver tracksuit with a sequinned rose motif on the breast. The top was unzipped, revealing a red swimsuit.

'You caught me on my way to aqua aerobics, my dear.' She opened the door wide. 'But your company is infinitely more enjoyable. A drink?'

Georgie declined. She was working against the clock but owed Pam a personal update, not another phone call. As she filled in recent events, Pam worried a chunky diamond ring on her right hand. She blanched and her face blended into its frame of white hair. Her left leg, crossed over its partner, twitched.

At the end of Georgie's explanation, silence filled Rose Cottage. Without the customary big band backing and Pam's cheerful chatter, the tense hush was even more tangible than McGuire's uneasiness.

Pam reached for Georgie's hand and gripped it. She asked, 'Will the police find Susan soon?'

Georgie shrugged unhappily.

'Do you know where she is?'

'No, but I have an idea of where she's been. Maybe I'll get inspiration from that. I'm clueless what else to do...'

'Bring her back, Georgie.'

A tear dripped. It stained Pam's silver pant leg. 'I miss her so badly.' Her voice trembled. 'At my age, people drop off all too often. But I'm too young yet to lose my best friend.'

The word *lose* pained Georgie as much as it did Pam. It constricted her chest. She rose and hugged the sweet lady and left the cottage charged with a heavier burden than when she'd arrived.

———

'Why'd she freak out?' Scott Hart asked.

Franklin steered past a blue-metal truck and automatically assessed its load. It looked about right. He glanced at his mate and replied, 'I think Cathy hit the nail on the head when she commented on Blyte having been a widow as long as she'd been a wife.'

'*That* pushed her from writing the sicko Solomon letters to throwing rocks at Christina's place and abducting Tyson?'

'Not in itself. It seems to have been a combination of things.' Franklin lifted one finger for each point. 'She's still mourning for her hubby and not having her own kid. She felt the single mums had ignored her warnings to change, which signalled horrific doom for society in her eyes. And she especially lost it because Christina hadn't stopped tarting around; it's not just *one* married bloke she's screwing.'

'Did Blyte really go on about Christina's tits?' Harty cupped two imaginary basketballs to his chest.

'Yep.' Franklin chuckled. He turned left towards Castlemaine and cruised under the speed limit. They'd patrol the highway for another ten or so kilometres before returning to town.

'How are Cathy and the bub?' his mate asked.

'They're fine. Overall.'

They were quiet for a few moments, then the constable spoke. 'Did you freak out when she attacked Blyte? I mean, I get the idea of doing whatever it takes to snatch Tyson, but then Cathy continued beating up Blyte, didn't she?'

'It was freaky but happened so fast. Cathy reckons she flipped. She only intended to disable Blyte and grab Tyson. But then, when she'd got the first strike in, she remembered all the stuff she'd learnt in a self-defence course. All the stuff she should've done during her rape.'

The men fell silent, weighed on by the sexual assault on which the Daylesford team had been necessarily briefed. In his peripheral vision Franklin saw a flash of emotion replaced by a grimace. But he forgot his mate as he recalled the young mother's broken voice. Her vulnerability as she revealed the rape to Blyte. Her pain at the older woman's scathing blame. With that type of prejudice in the community, Cathy's refusal to press charges made some kind of sense. Public scrutiny and cross-examination by a ruthless defence lawyer would be her second rape.

He continued the conversation. 'With Blyte misjudging her, it cemented her idea that a lot of people hereabouts are gossiping about or even condemning her. It made her lash out. Mind you, Cathy was devastated when she found out she'd broken Blyte's front tooth and nose.'

'After what Blyte did to Tyson?'

Franklin nodded, his eyes fixed on the car ahead. He

planted his foot, maintained twenty metres from its tail and clocked it at eleven clicks above the limit.

He flicked strobes and gave the siren a short yelp.

———

The driver ignored him for sixty metres, then drifted to the verge.

Franklin approached the driver's side, face set. 'Are you aware that you were exceeding the speed limit?'

'Was I?' Georgie Harvey appeared surprised.

Franklin noted that preoccupation topped her usual cockiness but said, 'You know it. Licence?'

He held out his palm, received and checked her plastic card. 'Any reason for your excessive speed?'

She gave a slight shrug.

'Have you been caught speeding before?'

She looked up. A smile twitched her lips but didn't reach her eyes. 'I shouldn't tell you this. Yes, several times.'

'Why should I let you off, then?'

'Well, I've maxed out my demerit points and would lose my licence, which'd be a pain in the arse. But I don't have kids or an invalid mum to cart around. All I can say is, sorry. I *really* didn't realise I was speeding, didn't mean to, and although I can't swear I won't ever reoffend, I'll try not to.'

Her frank response surprised him; his chuckle was involuntary.

While he chewed over his options, he switched track. 'Did you see Helena Watkowska yesterday?'

'Yeah.'

'You didn't call.'

She became edgy. 'Sorry, I need to go. I'll give you a bell later and fill you in.'

'Where're you off to in such a hurry?'

'Sch–' She broke off. 'Castlemaine.'

He propped his elbows on the open window and eyed her sternly. 'All right. You go to Castlemaine and call me later. I won't give you a ticket, this time. But if anybody on the Daylesford team catches you again, look out.'

Georgie touched his forearm. It shocked his senses. 'Thanks.'

'Whatever. Just be careful. Too many people think *it can't happen to me* and I end up having to knock on their family's door to give them the worst possible news. Unless you've got a death wish, don't speed.'

'Yessir,' Georgie mocked.

'I mean it. You've got to think of the consequences of everything you do.'

'But you've got to *live,* don't you? Not as if you expect to die young, right?' she asked seriously.

'Everything okay here?' Harty interrupted as he approached the convertible.

'Yep,' Franklin replied, then said to Georgie: 'Take care?'

She nodded, indicated and pulled away. Quickly but not excessively.

The cops watched her Alfa recede.

'What's she up to now?'

Franklin brooded. 'That's what I need to know.'

'You wanna follow her?'

'It'd piss her off and get us nowhere.'

'She must be in the area for a specific reason.'

A car whizzed by, filling the lapse.

Franklin contemplated Georgie's question on mortality and said, 'Yep. But what?'

———

Even another encounter with John Franklin barely registered in Georgie's psyche minutes later. Her focus was absolute, resolute.

It took her to a property with dirt roads on two sides: Rampage Road and One Mile Track. The neighbouring land was bare, raped by farmers or gold prospectors and a direct contrast with her destination. A large, secluded bush block, difficult to judge in size but upwards of twenty acres certainly.

Schlicht's driveway terminated at Rampage Road. Georgie looped past and parked at a lay-by adjacent to a creek about a ten-minute walk away.

Suddenly superstitious, she patted the Spider's hot bonnet and whispered, 'See you later, safe and sound.'

CHAPTER THIRTY-NINE

AFTER SHE'D ABANDONED THE CAR, GEORGIE FELT conspicuous and vulnerable in the deserted countryside. A fluorescent hot-air balloon floating across the horizon wouldn't have stood out more.

She strode faster.

A section of Schlicht's barbed-wire fence leaned towards One Mile Track. Georgie threw her bag on top to weigh it down and climbed over. Spikes dragged the skin under her jeans. She swore, then dashed for the nearest clump of trees.

She skidded on damp undergrowth. Legs split. Hands thrust forward to break the fall. Mouthful of dirt, skinned chin. Bruised pride, no major damage. She dusted herself and listened. Isolated birdcalls, occasional animal mutterings, nothing else. Not even a distant engine.

Georgie straightened. Was she mirroring Susan's movements? Of how long ago? Four, five days?

'What did you find, Susan? And where are you?' Her hushed words pierced the quiet.

She strained to scan the landscape.

Georgie approximated the direction of Schlicht's driveway and house. She trudged through scrub, blackberries, rocks and fallen tree limbs. Clouds and the gumtree canopy diffused the sunlight to a spooky gloom. As she extracted a pair of antique binoculars, she recalled with a brief twinge her dad handling them. The glimmer of a metallic object, perhaps a water tank or rooftop, caught her eye and she tramped another few hundred metres.

The next scan revealed a clearing. Georgie peered down on a four- or six-car garage, which obscured a house and twin water tanks. She dropped to her belly and slithered to a better vantage point.

Natural bush ended at the tall, cast-iron fence that circled the house block. Inside the compound, the grass was high and clumpy and gravel driveway potholed. White pillars and a sweeping external staircase adorned the faux-Georgian rendered brick residence – all it lacked were stone lions. The garage sat right-angled to the main building. The place looked deserted or at least neglected.

Drizzle fell.

Georgie's eyelids closed.

She deliberated the next move.

———

A dog—no, more than one—erupted into barks. She jerked alert. Car doors slammed. She centred the binoculars. Saw a mastiff and white pig dog straining against tethers attached to the house. The dogs leaned for the utility at the entrance.

Georgie ran the sights over the ute. A Ford F-150.

Battered. Black.

She adjusted the focus.

Familiar.

Her stomach knotted. She'd seen that ute last week. After her first visit to Margaret Pentecoste's home, it'd played leapfrog with a Skyline between Ballarat and Daylesford. Only now, it was obvious they'd tailed the Spider.

She gulped. Acid burned her guts.

The ute had also tailgated her yesterday as she'd returned from Helena Watkowska's. Had Schlicht's henchmen stalked her on other occasions? Seen every place she'd been? Followed her home?

She flinched as her mind fired.

Helena may have conspired with the F-150 driver. Or, on the flipside, she'd been forced to explain Georgie's visit and faced consequences for helping her.

She shook her head. No, they wouldn't dare rough up the boss's wife, especially with his release imminent.

A gruff bellow silenced the dogs. They dropped to their haunches.

Two men exited the house. The first guy was a rotund baldy. His buddy was scrawny but otherwise nondescript. Both Caucasian.

She'd definitely seen the first one before. Behind the ute's wheel. Anywhere else?

They departed with a skid of gravel.

―――――

Georgie evaluated her options.

Leave. Contact Franklin and suggest he get a warrant to check Schlicht's place. To find what, though? On what grounds? That Susan *might* have been there.

Or complete a tour of Schlicht's property, retrace Susan's steps and hope for a clue to her current location.

The thugs would be out a while.

'No brainer.' Georgie stamped out cramps in legs and butt and scrambled down to the clearing.

The dogs exploded into intruder-bark. She ignored them; easier done than shaking the guttural voice inside her: *Get out, get out, get out.* The chant swelled with each step.

Close now, she muttered, 'While the cat's away, huh?'

The Iceman would be irritated by the neglected lawn and the weeds that choked the driveway. But he'd be ropable over his boys' slipshod security. They'd left the gates wide open, rendering useless the high fence intended to deter intruders.

She tried to channel that into a good omen but grew more pensive with each step.

The front door provided little resistance to a twist and push.

Georgie froze. Would there be an active alarm system?

She risked it.

The living room with its once-posh furniture stank. Bags of putrid rubbish spilled over. Feet or fists had perforated the plaster walls. She saw pizza cartons growing fur, smoke discolouration to paintwork and carpet stains, even a dog's turd in the corner. Georgie gagged, pinched her nostrils and did a rapid search of the rest of the house.

Schlicht's opulent home would need major work before his release, thanks to his pals. On the upside, there was no sign of Susan or Roly Pentecoste.

Outside, Georgie gulped fresh air. She killed a few moments, then skirted the mastiff and headed for the garage.

She edged open the side door and crept through.

Wall one: a selection of tools, oils and fluids, a couple of jerrycans alongside a messy bench.

She scanned clockwise. Took in a pearl-white XJ6 Jag-Daimler – the means of Bigagli's murder.

Her gaze flicked over a Corvette shell and one empty berth. She halted at the other occupied car space. Large shape, shrouded in a dust cover.

Georgie held her breath. She grasped the front-centre of the cover. Inched it upwards. Speed-read the number plate.

'Ah. Fuck.'

Her hips swayed and her legs began to shake. She needed to be sure. She tugged off the cover, double-checked the make and model.

Susan's Land Cruiser.

She tried the handle: locked. Afraid, she peered inside.

Empty.

Clumsy hands retrieved her mobile and dialled a number. The phone pipped and cut out.

Zero service. Zero help.

Her breaths shallow, she couldn't fill her lungs.

Pam Stewart's earlier plea resonated.

Bring her back, Georgie.

A tear streaked Georgie's cheek.

I'm too young yet to lose my best friend, Pam had said.

I'm so bloody sorry, Pam. This doesn't look good.

Georgie's body quaked. Her blood turned glacial. Teeth chattered. Feet embedded into the ground.

———

'Mate, you're driving me insane.'

Franklin glanced at Scott Hart. He followed his glare to the steering wheel. Noted his fingernails drumming it and grimaced an apology.

'If you're so worried about Georgie, why don't we go to Castlemaine? We're nearly halfway.'

'And look where, Harty? She's had a huge head start and could be anywhere.'

A tension headache pulsed and Franklin rubbed his temples.

His eyes tracked a car as it snaked the highway. It was silver, the new white for cars, and merged with the gunmetal sky. The bleak outlook amplified the clenching in his guts.

'It's gotta be better than doing nothing,' Harty insisted.

Franklin planted his foot. With a glimpse forward, then in the rear-view mirror, he overtook a motorcyclist.

'You're right. Something tells me we've got to find her. *Now.*'

CHAPTER FORTY

SENSATION FINALLY RETURNED TO HER LEGS. FEAR OF discovery overrode all else. Survival instinct kicked in.

Georgie faltered outside Schlicht's garage. The most direct route was the driveway. But if the thugs turned up, she'd be dead. It seemed sensible to retrace her steps through the bush. Sensible but protracted. She looked in the opposite direction and caught a glimpse of metal. If it was the neighbour's roof, it presented the safest exit.

If. If. Too many ifs.

She pushed through the undergrowth. Stumbled, hauled herself upright and levelled with a bunch of broken stems on a shrub.

Here, there, she spied torn foliage. She crept forward, followed a corridor of damage. The wounds in the brush were clean, bright, recent. How recent? Today? Yesterday?

She noted scuffmarks. Narrow trenches, more or less parallel and set in the near-dry ground. Something, or someone, preceded her.

Minutes later, she quit the scrub and faced a brick chimney, incongruously erect while the rest of the cottage tumbled inwards. The warped rust-stained iron roof accounted for the metallic glint she'd glimpsed. The stone walls and support timbers were a jumbled mess, yet the doorway remained intact.

It beckoned Georgie. Or, more accurately, the drag marks to its mouth defied ignoring.

———

Self-preservation assumed second place to curiosity. Not inquisitiveness – a cheerless, gut-wrenching need to know.

She reached into her pack, desperate for a cigarette. Then she paused. A smoke changed nothing. This wasn't a time to procrastinate. Georgie tugged the strap over her shoulder and sidled through the door.

In the tiny cottage, she climbed under and over various obstacles with urgency tainted by dread. She pushed aside sticks of abandoned furniture, kicked an old pan and its lid by the hearth. Among the forest of timber and junk, it was impossible to discern drag marks beyond the doorway.

Despite the implications of Susan's vehicle in Schlicht's garage, she felt a twinge of optimism. Hunch proven wrong; Susan's not here. Yay, right?

Georgie hunkered and rescanned the ruin. She noted fewer animal droppings in one area and that the array of timber appeared less haphazard there than elsewhere.

She started to kneel, remembered the rat shit and sank into a squat. When she lifted several loose planks, her stomach lurched. And her pulse went berserk.

A hole. Access to the cellar. Close call. She slowed her breaths to clear her head.

She swung her mini-torch into the gap and cursed its tiny beam. With the Maglite clenched between her teeth, she descended. Rung by rung; each step tentative. In parts, the ladder had disintegrated, and Georgie scrambled and stretched for the next foothold.

A rung broke underfoot.

'Shit!' she swore around the torch in her mouth.

She lost balance and dangled by one hand. That impact hyperextended her shoulder and elbow. She gasped with the stab of pain. Eyes wide with fear, she panted and felt around for the next rung.

A few heartbeats later, she continued the descent, her armpits damp with perspiration.

Georgie sniffed. A rank odour overlaid the cold cellar.

She thought about Michael and Ruby and Pam. She felt obligated to them but wanted to beat a retreat.

She pictured the Noonans and Helena and was still tempted to run.

If she hadn't owed it to Susan herself, hadn't felt bonded to the woman, Georgie may yet have fled. But as her feet struck the brick floor, she shrugged off the oppression.

Quick. It mightn't be too late.

Using the Maglite, she located a door. A cupboard? Or a passage? On opening it, she tripped. The torch dropped and rolled. She fell, one arm extended and the other protecting her head.

Instead of the impact she expected, something broke her fall.

Georgie shrieked.

She retrieved the torch and shone it over the floor.

Her hand quivered. She used a double grip.

Illuminated legs splayed at impossible angles. Puffy face and neck. Rainbow of bruises.

Georgie moaned. Reluctantly, she reached and lifted a cold hand. Limp. Aware of the futility, she pressed the neck.

This close, the stench made her retch. Pulseless. Lifeless. Susan's body sagged under her fingertips. Flesh slack; rigor mortis must have passed.

She just managed to turn away before spewing a stream of vomit.

Still gagging, Georgie ran the torch over Susan again.

A tyre lever protruded under Susan's hip, incongruous among the debris.

Georgie arched the beam along the woman's other arm. To her hand.

She recoiled. Made a mewing cry.

Within her musty tomb, Susan gripped a skeletal hand.

Little remained of what must be Roly Pentecoste. The dashing, silver-haired, smiling man in his navy cardigan – reduced to a gold wedding band, inert watch, snags of cloth and leathered skin.

Georgie backed up to the ladder. Slipped, banged and bruised her body in frantic haste. Guessing their original position, she dumped the timber planks back over the pit, then she ducked and weaved through the ruin and into the scrub.

———

It was pouring rain. Charcoal clouds blocked the afternoon sun. Instinct drove her, hopefully towards One Mile Track and her Spider.

About five minutes later, unsure if she travelled in the right direction, Georgie halted. She retrieved her mobile and checked for service: weak but present.

She dialled. The phone pipped and cut out.

She ran on, desperation and smoker's lungs making her

wheeze. She dropped to the ground and tried the phone again.

This time it rang. *'John Franklin.'*

'Fuck, fuck, fuck. John, you have to get to Schlicht's place.' Belatedly, she added, 'It's Georgie. I've found Susan and Roly at Schlicht's place on Rampage Road, outside Castlemaine.'

'Are they –'

'No. They're both dead!'

'Where are you?' he shouted.

His voice stabbed her eardrums. Georgie pulled the phone away. 'I'm getting out of here.' She told him where she'd left the Spider and gave directions to the property.

Franklin said, *'We're actually nearby. But don't delay. Get out. Right now. And wait for me at the station.'*

'Okay.'

'Promise me!' he demanded.

Georgie freaked out even more. 'I promise!'

Her hands shook so hard it took both to disconnect. She sprinted and soon came to a barbed-wire fence that bordered a dirt road. With luck, it was One Mile Track.

Georgie's saturated clothes dragged her body. She recognised landmarks and fumbled for her keys before sighting the Spider.

She tried to insert the key into the driver's door.

'Come on. Get in. Shit, shit. That's it. Thank –'

Both her arms were yanked from behind. She hadn't heard anyone approach or seen their shadow in the torrential rain.

She twisted. Saw Baldy and Nondescript on either side. A third assailant materialised. Slammed her skull into the car.

Georgie screamed, agony and fury equal. She recalled

what an instructor had told her. The most important rule of self-defence: hit the bitch switch.

'Stop! BACK OFF, FUCKERS.'

She pivoted, tore her arms free and swiped at Baldy. He punched her guts. Winded, she gasped.

Nondescript snagged her arm behind her back. The other person, a female, laughed. It sounded cruel, vicious. Georgie's left shoulder popped. A score of red-hot darts punctured the muscle as the tendons ripped.

Eyes smarting, she couldn't see who pounded her face. Tossed airborne, her hand crashed into the car. Glass shattered.

Loud, desperate screams tore her throat. Metallic blood merged with rainwater in her open mouth.

Georgie slumped. Her attackers loomed again. She kicked back, towards the groin. Slashed forward, connected with someone's jaw. Raked fingernails across skin and thumped the heel of her hand to their nose.

Her other shoulder cracked as she was pitched to the ground and kicked. To the torso, head, maimed shoulders.

She could struggle no longer. The pain was too extreme.

CHAPTER FORTY-ONE

Rain whipped the windscreen. Set against a turbulent sky, visibility cut to eighty metres. The truck's headlights illuminated an obscure shape.

As they approached, the mass divided.

Three combatants.

And one in the middle.

Georgie, being pulverised.

Franklin yelled, 'Bloody hell. Get them to send backup *here*, not Schlicht's. And a fucking ambo.'

Hart radioed D24. Franklin planted his foot.

They'd cut strobes and siren before they slipped down One Mile Track, planning to confirm that Georgie's car was gone, then await backup for the advance on Schlicht's property.

That strategy detonated, Franklin hit various switches. Colour and noise resonated. The distance to their target seemed impossible.

'Jesus. They're going to kill her,' Hart shouted over the clamour. He shucked off his seatbelt and gripped the dashboard.

Fifty metres.

Barely breathing. Stares intent. Eyes fixed on the black convertible and the thrashing silhouettes in its foreground.

Forty metres.

Franklin braked.

———

'She's down! Nooo!' Hart exclaimed and physically winced with the barrage of strikes.

Close enough. Franklin killed the engine. The cops lurched from their vehicle.

The female kicked Georgie's prostrate torso.

Franklin drew his weapon. He bellowed, 'STOP. POLICE.'

Hart darted to the right, gun raised. The attackers swore and scattered three ways. Franklin hesitated, torn between pursuit and checking Georgie. Meanwhile, his partner sprinted after the large, balding offender. The female fled.

Franklin checked Georgie's pulse and breathing. Thready but present. He scooped her into the recovery position, further from the road, clear of strewn glass and debris.

'Hang in there. Ambos are coming,' he said into her ear.

No response.

Franklin squeezed her hand but looked away from the bloodied mess.

He stood.

His gaze swept the roadway.

You arseholes aren't getting away with this.

He spotted the smaller, skinny offender scurrying towards Rampage Road and raced after him. His feet landed hard and splattered mud over the uniform already stained with raindrops. His knee popped; the ancient football injury shot pain up his thigh. Eyes fixed on his quarry, none of this mattered.

A car fired nearby, startling Franklin. He dived to the verge as an iridescent blue WRX passed by whiskers. As he hit the ground, his right shoulder took full impact. He rose, clutching his bruised side. He glimpsed the driver, the female attacker. Noted the Subaru's vanity plate began with 'SXY'.

'Got you, you bastard,' Hart yelled in the distance.

Franklin heard scuffling, assumed his partner had restrained the balding thug. He saw the skinny crook to the fore. The man gaped at the diminishing WRX taillights. Looked like a drenched rabbit.

Franklin roared and charged. Rabbitman pivoted though remained rooted.

He started to run, sluggish with shock.

Franklin closed.

He hurled himself and forced Rabbitman down onto the muddy road. They squirmed. Franklin pushed his knee into the scumbag's spine. Rabbitman arched, delivering a reverse head butt to Franklin's face. Franklin ignored the pain and ground his knee into the spine below.

The man cursed and bucked. Franklin slid an arm around his neck. Applied a headlock. Squeezed the man's Adam's apple until the offender yielded. Then he slapped on handcuffs.

He pulled the bloke upright. They glared, a foot apart.

'You're fucked.' Franklin's headshake silenced Rabbitman. 'Don't worry, I'll read you your rights...and we'll do this by the book, down the station. But take it from me – you and your mates are fucked.'

PART IV

TUESDAY 23 MARCH

CHAPTER FORTY-TWO

EVERY NERVE SCREAMED AS GEORGIE WAS transferred to yet another trolley. It replicated painful yet blurred memories.

Flashing lights burned. Colours flickered against the dark sky. A transitory flare added white to the blue and red lightshow. The lightning illuminated Franklin, his face grey, matching the outlook. Excruciating to breathe. Impossible to move.

The next wave of pain brought blissful oblivion.

The blackout, like the others before it, was short-lived.

I'm thirsty, she tried to say. A mumble came out. Frustrated she silently cried and drifted into unconsciousness.

'She's stirring again,' a woman said, her tone brisk and crisp.

It was all too hard. Georgie passed out.

Time elapsed. How much, she remained clueless.

———

'How bad is the pain, Georgie?' another female asked, her voice soothing iced chocolate.

Bad. Terrible. Worse than anything I've ever felt.

Georgie prised an eye open. The white busyness overwhelmed her. She dropped the eyelid.

'Can you rate it out of ten? Ten being excruciating, one being okay.'

A hundred thousand.

'Squeeze my hand if you can't talk. I'll work up from five. Five, six...seven...eight. Still not there? Nine. Ten.'

Georgie pressed the soft hand.

'Welcome back, Georgie. It's good to hear from you, even if it's just a squeeze. Ten out of ten? I'll get you something for that pain soon.'

The nurse prodded and probed. She talked incessantly. It hurt Georgie's brain. She tried to curl away, into the foetal position.

Pain stabbed from every direction.

She willed the nurse away. The lights to dim. The noises to fade. The pain to go.

It did for a bit.

———

My teeth are hurting. Everything hurts. What the fuck is going on?

'We're popping you into surgery now, Georgie. This is your anaesthetist. He'll talk you through the process...'

Later... 'Are you all right, dear?' A male voice. Young, sympathetic, effeminate.

A tear plopped through a crack in her eyelid. It streaked her cheek into the side of her mouth. Salty. Warm.

Where's AJ? Livia? I want my mum.

'We can't have tears, Georgie-Porgy.' After an efficient swipe of her cheeks, the man crooned, 'There, that's better.'

Better for who?

The nurse left. Georgie battled psychedelic images.

Susan, Roly, an underground tomb. Her frantic call to Franklin. Key in the door, home free.

Hands rotated her body. Slam. *Her head into the Spider. Panel dinted.* Slam. *A fist to her face. Arm flung back, shattered glass sprayed.* Slam. *A boot to her ribs. Another to her already raw shoulder.*

Someone laughed, crazed. NOOOOOO! *Her scream gurgled. Brief hope shrank to despair.*

NOOOOOO! *Beyond caring. The lights extinguished.*

———

Franklin brushed past Paul Wells as he tagged behind Lunny.

'Looks like your neck is finally in the noose,' the constable goaded.

'Sorry?' Franklin challenged.

Wells smirked and sauntered on.

Cockhead, go back to the big smoke. Better yet, accidentally discharge your gun into your ugly mug when you clean it.

Furious, Franklin dropped onto a chair in the sarge's office.

'...be careful what you wish for,' Lunny commented dryly.

Franklin rubbed a hand over his jawline. Did Lunny know what he'd been thinking?

The sergeant steepled his fingers. 'It's kinda crazy out there, isn't it?'

He referred to the station, crowded by the full complement of Daylesford members, along with transients from homicide and CIU.

Franklin stifled a yawn and nodded.

He and Harty had watched the ambos whisk Georgie Harvey to Castlemaine then driven in the opposite direction, towards Daylesford, with their two prisoners, Baldy and Rabbitman, aka Broadbent and Scott, on board.

There, he'd kept his oath to Scott and conducted the initial interview by the book. They then cleared the holding cell of the miscellaneous junk stored within and confined the crooks until they were transferred to Melbourne for further interrogation.

As uniformed members, Hart and Franklin had Buckley's of getting anywhere near Susan and Roly Pentecoste's crypt except to direct traffic or fetch coffee for the detectives. Thus, they'd joined the search for Schlicht's lover, Ariane Marques. The third felon was on the run in her swanky blue WRX.

Their hunt proved fruitless.

So, much later on, Franklin drove by Schlicht's property, which was illuminated like the MCG and swarmed with police officials. Next, he went to the hospital. There he camped overnight, alternately dozed and demanded information on Georgie's condition while avoiding her gathering clan and the media vampires.

Occasionally, he phoned the station for updates. Each time he insisted on attachment to the connected homicide and assault investigations.

Be careful what you wish for.

Since his secondment to the homicide squad, Franklin fielded tireless inquisition by the high rollers from town and now awaited an interview with the district inspector.

Be careful what you wish for.

He'd wished all night that Georgie Harvey would stabilise and, after that, for her quick and complete recovery. Next week he'd probably regret those stolen prayers when she'd be swanning around, being the usual pain in the neck.

Then again, with Susan found, why would Georgie return to Daylesford?

———

'...John, are you with me?' Lunny said.

Franklin snapped out of his trance. 'Huh?'

'District Inspector.' The sarge jumped to his feet as the door opened.

After they all shook hands, DI Knight took Lunny's seat. He faced Franklin and the sergeant across the desk. 'I don't know whether to slap you, sack you or give you a medal. I'd find myself reprimanded for the first, hands tied on the second, so I may as well say bravo, John.'

Franklin forced a calm façade. He'd expected his arse hauled over the coals, not congratulations.

'What for, sir?'

'Wrapping up the Valerie Blyte-Solomon case. Tim here,' Knight's head inclined towards Lunny, 'filled me in on the matter. It seems you put it all together in the eleventh hour.'

'As it turned out, Cathy Jones had the situation in hand,' Franklin said honestly. 'I only helped with the mop up.'

'Far too modest. Who knows what would have happened if you weren't there? Jones may have continued her attack on Blyte. Or suppose Blyte recovered the knife; the outcome could've been catastrophic.'

The men exchanged glances. Lunny's eyes widened as if he'd visualised a different result.

Knight continued. 'Notwithstanding that, I'm *certain* the outcome for Georgie Harvey would have been dire if you and Hart hadn't arrived when you did. If you hadn't acted so swiftly. Such a brutal attack. Is it more shocking when a woman batters another woman, do you think?' He stared at Franklin. 'And she was laughing? Truly evil.'

With a headshake, the DI muttered, 'Terrible, terrible. Marques tried to drive you down. And I believe she would have ploughed straight over Georgie Harvey if you'd left her where she lay, is that right?'

Franklin shuddered.

Thank God I moved her.

'So, first-rate actions. Good job.' Inspector Knight adopted a stern air. 'Having said that, you've made a heck of a lot of mistakes over the past few weeks, Franklin. I can't abide shoddy work, and that extends to officers withholding crucial evidence, entering dangerous situations without backup and involving civilians in official investigations. Just to name a few of your recent transgressions. Do I make myself clear?'

That's more like it.

Amused, Franklin said, 'Yes, sir.'

'Eddie,' the DI corrected. 'We don't need to stand on formalities.'

Franklin's brow wrinkled. One minute, his arse was kicked and in the next one, licked.

'I hear Georgie Harvey is fighting back well,' Knight commented.

'That's great news,' Lunny interjected.

'She's young, the injuries not too serious; she'll recover quickly, I'm told.'

The hospital should have told me that.

To be fair, maybe they'd tried while the hommies had him buttonholed, mobile on silent.

'Now. I hear you're keen for a try at the suits, John.' Knight smiled.

Franklin frowned. 'You mean this secondment thing?'

'No, I mean you want a crack at CI.'

Franklin glared at Lunny, who grinned and flushed.

'I haven't decided.'

'Don't procrastinate. None of us are getting younger.'

'I've got a number of things to work out, sir; Eddie.'

Knight rose, extending his hand. 'I'm aware that you're a single dad and you've issues with your daughter. They can all be worked through – Tim will do whatever he can, won't you?'

Lunny bobbed his head. 'Maeve and I are always happy to look after Kat, you know that. She already half lives with us, and she's a good kid. Whatever you need, we'll help.'

'Good, good. John, I think you've proved an aptitude, but the ball's in your court. When you're ready, I'll sign off the request.'

———

Dismissed, Franklin tracked down Wells at the front counter. He knocked the constable's writing hand and a black line marred the pristine report.

'Whoops. Sorry. *Mate.*' Franklin winked.

Wells scowled.

Franklin hitched his service belt and tapped his holstered revolver with exaggerated swagger; you don't hang onto your weapon while suspended. Wells's shoulders slumped.

When he left the station, Franklin's grin dropped. He winced at Lunny and Knight's confidence, their certainty that he'd request the promotion and make a good detective.

He didn't know what he wanted. One part craved change. The other shrank from it. Consider how sure he'd felt about Donna, only to scrape the remnants of their relationship—all except their daughter and the bloody cottage—into the bin a few years later. Maybe he'd regret whatever he did now equally in the future. But maybe, just maybe, it'd feel far worse not to try.

It was more than career choices that Franklin contemplated.

WEDNESDAY 24 MARCH

CHAPTER FORTY-THREE

'Ruby's beaten you home, George.'

Still woozy with anaesthetic and analgesics, Georgie weighed speech, a smile or nod. All involved too much pain and effort. She grunted.

Perched on her bed, AJ went on, 'We were worried how the news would affect her. I suggested not telling her about Susan and Roly until she was totally well.'

Georgie tried to lift an eyebrow but it didn't move.

Perhaps it did fractionally, as AJ chortled. 'Yeah, that went down like a lead balloon. Michael waved around his walking stick, even stamped it on the floor.'

He jumped off the bed, which bounced Georgie and set off a domino of twinges. His arms and legs flailed as AJ mimicked their aged neighbour.

'I've never seen him spit it before. He told me and the doctor Ruby was bound to find out soon and there'd be hell to pay if she heard about it from the TV or someone else. And it would either kill her, or she'd kill him, if she missed the funeral. The doc had staff on standby in case Ruby took it badly, but it seemed to make her suddenly stronger. As if she willed herself well for the funeral. Bizarre.'

Georgie lifted a hand. She wanted to say, *Yeah, but she was already kicking goals. The doctor said she'd be home in a few days when I saw her last. On Monday.*

'I know, I know,' AJ answered her thoughts. 'She was getting better every day. But the shock could've been a real set-back. A disaster, even.'

He chatted about a number of mundane domestic matters. He prowled the hospital room, sniffed floral arrangements and read aloud cards. He chuckled over the array of dark chocolate assortments; people knew her weakness.

———

Georgie drilled him with an exasperated look and finally he quit dodging.

'The surgical realignment of that pretty nose of yours went without hitch. Quite straightforward as far as operations go.' AJ tried for a light-hearted tone but botched it.

'Overall, you've been lucky. Fractured collarbone, dislocated left shoulder, tendon and ligament damage and bruised ribs. With strapping and rehab, they'll heal fine. It could've been a lot worse.'

Georgie blinked. Tears stung. She gasped, which made her torso shoot with pain.

'George! Are you okay?'

Reassured by her mumble, he said, 'Seriously, you've come out of this lightly. I can't believe you went onto Schlicht's farm without a second thought. It was stupid. You could have...'

He broke off. Georgie saw him gulp.

Still in an unnatural pitch, he said, 'You should be out of here in days. Although it'll...it'll take a few months to recover properly.'

You're lying. There's more isn't there?

He turned away. Georgie stared at the back of his head for a moment, then dropped to the pillows, shut her eyes and blocked the stark whiteness. She couldn't mute the hospital noise so easily: buzzers, laughter, clatter and a telephone that nobody answered. Her body and brain started to numb. Soon her chin sank to her chest.

———

'Bron and Jo will be in shortly.' AJ's voice jerked her awake. 'They've been here on and off since you were brought in. All of us have. And half the police force.'

He laughed, but the word *police* jolted Georgie. She shifted; her body cried out. She reverted to the original position.

Really?

'The nurses reckon that the cop who saved you visits every spare chance. And they said even the district inspector stopped by. You didn't know? You must've been out of it.'

She sighed, too exhausted to converse.

'Livia's asleep down the hall, but she'll turn up again any minute. It's amazing how fast everyone's sent flowers. Even David Ruddoch and his crew have been thinking of you – they sent that...'

AJ pointed to a tall spray of cream blooms. No doubt its fragrance matched its elegance, but Georgie wouldn't smell much for a while with her mangled nose. Fancy David Ruddoch having a soft spot for her after all.

As he paced, Georgie thought, *There's definitely something you're not saying.*

'AJ?' His name was a rusty whisper through split lips and swollen jaw.

He drew nearer and reached for her closest hand. Mid-movement, he changed direction and took the right one. As he kissed her fingertips, her gravel-rashed skin stung. She flinched, then wondered about the bandaged mass to her left.

What's with my hand?

AJ spoke quickly. 'I've a bone to pick with you... What an elaborate way to avoid lunch with my parents!'

She figured he was joking.

After a pause, he said, 'And I remember you promising you'd do nothing, what was it? *Heroic or stupid.*'

Pissed off, Georgie tried to sit up. The effort too great, she fell back.

'Fuck off.'

'George, you promised to be careful. To check out a few things and then leave it to the police.'

She glared at him.

He mirrored it.

'I tried.'

'Huh? You tried, what?'

'To –'

'I'll tell what you tried to do,' he interrupted. 'You tried to get yourself killed, that's what!'

Georgie felt nauseous. Her stomach churned with fury and guilt. She slowly, painfully retorted, 'I tried to get away. Trust me.' The words came out muffled.

'I do, George. It's really a question of when are you going to trust yourself?'

The nose cast pinched with her confused frown.

What are we talking about now?

'You went drinking after court. You drove to Daylesford, drunk, I'll bet. You sent me a weak SMS to say you were staying there. Because you were avoiding me, right? Because you didn't want to deal with the Big M—as you call it—true? I bring up marriage, kids and off you run. But if you trusted me and yourself a bit more, you'd realise there's nothing to be worried about.'

Georgie gazed at the people who bustled past her open doorway. She yearned to join them.

AJ laughed abruptly, mirthlessly. 'And where'd it get you, George? Here.' He motioned contemptuously and added, 'In *that* state.'

She hummed inside her head. A soccer-like chant: *Here we go, here we go, here we go.*

He exclaimed, 'What, am I talking to a brick here? Trust. T-R-U-S-T. It isn't a difficult word to master. We've been together long enough for me to know that I want you and you want me. For the long term. I want to marry you, even knowing that you and my brother slept together.'

Georgie shot shocked eyes towards his.

'*Surely* you didn't think that Matt could keep it from me? But to be fair, we'd separated. And it was just one night, right?'

'Yes,' she whispered.

'Okay, so you've never cheated, although you are a hopeless flirt. But I'm convinced you love me, and the other day, you said you were close to committing.'

He waited. She turned away.

'I think you keep inventing distractions to avoid commitment.' He sounded fatigued.

'I didn't invent this,' Georgie snapped. She rolled her eyes to imply injuries and hospitalisation.

'I know!' AJ threw up both hands. 'Look, this isn't the right time or place. You need to get better. We'll sort this out later.'

He sighed deeply. Silence expanded like foaming fill-a-gap.

She searched for what to say to make it better. Her head pounded with discordant emotions.

Eventually, he sat on the bed and fixed Georgie with a hound dog gaze.

There's something more, isn't there?

Georgie's lips were poised to ask when Livia entered with a wave of energy. The moment was lost, so Georgie sank into the pillows and watched two of the most important people in her life chatter: her mum and her man.

Things would work out.

Wouldn't they?

THURSDAY 25 MARCH

CHAPTER FORTY-FOUR

'WHAT ARE YOU LOOKING AT, DAD?'

'You, kid. You haven't turned out so bad.'

'Thanks heaps,' Kat whined, yet a smile lurked on her lips. 'What brought that up anyway?'

Franklin sipped from his mug. 'I don't know. It occurred to me that we've been pretty lucky. And as kids go, you're bearable.' He laughed at her indignant expression. 'All right, you're *pretty cool*. Is that better?'

She smirked and stacked the dishwasher.

'This place isn't so bad, is it?' Franklin commented.

Kat shrugged. 'It's home. It's okay.' After a sly peek she added, 'Wouldn't mind a pool though.'

'Wouldn't we all,' he replied dryly. 'I've been considering selling.'

'You *can't*.'

'Why not?'

'Because it's home. All our memories are here.'

'Memories are portable, Kat. They don't stay locked inside four walls.' At her horrified face he hastened to say,

'Don't worry. I *was* thinking about selling but changed my mind. But it is definitely time to re-do the kitchen.'

'What, and get rid of this lovely pink?' She gestured facetiously.

'Yep. I'm thinking neutral walls –'

'Imagine my dad talking about neutrals.'

'...and cupboards, with stainless appliances,' he continued. 'How's that sound?'

'Are you serious? Can we afford it?'

Franklin chuckled and nodded. His kid surprised him no end. Sometimes shallow and selfish, sometimes sage and sensitive, she was a chocolate box without descriptions. And he loved the whole assortment.

'Don't you think we should finish the other projects first?'

She referred to the half-dozen or so renovation ventures he'd abandoned at ninety per cent done. Stuff being sensible; if they kept the cottage, it was imperative to eradicate the last traces of Donna.

'We should, but we're not going to. I'll pick up a bunch of paint charts.'

He watched her retrieve a lunch bag from the fridge.

'What's on today?'

'The usual boring shit.' Kat grimaced. 'And a careers talk this afternoon. At least we get out of science for it.' Now she grinned.

'Are you any clearer on what you want to do after you finish school?'

She shot him a cunning glance. 'Maybe I'll follow in your footsteps.'

Stunned, his automatic reaction was to say, 'You'll have to keep your nose clean from now on, then. No more shoplifting or trouble at school.' Then his forehead knit. 'Really, though? A cop?'

She wiggled her brows. 'Potentially. You like being a copper, don't you? Mostly.'

Franklin pictured the recent few weeks. A multi-fatality smash, close call with a Bible-basher-come-abductor-and-aggressor and missing person case turned triple homicide that had left a woman hospitalised and him in cahoots with the hommies. It amounted to the most exciting and harrowing period in his career. He wanted better for his daughter.

'I don't think it's for you.'

'That's hypocritical,' she censured. 'And what about *you*? At the start of the year, our coordinator said to expect a minimum of three major career changes in our working life. You're still on Job One.'

'I'm happy enough.'

She curled her lip.

'Perhaps I'll stay with the force but do something different.' He thought he'd managed to sound casual, yet his eyes were riveted on Kat. How would she take it?

'For real?' She dived onto the seat opposite.

'I'm chewing over CI. It'd mean changes for us...'

'You've always said I can do whatever I set my mind to. My turn to say it back. If it means that much to you, Dad, *do it*.'

———

Kat's advice ricocheted on the way to the hospital.

'Brian, Helen,' Franklin greeted Inspector Mitchell and his offsider Kyriakos of the homicide squad.

They shook and strolled in sync towards the ward, while Kat's words continued to shimmer.

'You've got visitors, Georgie-Porgy.'

Surprised that she let the nurse get away with the moniker, Franklin viewed Georgie's grimace.

'You'll keep, Wayne-Pain.' She wiggled her fingers at the departing nurse, then surveyed her guests.

'Uh-oh, am I *assisting police with their inquiries* again? Or are the troops out there, ready to bundle me into the divvy van and escort me to the interview room, where you'll grill me until I confess all, then arrest me?'

Franklin observed the effort behind her jocularity. Georgie's skin had more colour and her eyes more sparkle, but exhaustion and multi-hued abrasions marred her features.

Inspector Mitchell laughed as he placed a bunch of yellow roses on the crowded bed trolley. A vase atop the bedside cabinet held the mixed bouquet that Franklin had left anonymously. While less glamorous than many of the other arrangements, they were pretty and cheerful.

The detectives sat on Georgie's bed. Franklin lingered at the foot.

'Before you start,' Georgie said, 'I want one of you to tell me, what's with this hand?'

She lifted her bundled appendage.

Kyriakos gave a surprised, 'Oh.' She glanced at Mitchell. They both fixed on Franklin.

'They haven't told you?' he said, appalled.

'No. They're either patronising or dismissive. Saying the phantom doctor—who only seems to visit when I'm asleep—will explain. It's pissing me off.'

'I don't blame you. Well, here it is.' He drew a breath and a line across his palm. 'Your hand was sliced to the bone

425

from the heel of the palm to the base of your index finger. There's nerve damage...and no guarantees how it'll heal.'

'How bad does it look?'

He shrugged. 'I haven't seen it but believe it's nasty. Cosmetic surgery might reduce the scarring.'

'Georgie,' Mitchell interrupted. 'Sorry to push this along, but time's of the essence. We'll have questions for you later. Lots of them. Meanwhile, I guess you'd like us to fill in some blanks?'

'Hell, yes.'

'You realise you've got this guy to thank for being alive?'

He indicated Franklin, who felt himself blush. Georgie lowered her chin and mumbled.

'Right then. Your attack. Two coppers eye-witnessing it and plenty of DNA via skin scrapings from your nails –'

'Remind me not to pick a fight with you,' Kyriakos said.

The detective inspector continued, 'So, in relation to what happened to you, we'll get all three offenders on aggravated assault, if not attempted murder. You're aware Hart and Franklin nabbed two at the scene but Ariane Marques got away?' At her nod, he added, 'She's now in custody.'

'Good!'

'The bad news is that we've a your-word-against-mine scenario between the three where it comes to everything else. They're all blaming each other. Marques even blabbed on her lover. She wanted immunity, but I wouldn't cut her a sandwich, let alone a deal. When she found out Schlicht is still chummy with his wife, she spilt the whole lot anyway. But we need a lot more than the conflicting say-so of this lot.'

'I don't get it.'

'Georgie, most of what we have so far is circumstantial

or hearsay. The DPP needs enough physical evidence for a jury to convict or he won't indict. Ever heard of double-jeopardy?'

'Sure.'

'Well then, you know the prosecution gets one shot in court. There are only two possible outcomes, and the jury's verdict has to be not guilty if they have sufficient doubt. As a result, no conviction and no opportunity for a retrial. So the DPP chooses the winnable battles and concentrates on building the strongest of cases.'

Kyriakos agreed. 'We have to get it right for the Pentecostes.'

Franklin noticed Georgie clutch her bedcovers. She began to speak, faltered, then in a faint voice asked, 'What happened to Susan and Roly?'

'I'm sorry to say they were both murdered.' Mitchell's face contorted. 'There's enough left of Roly to confirm he'd been tortured before having his neck broken – which corresponds with what Angelo Sartori claimed before he suicided.'

Georgie made a strangled sound.

'And Susan died from a stroke several days after a horrendous assault –'

'*Days?*'

The inspector said grimly, 'Yes, regrettably. Whether Roly's death was as slow as hers, we'll never prove.'

Georgie swore and screwed her eyes but not before Franklin saw them fill.

Mitchell checked his watch. 'I'll have to make this quick. We'll give you the details later. Or Franklin will.

'In brief,' he ticked off the points, 'it's stacking up against Schlicht on Bigagli's hit-run. So far, we have nothing to directly pin Marques to Margaret Pentecoste's murder, although there should be enough to convict Scott and Broadbent on that. As for Susan and Roly, crime scene techs are still sifting evidence from the cellar. And my team's the best, not a bunch of muppets. We'll work every angle into the ground.'

His nostrils flared. Mitchell declared, 'But Marques is going down anyway.'

Georgie's head jerked.

'She shot and wounded one of ours at the scene of her apprehension. She made the mistake of leaving witnesses. Again. We're putting together a watertight brief, and Ms Marques is going to be old and wizened when released.'

'Good,' Georgie repeated but with less gusto this time.

It wasn't good enough.

Franklin knew it. Everyone in the room knew it. Their expressions told the story. They wanted retribution for Roly and Susan. And even then, it wouldn't bring them back.

Georgie shut her eyes and the detectives departed, pulling the door to.

———

Franklin eased into the visitor's chair and studied the rise and fall of Georgie's chest. He mused on everything she'd endured through commitment to the Pentecostes and their mates, plus a strong conscience and yes, bull-headed character.

'Thank you,' she said without opening her eyes.

'I thought you were asleep.'

'Nah. Just resting.' She looked at him then, her tired smile highlighted by contusions and dressings.

He didn't have to see the *Get well* balloon and expensive floral arrangement from her live-in lover to appreciate she was off limits. Yet, in her unflattering hospital gown, swathed in bandages, he'd never encountered anyone more pitiful, and beautiful, than Georgie-bloody-Harvey.

If it means that much to you, do it, Kat's words rang.

Franklin hesitated. He stared at his fidgeting fingers.

If it means that much to you, do it.

He met Georgie's gaze. He rose and brought his face towards hers. Their eyes locked; he leaned in. His heartbeat was the bass of a rock anthem in surround sound. She didn't shift, even as he pulled away and tilted exaggeratedly to avoid the nose cast.

Now, their lips met, parted and their breaths merged. His senses fired with peppermint and white musk. Electric pinpricks covered his body.

Georgie slipped her tongue between his lips, sensuous as satin sheets against naked skin. His groin warmed; legs weakened.

Their tongues tentatively touched and the heat escalated. He cradled the part of her face not marked or bandaged. She moaned. They broke away briefly as he scanned her. Had he hurt her? Did she want him to stop? She outlined the cut of his jaw, his nose, cheekbones. Her hand brushed his ear, circled his skull, drew him near.

Franklin gently kissed her eyelids, and Georgie's eyelashes were butterfly wings caressing his lips. She lifted her face and they fused. This kiss was longer. Deeper. More urgent.

'Oh, Jesus,' he whispered. The reality of finally kissing her exceeded his imagination. Infinitely.

She silenced him by covering his mouth with hers. They explored. The bulge in Franklin's pants swelled and hardened. Their breaths were gasps and groans that overloaded the erotic thermostat.

He pulled back and stared. His brow furrowed; he withdrew further. His fingertips traced her jaw to chin, hesitated at the small cleft. Then he straightened and severed contact.

Neither spoke, their eyes linked. In a zone where the scurrying clamour within the hospital—nurses and doctors in soft-soled shoes, the scratchy sound of wheelchairs or trolleys, conversations, arguments and televisions—didn't exist.

A shadow crossed over Franklin.

What the fuck am I doing?

He shook his head. Georgie stretched her good hand but he retreated. Pivoted. Strode from the room.

The door snapped shut.

SATURDAY 3 APRIL

CHAPTER FORTY-FIVE

The melody of a lone bagpiper drew Georgie and AJ beyond the aged timber St Andrews sign, along the curved steps and through a cottage-style garden with its cascades of seaside daisy.

Douglas Macdougall stood apart, in full highland getup, blowing mournful fingers of music that twisted heartstrings and lingered in the chill autumn air.

At the top of the stairs, Georgie turned to look down on Daylesford.

So much for a sleepy country town renowned for romantic weekends.

She blinked back tears and swivelled. Clouds travelled swiftly behind the neo-gothic Presbyterian Church. Weak sunlight illuminated its slate roof and leadlight windows. Beautiful, yet depressing. Like the bagpipes.

Despite a cocoon of pillows and tripled-up painkillers, the journey from Melbourne had been akin to an endless row of rib-jolting speed humps. Emotionally battered, too, she took AJ's hand. They leaned together and stepped through the arched entrance. Ruby and Michael Padley trailed and they all squeezed onto the end of a pew.

The bagpipes ceased. An occasional sniffle or shuffle punctuated the descending hush.

A black-cloaked preacher glided through the internal door, as Macdougall hurried up the aisle. He joined his mates Lewis Davis, Bill and Gabby Noonan and Pam Stewart in the front row, below the pulpit.

Georgie braced herself for the obligatory heaven, hell, fire and brimstone religious bullshit.

'We are gathered here today not to mourn the deaths of Susan and Roland Pentecoste but to celebrate their lives. What more fitting farewell than to rejoice in the gift of their mateship, their benefaction to the community...' The minister gazed over the pews. 'I don't think I'm alone in thinking that it is especially poignant that we are here today on Easter Saturday.'

He let his words sit and nobody fidgeted.

'I'm Minister Malcolm.' He cleared his throat and waved to the coffins. 'These are my friends, as they are yours. So, let us step outside convention. Who wants to speak? Suggest a song, a hymn? This is your service today.'

Bill flanked the minister and pointed. A full house followed the old copper's finger.

Georgie twisted with them. Confused, she sighed.

'Stand.' He lifted his hands.

The congregation rose. Georgie tried but gave up.

'Show your respect for Georgie Harvey,' Bill demanded. *What the hell?*

'For what she went through for Susan and Roly and their Margaret.'

They applauded, and Georgie wished for a trap floor. She shook her head. Then grimaced with pain.

'Three cheers for Georgie.' She identified Gabby's voice. 'Hip, hip, hooray.'

At the third hooray, Georgie's mortification gave way to an embarrassed smile. She struggled up and said, 'No, please. It's not about me.' She waved the congregation to their seats.

Macdougall replaced Bill.

'Susan and Roly were grand chums, and I'll sorely miss them. Every Wednesday the boys and I play a few hands of cards and enjoy a wee drop of single malt at my place. We'll keep a spot at the table for Roly.'

There were several chuckles as he returned to the pew.

The steady succession of eulogies ranged from elaborate to impromptu by characters as disparate as the content. Meanwhile, Georgie's body uncoiled, apart from her clenched, throbbing jaw.

After a hymn that Georgie mimed, Davis and Pam Stewart shuffled to the altar. They stood with their arms touching. They smiled, yet tears streaked their cheeks.

Pam glanced at Davis, who nodded. They looked to the caskets laden with wreaths. She said, 'Most of you will know that this is Roly and Susan's favourite.'

Georgie stiffened. She expected a soppy poem.

Pam inhaled a deep breath and sang in the sweetest of voices. Georgie recognised the tune from her first visit to Rose Cottage and her mouth gaped. When Davis joined in, his was a gravelly timbre, not dissimilar to Louis Armstrong's.

Pam crooned, Davis echoed. And *That's My Desire* tore at Georgie's heart.

While the friends sang, Georgie pictured Roly and Susan in their twenties, twirling into their middle years, then older age, yet still gazing at each other with the excitement and love they'd felt on their wedding day, as captured in the photograph that'd stood on their bedside table.

As she listened to the lyrics, Georgie realised she'd never be able to hear them again without seeing the couple dance. And that the song would always make her heart sing and sob at the same time.

The friends finished to cheers, foot stamps and claps. Pam dashed away tears. Georgie felt her own hand do likewise.

'It's too soon to say goodbye. But the music doesn't die,' Pam said when the crowd quietened. 'Neither do…' She faltered. 'Roly and Susan.'

A sombre lull ensued. Minister Malcolm filled it with his personal reminiscences, then thanked everyone for their contributions and extended a welcome to the final farewell.

Georgie coaxed her sore muscles and joined the exodus, hobbling next to Ruby. They picked their way to the car and fused with the slow convoy.

Over the hill, beyond bungalows, the Wombat Arms Hotel and pastureland.

To the cemetery.

———

Georgie spied the arrival of various cop vehicles, headlights on, their red and blue lights flashing mutely. Her mood fit the leaden sky overhead as she scanned the milling men and women in blue. He had besieged her thoughts for the past week.

She could feel his lips even while asleep. And the sensation ramped up as she huddled among the fresh tombs in the old part of the Daylesford Cemetery.

The bagpipes began to cry, and the minister's speech drifted. To avoid Franklin and the reality of Susan and Roly's deaths, she focused on neighbouring graves. A rusty wrought-iron structure that resembled a cot; several grassy unmarked mounds.

AJ's tug on her hand startled her. The caskets had disappeared into their deep voids and the mourners disbanded. Peripherally, she caught a wave from Helena Watkowska and a younger man, her son. They shunned the media greedy for a story on the Iceman's family and departed with paparazzi in pursuit. Matty Gunnerson saluted Georgie. He jostled counterparts to his car, mobile to ear, undoubtedly dictating to the news desk. He ignored the *Advocate*'s Jennifer McGuire.

'Ready?' AJ asked.

She sidestepped out of his reach. They paced after Ruby and Michael, two stones sporadically rubbing. The longer the silence stretched, the greater the aura of hurt exuded from AJ.

AJ's misery increased the intensity of Georgie's guilt.

She was guilt-ridden over her survival where the Pentecostes had perished. About the stolen kiss. Because she took from AJ although offered him little. All that and some.

The more her mood darkened, the more isolated she and AJ grew. They separated at the wake.

———

Georgie bee-lined for the Noonans and skolled a beer; AJ lurked on the fringes, acquainted with few. Even as she took another bottle, the alcohol and analgesic cocktail already blurred the edges of Georgie's pain.

Ruby and Michael huddled with Ann Campbell, Susan's sister from Sydney, the women renewing their acquaintanceship of decades ago. Georgie spoke with Gabby and Bill and noticed an old man. He snuffled into a large navy hanky, drifted to the food table and picked at morsels.

She forgot him when Franklin materialised.

'Georgie,' he said, dipping his head. That mouth, a forced smile.

He turned aside and beckoned. 'Kat, Georgie.'

So, this is Kat, his daughter. She's a knockout.

Fuzzy-headed, Georgie gazed at Kat.

Oh my god, she's got his eyes. She's seeing right inside me.

She strained to concentrate. Uttered something – hopefully it was sane, polite. Her mind obsessed.

Does Kat know about us? What's there to know? Nothing happened, right? Is he okay? Does he regret it? There's no us, is there? There's an AJ and Georgie, but there ain't no Georgie and Franklin. Not that there should be either.

Georgie slugged a long draught of beer and caught Franklin's stare. It held regret and the same kind of longing AJ's retriever, Molly, assumed when she begged scraps. She severed the connection, scanned the room. Saw the old guy in animated discussion with Ruby and Ann and AJ chatting with Michael and the minister.

She spotted Pam Stewart, made excuses and ducked away.

———

'Pam!'

They hugged gingerly. Pam patted Georgie's back.

When they broke, Georgie caught her friend's hand in her good one. 'How are you doing?'

Pam flapped her free wrist. She gulped and managed, 'I woke up this morning and I'm still here.'

They both smiled at her weak joke.

'But more to the point, how are you, dear?'

They'd talked since Georgie's discharge, well aware that each glossed over their feelings to be a rock for the other.

Georgie's eyes rolled to her strapped ribs and bundled fist, and then crossed downwards to her nose cast.

As hoped, Pam laughed. Then a thought struck Georgie. 'How's Oscar?'

Pam sobered. 'Similar to the rest of us. Fretting, lost some appetite.'

'Aw, poor little thing.'

Pam clucked and assured her, 'Don't you worry, we'll make sure he comes good. He'll stay on the farm, of course. He's a Pentecoste and belongs at Abergeldie. With Roger and Mick inheriting the place, they'll move in and be three bachelors together.'

While Georgie was imagining that, Pam unexpectedly said, 'You and John Franklin seem chummy.'

King-hit, Georgie flushed. 'He's not so bad. I guess I owe him.'

Pam searched her face, tone gentle. 'You know what they say about relationships with those you meet under extraordinary circumstances, don't you?'

'What's that?' Georgie asked, not really wanting to know.

'That danger can be a powerful aphrodisiac but it wears off. You might think it's love but it can't last.'

'I don't know what you're talking about,' Georgie muttered.

Was it love, or did she just want to jump Franklin's bones?

'Yes, you do, my dear.' Pam sounded sad. After a pause, she remarked, 'Your young Adam is quite a spunk.'

Georgie laughed unhappily. The fine lines above her nose deepened as she mulled over what exactly Pam suspected.

Not prepared to let up, her friend murmured, 'I'm only interfering because I care. Choose whoever will make you happy.'

Georgie raked the room for another escape opportunity. Ruby filled one of the Noonans' armchairs and appeared to be asleep. The old man and Michael Padley were drinking in a corner with Roger and Mick, Abergeldie's lessees. Lewis Davis was pissed, and he and Doug Macdougall alternated between maudlin and jovial. There were dozens of people she didn't know who were familiar with each other.

She glanced back to Davis and Macdougall and glimpsed the big Scot run his hand over the other's cheek. His thumb brushed at tears and lifted the corner of his mate's mouth. Weird.

'I've often wondered,' Pam whispered. Her discreet twitch indicated the two men.

'You mean?'

She nodded. 'We're branded a gay-friendly town, but I suspect that tolerance doesn't extend to the bank manager.'

Georgie huffed and simultaneously supposed it may explain the men's initial caginess.

Michael Padley, AJ and Bill Noonan now perched on the couch.

———

The old man sat alone. He swiped his eyes with his blue hanky.

'You must be Jack?' Georgie said, arriving at his side.

The sad old man looked surprised. 'Yes?'

On a roll, she said, 'And you've loved Susan Pentecoste since you were kids in Wedderburn?'

'Wychitella actually. My folks owned Wychitella Produce. Hers had a farm out of town. You have me at a disadvantage, young lady.' He peered at her. 'You were the lass everyone cheered in church. Georgie?'

She nodded. 'Yes, Georgie Harvey.'

'You're our Ruby's friend.' They shook hands, as he added, 'I'm sorry I was a bit slow to place you. I've been so overwhelmed since the news about Susan and Roly.'

'You have nothing to apologise for.' Georgie admitted, 'I fluked a few lucky guesses about you there, myself.' Her throat constricted. She regrouped. 'I'm sorry for your loss. And that I couldn't help Susan.'

Jack blinked rapidly. Eyes watery, he asked, 'So, how'd you know about little ol' Jack Henry then?'

'I found a bunch of letters that didn't say much yet seemed to have plenty between the lines. Unfortunately, you didn't date them or include your surname and address. They were important, or Susan wouldn't have kept them in the bottom of her robe. So, "Who is Jack?" has been one of the burning questions for three weeks.'

Is it really only three weeks?

'I'm flattered she kept them. And I beg your pardon that my dull letters became a time-wasting riddle.'

Georgie waved off his apology. She hesitated before saying, 'This is none of my business, but I'm curious. It's an occupational hazard.' Relieved when he laughed, she blurted out, 'I gather you thought you had no chance of more than a platonic relationship?'

Jack replied quickly, 'What I believed and hoped were two different things. While you live and breathe, never stop wishing for the things that matter. You don't want regrets when it's too late.'

Georgie scuffed her toes, knotted with emotion. She thought there couldn't be anything worse than the old man's misery. Then she fixed on AJ. With a roller-coaster plunge in her guts, she realised her mistake. It could be much worse. And *was*.

In the red corner: AJ and John Franklin conversed intensely.

SUNDAY 4 APRIL

CHAPTER FORTY-SIX

'GET UP.'

The mattress bounced. Her stomach dropped.

'Come on.' AJ prodded her leg.

'I can't, I'm dying,' she muttered, motionless bar her mouth.

He scoffed.

She moaned, head imploding. 'Go away.'

TV and radio clamoured in competition with AJ.

'And turn off the damn noise.'

'No sympathy.' He prodded harder. 'It's self-inflicted.'

Georgie remembered downing quite a few beers at the wake, plus a number of scotches and glasses of red wine. Between that and the painkillers... He could be right; she may have overdone things.

You think?

She jumped to the present. Swallowed, nauseated. It was insensitive and brainless to put a hangover and death in the same category – even the worst hangover in history.

Hangovers and death. Stale and foul. In her mind, time

transferred to the cellar. To her fall. To the discovery of the dead Pentecostes. She flinched, forced her thoughts forward but ended up back at the wake. And faced with a living nightmare.

Oh, shit.

Across the Noonan's lounge room: Franklin and AJ in debate.

Georgie fell out of bed and blindly bolted to the toilet. She heaved the contents of her stomach into the bowl. She stared at the vicious mixture. Vomited again until her throat burned and the liquid turned black.

'You finished in there?' AJ called, all too noisy and cheerful.

Georgie saw his high spirits as a good omen and brightened. He couldn't know about her and Franklin.

Could he?

She flushed the loo and leaned on the cistern.

That bloody kiss.

While their lips had locked, pain didn't exist. When Franklin had pulled away, it returned, merged with erotic volts. Desire and pain were powerful antagonistic forces; an apple that tasted sweet and sour in the same mouthful.

Her stomach turned and hurled up more bile until nothing remained. She shuffled into the bathroom. After glowering into the mirror for a few moments, she brushed her teeth, gargled and stood under the shower rose with forehead pressed onto the wall.

Just as well he didn't see me cry as he left. I don't even know why I cried. I mean, the guy's a bloody good kisser but a dickhead more often than not.

She rotated and water pummelled her front.

How did life become so fucking complicated?

AJ gagged for marriage, and a man she scarcely liked

filled her thoughts. It wasn't fair to AJ, and she ought to cut him loose.

'You want some help with the soap? Must be tricky with the freaky-beak and bandages.'

She slit an eye and saw AJ perched on the vanity. She ignored him.

'George, I've been thinking.'

She faced away. A deep and meaningful was the last thing she needed.

With a wrench of the hot tap, she growled, 'I'm not in the mood.'

The water steamed. It blotched her skin.

Unperturbed, he said, 'Do you think Susan and Roly are together now?'

'Yeah, *sure*. In the ground –'

'I don't mean physically.'

'Where worms and bugs will eat them –'

'Cut it out.'

Georgie twisted the taps and stood dripping. She swiped vapour off the screen and regarded him through the circle. 'You know I don't believe in that afterlife crap.'

'But some of us do, George.'

She towelled off. Where was this conversation going?

'Maybe Susan's glad she doesn't have to be alone any longer.'

Georgie stopped mid-rub. 'You don't seriously believe she's *glad* she was murdered?'

He flushed. 'Well –'

'I mean, *how* ridiculous,' Georgie lashed out. 'Who the hell understands what Susan went through? All I know is how bad I felt, especially for those first few days in hospital, and I got off lightly in comparison. She was tortured, knee-capped and left in a cellar with her husband's corpse, copped hypothermia and finally suffered a stroke. Do you think she's planning to write thank-you notes in the near future?'

Angry and horrified, she wanted to hurt him for making her think about Susan. Not that many minutes in the day passed without her mind fixated on the woman's gruesome death or illicit fantasies featuring Franklin. Or without her wishing she'd met the farmer in life and that she'd never encountered the copper.

AJ's voice quaked as he said, 'I don't know why I bother.'

He slammed the bathroom door. A moment later, he rattled the lead and exited with Molly.

———

Georgie sank to the floor and accidentally bumped her hand on the tiles.

'Fucking, bloody, shit.'

The damaged nerves convulsed. Her eyes brimmed and gave way to tears. She vented emotional and physical pain in deep, racking sobs that hurt her body, fuelling the hysterics in a cruel catch-22.

Three weeks ago, Georgie had starred in her worst nightmare. Or so she'd thought. The encounter with Magistrate Narkin and conflict with AJ turned out to be tame appetisers for events to follow – with the extra complication of a certain man.

And what a complication. Something that would have been laughable: *her* falling for a country cop, an older guy with a kid to boot. Huh.

She tried to convince herself that Franklin hadn't revealed their kiss to AJ. Why would he? It couldn't have

SANDI WALLACE

meant much to him. So, they were in the clear. Just as well, because she couldn't envisage life without AJ.

Yet Franklin clouded their relationship. All because of one damn kiss and the danger that had acted as a powerful aphrodisiac.

Georgie dressed while she listened for AJ's return. She couldn't secure her bra one-handed, so went bare. Had trouble raking her hair, so left it in a bird's nest.

Restless and waiting, she caught Susan and Roly's borrowed wedding photo in her peripheral vision. She'd found the Pentecostes yet unearthed nothing but pain. Miserable, she turned the photo face down.

Sometimes winning is still losing.

Dear reader,

We hope you enjoyed reading *Tell Me Why*. Please take a moment to leave a review, even if it's a short one. Your opinion is important to us.

Discover more books by Sandi Wallace at https://www.nextchapter.pub/authors/sandi-wallace

Want to know when one of our books is free or discounted for Kindle? Join the newsletter at http://eepurl.com/bqqB3H

Best regards,

Sandi Wallace and the Next Chapter Team

The story continues in:
Dead Again by Sandi Wallace

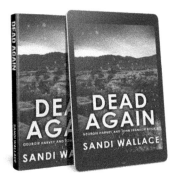

To read the first chapter for free, please head to:
https://www.nextchapter.pub/books/dead-again

ACKNOWLEDGMENTS

Although several of the places and businesses in this book exist, all characters and events are fictitious and I've taken some liberty with setting. For instance, St Andrew's Presbyterian Church on Camp Street was sold for redevelopment some years ago. Today, the church is hidden behind locked doors and surrounded by unruly gardens, and squatters allegedly shelter in the small hall out the back. Its copper spire may be tarnished but this neo-gothic church is a prominent Daylesford landmark, worthy of resurrecting in this story.

I am grateful to the many people who helped with this book. Any mistakes are my own.

Firstly, warmest thanks to the team at Next Chapter.

Next, my thanks go to Brian Rix, Chris McGeachan and Tony Haining, who were generous with their insights into policing in the homicide squad and general duties at Daylesford and Olinda, while Tessa Jenkins was a gem for police information.

I'm grateful to the original publisher and editor of *Tell Me Why*, Lindy Cameron of Clan Destine Press and Liz

Filleul respectively. Also cheers to the convenors and members of Sisters in Crime Australia who are passionate about the crime writing art (and for the nod to *Tell Me Why* with the Davitt Award Readers' Choice).

Thanks also to Kerry Greenwood, Andrew Rule and John Silvester, along with Ruth Wykes, Judy Elliot, Raylea O'Loughlin, Sharon Gurry, Ray Mooney, the late Anne Calvert, Maurice Gaul, Mandy Tannenbaum, Seamus Anthony, Nola Brooks, Jacinta Butterworth and Alex Petrakos. My appreciation also goes to Ruth Kennedy.

A big shout-out to my family and friends for being a patient cheer squad, and thanks to *you*, my readers! I always treasure your messages and reviews letting me know you've enjoyed my stories. I'd love you to join me on Facebook and Instagram or follow my website.

Lastly, an ovation to my partner and best mate, Glenn. Without him, this novel and those after would not have eventuated.

ABOUT THE AUTHOR

Sandi Wallace's crime-writing apprenticeship comprised devouring as many crime stories as possible, developing her interest in policing, and working stints as banker, paralegal, cabinetmaker, office manager, executive assistant, personal trainer and journalist. She has won a host of prizes for her short crime fiction including several Scarlet Stiletto Awards and her debut novel *Tell Me Why* won the Davitt Award Readers' Choice. Sandi is currently at work on a psychological thriller and a second collection of her short crime stories. She is still an avid reader of crime and loves life in the Dandenong Ranges outside of Melbourne with her husband.

Connect with Sandi at

Website www.sandiwallace.com
Amazon www.amazon.com/author/sandiwallace
Goodreads www.goodreads.com/author/show/
8431978.Sandi_Wallace
Facebook www.facebook.com/sandi.wallace.crimewriter
Instagram www.instagram.com/sandiwallacecrime
Pinterest www.pinterest.
com.au/sandiwallace_crimewriter/

Lightning Source UK Ltd.
Milton Keynes UK
UKHW020239041220
374592UK00012B/865/J